COYOTE

A Novel by J. M. Nelson

ISBN: 9798581526590

Front Cover by Joseph Feely

First Printed Edition 2021

www.jmnelsonfiction.com

www.twitter.com @JMNelsonFiction

www.facebook.com/JMNelsonFiction

www.amazon.com/author/jmnelson

www.reddit.com/JMNelsonFiction

"Man is the cruelest animal...At tragedies, bullfights, and crucifixions he has so far felt best on earth; and when he invented hell for himself, behold, that was his very heaven." — Friedrich Nietzsche

COYOTE

Chapter I
The Farm
1875

A swirling grey anvil cloud sat at his back as his horse carried him across the plains. The sun hung somewhere overhead, but it could not be seen through the thick overcast. The rider swayed with each trotting hoof. The wind blew the once bright vibrant yellow grass that now sat greyed and thinned, almost ashen in appearance, as if more than age withered the earth. The rider knew not where he went. He bundled himself under the thin buckskin jacket when another burst of hot muggy air washed over him. A chill went down his spine, sending a shockwave of muscle spasms beneath his pale skin. He removed his black flat brim hat, wiping away the sweat from his young, yet hardened, face.

He believed himself a dead man, but he lived enough of a life in his youth that he did not mind much. He dreamed of places he wanted to go, things he wanted to see, but he accepted years ago that he'd never see such dreams come to fruition. His time East broke him down, while his time West laid ruin to what was left. Though he was young, 19 to be exact, he knew not the number or how to count to it. He possessed no education. He held no piece of land to his name. He was a wanderer, and he felt that he would forever be so.

The rider kicked his leg in the stirrup, giving his horse a pickup in speed. He adjusted his body in the saddle, for his swaying became heavier and he dared not fall onto the dying grass. He knew that if he fell, he'd be unable to find the strength to get back into his saddle. He wandered for days after the sickness took him, but he wandered long before that. When he ran from the Appalachians, he found himself lost to the world. Many nights he sat in the dark by a barely burning fire, wondering if he should ever turn back. He couldn't. His life was his and no longer belonged to his father, nor the memory of his mother. Those days were long gone to him, but he thought of them from time to time. They felt as if he dreamed them from another soul. His time on the plains, with his business, with his new siblings and father, ones he chose, were all that belonged to him. Though, those memories served him no purpose and most times only brought him grief. He believed he made the right choices, that his choice would always be better than what was inherited, as most young believe. He learned from those mistakes, or at least he believed it to be so.

The past year he spent alone. He knew people, spoke with a few, but carried no company with him. He learned that he worked better alone, worked better without that constant pressure of watchful eyes of judgement. He told himself so each night as he slept in his bison furs with his eyes wide open. Though, he knew it different, the harsh truth of loneliness, deep down. The judgement of others mattered not, but he knew himself too weak willed, too stupid in his own eyes, to know better before corruption set in. He saw his relationships, those good and bad, to be nothing more than a poison that ate his soul, who he truly was. Anything he told himself, however, was nothing but an excuse. He lost his true senses of who he was long before he ran from his Appalachian home, long before he wandered the streets of New Orleans for a day or two, long before he went to Dodge, and long before he became a hunter. It was engrained in him to know the kind of man he was, but he'd been searching for it since, and figured he'd be searching into the hereafter.

On the horizon, as if it were some last beacon of hope to the sick rider, a small fence post broke over the dying grass. The post, worn and cracked through such terrible hard times on the plains, held no boards to connect it to another. As he rode closer, he noticed that the post belonged to a worn and broken fence line. Around fifty yards from that first post he spotted, a few fields of wheat stood, lining a downward slope to a great flat land. On that flat land, sat a small house, nothing fancy, nor modest. The home itself appeared abandoned and had it not been for the waving wheat, he would've believed it so.

On the other end of the farmland, a large oak tree stood and from within its shade, a man stepped forth to the young rider. His gait seemed weak. What little sunlight that broke through the overcast glistened in the man's silver hair as he approached the sickly rider atop his horse at the far end of the farm. In the farmer's hand, he carried a worn double barrel, something the kid knew had the potential to misfire due to its condition. The rider thought nothing of the man, nor the weapon he carried with him.

The farmer stopped when he stood about ten feet from the rider. His voice was solemn, old, and seasoned, "Who the hell are you?"

The rider did not respond at first. He thought for a moment, thinking of taking his reins and pulling away from that man's farm. To speak to another person opened himself once more, something he wished not to do. He smacked his lips, rubbing his dry tongue to his teeth. His canteen ran out some time ago. The pale kid loosened his grip on the reins, slowly raising his hands to his shoulders, palms out. His voice, as dusty as his appearance, shook as he replied, "Orson Newkirk."

The old farmer looked the stranger up and down. His aged fingers danced across the hammers of his coach gun as his eyes studied. The weaponry hung at his side as he looked to the kid's pale face, his sluggish demeanor, his empty eyes. He didn't know if Newkirk had been sent there for him or if he was some lost rambler. As he thought on it, and the silence between the two grew, Orson spoke again, "Don't worry, old man. I ain't lookin' to hurt no one."

The farmer raised his thick peppered colored eyebrow, "Old man? You lookin' to get hurt with manners like that."

Orson squinted. His fingers tapped the air as he kept his hands raised. The farmer knew him to be ill and asked him, "What do you want?"

"Water, if you have any," the kid answered.

"Askin' for stuff when you talk to people like that..." The farmer muttered to the kid.

"Like what?"

The eyes of the farmer danced across the kid's horse, seeing the .36 caliber revolver strapped to Newkirk's leg. It was then that he caught the .50 breech loading rifle holstered behind the saddle. He thought to turn the kid away. He didn't know him. He knew better than to deal with such a person, such an armed person. The sickness in the kid radiated into the air. It smelt sweet of death and his heart broke for him, for he'd seen sickness and death before. He figured the rider would die if he turned him away.

Orson spoke again, "I said like what?"

"Old man..." the farmer reminded him, not tearing his eyes away from that breechloader.

"I didn't mean no offense," Newkirk responded.

"Just because you don't mean none, don't mean there ain't none."

Orson nodded. He felt the sweat drip from his face onto his saddle, "Alright then...may I have some water?"

The farmer lifted his eyes from that rifle, staring into the young rider's gaunt face, "You leave that pistol there, and that horse too. I'll get'chu some water."

The young rider sat on the farmer's worn-down porch. His eyes danced around, staring at the dilapidated wood, out towards the lush waving wheat, then to his horse which stood hitched to a fence post on the far side of the property. The farmer, who gave his name as Thomas Daniels, approached the young man.

Daniels watched as the young man dipped his hand in a small bucket of water that sat near his cherry wood chair, then began ladling the lukewarm liquid over the back of his neck and onto his face. Thomas saw a shake in Orson's hands. He noted the dirt and grime they accumulated too. He said nothing on it though, "Where are you headin'?"

Orson did not break his sickly gaze from the water as he began to sip it from his cupped hand, "West."

"Where West?" The old farmer pried.

The kid finished his water, shaking his hand dry. He leaned forward in his chair, eyes dancing across the property. He placed his hat on his knee, wiping the sweat from his forehead with a small blue and white bandana. He cleared his throat and spat, "I don't know. Anyplace, I guess."

"Why?" Thomas continued to pry. He leaned against one of the support beams of his porch. It creaked as he shifted his weight.

"Always wanted to, I suppose. Ain't never seen the ocean."

"They got oceans East. They got oceans South too," the old man informed the youth.

The kid shifted his eyes upward, staring into Thomas's pale blue gaze. Orson placed his hat back on his head, throwing his eyes back under the thick shade of the flat brim, "I want to see the one West."

The old man nodded, stepping back down from the porch. He knew the next question he wanted to ask the stranger and he knew the answer but found it difficult to press. He turned his back to his porch, staring out across the wheat. He mustered the courage as he stared off towards that oak and its shadow on the boundary line of his farm, "You sick?"

Orson watched the old man closely. He looked to the far beam of the porch, noticing the coach gun resting against it. The farmer stood before him, unarmed. He too lowered his guard as the farmer turned to him, slowly. The kid gave him a slight nod as he spooned another cup of water with his right hand.

"With what?" Thomas asked, now facing him fully.

"Not sure," Orson admitted. "I think I got something, hot to cold. You know?"

As Thomas Daniels stared onto the young man, watching as Orson once again removed his hat to wipe sweat away from his brow, a patch of sunlight came through the overcast, illuminating the farm in such a bright glory. In that light, he saw the true paleness of the kid's face, and not only that, but also beyond it. He saw years of hardship, years of trials and tribulation, years of uncertainty, and what short years he truly lived. With a quick snap of his eyes to his beloved oak tree, he asked another question he found difficult, for he too had become accustomed to being alone, "You eat recently?"

Orson leaned back, "I had some rabbit a day or two back."

"I've got some stew I'm plannin' on cookin' tonight," the farmer informed.

Orson lifted his eyebrow to the thought, hearing only the words and not the infliction in the man's voice. He only knew one kind of man and one kind of hospitality, to which he responded, "You rubbin' it in?"

Daniels scoffed at that as he stared down the young Newkirk, "I'm invitin' you, boy."

Orson's eyebrow dropped as he leaned forward. He didn't know how to take the gesture of kindness, because he had not seen kindness in such a long time. He basked in the silence for a moment, just watching the wheat roll in the small bouts of wind that came sweeping through the farm. It was only when all light became hidden by the low hanging clouds once more, did he realize what the old man called him, "Boy?"

Thomas knew the young man took offense by the look of his face. It took a moment to settle in, as if the gesture outweighed any type of insult. He didn't think much of the term, but saw that Newkirk, for whatever reason, cared not to be called anything that applied youth. He saw many things across the plains, Daniels figured, and those things probably aged that young man past his own age. He dared not allow that kid to leave though, because he knew that fever would take him before long and he knew that he would feel that guilt. Thomas defused with a smirk, "Oh, I didn't mean no offense."

The overcast cleared sometime after nightfall. The light of the full moon glowed down onto that small farmland with such a vibrant glow. Orson sat within Thomas's small shack, at the worn table that took up most of the space within the home. At his back, a small bed laid within a small cubby of wood. Before him, the fireplace crackled as the men basked in the infernal glow. Yet, though the flames appeared to be intoxicating, Orson dared not break his gaze from the small makeshift window that presented the plains he knew cooling in the moonlight.

Thomas spooned the recently cooked stew into two bowls. The steaming cauldron of brown muck sat atop a small woven blanket on the slightly crooked counter. The smell of the stew was nothing much, and Thomas knew it to be a bland concoction, due to salt being the only seasoning he still owned and with such little left around, he used it sparingly. He approached the table, sliding the stew towards the young wanderer.

Thomas sat across from the young man, waiting to bite into his food until his guest did so. It took Orson a moment to finally snap out of his moonlight trance, but when he did, he smirked upon the sight of hot food. Sweat still dripped from his forehead and he wiped it away again. A slight cough slid from under his bottom lip as he took his first bite. Thomas then too took a spoonful of his homemade mud and placed it on his tongue. Too little salt, he cursed himself. Though, Newkirk did not mind.

Orson swallowed another mouthful of stew, "Just you out here, Thomas?"

Thomas stared down at the brown murky water at the bottom of his spoon. His hand shook slightly, causing the oils atop the stew to swirl, something he became lost in. He'd been alone for a long while. He thought of the times before that often, but never cared to stop and realize they were distant memories, dreams to him now. His eyes shifted to the kid, giving a slight nod.

"It always been that way?"

Thomas did not care to be on the receiving end of the prying. He wanted to wave the question away, as if it were nothing more than a pestering fly. He feared what lied within him when he answered such a thing. He felt the frog burrowing in his throat. He shook his head quick, clearing his throat after a quick drink of water, "No…had a wife…a daughter…"

Newkirk looked down to his stew, realizing quickly that he made a mistake in his question. Out of the edge of his eyes, he watched Thomas struggling with what was asked. Orson soon realized that there was a reason he hardly spoke to anyone, even those that offered him kindness. He could not find a way to relate, could not find a way to speak to people with the right social context. He felt ashamed by his questions, his prying, because he too knew how it felt to be vulnerable.

Thomas continued, "Cholera, the both of 'em. I…don't talk about it much."

The old farmer lowered his head and Newkirk believed him to wipe away a tear with a piece of the tablecloth, but it could've been a bit of food. As Daniels thought on his wife, his child, he only remembered their blue faces riddled with the sickness. That frog burrowed deeper in his throat, for time healed the wounds of their death but the scars ran deeper than he believed. Thomas changed the subject away from him, "So, how long you been alone?"

"A year, maybe less," Orson responded, forthcoming with any information for he felt the old man deserved it as payment for answering his questions.

"So, it always ain't been so?" Thomas realized he was prying once again and felt the urge to change the subject. He opened his mouth to speak.

However, Orson responded quickly, "No, I rode with some fellers a while back."

"Rode with 'em?" Thomas laughed at the sound of that. The kid sounded like a true cowpoke, a real character from a newspaper story or a dime novel. He asked, trying to not sound mocking, "You some kind of outlaw?"

Orson chewed a hunk of potato for a moment, staring down the old man. He knew he meant no offense, but still took some.

He dared not be awkward with the farmer again, so he smirked and let out a halfhearted scoff, "I hunted."

"You look young to be a hunter."

"Ain't no age limit," Orson said quickly.

"What'd you hunt?" Thomas laid his spoon down in his bowl, folding his hands over one another. He really found interest in the young man across from him and found that the conversation moved away from anything with the potential for pain.

Orson noted the older man's demeanor but continued to eat, "Bison, mostly."

"Good money in it?" Thomas asked without thought. He felt himself lost to the wonder of being a hunter on the plains. He heard of such things before. He lived in Kansas long enough, been to Hays enough, and Dodge once before, a long time ago. He'd seen rough looking men of the plains, their long hair and beards, and sometimes wished that life of excitement for himself. He knew he couldn't hack it, but the thought of something different, something without the bindings of the civilized world sounded enticing as he laid awake most nights.

"Some days," the kid responded quickly.

Somewhere outside, off in the distant night and across the plains, a coyote let out a quick yap. It drew Orson's attention as he chewed a bit of carrot from the stew. As his head turned to look out the window across the plains, Thomas noted the sweat raining from the kid's neck and from his forehead. The beads of sweat flowed like rivers behind his ears. As Newkirk swallowed his food, a slight cough slipped from his lips again. Another followed. And another. He leaned forward, holding his chest.

Thomas stood quickly. He'd seen sickness before and felt that panic grow within, "Are you alright?"

Orson nodded, coughing while doing so. His head tilted forward, then back, repeatedly. All the while, still coughing. He threw his arm out towards the farmer, fingers pale as if they were Death's. Thomas stood before the coughing boy, watching without knowing what to do.

Orson continued to nod, his vision blurring, darkening around the edges of his eyes. He felt his knees buckle as he stood away from the chair, trying to make his way to the door for fresh air. He heard that coyote yap again somewhere out in all that dark. He feared it. He feared that sound. He feared what it meant. He feared what retribution came with it. His legs gave out with his second step and the young man collapsed onto the floor.

The harsh unpolished wood of the Daniels farmhouse felt like needles in his back as Newkirk writhed like a decapitated serpent for a quick moment. Thomas knelt next to the sick young man, resting his cold hands against Orson's scorching face. The whites of his youthful, yet harsh, eyes took over. The deep grey irises were no longer visible as Newkirk's eyes slid into the back of his head. He shivered for a moment, before going still. Thomas felt his heart stop, for he feared the worst.

The sun had not risen above the thick Appalachian forest. A purple haze clouded the sky. A thick fog rolled, ankle high, between the oaks. Something stirred within the thick shadows between the trees. Orson could not see them from where he stood, but he could hear the slight rustle of the leaves. He held his breath, watching, waiting for what came. From the darkness, two glowing dots appeared, reflected with what little light hung in the air. It took him a moment to realize that he stared into the eyes of some creature, and it stared back. Then more appeared behind it, and with them, a haunting yap…

Chapter II

A New City, A Familiar Life

1873

The city sat on the plains, glistening like a small jewel under the low hanging sun. As the locomotive rolled through the station, thick bellows of smoke flowed from its chimney, darkening the blue sky overhead. People lingered all around the platform, dressed fancier than the kid had ever seen. Women wore elegant dresses of silk and lavender. Men wore suits with ties that cost more than the kid could earn in a year. As he peered out of his lower-class car, he envied all their attire, wondering if he, someday, could make money as they did. The breaks squeaked, ripping a loud haunting song into the air as the locomotive came to a complete stop.

Orson's first step into Dodge City was on that platform. He was young then, not just by years, but by soul too. His eyes, as they danced across all the possibilities seen in every face on the platform, were filled with such light, a light that would eventually wither out on the plains. He stood still, wearing his cheap cotton shirt, tucked into a pair of worn corduroys. It wasn't until a man with a smoke grey three-piece suit brushed by him, that the foolish young boy realized that he blocked the exit from the cars. He stepped away, looking all around the platform. He saw the city out of the corner of his eyes. The buildings were tall, not all of them, but enough to make him feel as if he entered a new world.

As he felt swallowed up by the large amount of people at the station, a station worker stood atop a box not far away. He directed those with tickets where they needed to be, and those without where to find a place within the city. Sweat rolled from beneath his small billed cap as he pointed the patrons wherever they desired. Orson, upon seeing the man, thought of him as a beacon of hope. He knew not where to go, what to see, what to do.

The young man approached the station worker, who stood tall and mighty over him with his blue suit, his red tie. Orson kept his hands tucked into his pockets. He rolled his index finger over a small hole at the bottom of the inner seem. He felt a nervous shaking in his voice as he approached. The station worker began to direct with his arms as he shouted to the growing crowd, "Clear the way! Please, clear the way if you are waiting to board!"

Orson stood at the man's side. He looked over the man's fading red hair, his reddening skin. He opened his mouth to speak, just as the worker gave more orders for those wishing to board the train. Newkirk paused, mouth still open, but finally mustered the courage in such an unfamiliar place, "Sir, I am lookin' for work."

The red-haired worker shifted his eyes to Orson, looking him up and down. He could tell the kid shouldn't be in such a place. The cheap shirt, the worn pants, the lost look were enough to forgo any second thought he would give the kid. He turned his head back towards the crowd, which the worker felt grew in just a matter of seconds. He noted those not obeying his earlier commands, so he shouted again, "Clear the way, folks! Please, if you are waiting to board, you need to clear the way so we can get those arriving off the platform!"

Orson noted the quick side glance the worker gave him. He thought of turning and walking off, finding a way on his own. He did that for some time, and somehow managed to make enough money to go as far West as he possibly could. He believed it possible to do again, if he wanted. He hated the things he did for that money though, the dignity lost. He wanted a fresh start and all he needed was some guidance, someone to tell him what was right. He was young, impressionable, needing a hand to point the way. He knew that. He was honest with himself then. He spoke up, "Excuse me, sir. I asked if there's any work about? I'm lookin' for some."

The station attendee turned his head, looking to the young man. He didn't think the kid had it in him to speak his mind once again. He took the poor looking young man at face value, lost and weak. He smirked at that though, but that turned quickly into a scowl as more people flooded by the arrivers to board the train. His eyes shot back to the kid, realizing that he had his own work to do, and not help some poor assumed runaway get by. He shook his head wildly to the young boy, frustrated as all be, "Take a look around. You'll find something somewhere. Now, leave me alone, kid."

And so, Orson did.

The kid wandered those streets for days. Contrary to what the station employee told him, he found no work. Nobody was willing to hire some young kid that didn't even have a spare change of clothes. He wanted to sweep the floors of one of the many saloons or casinos, but they would not have him. People held those jobs already. He wondered if he could deliver the mail or be a lamplighter. Those too were taken, and nobody saw need for some fresh-faced kid from the East.

He thought of leaving that place, but he would need money for that. One night, he wished he never left New Orleans, but the more he thought about it, the more he realized he was wrong. He found a nice warm spot behind a casino, in one of the back alleys, where he setup camp with a worn blanket he stole from beneath a random saddle. It smelt of the American Paint it laid on, but he needed it more than the steed. It grew cold on the plains, especially at night, and he didn't think it would be so.

To eat, he foraged through the garbage outside of businesses to eat the scraps. He witnessed other urchins, young and old, do this. The dirt on their faces, the loss of light in their eyes, made him realize what he was becoming but he had no other choice. It was then that he wanted to leave. He wanted to escape because he was living the same life he had East, after he ran from home. He needed money and he did have a trade he picked up outside of Chickamauga, and that was thieving.

He wasn't a good thief, but he knew what people would buy. He knew what he needed to do to survive, but still found it difficult. By day, he wandered the streets, looking at the casinos, the saloons, the restaurants. He watched people come and go, imagining what it would be like to be in their shoes, to acquire such wealth and to live that lifestyle. As he looked into those patrons' eyes, he could not pick their pockets. He refused because he wanted an honest living. At night, the kid wandered the streets, finding food any place he could. He lived in the shadows of the city, one that would rather eat him and spit him out. For days, he told himself he would not pickpocket. He needed to find work. He had to find work. There had to be a way for him to make it in such a harsh plains town. Though, the idea always hung at the back of his mind. Then, hunger struck and the desperation for survival devoured any desire for honest work.

On a cool evening, not long after the sun went down and a light breeze rolled through the streets of Dodge, Orson wandered alone. He looked to the casinos first, noting all sorts of men and women inside. He saw hunters, gamblers, and whores. He saw pocket watches, guns, rings, chains, necklaces, and anything else he thought would fetch enough food to last him another night. As he peered through the window, he felt eyes staring back at him. They were. Off towards the door of the casino, a man leaned in the doorway. His red vest glistened in the early moonlight. He crossed his arms as he looked to the young man. He shook his head, "Go on, get."

Orson didn't question it. He gave a nod, moving away from the building and wandering down the street. He saw higher end saloons. He knew they wouldn't allow him in. He knew the poorer ones wanted a drink purchased and he carried no cash. He would have to linger in the shadows of such a place, but it wasn't anything he wasn't familiar with.

He staggered a bit as he walked. His hands shook, not from nerves, but from weakness. He felt his body consuming itself. His ribs, wrapped tightly under his pale flesh, rose and fell quickly with heavy breaths. A bead of sweat rolled from his forehead, dancing around the edge of his sunken eyes. If he were to see himself, he knew he would look like a dead man risen. He passed a lonely saloon towards the end of the main stretch of the city.

He eyed the few folks that lingered around outside. They were drunk. Easy pickings, he thought to himself. He noted a man's pocket watch. It appeared to be a worn tarnished silver, but he knew he could get a few dollars for it from the right person, if he found the right person. He watched as another man held his lighter under a woman's face as he lit her cigarette. The lighter was brass. It might fetch him something, not much, but something. He eyed the men and knew that he was not fast enough to take them if caught. He staggered again, wondering if he could grab them and run, but those men looked rougher, tougher than he and he knew he did not stand against them. He needed a quick escape and the opportunity presented itself to him as a lone drunk man leaned against the side of the saloon. His head tilted forward as he pissed off into the darkness down the alley. The man staggered as he threw his head back, letting out a deep grunt. His hat barely hung on his head. It was nice, a good quality felt, and a fine turquoise ribbon rested around the base of the crown. Orson stepped forward, wanting to take that hat. He knew it wasn't much, but it was something. Quickly though, the man finished pissing, buttoned his fly, and turned to Orson. They met eyes and Orson regretted ever having the thought as he stared into those deep emerald greens. The man tipped his hat to the boy, then staggered off down the street.

The sound of spurs against the saloon's wooden porch drew the boy's attention away from the drunken man and his hat, who now stumbled down the lonely lamplit streets. A lone lantern dangled from the overhang, lighting the saloon porch. Beneath it, a man stood. He chewed an unlit cigar. His hat, flat brimmed and wide, covered his eyes in a thick shadow as he basked in the low light of the burning kerosene. He wore a thick coat, one too thick for the heavy heat of the plains. It was long, a coat for the trails, and covered in thick brown fur. Elegant to a degree, but not practical for hot weather in the slightest. A fashion statement, nothing more, nothing less. The man dug into his jacket pocket, removing a match that he lit on the sole of his boot. He held it to the cigar, and his face flickered under the hellish glow of each puff of smoke.

Orson eyed the man for a moment, staring into those seemingly empty shadow covered eyes. That faded though, for the man threw back his furry duster for a moment, letting the cool breeze wash over his sweating body. His clothes were rough and worn. He did not possess a lot of money by the looks of him, but on his left, sitting in a weathered cross-draw holster, sat a nickel-plated Colt Navy. The silver finish glistened under that infernal lantern glow. The worn ivory handle, yellowed and cracked at one edge, drew Orson's gaze. His stomach rumbled as he stared into it, thinking of how much he could sell it for. Any man on the street in Dodge would have need for a pistol like that, though it was dated, he knew such a thing would still find value among those who desired a weapon of that sort. The engravings, a floral pattern, wrapped around the grip of the weapon and he examined some around what little bit of the barrel hung out of the end of the holster.

He needed that pistol. He needed it to eat. The man looked drunk. He swayed a bit and if Orson could get the revolver fast enough, the man may just let him have it if it were loaded and pointed at the stranger. He didn't know for sure, but that hunger moved from his stomach into his heart, and the boy needed it. He needed to survive.

Newkirk moved slowly up the side stairs of the saloon's porch. His worn boots echoed with heavy steps on each plank. He kept his eyes on that revolver, staying focused on the target, something his father taught him about hunting as a child. The man turned his back to one of the support beams, leaning against it. He threw his head back. His hat's crown receiving a deep dimple in the process. Orson watched as the man removed a small silver flask from his pocket, sipping from it as it glistened under the lamplight. The kid thought for a moment of taking that, but he knew better. That pistol would fetch far more, and if he sold it, he would eat for a few days.

Orson stepped towards the man, unable to see the revolver with the man's back turned towards him. He'd get him by surprise. He would run by, quickly grab that revolver from across the man's hip and dash off down the alley. It had to work. The man appeared drunk for he swayed as if the wind would knock him over. There'd be no way he could follow the kid into the darkness of the alleys. Newkirk had the drop on him too, he'd get away. At least, he thought so until the man's raspy, emotionless voice boomed across the saloon porch, "Wha'chu want, boy?"

The kid heard the man but cared not. He thought for a moment that he spoke to someone else, maybe someone inside, maybe someone lurking out of Orson's eyesight. Then, it hit him as he took another step and the man peered back to him, eyes piercing through the shadows beneath his hat's brim. The boy stopped in his tracks, eyeing the man as the stranger tipped his hat upward, lifting the shadow out of his eyes. They were a deep blue, haunting. They sat within deep sockets, dark around the rims from lack of sleep or too much alcohol, or maybe a bit of both.

The stranger waved the flask in the air. A soft slosh of alcohol rattled within it. He asked the kid as he turned towards him, no longer leaning on the post, "You after this?"

Orson didn't speak. His eyes glanced down towards the revolver as if it still held some trance over him. The man noted, smirking as he watched the defeated teen before him. The stranger rested his hand on that glistening ivory grip, "This? This what you after, boy?"

Orson still did not speak, but as the man's hand rested on the grip, the spell of the weapon vacated his soul. He looked to the man's haunting eyes, lost within them, vulnerable, bare.

The man spoke quickly, "What'chu gon' do with it? Shoot me? Shoot yer'self?"

No response was given from the kid.

"I asked you a question, boy," the stranger pressed. "It's only polite of you to respond, seein' as you was gon' rob a man who is only enjoyin' his evenin'."

Orson finally mustered the courage. He looked away from the man though. He felt forced to look off towards the inside of the saloon. He watched as people drank, gambled, whored, and laughed. He spoke softly, "I was goin' to sell it."

"Sell it?" the man laughed, "It ain't worth all that much. What'chu gon' sell it for?"

"Maybe trade it..." Orson replied, still lost to those enjoying their evening inside.

"Trade it? And what was you plannin' on tradin' it for?"

"Money...food...I don't really know..." the kid responded.

The man's boots echoed across the porch as he began to walk around the kid. He shook his head, trying to clear his mind from the whiskey, "So, you some starvin' thief then? That it?"

Orson's stomach growled and turned at the thought of food.

"Cain't be any good at it," the stranger continued, "I saw you eyein' that feller's watch and that poor sum'bitch's hat. You really gon' steal a man's hat?"

Newkirk hesitated. The shame shook his voice, "Thought about it."

"You ain't no thief," the man claimed. "At least, not no good one."

"I'm just hungry."

"We all hungry, son. I'm hungry for whiskey, women, and money. Wha'chu hungry for?"

Orson thought for a moment. He wanted something clever to say. There were plenty of things he wanted. Money being the first. But as he glanced to the inside of the saloon, he realized he was hungry for fun, excitement. He was hungry for an honest living.

He was hungry for a life better than what he had. He was hungry for a family, or at least a different one than the one he had back in the Appalachians. As he poured over the thoughts, he simply said, "Just…food…"

"Just food? Shit, boy, I have food," the man smirked.

"Can I have some?"

The naivety made the stranger belt out a harsh sounding laugh, rough with smoke and booze. He took another puff of his cigar before standing in front of the boy, towering over him with such an ominous presence, "And what the hell do I get, boy?"

The question scathed its way into Orson's core. He'd heard it before, back when he kept a portion of his dignity intact. He didn't leave the East the same and he figured, deep down, that he probably wouldn't leave the West with any of his dignity in tow. He lowered his head and said, "I guess…whatever you think is fair."

The stranger took a step back. His eyes widened in his drunken stupor. The question itself did not hold any implication to him, at least, not until he heard the boy speak. As he looked down on the kid, he felt sorry for him. He too had been in a similar situation when he was young, that was a long time ago, but never did he give up his dignity. Before him stood no man or child, but a calf, lost to the world.

The man dug into his jacket and removed a small piece of cloth. He tossed it to the boy, "It's all yours."

Orson quickly peeled back the cloth. He stared into a small pile of jerky bits. He took the largest and tore off a quick bite with his teeth, smacking as he chewed.

The man watched him. He knew the kid was hungry, but he figured he was exaggerating the claim. He'd been cheated and burned before by those he invested in, but something came from the kid that he didn't expect, honesty. He asked the boy, "So, you's a crummy thief. You good at anythin' at all? You ever work? Daddy teach you some skills?"

Orson lifted his shoulders in a shrug as he tore into another piece of jerky.

"Fuck-sake, kid. You ain't good at shit?" the man pressed, wanting some form of answer.

The kid spoke without thinking between his chews, "Daddy never said so."

The stranger let out another raspy laugh. The honesty he admired reared its head again. He too became honest, "My daddy said the same shit too."

The man watched as the kid smacked his food, licked his fingers. The kid did have a hunger. He saw beyond the starvation. As a boy, the man too faced hard times, saw rough days. He sympathized with Newkirk. The honesty the teen spoke too struck a chord with him. That, as simple of a quality as it can be, became a rarity in life among the plains. The stranger was no honest man. He knew that about himself, but he tried to be honest with those he cared about. He foresaw something within the boy's honesty, and for a moment thought maybe that it too would rub off on him. As the kid took another bite of jerky, the man spoke, "Say, I uh...probably wouldn't ask this sober, but uh...I lost a feller out in the field not too long ago. My crew could use an extra rifle. Can you shoot?"

Orson thought nothing of it, "I've shot before."

"That's all experience need required," the man told him. "Ol' Ben couldn't shoot for shit. So, I guess you'll make do."

It finally hit Newkirk. He turned his head, staring to the man before him. He stood silhouetted to the lantern overhead. The beams of the flickering flame wrapped around the edges of the man's hat. He still saw the man's face beneath the shadows of the night and those cast by the lantern. He smirked to the boy. As Orson chewed, he felt relief. He felt that for once, an opportunity presented itself to free him of the invisible chains he latched onto himself. He swallowed the jerky, "You offerin' me a job?"

"My sober half says no," the drunk stranger replied with a grin. "But my drunk half don't like him too much."

The stranger stared into those bright eyes of the boy. The dirt and muck on the young man's face became almost nonexistent to him as the boy stood in his elongated shadow. He saw the hope swirling in them. He heard the honesty and excitement in the kid's voice. The whiskey swam around the edges of his eyes as he stared into the boy, and any sense of doubt of receding the offer vacated his mind. He said to the kid, "Yeah, boy. I guess I am offerin' you a job. It ain't much money, but it's honest money. More honest than tryin' to steal a man's hat, that's for sure."

Orson did not know how to take the man's offer. He just looked down to the empty cloth in his hand and folded it back over. He extended it towards the stranger, who took it quickly, placing it back into his jacket. The man swayed a bit, staggering with a quick step of his right foot. He shook his head as he muttered something under his breath. He felt awkward and the kid sensed it. There existed something about the man and the offer that he could not refuse. Somehow, someway, the kid felt the man wanted his best interest, whether it be out of pity or out of drunken stupor. Either way, the presence of the man felt similar to when he was out in the Appalachians, a small piece of home, something he ran from but desired to find elsewhere.

The man spoke quickly as he brushed by Orson, "Meet me here in the mornin' and we'll get you squared away. I cain't promise you nothin'. I'm pretty drunk, kid. I might not remember. I might, though. Meet me here and I'll make sure you ain't goin' go hungry."

And with that, the man stepped down from the porch, the light of the lantern no longer reached him. He wandered off down the street, passing beneath the lamplights every so often. He staggered and sang. Smoke of his cigar lingered in his wake. Orson watched him as he went, standing all alone on that saloon porch. He knew not to get his hopes up. The man, more than likely, was just being polite and Orson, with the knowledge of what men he did know since being out on his own, did not expect him to return come morning. That said, his heart fluttered with the idea of getting away, making an honest living, making a name for himself, even if it be with those closest to him.

He knew not what work the man offered, but he did not care. He wondered if it would be a life of excitement, one of the outlaws he heard about growing up. Maybe he would hunt the scalps of Indians. Maybe he would be a deputy or some type of lawman. Maybe he would find friends. Maybe he would find a life worth living. Maybe, just maybe, he would find what he was looking for since he ran away: a home.

He told himself under his breath that it was all wishful thinking. He knew better. The man was drunk, and he'd probably never see him again. And with that thought, the young Orson Newkirk stepped down from the porch of the saloon. He too wandered down the shadow swept road. Though, he owned no bed to return to, no place to go. He laid in that alley all night, never gaining a wink of sleep as he kept thinking of all those possibilities.

Chapter III

Waiting

1873

Orson stood on that saloon porch since before the sun came up. He watched the sun break behind the low hanging clouds, basking the city in such a gorgeous purple haze. The streets began quiet, hardly anyone stirred. It wasn't until an hour passed that most began their daily routines. The kid lingered on the wooden planks of the porch, nodding at folks as they walked by. They minded their business, not him. A man in a fancy hat and three-piece suit walked by. His cane carried his weight and he looked off into the morning light. Orson asked, "Got the time, mister?"

The man shot a quick glance to the boy, then dug into his vest pocket with his index finger and thumb, removing a small silver pocket watch. Orson thought of the money that could bring if the opportunity with the man from the night before did not present itself. The stranger looked up to him. His lip twitched under his mustache, "Just a bit after nine, son."

He went on his way and Orson stayed put, waiting.

The saloon sat quiet all morning but picked up around noon or so when the proprietor entered with his sweep boy and a dapper looking bartender. Orson still waited. They offered him a drink a little after one, but he declined. He waited. The thoughts of those possibilities began waning.

He grew tired of watching the sun moving across the sky. The young dreamer sat in one of the chairs on the porch. He looked down at his shadow, finishing off the last bit of a cigarette that a passerby gave him. He took his time smoking it, telling himself he would only go once it was done, biding as much time as he could justify to himself. He threw the cigarette down onto the worn wood planks, watching as the grey ribbons flowed from each end before bringing his boot down onto it, crushing it with a side-to-side motion.

A shadow grew over him, one that came with the echoing of boots and the slight twinkle of spurs. A drawled, sweet voice came before him, "You Jack's boy?"

Orson looked up, seeing the stranger standing before him. They wore a worn buckskin jacket. The fringe appeared torn in places, dangling by a few threads. He wore a decently made gun belt. A Colt .44 Open Top sat in the man's cross draw holster. The man, who appeared to be just as rough as the one Orson met the night prior, looked to be in his late twenties, maybe younger. A small beard accented his face. Those dark brown eyes stared down on the young boy under a wide brimmed hat.

Orson replied, not getting up from his chair, "I'm sorry?"

"I been watchin' you for about fifteen minutes. You ain't had no drink, nothin' to eat neither. You Jack's boy?" the man asked, leaning to his right side with a slight frustration.

"Jack who?" Orson asked.

"Jack Tanner."

Orson felt confused by that. It was then that he foolishly realized that he never took the man's name the night before, nor gave his. He told the stranger as much, "I met a man last night. He offered me a job…I didn't get his name."

The buckskin clothed man scoffed at that. He spat, "Jack done hired you but didn't tell you his name? He tell you what he did? What he hired you for?"

"He made it sound like he was a shootist," Orson admitted.

The young stranger threw his head back, letting out a chilling, demeaning laugh that rolled over Orson. The stranger spoke, "He ain't no shootist. Don't let that ol' bastard fool ya. C'ain't believe he hirin' the likes a you to replace Ol' Ben."

"He said he needed a rifle," Orson told the man, standing from the chair. He did not want to lose the opportunity so quickly, without even a chance to prove his worth.

The stranger spat again, "Not for no shootist. Huntin'…the big stuff too, bison, wolves, sometimes other things. Buffalo mostly."

"Ain't bison and buffalo the same thing?" Orson asked, not sure and feeling a bit ashamed with the question.

The stranger gave a slight nod, "I think so. Fuck if I know.

They all fall down the same, that f'er sure. They fetch a good price too, three dollars a pelt. You can get fifty cents a tongue too, but we ain't sell much of them."

Orson began to press, "The man that hired me…"

The stranger finished for him, "Jack."

Orson nodded, waiting for him to give the full name, so he could remember it.

"Jack Tanner. His drunk ass is named Jack Tanner," The stranger spat from the small pouch beneath his lower lip.

"Jack Tanner," Orson said aloud. "He didn't give much specifics."

The stranger put his hands on his gun belt. He rolled his fingers over the .44 ammunition that sat within the loops, "He didn't give no specifics on you neither. Had he told me I was pickin' up some scrawny lice-ridden orphan boy, I'd probably have told him to shove it. There's a thousand fellers here, all of which would do a better job than the likes a' you."

Orson heard everything that came from the stranger's mouth. He cared not for what he thought of him, thought of what he had to say. The thousand other men around Dodge probably could shoot better than him, probably didn't hesitate behind the sights either. Though, one word shook the boy because it was not true. He had a family, though he left them far behind. Orson said quickly, "I ain't no orphan."

"You look it," the man said, still rubbing the ass end of the cartridges in his belt.

Orson grew angry. The word heated him so, as if it were the sun that lit the city, "Well, I ain't."

The buckskin man leaned into Orson a bit, lowering his voice. His eyes widened a bit and he spat towards the boy's shoe, "You gettin' lippy with me, boy?"

Orson cared not of the man's growing intensity, for in his anger he lost sight of any repercussions. He said, behind grit teeth, "I ain't no orphan."

"And I said you look it, orphan boy," the young man said, now pushing his finger into Orson's chest. He continued, "Don't chu be getting' cute with me, ya hear? I'll knock your god damn teeth out. Jack calls the shots, but if he ain't here, I do. Got it? I say you look like an orphan, you shut your fuckin' mouth and nod."

Orson said nothing. He just stared into the beady brown eyes of the stranger who stood only inches from him.

The stranger said again, "You look like an orphan."

Orson didn't respond.

The stranger spat, "Now, fuckin' nod."

Orson balled his right fist. He stared into the man's eyes, seething with such an anger. It grew within him, consuming him. He didn't need to listen to this man. He didn't even know who he was, or if he really worked for the man he met the night prior. He wouldn't take it. He traveled too far, ran from an attitude similar, and did not end up in Dodge City to listen to it yet again.

"Parker," a familiar voice called from off the side of the saloon.

The man before Orson turned his head, calling out to the

voice, "Hey, boss—"

Before Parker even finished his sentence, Orson took his opportunity. He brought his fist back, then forward in one quick motion, hitting the man across his right cheek with a wild, uncoordinated haymaker.

Parker staggered, rubbing his cheek. He spat again. His eyes were wild as he looked back to Orson. He muttered, "You lil' sum'bitch!"

He leapt onto the kid, grabbing ahold of his shirt. Orson heard laughter from off to the side of the saloon, out in the street. Parker raised his fist, his left hand still gripping onto Orson's tattered shirt. Orson braced himself for the blow that was about to be thrown. He knew he would lose the fight, but he had to at least try.

The familiar voice came again, "Nathanial!"

Parker lowered his fist, turning to the man who approached the saloon porch. Orson shifted his eyes towards the man as well, once Parker let go of his shirt. Jack Tanner, the man from the night before, dismounted from his bay Standardbred. His long bison fur coat blew in the wind as he approached the two on the saloon porch. He wasn't alone though, for a two-horse wagon sat behind his horse. In the driver's seat, a thick man sat. A beard accented his face and his long hair glistened, slicked back and resting on the back of his neck. The big man chuckled to himself as he eyed Parker from beneath his floppy hat.

Riding shotgun in the wagon sat a younger man, maybe a

few years older than Orson. He possessed a soft face. He checked the time from a pocket watch that he kept in his leather vest. A head peered out from the back of the cart. Soft eyes looked onto Orson. A young man, of Orson's age, maybe younger, sat in the back of the wagon. He laughed out loud as he watched Parker turn to face Jack's approach.

"He hit me boss," Parker told Jack, but Jack walked right by him towards Orson.

Tanner leaned into the boy, "Why you hittin' my friend, boy?"

The honesty that Jack admired spewed from Orson's mouth, "He called me an orphan."

Jack opened his mouth to speak, but Parker turned, stepping quickly towards Jack. He looked panicked, as if he were in trouble, "I said he looked it. I never said he was one."

Jack nodded to Parker, then turned to Orson, "Is you an orphan?"

Orson felt a stinging in his heart by Jack's question. He hardly knew the man, but it still felt as if it were a betrayal. It was as if that honesty that Jack loved about the boy came into question. Orson's voice shook, "No. Pa's alive, I think."

"You think?" Jack asked, raising an eyebrow.

Parker chuckled, turning his back to the two. He faced the men on the wagon and threw his arms out as if to present Orson to them, "I knew he was an orphan."

Orson took a step forward, fist balled again, ready to strike Parker once more. He felt a hand on his chest, Jack's, who gave him a slight push back. Jack spoke to Parker, but still stared unto Orson, "That's enough. We all have to get along now."

Parker turned back to Jack. Orson saw the disbelief in his eyes as he asked, "You still hirin' this fool? He just sucker punched me like a gah damn coward!"

The broad man at the reins of the wagon belted out a deep laugh. He shouted down to Parker, "You deserve a good smack in the face, you asshole!"

Parker turned quickly, pointing his finger to the broad man, "Shut yer gah damn mouth, Bill! Ain't nobody talkin' to you!"

The broad man, Bill, just laughed back at Parker.

Jack turned to the distraught young man, placing his hand on his shoulder, "Yer hot, Parker. Go to the wagon."

Parker responded, "I ain't happy."

"Yeah, well…you called him an orphan. He ain't." Jack told him, pointing to the wagon as a final order.

Parker spat, "He is."

Jack did not speak another word to Parker. He just held his arm out, pointing towards the wagon with such authority. The young Nathanial Parker hung his head, walking over to the wagon. The young man next to Bill climbed down from the passenger's position, moving into the back of the wagon with the other youthful companion. Parker took his spot next to Bill who still held back some laughter.

Jack turned to Orson, "You hit him, or any of my other boys, without them lookin', I'll gut you. Understand me?"

Orson heard the shift in the man's voice. He did not think he exaggerated. A quick thought of him bleeding out on the plains with a knife wound terrified him. He nodded to his new leader, "I'm sorry."

"Don't be sorry," Jack told him. "Not if you meant it. He's an ass. I get that. He's loyal though and he brings in money."

"I won't hit him," Orson clarified.

"I didn't say you couldn't hit him," Jack smirked. "He deserves it sometimes. Hell kid, we all do. Just don't do it while he ain't lookin'."

Orson nodded, "Alright."

Jack nudged his head towards the wagon and his companions, "Get in. We's leavin'."

Orson did as instructed. He stepped down from the saloon porch, passing by the front of the wagon towards the back. Parker stared down onto him, a tower of seasoned authority. His beady eyes still seethed with anger towards Newkirk.

Orson looked away, unable to look upon that gaze anymore. He climbed into the back of the wagon with the two younger men. The one that originally rode upfront with Bill sat towards the back wall of the carriage. He tilted his hat forward as if he were going to sleep. However, the younger of the two stuck his hand out to Orson once Jack mounted his horse and the wagon began moving. The young man smiled, "You new too, huh?"

Orson shook the small hand of the young man. He didn't state the obvious.

The young man continued, "I ain't never been on a hunt with these fellers yet."

"Where'd they pick you up?" Orson asked.

"Just outside Lawrence."

Orson saw the brightness in the kid's eyes. He knew then that the young man was younger than he. If not in age, then in experience. He hadn't seen the hard times that Orson had while trying to hack it alone. He smelt the kid's dignity still intact as if it were a potent perfume. Orson nodded, "That's a long way with no huntin'."

"Ol' Ben got sick," the kid stated. "We's just tryin—."

Parker turned around from the top of the wagon. He interrupted the kid, "Charlie, I ain't gon' tell you again. Shut yer gah damn mouth!"

Charlie turned his head, then lowered it as if a beaten dog, "Sorry, Parker."

Parker then looked to Orson, "You shut up too."

Orson didn't respond. He just watched as Charlie leaned against the side of the wagon, too ashamed to look to his new acquaintance. He just looked out over the horizon. Orson too leaned against the side of the wagon. He looked out behind them though, watching as Dodge City slowly faded from view, hidden beneath the dust of the plains and the waves of heat that radiated from the ground. He felt nervous, scared. He wanted to prove himself to Tanner and his party. He wanted to show them that he could hack it, that he was a worthy employee. He cared not for the sport of hunting but needed an honest living. The wagon bounced around and he shut his eyes, trying to think no more of it.

The Appalachian sky sat with that haunting purple haze. Orson looked out across the clearing. He saw the fog seeping from the forest on both sides of the open field, watching as the pale crept across the field as if it were Death itself coming to claim the firstborns. A shadow moved within the tree line. Those glowing eyes, red and purple with the reflection of the light, blinked as they stared out across the field. Ears perked up from the mass of darkness, and slowly the silhouette of the coyote slithered out from beyond the tree line into the glade. It was not alone, for five more came with it. They moved together, trotting through the early morning fog…

Chapter IV
The Job Offer
1875

Orson awoke in a pool of his own sweat. The damp sheets that he laid covered with stuck to his clothes. He sat up quickly, breathing heavily. The spinning in his head vacated sometime during his slumber. The deep inhales he took as he eyed the Daniels farmhouse felt smooth in his lungs, no rumbling of phlegm. He let out a small cough from habit though, but his lungs no longer felt as if they were going to be hacked from his chest. He wiped his brow as he examined Thomas sitting in his rocker near the fireplace.

The old man stood from his chair, turning towards the young man. He gave him a nod, "You was mutterin' in your sleep."

Orson slid his body out of the bed, sitting on the edge. His pants clung to his sweaty legs. His feet, pale and gaunt, touched the harsh wood floors of the home. Next to them, he saw his worn boots with his damp socks hanging from the inside of the shafts. Orson paid no attention to what the man told him at first but did take interest as he realized that his fever felt broken. He asked, "What?"

"You been mutterin' in your sleep," Thomas repeated. "I never thought I'd nod off with all that gibberish you been spoutin'."

"I don't feel well," Orson admitted. While he did feel better than before, he still felt off in his bones. His lungs felt normal. His head no longer spun. The sweat though, that made him uncomfortable, nervous even. He bent over to put his socks and boots on, noting the creaking in his back and arms as he performed the action.

"I think your fever broke. Should be all downhill from here," Thomas stated. "Not sure what you had. Maybe just a cold? Ain't sure. All that coughin' had me worried you had the T. B."

"I ain't got no T. B." Orson replied, finally sliding his socks on. He began to rustle with his boots, "At least, not that I know of."

"Nah," began the old man, "you're clearin' up. I ain't no doctor though. I say that fever is broken. It's been long enough."

"How long I been in this bed?" Orson asked.

"Long enough," the old man joked. "A few days."

Orson nodded after his boots were on. He slid his jeans over them as he stood. He took a few paces, feeling the weakness still within his legs. He shook his head and told Thomas, "I should be headin' out."

Thomas watched the young man pace around the bed, trying to

find his bearings. He sensed the weakness in him. He too heard the bones cracking. His eyes did not break from the bandana that Orson used to repeatedly wipe the sweat from his forehead. He knew he couldn't have the young man go off just yet, not in that condition. "You ain't ready, yet."

"I ain't here to take your bed or steal your food. I just needed water, that's all."

Orson began to move towards the door. Thomas stepped towards him with a halfhearted attempt to block the way. He spoke quickly, "But you're sick, boy."

Newkirk felt a shudder through his body as the word "boy" left Thomas' mouth. He felt the sweat flood from his forehead. He felt his heart pick up pace. He felt his nostrils flare as he took another deep inhale. The word upset him. He shook his head and raised his voice to Thomas, "I ain't no boy, old man!"

He brushed by Thomas, opening the door to the farmhouse. Daylight flowed into the home, drowning the two men in its bright vibrancy. Thomas felt his heart skip a beat as Newkirk took a step out the door. He didn't mean to upset him. He truly didn't. He realized his mistake after the word left his mouth. The young man lived a far more exciting life than he, and he knew that somehow, he was jealous and somehow he forgot, in the heat of the moment, during the fear of being alone once more, that the physical age of the young man was a broken meter. His spirt was older, maybe older than Thomas'. He spoke sincerely, "I'm sorry."

Orson didn't stop. He continued out onto the man's porch. He grabbed his waist cut jacket that he left on one of the chairs days prior. Dust sat collected on it, and he beat it away as he threw it on, followed by his hat. He heard the sincerity in Thomas' voice, and matched it with his own, "I appreciate your help, Thomas. I do. But, I told myself I'd go as far West as I could and I ain't done it."

"You need rest," Thomas pleaded. He doubted the young man would die out on those plains alone. He didn't seem like the type to worry about a home to return to. Though, he did fear the sickness would return or grow within Newkirk without him knowing. He feared of illnesses. He feared of what they could do, for he'd seen one of the worst.

Orson stepped down from the porch, hating that the old man continued to press him to stay. He didn't want to. He didn't want to be a burden or feel as if he needed to be taken care of. He was his own man now, and he dared not take what he deemed charity. He said, "I ain't taken orders from no one no more."

Thomas watched as the young man moved away from the porch. He followed after him but stayed near one of the posts. He risked not losing his elevated position, "I guess I can't stop you, that's your choice."

Orson stopped and turned. He used his index finger to lift the flat brim of his hat in order to take a good look at the old man. He shook his head at the sight. It reminded him of his childhood in a sense. His father would lean against the porch like Thomas did. He would scold him as he did so. The sight alone boiled the young man's blood. He spat, "Stop actin' like you owe me some favors or somethin'. I don't know you."

"Owe you favors?" Thomas voice rose a bit. He barely knew the kid, but he refused to have his death on his conscious, not like those in the past. He couldn't let him walk out. He was angry though, truly. Orson appeared ungrateful, and without him, the kid would be dead. He didn't want praise or grand thanks, but he did want some recognition. He continued, "Hell, Orson. You owe me favors. I gave you rest when you needed it. I gave you food. You ain't even acknowledge it."

"What you sayin'?" Orson asked.

Thomas watched as the young traveler stopped at his horse. His right hand held the reins while his foot sat in the stirrup, as if he was ready to mount up. He looked back at Thomas, watching him and waiting for a response. All Thomas truly wanted was the kid to stick around, that's it. He wanted him to heal. He feared the worst for the boy, where he wanted to go. He thought of something quick. It wasn't a lie, for he could use the help, but he would've never offered had he not believed Newkirk to have the potential of worsening his sickness. Thomas spoke quickly, "Harvest is comin' soon and it's just me here."

Orson grabbed ahold of his saddle horn, ready to throw himself upward onto the horse, "You'll do alright."

"I won't though," Thomas admitted. "Last harvest…my

first without Betty…wasn't too good. I need this one, Orson."

Orson stopped, staring at the old man who still stood on his porch. He watched as Thomas crossed his arms, looking out towards the tree on the far end of the property. He didn't want to stick around with the farmer. He had things he wanted to do, places he wanted to see. He felt the weakness in his body creep back up, but he dared not tell the old man he was right. If he stuck around, it would have to be worth his while. That's the way he was taught. He asked Thomas, "You payin'?"

Thomas thought on that. He wouldn't use the kid's services for free, he knew that. However, the ungratefulness of the young man reared its ugly head. He would pay if it meant that his conscious remained clean. He made a plea to the boy, "I was goin' to ask you when the time felt right because I'm not one to ask for nothin'. I just thought that, maybe since you're here, you could lend a hand."

"I ain't no farmer," Orson chimed.

"It ain't that hard," Thomas reassured. "Wheat ain't that bad."

Orson let go of the saddle horn as he slipped his boot out of the stirrup. He looked over his horse, eyeing his old hunting rifle, eyeing what little provisions remained. He might get enough for a train ticket in Hays, he thought to himself. He may have to sell the horse, but even then, it would be difficult. He wasn't good with numbers. He didn't want to stay though. He wanted not just away from the farm, but away from Kansas all together. He had enough of it, and it only brought him grief.

Thomas pressed, "I'll give you a quarter of what we pull."

Orson turned, "That a lot?"

"It's fair, I think."

The greed instilled in Orson grew. He wanted to assure his exit from that place, "What's more than a quarter? A fifth?"

Thomas smirked at that, "A third."

By any usual means and by any form of education, the boy would have known Thomas' sincerity. Though, life on the plains, living in back alleys in Dodge, wandering in New Orleans, running from home at a young age, made it impossible for Orson to distinguish earnestness from manipulation. He saw it before. He fell for that trick in days past. He kept his guard up, "When's harvest?"

Thomas knew the boy truly contemplated sticking around, "A few weeks out. I've got my buyers lined up already. All you have to do is help me."

Orson couldn't glance back at his horse. He knew the opportunity to make a fourth or a third of the farmer's profit would be enough to get him away. He just feared that if he didn't leave in that moment, he never would. He held himself up for far too long, helping others when they asked, helping himself to whatever he delighted in the moment but not at heart. He felt himself weak in the knees. He thought it the sickness, but he wondered if it was his soul telling his physical body to flee. He couldn't though. He needed the money, but only if Thomas truly needed him.

Orson looked up to the older man, "You really need the

help?"

Thomas nodded.

Newkirk's hand tightened on the reins. He wanted to go. He had to go. He tried to reason with himself that it would only be a few weeks and then he'd leave. Yet, through experience he knew that to be a farce. It took him too long to get to Dodge when he first came. It took him too long to break free of the binding of others once he realized what he really wanted. He shook his head at the thoughts, knowing money was more than anything to him. It's what he learned and if he wanted anything, it would come through money.

Thomas watched as the boy contemplated. He knew he wouldn't get the answer he desired if he let the boy stand and stew for so long. The kid was a traveler. He didn't know what that meant deep down, but he knew that he wouldn't stick around forever. He knew that he was jealous of such a life. He nodded again, staring at the boy.

Orson looked up to Thomas. His eyes danced, conflicted, that much Thomas saw under the shade of the young man's flat brimmed hat. The young man took his horse's reins and tied them to the hitching post. Thomas reassured him, "Come on in. I'll start supper. We can start in the mornin'."

The old farmer turned his back to the kid, walking back inside the house. His boots echoed across the weak boards of the porch. Orson thought on it, looking back to his now hitched horse. He shook his head as he took his hat off. He cursed himself under his breath. He felt tired of helping others, tired of not doing what he wanted. Money is a powerful thing, he thought.

He followed Thomas inside, wondering if it would be stew again.

Orson watched as the sun fell over the small tranquil homestead. He rested his arm against one of the chairs on Thomas' porch. The way the orange vacated the sky left him in amazement as purple and navy blue began to overtake all colors. He felt as if it were a door closing before him. He wondered where he would be if he left. He thought he would be halfway to Hays. He wasn't sure. He was sure that he'd be hungry though.

The door to the farmhouse opened and Thomas stepped out holding two beers by their necks. Orson turned, accepting the drink from the old man who said, "Nothing like a beer after dinner."

Orson nodded at that but dared not speak his mind. He made an agreement with Thomas, a fourth of what was brought in. He didn't want to let him down, let him know that he second guessed his staying.

Thomas knew. He knew that the boy contemplated his choice. He saw the doubt. He felt bad about it, though he told himself he did it for the young man's best interest. The sickness would completely vacate him eventually, but he was still going to make him work, which he feared would make the sickness grow. He at least had a place to rest and the crops they yielded would not just help him pay what he owed in Hays, it would at least get the boy a starting chance heading West.

He watched as Orson took a sip of his beer, still staring out at that sundown. He knew he thought about going West. He wondered if knew that he stared out over his desire, "The sun sets West."

Orson shook his head, scoffing at that, "I know. I ain't stupid."

As Thomas sat in one of the chairs, he tried to justify his comment, "Sorry, it's just you didn't know fractions. Wasn't sure if you knew about that sun."

Orson rolled his eyes at the thought. Of course, he knew the way the sun moved across the sky. He lived out on the plains. He had to know. He also knew the stars. He knew which way was north in pitch darkness. As he thought of that, he processed whatever else Thomas told him, "Fractions?"

"Forget it," Thomas replied. "Just tryin' to make small talk."

Orson turned his back to the sunset, facing the old man. He leaned against the chair behind him, crossing his arms casually, "I ain't one for talkin'."

Thomas assumed that much. He always thought himself as quiet too, but when he sat in the presence of company, he found that he could not stop talking. He took that moment to hold his tongue, reflecting on trying to enjoy the silence, the sunset. Though, as he glanced at the boy, he examined some seeds of another life planted behind those eyes. Thomas couldn't resist pressing, "Why's that?"

"My daddy always said small talk is to fill the emptiness." Newkirk responded quickly, as if hammering the final nail into the conversation.

Thomas found some truth to that, deep down at least. He was empty. He tried to fill that gap with company. Maybe that's why he wanted the kid around. He had a taste of something other than loneness and he couldn't let it go. He waved that thought off, cracking a joke, "That supposed to mean something?"

Orson laughed at that. Though he found truth to his father's old statement, one that he held onto dearly, he realized he never bothered to think about it. When he did, he too realized that it held nothing but the emptiness of their relationship. It held nothing but the words he spouted as wisdom, false wisdom, for he saw his father as a fool. He saw himself as a fool for even attempting to impersonate him with his own words. He shook his head, chuckling to himself, his false wisdom, but dared not admit his shame, "I think it is supposed to mean something. I don't know. I could be sayin' it wrong."

The young man took the chair he leaned against, flipping it around, and sat down across from Thomas. He still looked out over the sunset, turning his head to do so as he drank another sip from his beer. Thomas asked, "Your daddy still alive?"

Orson kept staring at the orange orb that sat covered two thirds of the way by the tall grass over the plains, "Probably not, no."

"You don't know?" Thomas pressed, realizing it a bit too late. He wished he could take the question back.

Orson turned his head, looking downward. He dared not look to Thomas as he spewed his guts, "I left home, couple years back. He was mean. I was weak. Didn't see myself bein' 'round much longer with him."

"I see," Thomas said, leaving it at that. He sat in silence for a moment, finally learning to put his foot in his mouth. Birds chirped off in the distance. He focused on that.

Though, out of the silence of the porch, Orson continued, "He got sick. I left. That's that."

The two continued to sit silently together. Orson did not wish to continue the conversation. He felt ashamed just saying what was truth, why he left. He felt that Thomas judged him. Thomas didn't and he wanted to keep talking, but he knew that prying too much caused problems. He changed the subject, "So you come to Kansas then?"

Orson nodded, looking back out to the falling sun.

"Been anywhere fancy?"

"Fancy?" Orson questioned, wondering what the old man meant by that.

Thomas smirked, allowing himself to open up a bit too, take the awkwardness away from the previous conversation, taking the shame he smelt seeping through the young man's pores, "Yeah, I ain't never left Kansas since I came from Nebraska. This farm is all I really know."

"I'm not the kind they let in fancy places. Never really ran with those types neither."

"But you've seen fancy places, right?" Thomas really wanted the answer. He wasn't lying when he told the kid he hardly ever left the home. Before the sickness came, he cared for his family. After they left, he just saw no need to go anywhere else other than Hays when he needed.

"I did see a mansion when I was in New Orleans."

"What's that?" Thomas knew. He knew what a mansion was. He'd heard of them. He hadn't seen one, but he knew. He subtly tried to make up for his sunset comment before.

"It's a big house, bigger than this whole farm here, all the land. It was meant for one person. Can you believe that?" Orson turned, looking to the old man. He smiled.

Thomas smiled back, "I can't."

"I ain't kiddin' neither. It was big and only one man lived there. No kids. No wife. Just him."

Orson turned his head. He wiped the sweat from his brow with his handkerchief. He took a cigarette from his pocket, one he rolled a few days back. He plopped it in his mouth and lit a match under his boot. Thomas watched him, finally enjoying the silence.

The sun finally fell behind the horizon. The majority of the sky sat with such a vibrant purple hue. Though, orange streaks and hellfire red accented the lower portion of the horizon, right near what appeared to be the end of the earth for Thomas. He saw the reflection of that light in Orson's eyes. He daydreamed about something, he wasn't sure what, but he had a feeling. He watched as the smoke bellowed from the kid's mouth and he coughed a bit. Those lungs weren't fully healed and that made Thomas not regret his persuasion of the kid to stay.

Thomas opened his mouth to speak but chose not to. He liked the silence. He knew Orson did too. He learned, finally, to hold his trap. All he wanted to do was comment on the obvious: Orson saw some things.

Chapter V
The First Hunt
1873

The Tanner Party stood around the wagon. Timothy Masters, the other young man that accompanied Charlie and Orson in the back of the coach for most of the journey, now sat at the reins smoking. He looked back to Orson and Charlie, who stood awkwardly a few meters away. Bill and Parker whispered to each other near the horses of the wagon. Orson tried to listen to what they said, but they kept their voices low. He heard them speak, but not their words. Charlie glanced to Orson with uncertainty, and Orson reciprocated the look. They all waited for Jack's return.

Orson's legs ached. He sat in the back of that wagon for two days, heading north out of Dodge. They didn't stop once, cycling through those Jack trusted most at the reins. Orson and Charlie of course never received the chance to get out of the cart. He felt as if he was just a piece of a cargo, stocked next to the rifles, ammunition, and food stores. He felt the stiffness in his legs and stretched them with small motions as he stood next to Charlie. He did as he was told, stay quiet and wait.

Before the party, a large hill stood and on it, a silhouette appeared on horseback. Orson looked upon the figure in such amazement. The blue sky glowed vibrant behind the shadowy rider. The grass, so lush and golden, waved as a large gust of wind came rolling across the plains. The rider and his horse stood for a moment, but soon he kicked his heels into the sides of the horse and down the hill they ran at full gallop. He approached the party and soon the sunlight lit him as he approached. It was as if Orson didn't recognize him at first, so amazed by the sheer mysterious awesomeness of the silhouette. The rider slid from his saddle as his horse slowed. He tipped his hat back and Orson knew for sure then that he looked upon Jack Tanner.

"Just over that hill there. A decent sized herd, they's standin' still," Jack said, wiping sweat from his brow with the sleeve of his fur lined duster.

Parker spat as he turned, walking with Jack towards the back of the wagon, "What's the call, boss?"

Jack moved past Orson and Charlie, not even giving them a glance. He stood at the back of the wagon where he removed one rifle. He slung it over his shoulder and removed his canteen. He took a quick sip. His face grimaced as a small trail of dark brown liquid rolled onto his chin. He rubbed the liquor away from his mustache, "Get the rifles. We can pick 'em off as they's standin' still. We can show the new boys how to shoot."

"C'ain't they stay with the wagon? We can take Timothy," Parker argued.

Jack finally shot a glance to Orson and Charlie who stood awkwardly on the outskirts of the conversation. He gave the two a smirk, then moved past Parker, heading back to his horse. He spoke to his young lieutenant without looking to him, "Timmy will stay with the wagon. The new guys need experience."

Timothy Masters finally spoke up. It was the first Orson heard him speak in the two days since they met, "Why I gotta stay?"

Jack stopped at his horse, turning slowly towards Timothy at the reins of the wagon. His presence was dominating, even though the young man towered above him, Jack stood as if he were ten feet tall. The leader told him, "'Cuz I said."

Parker continued the argument, "It'll be better with Masters up there instead of the orphan and the dipshit."

Jack wanted none of it.

As Parker shot a dirty look towards Orson and Charlie, Jack spoke with a harsh tone, "They gotta learn sometime. Listen, there's a lot up there and we can kill plenty and make it back to Dodge quick."

Bill chimed in with agreeance, "Fast money."

Jack turned to the broad, bearded man. He gave him a wide smile, "Tha's right, Bill."

Orson and Charlie gave each other a small nod in understanding that this would be their moment to prove themselves to the others. Orson felt a weight in his heart. He hadn't hunted since the days of being a small child. He never cared much for it, even with his father's great disapproval. He would prove himself though. He wouldn't let Jack down the way he let his father down, or so he felt.

Jack called over to the boys, "Hustle up now. We're going to do damn well today."

Orson and Charlie stood at the back of the wagon. Bill and Parker were in front of them, rummaging through all the supplies to get what they needed. Parker grabbed a fine-looking breach loading rifle. He handed it to Bill who slung it over his shoulder. Bill took hold of a bag and began to remove brass cased cartridges. He handed a few to Parker, then turned and gave some to Orson and Charlie. Orson felt the coldness of the brass in his palms, reading the small markings on the ends. He realized they were hefty fifty caliber rounds.

Parker reached into the bag that Bill held, grabbing even more rounds and stuffing them into his pockets. He spoke quickly, "Get some boys. Jack ain't gon' let you run back down for ammunition."

Charlie quickly reached into the bag, grabbing as many rounds as he could. The lead tips hung out from between his fingers. He stuffed them in his trouser pockets. Orson did the same. Parker turned, handing Orson another breach loading rifle. Then, he gave one to Charlie. Orson studied the disappointment in his face. It mirrored that of Timothy who still sat at the reins of the wagon with his head turned, watching from afar. Parker looked over Orson and Charlie, who held their rifles awkwardly at their hips. He knew they weren't experienced shooters but when he saw them standing there without a clue of what to do, he felt that Jack made a bigger mistake. Nobody could replace Ol' Ben, even though the old bastard couldn't shoot either.

Parker didn't speak to the boys. Instead, he glanced over to Bill, "You ready?"

Bill nodded, throwing the pouch of ammunition into the back of the wagon carelessly.

Parker turned, walking around the side of the wagon. Bill followed him. Orson and Charlie paused a moment, unsure if they too should go. It wasn't until Bill turned back and gave them a slight motion with his head, a signal for them to get moving, that they began to scurry after the two seasoned hunters.

Orson watched as Bill and Parker broke over the crest of the hill first. He and Charlie lagged behind a bit, a few paces, all because of their nerves. Orson slung his rifle over his shoulder as they reached the top. He didn't want Jack to see his hands rattling on the barrel of the rifle. He wanted to act like he was ready, a good hunter, emotionless. He wasn't. He hated hunting. Though, he told himself it was the most honest living he'd seen since he left home.

Once the two boys reached the crest of the hill, Jack Tanner stood idle, greeting them with a quick turn of his head and the flash of a smile. Parker and Bill stood off to his side while Jack looked out, downward across the other side of the hill, across the shallow slope. His rifle rested across his back. His long bison coat flapped wildly in a gust of wind. His hands rested on his gun belt. He chewed an unlit cigar as he stared at the massive herd of bison before him.

Orson had not seen anything like it. He was too captivated by Jack's dominating presence to realize it at first, but the herd of bison stood at the base of the hill. Some moseyed along. Some grazed. They groaned and communicated with each other. The herd itself stretched on for what appeared like miles. Orson thought of counting them, if he could, but he made a rough estimate of more than a thousand for sure. The beasts stood close to one another. The golden grass they stood atop was hard to see under the various blacks and browns of their pelts huddled side-by-side. The young Orson felt his jaw drop as he stared out across the vastness of such a wonder.

The party stood no more than fifty yards away from the massive herd at the top of the hill. Orson and Charlie moved closer to Jack and the others, still in awe of such a size. Orson heard of the bison and the scale of which they ran in. He just never really believed it, or at least thought about it. As he stared out, he felt his breath taken away.

Parker spat, "You was right, decent sized herd for sure."

Jack raised his arms, as if to present a gift to his followers, "Look at 'em, boys. They don't even know we're here."

Charlie moved past Orson, walking between Jack, Parker, and Bill. He stood on the edge of the downward slope towards the herd. He raised his rifle from his hip. He fumbled with it for a minute, struggling to keep the barrel pointed where he wanted the bullet to go. He had no experience. Orson knew the kid never touched a weapon in his life. It looked as if the young boy wanted to fire a round into the herd, seeing if it would hit anything at all. His rifle lowered as Bill put the flat of his palm on the barrel. He spoke quickly with a grin, "Would help if you loaded it first."

Parker let out a loud, demeaning laugh. He shook his head as he spoke to Charlie, "You lucky we's picked you up, you dipshit. You'd be dead already. How the hell you made it this far—."

"Load 'em and I'll tell you where to shoot," Jack interrupted his lieutenant to tell Charlie and Orson. He then turned his head towards the seasoned Parker, "Take Bill and head a little down the line. I'll have 'em watch you two first."

Parker spat his tobacco, soiling the golden grass of where they stood. He grabbed the strap of his rifle as he moved past Bill, heading a little ways down the slope towards the bison herd. Bill followed after him, unslinging his rifle and loading a round in the breach. Charlie's eyes watched as Bill loaded his weapon as he walked, and he tried to imitate the act but struggled with opening the breach at the top of his weapon.

Jack moved towards the boy, grabbing ahold of his rifle, opening the breach with ease, and slid a .50 caliber round into the weapon. He looked to the boy, first with a stern gaze, but that quickly faded as he gave the boy a wink and smile. Charlie looked to his leader in amazement. Jack admitted, "They don't know you ain't never shoot before."

Orson thought that odd, to hire a person who never shot a weapon in a career that required it. He asked without thought, "You ain't?"

He knew by the way that Charlie held the weapon, tried to load the weapon. He just felt shocked to hear it.

Charlie looked to Orson, shaking his head. He lowered it, as if defeated before the battle began.

"'Ay, don't pay no mind to Parker. He's as dumb as anyone. He's loyal though, when it counts. So, show him up today, you hear?" Jack told him, tossing the boy's rifle back to him.

Charlie fumbled with the weapon as he caught it, "I hear."

Jack's gaze then turned to Orson. He didn't speak, and neither did young Newkirk. He quickly unslung his rifle and opened the breach. He dug a round out of his trousers and slid it into the weapon, closing the breach. He looked to Jack. He knew that he appeared as if he were wanting affirmation, because he was. All that Jack gave was a quick nod.

A gunshot pierced the air. It drew the attention of both young boys as they looked down the hill towards Parker and Bill. Before them, the great herd stood idle as if nothing happened. Though, on the outer edge of such a mass, a great black bison laid dead. Crimson flowed from a wound in its side as the other bison moved ever so slightly away from it, continuing to graze.

Orson looked back towards Parker and Bill. They stood enveloped in a cloud of gunpowder. Parker reloaded as Bill took aim. He fired. The loud crack of the rifle caused Orson to jump. A massive bellow of smoke and sparks flowed from the end of the rifle, and on the other end of the cloud, another bison dropped. It too hit in the side. Those around it barely noticed, continuing to eat.

Jack pointed to Parker and Bill, resting his hand on Charlie's shoulder, "See 'em? They can kneel, stand, what have you, but they ain't goin' crazy blastin' away at the poor ol' bastards."

"Why ain't they movin'?" Charlie asked, his eyes fixated on the grazing herd around the dead.

"They big dumb animals. They don't know no better," Jack said, patting his hand on Charlie's shoulder. He extended his arm back out, pointing to one particular bison. He continued, "Now, look where he's gon' shoot it."

Orson's eyes zeroed in on the bison. Charlie's too. They watched as the bison ate a tuff of grass, chewing it with its mouth open. Those deep brown eyes stared downward. The sun glistened off its black horns. Its deep brown hide sat caked with grass and thorns. It buckled as a puff of pink smoke erupted from its rib cage. Blood flowed from an open wound as the crack of Parker's rifle filled the air. The bison fell dead, crimson flowing like rivers from the sucking wound.

"You ain't gotta shoot it in the head. Them thick skulls gon' bounce the round right off. Seen it half a dozen times," Jack told Charlie. He looked back to Orson, making sure he understood the information as well, "You ain't gotta shoot it anywhere but in the lungs. Shoot it there, it falls, the others ain't gon' panic."

Charlie watched as the recently shot bison kicked its hooves, entering its death throes. The herd around it remained undisturbed to the death that entered their sanctuary. The young kid blinked, trying to fight back the rising waters within his eyes. He shook his head subtly, muttering under his breath, "They just standin' there…"

Jack paid no mind to the boy. He continued on, "Easy three dollars per beast. If you see that herd disturbed, you best holler. These bastards get real mean when they runnin' for their lives."

"I can't believe they ain't movin'," Charlie said louder, his eyes still fixated on the dead among the living. He never saw anything like that before. He always thought that death was noticed, death was not just feared, but avoided. The bison paid no mind to it. He couldn't fathom that. He began to wonder if he too would die and if Tanner and the others would pay no mind, if that's just how life and death on the plains worked. He fought that thought, telling himself they were just stupid animals. He lost that fight though.

Jack stared the boy up and down, taking note of the weakness rising within him. He'd seen it before. Parker was that way. Timothy was too. He'd seen it before them though, seen it back before he ever entered Kansas, back before he was a hunter of great beasts. He drew that weakness away from himself like a poison from his heart when he beat a man half to death. He'd seen it vacate countless others, including Parker and Masters on their first hunts with him. Charlie would be no different. He paid no mind to the conflict within the boy. It would leave him. He just had to pull the trigger, see that death meant nothing, nothing when it was an animal.

The leader removed his hand from Charlie's shoulder and told him softly, "If at any point you get nervous that they startled, you holler to me and make a run back to Timmy."

Charlie didn't respond to Tanner. He just stared ahead, lost to the gun smoke and the fury it brought with it. Jack noticed but said nothing. He just patted the boy's shoulder as if he looked for some sort of reply. All he received was a slight nod of the head from the young boy. He then turned to Orson, who gave a quick nod of approval and understanding.

Jack spoke quickly, "Alright then, let's go boys. You first, Newkirk."

Orson raised his rifle as Jack moved away from Charlie. He aimed down the sights of the weapon, lining up the small post at the end of the barrel with the side of a bison he randomly selected from the herd. His finger rested on the trigger, twitching with a few nerves.

Jack stood next to him, hands on his hips, his coat thrown open and behind him. He towered over the young man as he looked at his firing stance, looked at the way he aimed that rifle. He noticed the twitching of the kid's finger and he knew that he too was nervous like the other young boy. Though, he could tell from the shooting stance and the way Newkirk aimed that he'd shot before, that he probably killed before. He told Orson, "Aim for them lungs, boy."

Orson did as he was instructed, lining that post up to the ribs of the bison. He kept one eye closed as he stared down the length of the barrel. He imagined what it would feel like to kill such a thing. He hoped he didn't startle the herd or that the bison didn't moved last minute. He didn't want to miss. He didn't want to kill it, but he didn't want to let Jack and the others down. He told Jack, "I'm aimin' at 'em."

Jack studied that twitching finger. He knew it would come down to this moment. He would have to see if the kid could stomach it, if he had the guts for the work. If he couldn't do the easiest part, he couldn't do the hard part. He replied quickly, "Then wha'chu waitin' for?"

Orson kept his finger on the trigger. He didn't want to squeeze it. He had to though. At least, that's what he kept telling himself. He couldn't lose this honest work so early. He couldn't go back to trying to thieve, trying to scrounge anything he found in alleys. The bison he aimed at looked upward towards Orson. Those deep brown eyes looked right into his soul. They connected for a moment, something strange that the kid felt deep down, as if nature and he had become one just from that simple look. Though, he thought nothing of it in that moment because panic set in. The bison moved its head and he feared it would move its body too. He couldn't miss. It was his opportunity. As that bison stared deep into his eyes, deep into his soul, Orson squeezed the trigger. Those eyes closed behind a bellow of gun smoke.

The kid didn't know if his round hit home and his heart stopped. That all faded as Jack exclaimed, "Damn good shot, Newkirk!"

The leader slapped Orson on the back as he let out a cheer. Newkirk squinted his eyes as he stared out across the herd. They were undisturbed. None moved near the body of the bison he shot. A fountain of blood spewed upward like a geyser from the lung wound for a half second as the bison laid on its side. The kid looked away, opening the breach of his rifle and discarding the spent brass casing. It wasn't until he looked to Jack, seeing his visual excitement, his wide eyes and lifted cheeks with a massive grin, that Orson smiled back. He felt good. Not for the killing, but because of the approval he so longed for finally arrived.

"You next," Jack said, stepping away from Orson over to Charlie.

Charlie didn't turn to face the man as he stood next to him. He took his rifle, placing the butt of the rifle to his shoulder.

He didn't aim down the sights of the weapon. He kept his head straight forward, trying to gauge where the bullet would land based on where he thought the end of the barrel pointed. Jack told him, "Line up that little post on the end of the barrel. Line that up with the ribs."

Orson pointed his rifle downward, crossing his arms around the stock, resting while he watched his inexperienced acquaintance try his hardest. Charlie placed his cheek where the wood met iron on his rifle but raised away once he heard a slight grovel from Jack. He kept his head low, peering down the shaft of the rifle, looking at the small post at the end of the barrel. On the other end, he saw a bison lined up.

"It on the ribs?" Jack asked.

Charlie squinted, trying to focus on the post and the bison. The rifle swayed in his nervous hands, dipping downward, upward, and to the sides as if he were drawing small circles with it. He responded, "I think so."

"Do you think you can hit it?" Jack pressed, looking away from the boy and down range towards the bison herd. He gauged the distance in his head. Even an inexperienced shooter could make that shot, he thought to himself. Charlie would make it and that weakness would vacate his soul.

"Yeah," Charlie muttered, still fixated on that post. "I think I can hit it."

"Then hit it," Jack turned back to the boy with a wide grin.

Charlie lifted his finger, resting it against the warm metal of the trigger. He felt the inside flesh of his index begin to twitch as if his body refused to obey the command. He tightened the finger, yet it still twitched. The post at the end of the rifle doubled and Charlie felt his head go light. He closed his eyes for a moment. They too twitched as he felt a wave of relief in the darkness of his lids.

"Shoot," Jack told the kid once more.

Charlie opened his eyes, but they did not look to the post at first. They glanced to Jack. He watched the grin fade. He saw that doubt set into his eyes and he questioned whether or not Charlie was capable. The boy looked back to the sights. They were off the bison, pointed towards the golden grass at the back hooves of the beast. He raised the rifle, lining the post back up with where Jack told him to shoot. His finger tightened on the trigger for a moment, but he feared the sound it would make. He feared the fire that would spew from the barrel and the ferocity that came with it.

"Gah, dammit kid! Shoot!" Jack shouted. His brow arched in frustration. His eyes widened. He was not pleased by the hesitation.

Orson continued to watch the two from a distance. He felt the sweat in his palms as he gripped the stock of his rifle. He stared as Jack hunched over near Charlie, lowering himself to the same height as the boy. Newkirk had seen that hesitation before, because he too hesitated when he used to hunt with his father. He never cared much for killing, animals or otherwise.

He pushed that out of his mind to kill that bison though, to impress Jack. Charlie just had to do the same. They were nothing but animals, he told himself. That's it. It wasn't like Charlie would be killing a man. Maybe animals didn't have souls, and maybe that's how he could justify it to himself. Maybe they did, but bison were not men. Coyotes were not men.

"Shoot!" Jack screamed into Charlie's ear, no more than an inch away.

Charlie felt startled. His right ear rang with bells from the shout. He panicked, closing his eyes as if to hide away from the pressure forever. He squeezed the trigger. The rifle puked smoke and flame. The gun bucked upward. Charlie's grip was weak on the barrel and it slipped out of his hand and into the dirt at his feet. Sparks flew from the breach. He felt the quick sharp pain as they peppered his face, then faded away as if nothing ever happened. The smoke surrounded him. His ears rang with such loud bells that he dropped the rifle to cover them. Though they rang, he still heard the cries of agony rolling across the field.

Orson squinted, looking out towards the herd. Charlie missed the lungs. He hit the bison, but only hit it in the hindquarters. It screamed such a sound as it writhed around, trying to run. Those around it began to realize the danger they were in and began to stir. Jack quickly unslung his rifle from his shoulder, firing a round with such precision and skill, it looked as if he didn't aim. The bullet struck the bison in the ribs, silencing it. Those around the bison still stirred, clearing away but not too far. They continued to graze. Jack let out a sigh. He'd been holding his breath in nervousness, but now that the herd appeared safe for the slaughter, he turned back to Charlie.

The young man covered his ears still, digging inside his left with his index finger. Jack slung his rifle over his shoulder and in one swift motion, cracked Charlie upside the head with the back of his closed fist.

Charlie cried out, "Ow! I'm sorry!"

Jack didn't speak at first. He hit the boy two more times with his righteous closed fist. Orson watched as the man's face turned red as Hell itself as he started to scream to the young man, "Sorry? You know what you could'a done? That herd be long gone had I not been quick enough. You stupid lump a' shit!"

Tanner hit Charlie again. Parker and Bill no longer shot. They moved up the hill a little ways to get a better view of the berating of the green member. They smirked and joked under their breath. Orson stood emotionless. He'd seen this type of discipline before. He was just happy he wasn't on the receiving end.

Tears flowed from Charlie's eyes, leaving clear streaks in the dirt and gunpowder on his face. He sobbed, "I didn't mean to!"

"You told me you could do this, boy!" Jack screamed. "You fuckin' lyin' to me?"

Charlie's eyes stared on, wide with panic. Orson knew that the boy feared losing his job. He saw that the boy felt that he let everybody down. That panic, that fear, that thought of isolation and going back to the streets. He cried harder, "No, I can! I promise!"

Jack hit him again. This time, his fist connected with the boy's cheek, hard, knocking the distraught kid to the ground. He sobbed even harder, something that made Jack redder, more angry, more frustrated. He screamed himself hoarse, "Stop fuckin' cryin'! Now!"

"Hey, boss!" Parker shouted from down the slope of the hill.

Tanner turned to him, still fuming with that unchecked rage.

Parker laughed, "I told ya, he ain't got the stomach!"

Bill laughed too.

Charlie continued to weep.

Jack boiled over, "Shut the hell up, Parker! I'll bust your skull next, with that lip'a yer's!"

Parker cared not. He and Bill joked to one another as they moved back down the hill. They began shooting once again. That drew Orson's attention away from the commotion between his leader and his acquaintance. He found some sort of peace watching Parker and Bill drop a few more bison. It made his stomach ache, but he felt it better than be washed with memories he chose to forget.

Tanner drew Newkirk's attention with a snap. He told him, "Go on, shoot a few more."

Orson took his rifle from his resting position. He did not put it to his shoulder. He hesitated at the thought. His eyes were fixated on the herd, but his mind stayed focused on Jack and Charlie.

"Head back down to the wagon and send Timmy up here," Jack told the inexperienced kid.

Charlie pleaded, "I can do it."

"Not today."

"Boss...," Charlie whimpered, "please..."

Jack began screaming again, "I ain't your fuckin' boss yet, boy. Yer lucky if yer still employed once we get back to Dodge!"

Another whimper escaped Charlie. He so desperately wanted to prove himself, "Please..."

Jack hunched over, leaning into the boy. He spoke between gritted teeth, "Get Timmy Masters, right fuckin' now!"

Charlie turned his back to his leader, returning the way they came. He shot Orson a quick glance of defeat, but his eyes tore away quickly, staring back down at the golden grass at his boots. Orson watched him for a moment as he headed down the hill.

Jack approached, standing at the side of Orson. The young man felt the frustration and anger radiating from him. He dared not let him down.

Orson quickly raised his rifle, tucking it into his shoulder. He picked a bison out of the herd, lining the post with the ribs as he was taught moments before. He held his breath but dared not close his eyes.

"Don't hesitate, now," Jack told him.

He didn't.

Chapter VI
Two Calves
1873

The sun began to set. Thunder echoed across the plains as the remainder of the herd ran. Their hooves rumbled the surface of the Earth, sending vibrations every which way. A hellish haze stretched across the sky. A red hue rose from the earth, just along the edges of the horizon. Fifty dead bison laid stretched across the field. Crimson stained stocks of tall golden grass. The wind blew, and with it, the stench of iron filled Orson's nostrils as he stared down upon the site. His clothes smelt of gunpowder. His hands, sooty and black, shook from stress and exhaustion. He couldn't see his face, but he felt the grime on his cheeks, on his mouth, around the edges of his eyes.

He walked with Jack through the graveyard. A small cigarette hung from Tanner's mouth, smoke rolling around the edges of his smirk. He stopped and stood near a deceased bison. He tucked his hands into the loops of his gun belt. His rolling block rifle rested slung on his shoulder as he looked out across the field, off towards the retreating bison that disappeared over the horizon. Orson knew that the man was proud. He just wasn't sure of what, for Orson felt a sense of shame. That shame faded as Jack looked to the boy with a toothy grin that held his cigarette. Orson smiled back.

Timothy Masters approached from behind Newkirk. He held a large knife that glistened with the redness of the sun. Jack gave the young man a nod, saying something that Orson could not hear over the ripping wind. Orson watched as Masters knelt before the dead bison, kneeling in a pool of blood. He thrusted the knife into the gut of the dead beast, sliding the blade downward from the animal's sternum to its genitals. Such a great river of red spewed from the belly of the beast.

Jack spoke, but Orson did not listen. He only heard the wild winds as if the earth itself tried to drown out the opposition. His eyes laid fixated on that knife, that beast, Timothy. The young skinner threw his arms inside the beast, tossing out whatever he found, a liver, a heart, bowels, and those destroyed lungs. He flung them at his feet, and he stood in them as if they weren't there at all. His trousers were soaked in such a violent gore. His black boots dyed red. The smell of iron radiated from him and seeped back towards Orson, who turned his head away.

Newkirk saw Parker off in the distance, gutting and skinning, the same as Masters. He could not escape it. So, why fight it, he thought to himself. He turned back, watching as Masters began to peel the furry hide away from the body of the bison. The flesh and muscle beneath it glistened pink and white, so vibrant. Orson held back a gag as Jack helped tear the hide away from the bison. Once free from its previous owner, Jack held it in one hand above his head, so victorious in stance, as he eyed it for any imperfections.

Jack spoke to Orson as Masters began to cut away at the horns, "…then we take the hide. Then, we gon' salt it so it ain't gon' go bad on our trip back."

Orson did not speak, he just looked to Jack. His leader stared back, still holding that hide above his head. It fluttered in the wind. His eyes stared at Orson, waiting for some kind of response. He needed to know that he was heard. Orson gave three swift and shallow nods of his head. Jack grinned, spitting the cigarette from his mouth onto the skinned bison.

Once the horns were cut free, Masters held them for a minute in his hands as he looked over them. He raised his right cheek to a thought, then threw them into the dirt. He too looked to Orson. Orson found himself admiring the young man in some way. The way he stood there with his arms crossed, covered in such a foul sticky red, the gunpowder beneath it all. Orson wondered if he too could do that, if he too could find a way to escape his doubt about his honest living.

Timothy saw that Orson struggled with what he did. He assured him, "What? It's like skinnin' a big ol' rabbit."

Jack laughed, "It's a little more complicated than that, Timmy. I appreciate the comparison though."

Tanner dug into his jacket pocket, removing a small silver flask. He opened the top, taking a heavy drink from it. He wiped the liquor from his mustache as he handed the flask to Masters, who wiped his bloody hands clean on his bloody jeans before imitating his leader's action. Timothy handed the flask back to Jack, who took another sip before holding it out to Orson. The young man eyed the flask, seeing his reflection in the dark brown smudges on the outer rim of the container. He couldn't recognize himself beneath the soot and the grime, but he knew it was him. He took the flask from his leader, taking a heavy drink. He grimaced and coughed.

"Don't like whiskey?" Masters asked him.

"I didn't say that," Orson replied, handing the flask back to Jack.

"You look it," Masters smirked.

Jack moved over to Masters, patting him on the shoulder. He told him, "I appreciate you, Timmy. Will you fetch the shy one and the wagon? Just about needin' to pack things up."

Masters nodded to both Jack and Orson before turning his back and moving on through the field. Orson watched him in an odd fascination of admiration. The way he moved, so confident, so young, and the way that Jack spoke to him made Orson want that. Parker spoke to Masters as he passed him. He wasn't called a nickname or demeaned. Respect was demanded from him. Orson knew not how long he rode with the Tanner party, but the way it appeared was that their souls were interconnected long before this time or even before the world began.

"Come on," Jack told Orson.

Orson followed after him as they moved through the field once more. They stopped at another dead bison. Jack reached to the back of his gun belt, removing a large knife. He looked to Orson, handing him the blade. Orson took it without question, eyeing the fine craftsmanship of the worn weapon. It saw some rough times, probably made Jack plenty of money. Through all of it, it stayed sharp, still beamed with the brightness of the setting sun.

"You try. Don't botch the job, Newkirk," Jack told him. "You do, you lose three dollars of your pay. Got it?"

Orson nodded.

The kid knelt next to the dead bison. The wound in its side sat caked in thick dried blood. The dark brown fur laid littered with dirt and grass. Patches of loose fur covered the entire upper half of the large female. Orson stared into the deepness of those dark dead eyes. They still looked living, though he knew it to be impossible. He held the knife in his hand as he knelt in the gore before the beast, the same as Masters. He felt the sweat accumulate in his palms around the handle of his blade. It had to be a trick of the low light, for he swore he saw the ribs rise and fall as if the beast still breathed.

He took the blade, thrusting it just below the sternum. He half expected to hear a squeal, a cry for help. Nothing came though, nothing but the sound of steel against flesh. The puncture began to leak with scarlet. He held his breath as he slide the blade down the center of the bison.

"'Ey, Jack!" a voice called out. Orson turned his head, seeing Bill approach at a slow and steady pace. He continued, "Parker's got somethin' for ya."

"What?" Jack questioned.

Orson stood idle, waiting for his one-man audience to return. He kept his hand on the handle of the weapon as he paused his cut. Yet, the blood did not as it continued to flow from the gash.

"Something for the new guys," Bill said. He turned his head to Orson and gave a smirk, but still spoke to Jack, "He said you'd like it."

Jack turned his head to the young man, giving a wide smirk. Orson only stared upwards at him as he said, "Well, come on then."

Orson removed the blade from the gut of the beast. He handed it back to Jack who wiped it with a worn dusty cloth before placing it back in its sheath. Bill turned his back to the two and began to walk away without a word. Jack followed him, and Orson did too.

The wagon approached the graveyard from down the hill. Masters sat at the reins. Nobody was next to him, but Orson saw Charlie peering over the back of the wagon. Jack called to the two, "C'mon then, boys! Get down here! Parker has somethin' for us!"

Masters and Charlie dismounted from the wagon. Jack waited for them to approach, letting Bill head off to the other side of the clearing. Once they all stood together, no words were exchanged. They followed Jack over and through the dead that surrounded them. Masters stood at his side while Charlie and Orson walked together behind them. Orson glanced to Charlie, but the kid kept his head forward, only looking to Jack. His eyes were lost, staring not to the man but through him. Shame seeped from his pores more than the sweat that ran down his face.

Jack stopped at a circle of dead bison. Bill stood with Parker. The scrawny long body of Nathaniel Parker hunched over slightly. His arms were crossed, holding onto a small calf that wiggled wildly trying to escape. The brightly colored calf opened its mouth, wide enough for a yawn, but let out a small cry of fearful anguish. It was not the only one, for a dead female laid nearby and around it, a small red fur calf cried out as it pranced around its fallen mother. It nuzzled its nose against hers expecting a response, not understanding life or death. It screamed and cried as it refused to vacate the killing field.

Parker smiled to Jack, speaking over the screaming calf he carried, "Looky what I got."

Jack returned the smile. He gave a couple of shallow nods as he gave a glance to Bill, who too smiled back.

Masters chimed in, "I'll get the spokes."

Timothy turned quickly, rushing back to the wagon off on the edge of the hill. Orson turned to watch him for a second, but the screams and cries of the calves kept his attention more so. Charlie looked nowhere else but at Parker.

The calf screamed again, and Parker tightened his grip. He fumbled for a moment but stabilized and said to the two new members, "The thing is, I saw you two boys hesitate today."

Orson and Charlie stayed silent.

Parker nodded his head towards Charlie, "And if I heard right, this lil' lamb here cried his heart out."

Charlie only stared at Parker, who spat. Jack chuckled.

Orson spoke up, finding some courage to defend himself and his actions, "I killed plenty today."

"That you did, orphan," Parker sneered, "but, I saw that hesitation."

"You was a mile away," Orson told him, stone faced. He did not fear Parker or his attitude. He did enough to impress Jack, or so he thought.

"Wasn't no mile, orphan. I saw that first shot. You's weak," Parker told him. He then turned his head to Charlie, "Not as weak as this lil' lamb. But, you still weak and we gotta get that weakness out."

The calf in Parker's arms began to buck a bit. He struggled for a moment to hold it as the small brown calf swam in the air with its two front hooves. It wasn't going anywhere, for Parker, though scrawny and thin, was all the strength needed to hold it.

The other red calf continued to cry, and kept on as Bill swiped it upward, holding it in his arms in the same fashion as Parker. The little beast screamed. Its tongue slithered in its open mouth as it did so.

Charlie stood emotionless. His voice rattled in the back of his throat, hollow, "What is this?"

Orson turned his head, hearing Masters approach. In the young hunter's hands, he saw he held two wagon spokes. They were smooth, cut short too. They were probably made from the same shaft of wood. They were gnarled, browned and reddened on one side. He smirked to Orson who he caught looking.

Masters approached Jack, handing him the spokes. The leader then turned to Orson, handing him the shaft of wood. He then gave the other to Charlie, who took the spoke without question. Jack patted the young man on the shoulder and said, "You gon' beat them calves to death."

Orson thought aloud, "What?"

Parker spoke between his toothy grin, "Gotta get that weakness out."

Charlie's young eyes stared at the makeshift club. The dark brown bloodstains sat embedded deep within the light-colored wood. Chips and scuffs accented the shaft all the way down. He stood lost to such a brutal wonder, for he knew, just by the look of the weapon, that it had been passed down like an heirloom from one party member to another. He assumed they all had to do something similar. They all killed without question. He felt the weakness in his heart growing. That is what Parker called it. He tried to suppress it, focusing only on the club, and then the calf that he stared at locked in Parker's arms.

Jack's fingers snapped in Charlie's face, "All will be forgiven and you'll still have a job."

"No pay though," Parker chimed. "You ain't kill shit."

"I'll give him a buck fifty for half that kill he botched," Jack smirked.

Parker laughed loudly, squirming with the calf in his arms as he did so.

Charlie stared off, emotionless. He couldn't think of anything better than to be forgiven for his performance. He didn't want to let anyone down and he did. He knew the men doubted him, and he gave them a reason to do so. He couldn't hesitate this go around. He ran his thumb against the wooden spoke, rubbing a deep notch in its side. Each pass over the gash felt as if he removed that weakness from himself, wiping away any doubt he possessed. He couldn't let them down, wouldn't let them down.

Orson watched as Masters moved away from the group. He walked to the dead female bison, sitting atop her carcass. He dug into his pocket, removing a piece of jerky. He ate, waiting for the show to begin.

Parker spoke to Bill, "Ready?"

"When they are," Bill replied.

Masters licked his fingers, "They ain't gon' be ready. None

of you's was ready when you done it. Best get on with it."

Jack smirked to Masters then slowly turned back to Orson and Charlie, "You ready?"

Orson wasn't. He could shoot a bison, though he had second thoughts about it. He could skin it if it meant an honest living. Killing a calf held no value, it was only there for validity of his commitment to the party. He felt that he had no choice because he liked Tanner. He was the only man to give him a chance. It felt wrong to him though, more wrong than dropping those bison. It felt pointless. There was no reason. He argued with himself that they were animals, like Jack said and like his father said. They might fetch a price, he argued. He opened his mouth to speak, but Charlie belted out first, "I'm ready."

A yellow toothy grin stretched across Parker's thin face. His eyes widened as he stared at Charlie. He didn't think the kid had the stomach. He'd laugh as he failed, then he'd never see him again. He liked that idea, and he could tell Jack that he told him so for years to come. The thought raced through his mind and he let out a quick laugh as he let the calf fall from his arms.

The brown calf fell to the ground, buckling at the legs once it touched down. Its hind legs lowered, as if ready to spring forward. Yet, its footing was still off. It was young, weak, and not as agile as one would think. It stepped forward quickly, its back legs weaving inward and outward as it tried to find balance. It was too late for it, for Charlie was on the calf within a few seconds. The boy was surprised he moved so fast, and that was the only thing he thought of as he brought the spoke down onto the calf's head.

The calf cried out, mouth opened, tongue flailing.

Blood seeped from a deep canyon on its crown as it fell to its knees. Charlie looked down on it, his eyes staring into its. He paused for a moment with the club stretched back behind his head. He heard the excitement in Parker's laughs and that is all that consumed him. All thought left his mind. He couldn't doubt, not now. He brought the club down again, square between the calf's eyes. He felt a mist of blood pepper his face. He didn't think it would feel so warm.

The calf screamed, so haunting, so human.

He brought the club down again to try and silence it.

He didn't realize it, but he wept as he swung. He kept swinging, trying so hard to muffle those cries. They wouldn't stop, not even under the sound of cracking bone and the ghastly sound of smashing brains. There was so much blood, so many tears. He couldn't feel the difference between the two on his numb face.

Orson looked on in horror, watching as Charlie continued to beat that calf. It laid dead, and it fell silent some time ago, but he just kept swinging. He just kept crying.

Bill looked to Newkirk. They met eyes. He gave Orson a nod, dropping the red calf from his arms. His calf too buckled, but once it sprang to its feet, it did not move. It stood, throwing its head back and letting out a wail from deep within its throat. Orson hesitated. He took only one step, but it was the gaze from Jack who now sat next to Masters on that dead carcass that propelled him forward. He rushed the small creature, throwing the spoke behind his head, and then bringing it down on the wailing calf's muzzle. He felt a mist of blood on his hands, on his face, on his neck. He cared not, only thinking of what Jack would say.

The calf bellowed an odd sound, something Orson never heard before. He brought the club back down, splitting the skull wide open. He peered into it, so dark, so red, so painful. The calf collapsed on its knees, tucking them under its body. He brought the spoke down again, and again, making sure the beast was dead. It was, it had to be. It laid still, head cloven in two. Blood rushed from the wound, staining the golden grass. Orson wanted to look away, but he couldn't. He felt such guilt, such shame as he stared down onto it. His eyes became lost to the gory abyss within the calf's skull. In it, he saw a coyote, one that cried and wailed as it dug a bullet from its hind leg. With a quick blink, that image faded and all that remained was the dead calf, its broken skull, that bloody spoke.

All Orson heard was the thumping of the club against skull and brain. He feared he would never unhear it, for it continued, long after he stopped. He soon realized that it was not a memory or trauma, but that of Charlie who still swung viciously on the dead calf. Orson looked to the boy, who wept so uncontrollably. The spoke was brought back, then forward, over and over again. The brown calf's skull collapsed long ago, and Charlie just beat a pile of brains, fragments, and what little remained of the calf's jaw. His face shimmered, accented with blood. Orson saw streaks of his pale skin in the small trails left by his tears.

Parker laughed continuously, standing behind the dead calf. He too getting showered in the occasional mist of blood that flew from Charlie's club. He didn't mind. Jack, Bill, and Masters shared the flask atop that carcass. They talked about something, not even watching the madness unfold.

Charlie did not stop swinging until Parker grabbed ahold of him, throwing him down onto the soiled grass. He laughed in the boy's face, stepping in all the gore as he did so. He cackled, "Hell, Lil Lamb! I didn't think you had it in you!"

Charlie did not look to Parker. His eyes stayed fixated on the pile of brains and shattered bone. He murmured, "I did it..."

"Yeah, boy," Jack said, taking his flask back from Bill. He didn't even look to the boys as he said, "You did it."

Bill turned, drawing his knife and approaching another dead bison not far away from the calves. He began to skin it. Masters finished his small meal, and he too got up and began to return to work. Parker continuously roared with laughter. He was wrong about Charlie not being able to do the job, but that weakness was there and he would still tell Jack he told him so before long. He too left, returning to skinning.

Orson stood over his dead calf, looking down onto it once again. It had to be worth something, he thought. He glanced to

Jack, who drank and staggered off. He called out to his leader, "We skinnin' these?"

Jack didn't bother to look back as he walked away, "Ain't no point. They ain't worth a dime."

Chapter VII
The Creek and the Dream
1873

They slept in filth through the night. When awake, they passed streams and ponds, but Jack would not stop. Orson and Charlie sat in the back of the wagon, neither speaking to one another. They shared the occasional glance, their blood caked faces staring into one another, but often looked away, looking up into the stars but still seeing calves in the constellations. The hides of their kills laid tanned. They sat atop them, as if some sort of great victors. Nobody within the party spoke as they rolled through those open moonlit fields.

Come sunrise, Tanner allowed the boys to bath in a small creek while the others rested. The two boys entered the thicket of trees alone, stripping naked on the rocky bank of the small creek. The water wasn't clean. Orson knew that much by its dark brown appearance. Nothing lived in such a place, but he found some sort of small grace in that he would not soil the home of some innocent creature in his wake.

He stood on the bank for a moment, studying the blood on his nude flesh. He found flakes and dots in places he couldn't understand it getting to. So much blood, so much gore, sat attached to his precious skin which now itched and oiled from the film of red grime that covered him. He took a step into the water, feeling the first bite of coldness that faded away quickly. It felt lukewarm after that and he began to wade in.

Charlie did not. Orson turned back, studying his acquaintance on the edge of the water. The young boy was covered in far more blood than Newkirk, far more filth. He made out pieces of brain and other matter stuck to the boy's body and in his hair, something he hadn't noticed the night before, but saw in the basking orange glow of the sunrise. Charlie sat with his legs crossed on that rough stony bank. He took a few small brown stones, running his thumbs across their rough surfaces, the same fashion as he did with that chipped and gnarled spoke. They did not speak to him the way that makeshift club did. He saw no visions of the past, no understanding of what needed to be done, he saw no blood stains, no cuts and gashes, nothing at all. And yet, he found no peace in the stones as he thought he would. He began to cast them into the small creek, far enough away as to not hit Orson who waded in further.

Orson watched Charlie for a moment, wondering why he threw those stones and did not bathe. He knew the answer though, deep down, somehow, he knew for his soul spoke to his acquaintance for they were now bound by a single act and the blood that came with it. The water came to Orson's chest. It was the deepest the creek went, and his feet still stayed planted on the rough surface. He began to scrub his arms under the murky water. He felt the dried blood wash away, the flakes disintegrating in the dark brown that surrounded him. Though, once he raised his arms from the surface of the water, they emerged muddier, dirtier than before. He thought it a trick of the light at first, but he knew those streaks of brown that ran like rivers down his arm were truly there.

He dunked his head beneath the surface, closing his eyes as he did so. He stayed submerged for a moment, listening to the hollow splashes of Charlie's thrown stones beneath the surface. He wondered if he could stay there, beneath the calm dirty water, forever. He wondered why he couldn't. He wondered if it would make a difference to the party had he just stayed. He rose from the surface of the water once his breath ran out. He gasped for a moment, feeling those rivers of mud roll down his cheeks, roll down the edges of his eyes. He told himself it was better than blood, but he couldn't tell the difference in the way it felt.

His acquaintance still sat on the edge of the water. He had not moved and would not move. He and Orson both did not understand how he would get clean, but Charlie did not care. His mind did not race with any sort of thought. It sat empty, a black abyss that swallowed up all feeling or care. He no longer ran his thumb across the surface of the stones before he threw them. He saw no value to it any longer. They would not speak to him anymore as they did in his childhood. He often felt that connection, felt that history within the earth. As he sat on that bank, he felt it severed and as he held the last stone he collected in his hand, he stood. He stared down onto it, wondering if he should toss it into the creek like he did all the others. His blackened mind refused him any more thought on the matter, and with instinct over anything else, he threw the stone as hard and as far as he could. It crashed into the thicket of trees on the other bank, causing a ruckus as it tumbled downward, separated from where the earth placed it years or centuries before. There it would stay, he thought, the outlier forever and he no longer felt so alone.

Orson watched as Charlie sat back down on the bank, crossing his legs once more. He did not pick another stone, nor fiddle with whatever else rested on that shore. The birds chirped wildly, disturbed by his stone throwing. Charlie paid no mind. He saw nothing, heard nothing, cared nothing. He just sat, hands on his knees, eyes closed. Orson knew what the boy felt for he too experienced such a thing in his youth. He thought of telling him the story, but he knew it wouldn't make much of a difference. Both boys knew the story, for their souls recounted it to one another.

The sun began to rise, causing that purple to vacate the sky, smothered by a hellfire orange that slowly crept upward from the horizon. There were six of them, coyotes. Their grey and red fur looked matted, worn from living in the brush of the thick oak trees. One led forward, the biggest of the group. They moved silently down the hill. The low fog appeared to part before them, as if welcoming their carnivorous presence.

Orson watched. He gripped his small carbine tightly. His hands sweated as he wrapped them tightly around the stock. He did not aim it. He didn't want to. He looked upon those coyotes as they moved down that hill. They were dangerous, as his father told him. They would destroy their livelihood if given the chance. They had to be stopped. Though, as he watched them slink across that field, he could not help but admire their beauty in the low light of the sunrise.

"They are going to come in, alright. You will have to hit one before it gets a chicken," a voice echoed from behind him in such a soft whisper. "Understand?"

Young Orson Newkirk looked behind him, seeing his father crouched down. He sat in the shadows of the trees, watching his son do the assigned task. He did not like that he took his eyes off the prey and gave a quick wave of his hand to draw the boy's attention away from himself. Orson turned back, looking to the chicken coop that laid at the bottom of the hill. The fence was broken. The chickens pecked on the feed planted only an hour or less before. They clucked in rhythm with Orson's beating heart.

The young boy wiped his brow, staring down onto the coyotes as they approached the coop. His father said, "I need you to tell me that you understand."

Orson kept his eyes fixated on the coyotes, wondering which would receive his reckoning. He whispered to his father, "I understand, daddy."

"They comin'," his father whispered back.

The coyotes broke formation as they closed in on the coop. A few circled about, but that leader moved slowly, hunched down, ready to pounce, towards the opening in the fence. The chickens clucked wildly. They sensed the danger coming and for a moment, Orson wished the coyotes did too.

"That one," his father's hand reached over Orson's shoulder, pointing to the leader as it approached the coop. "You'll hit that one. He's too confident, the young fool."

Orson raised his weapon, aiming down the sights the way his father taught him days before. He prepared for this and he feared of letting his father down. His finger did not rest on the trigger though. He felt it writhing around the metal frame in a panic, as if it were a serpent strangling a mouse.

The lead coyote lurked in the pen. It lowered even more, something Orson never saw before. The chickens began clucking louder. They were just as panicked as Orson.

"Shoot it," his father whispered.

Orson finally placed his finger on the trigger, resting it against that warm metal. He felt it twitch and he raised it a little more, fearful he would fire before he was ready. He kept his eye down the sight. The post lined up with that big coyote. He saw it so clearly.

"Orson…" his father's voice shook. The rage began to rise.

The boy wanted to shoot. He truly did. He wanted to impress his father with a clean shot, a clean kill, just the way he taught him. But as he stared into those glistening eyes of that coyote, he could not find the heart to do so. He didn't know why. It had to be because he was weak, like his father told him.

"Kill it!" his father's voice rose.

In that second, the coyote pounced forth onto a big fat chicken. Its jaws clamped down onto the white feathered throat of its prey. It flung it around, gnashing its head side-to-side. Feathers and blood and gore and clucking and chaos filled the pen. Orson could not look away, and his heart felt heavy for he did not shoot when told and something else perished because of his mistake. Though, he feared his father's justice more.

A crack and a sharp pain rolled across the back of Orson's head. He knew he had to fire. He had to. No other option presented itself. He closed his eyes, fearful of where the bullet would strike and fearful of the debris from the carbine. He pulled the trigger.

The weapon bucked upward in his hands. Smoke and powder blinded him as he opened his eyes. His ears rang with such a vibrant hum. That faded though, and all he heard was the painful yapping of the coyote.

The boy stood, looking down on his target. He hoped for a clean kill, but he did not receive it. He struck the leader in the hind leg, and it panicked as it tore its head backward, not running, but trying to dig the bullet from its back leg. Its teeth gnashed, not violent like it had with the chicken, but out of sheer terror for it knew its time came to an end. All beings did such a thing, for though death was inevitable, there was always a desire to resist.

Orson lowered his rifle as he stared down on the wounded coyote. The others that circled the pen dashed off quickly into the low light of the early morning. They left their leader to suffer alone, writhing in such pain, in such panic. His father brushed past him, rushing down towards the chicken coop which drew Orson's attention away from the fleeing companions. His father drew his revolver, aimed it, and finished the coyote with one shot to the head. The coyote fell still. It laid next to the chicken. Steam rose from the warm blood that seeped from their bodies.

"Get down here," Orson's father beckoned between gritted teeth.

Orson did as his father commanded. He moved to his father with his head hung low. He knew he disappointed the man. He knew he deserved whatever his father said or did. The two stood over the dead coyote. Orson did not look away from those still eyes as they stared off into the vast nothingness of death.

"Do you work?" his father asked him.

Orson thought that a peculiar question, but responded, "No…"

"You can't buy me another chicken, can you?"

"No…"

"Of course not," his father began to scream, "'cus you too

stupid, too worthless, to replace my *property that you let get killed!"*

"I'm sorry…" Orson muttered, still fixated on that coyote. He stared at its head wound. It seeped with a vibrant red. He looked to its hind leg, where it chewed through fur and flesh to remove that bullet that created a deep crimson crater in its thigh. He still heard that yapping, that panic, that fear.

"You too worthless to get me money for another one. How the hell are you going to get me another chicken?" his father asked.

Orson did not answer.

"Answer me," his father pressed. He placed his hands on his hips as he stared down at the boy.

"I can't buy you chickens," Orson continued, "I can't do anything."

"So why didn't you do what I asked?" his father asked.

"I don't know…" the boy muttered again.

"Look at me," his father commanded.

Orson did and was met with a quick backhand across the face. He fell to the ground, trying to scramble to get up. His father stepped forward, towering over him. Orson knew better than to stand so he just stayed put, resting his weight on his wrists with his arms behind him.

His father screamed, "Because you're fuckin' stupid. That's why! You aren't going to be a man if you can't listen, can't shoot when told! Understand? If you can't kill what destroys your property, you won't make it long in this world! You won't ever make an honest living if you can't be a man!"

"I'm sorry!" Orson sobbed.

His father reeled his fist back, then brought it down onto the top of his son's head. Orson's brain felt as if it rattled around in his skull. He cried harder.

"You're always sorry! Dammit, Orson! Damn you! I'm down a chicken because of you! All you've done is caused me grief!" his father continued to scream.

Orson did not speak. This was not the first time his father lost his temper because of a mistake from the boy. Things were hard after Mrs. Newkirk passed and his rage became untethered. His voice shook, his face was red as he yelled to his son, "Stop crying!"

Orson couldn't. He lowered his head, trying to keep his sobbing muffled, quiet as to not upset his father.

It was as he looked down on his boy, that the father realized that his son would never be what he wanted him to be. He hated that, but he could not fight it. The boy was weak, he would be consumed by the vicious world, one that he had seen pure evils in. He would lose the boy the way he lost his wife. He wondered if he would be alone in the world, wandering till the ends of time because he failed his family. He shook his head at the thought, and calmed himself before telling Orson, "I'm hard on you because you need it. Everything I do, I do for your benefit."

Orson's father then turned his back and began to walk across the property towards their small cottage. Orson stayed put, looking up when he heard his father's footsteps leading away. He cried louder then, thinking his father couldn't hear. He needed the tears to leave his body. They were poison and they had to be removed for him to survive.

The boy's eyes were drawn to the coyote that laid next to him. Its crown was crushed under the weight of the bullet. Red streaks flowed from its two wounds and from its maw. Its tongue hung out into the dirt. Those eyes though, those empty yellow eyes, looked to the boy and he swore he heard it yap again…

Chapter VIII
Carvings in the Oak
1875

It must've been around noon. The sun hung in the center of the sky. Its glowing yellow rays stretched outward across the infinite blue overhead. Not a single cloud lingered in the air. No shade would be given to Orson as he looked upward, adjusting his hat. He wiped the beads of sweat that rolled down his face with his bandana, then took it, wrapping it around his neck to keep the sun from his nape.

A light breeze rolled through the Daniels farm, sweeping across the plains. The wheat surrounding Orson waved, as if he stood in a vast ocean of gold. He inspected the stocks, the soil from which they grew. Thomas told him to make sure all the wheat appeared reapable come a few weeks. He didn't really know what he looked for, but he gave Thomas his word and would keep it.

He peered out beyond the field where he stood. He saw that lone oak looming in the distance. Not far from it, the fence that lined the property caught his eye. He saw that two posts stood cracked, one split right down its center and the top rail of the fence had collapsed into the dirt, leaving the bottom rail only. He approached the fence slowly, taking a break from all that wheat inspecting.

The fence stood broken, but not too bad. He didn't think much of it. Time and weather wore that section down. He grabbed the fallen top rail, trying to place it back into the split post, but it would not go. It needed replaced. He thought no more of it for a moment, but as he placed the top rail where he found it, he noticed paw prints within the dirt. He knew what they belonged to just from experience. He looked at them for a while, wondering why such beasts would be on that property. It was then that he saw the coop not far from the Daniels home, nothing stirred within it.

Thomas too inspected stalks of wheat. The field in which he stood was far larger than Orson's. He still took the blunt of the load when it came to work as to not wear the young man down after recovering from whatever illness plagued him. He removed his straw hat, wiping his brow, then placed it back on his head. When the shade from the brim met his eyes, he clearly saw Orson approaching him quickly. The young man hollered out across the farm, "Yer fence is broken!"

The man's hearing wasn't all that good. The wind drowned out a piece of the young man's sentence. He asked, "My what?"

Orson stood in front of Thomas before he spoke again, "I said, yer fence. I see you must'a had somethin' comin' through. That why all your pens and your coop are empty?"

"No," Thomas told the young man. He felt weak from the sun and wondered if he could continue for the day. He pushed the thought away as he told the boy, "Those are empty because I sold 'em all. The hogs, anyway. Too much to maintain by myself."

The farm struggled without his wife. He hired no hand to help him until Orson came along. He did not pay a decent wage. He wished in that moment that he could pay Orson for each day of work but waiting until the crops were sowed would have to do. He would pay him, for sure, but he felt as if he scammed him in some way.

Orson looked back across the farm, staring at that chicken coop. Memories of his childhood swam across his brain. He asked, "And what about your chickens?"

Thomas didn't care. The chickens never brought him as much money as he hoped. The hogs were the real prize when he maintained them. The wheat became the main priority for him since alone. He could handle the amount he possessed, most days when the pain subsided. He told the boy matter of fact, "I ate some, something else ate the others."

"I can fix that fence for ya. Get you the opportunity to get new ones," Orson said.

"No, that's alright," Thomas nodded. "That fence on the outer end of the property ain't keepin' much out. Plus, I'll be done here after this last crop season. One last good haul."

Orson didn't quite understand that. He looked over Thomas, staring into his old withered face. He saw some youth still in those eyes, but his body looked worn and tired. His eyes spoke that too. He wondered what he meant by that, and assumed it had to be about the crops. Maybe the old man would move on with his life, get out of Kansas, head West the way Orson planned to. The plains were dying, Orson told himself. Everything needed to leave if it wished to survive, even the people. He needed that clarification. He couldn't just assume it so, "Done?"

"Yeah," Thomas said with a slight twitch of his upper lip. "Done. I'll be off to bigger and better things."

"Like raisin' pigs?" Orson asked, knowing the value of a good hog. The fact that Thomas used to own some along with chickens amazed him. He was a farmer of many trades, something that reminded him of his father, though he didn't despise the thought of Thomas.

Thomas laughed at that. He did not mean it at all. His farm held little value to him anymore. It held little value to almost anyone who saw it. He knew it. He just chuckled and said, "Maybe cows."

And with that, neither said anything else to one another. Thomas turned his back, staggering a bit from the heat that radiated from the sun overhead. He began to inspect his crops once more. Orson watched him for a moment, watched as the man struggled to stand. He saw a weakness in him, in his bones. Something that he hardly noticed before aside from his drastically aged appearance over his true age. He knew something was off with that man but hoped he could survive in such a place. He'd been told before that farmers were weak men, and he believed that for some time. He looked upon Thomas, wondering if his spirit was as weak as his body. He cared not for that thought, and in it he felt ashamed for even thinking such a thing. He turned his back too, walking off back towards the fence on the property line.

A well fit coyote could jump the fence or slink beneath it. Any feline predator could do the same. That did not bother Orson though as he stood at the collapsed portion of the fence holding a hammer and some long nails. He gathered some supplies from behind the old man's shack. Old wooden posts, most of which were rotted, had been piled up since he first built the fence. Orson found a few that only began to decay but could possibly make do for a while. It solved the problem short term, but it would need to be repaired again.

Orson cared not. The fence meant more to him for some reason. He wasn't really sure why. He knew it wouldn't stop much, but it was the boundary set across the farmland. It marked it as Thomas's to any man or animal that passed. It was his stake, his life presented for all the world to see and Orson could not let its walls be torn down.

He began by uprooting the first split post, followed by the second. The warmth of the sun overhead increased the difficulty of the task, but he told himself that he had worse. His loose-fitting clothes stuck to his sweaty skin, creating such an awful discomfort. He took the two new slightly rotted posts and hammered them into the openings of the earth. He brought the hammer down delicately onto their flat tops as to make sure he did not split them. He felt the wood mush and buckle under the pressure of his hands as he lifted them. They were not strong. He knew he would have to replace them at some point, but he told himself he would return to the farm to complete the task for the old man once he came back from the West. He corrected his thought, *if* he came back from the West. He didn't know why he doubted that. He still wanted to go, still wanted to stay away from such a place, but maybe he found a home amongst the dying plains. That thought scared him, for he knew the types that dwelled and died in such a place.

He took the top rail and fit it into the openings of the posts. The weight of the rail felt like nothing to him, but splinters and cracks began to form from where it rested in the slot. He knelt, examining them. He shook his head, realizing that any storm that came through with high winds or any amount of moisture could cause that to collapse a little more. He needed new wood. Hell, the whole fence line probably needed replacing. He thought of spending that money from the harvest on some wood. Thomas could raise those cows, pigs, chickens, or whatever else he truly desired with a good fence. Then, he told himself, he wouldn't have to come back unless he really wanted to. He would feel no obligation, though he rationalized that he still held no obligation. He was at the farm for money, and that was it. That's what he was taught.

He took a bit of rope, wrapping it around the slots of the posts. He made sure to not tie it too tight, as to avoid cracking the flimsy timber. He made it just tight enough that maybe it would withstand another storm before the top rail fell again. Maybe it wouldn't. He wasn't sure. Only time would tell, but he told himself it only needed to hold for a little while. He would fix the whole thing, he thought. Someday, maybe, he would fix it all.

He eyed his hours of work, looking at it for a few seconds. A rush of wind came and the rustling of the branches of the great oak drew his gaze. It sat so beautifully in the sunlight. The shade beneath it looked so calming, so cool. He thought he'd have a drink of water under that piece of tranquility.

"What'er you doin'?" a shout echoed from behind him.

Orson turned towards the voice, watching as Thomas stormed across the property.

"I fixed yer fence, Thomas," Orson told him.

Thomas eyed the fence, brushing past Orson to do so. He recognized the posts, those partially rotted pieces. He wanted to use them for firewood if he ever ran out, but he could no longer. He shook his head. That fence would not hold for long. He told the boy, "I ain't needin' it fixed. I already told ya."

Orson spoke truthfully, a trait he heard made him likeable, "You said you was gonna do bigger better things. Figured you'd need a fence."

The kid didn't understand. Thomas did though. He understood that the kid meant well but an afternoon's worth of work withered away on something that did not matter. The thought scurried across his mind, frustrating him deep within his heart, "I needed you out in them fields, Orson. How much time you spend on this?"

"I dunno," Orson thought. He tried to count the time in his head, but he truly had no idea upon recollection under questioning, "An hour? Maybe more. I dunno."

"And you look beat!" Thomas shouted. He realized he raised his voice, something he told Betty he would watch once Tabitha came into the world. He brought it down a moment, still trying to hold back his frustration but it seeped from his mouth like rain from an anvil cloud, "I needed you elsewhere. I asked you fer help."

"I did help," Orson argued, trying not to plead. He was done with all that.

"Not the way I needed ya to," Thomas shook his head again, still inspecting the fence, "I need this wheat, son."

Orson swallowed the frustration that Thomas spewed, honing it himself, "The wheat is fine! It's as golden as ever!"

"And I need it to stay golden!" Thomas shouted back, "It's been hard out here this season and I am worried it ain't gon' make it till harvest!"

"I think it'll be fine," Orson defended himself again.

The boy didn't know. He couldn't know what it all meant to the old man. Thomas seared with such an anger on the inside. He truly tried to hide it, but it was not going well for him. He reasoned with himself, knowing that the boy would make these stupid mistakes without the proper context on why the wheat was so important, why he sold his livestock, why it all mattered to him. He took a deep breath, feeling that warm air in his lungs as it flushed some of the anger away. He spoke softly, "It's been tough, Orson. I need this. I'm trying to pay off debts and things."

"Debt?" Orson asked. He'd heard of it, or the concept of one man owing another.

"I owe money," Thomas's voice shook. "I owe a lot of money for this farm here. I owe money on this wheat too. I need to make my money back."

The concept of debt, especially with money and how that could be somewhat scary for a person, especially an older weak man, finally sank into Orson's mind. He only said, "Oh..."

The lack of empathy, the lack of understanding, the lack of an apology from the young man turned into more rage within Thomas. He just mocked the boy, for that's all he thought of to do, "Yeah...oh..."

Orson felt the mock's sting. Thomas saw it in the boy's eyes. He hated that he did that. He could not control his frustration, but he had a visitor on his land, and one that wished to help him. He tried to reason that the fence wasn't all that bad, but it was just another wasted day like all the wasted days when he was in too much pain to work his own fields. He felt nervous for his future, nervous for his farm and what was to come but he took it out on the boy. He told himself that wasn't fair and then told Orson, "I need to step away. I just...I'm nervous is all."

With that, Orson watched as Thomas turned his back, heading down towards the small house at the center of the property. As the old man moved, he saw the pain in his gait. He felt the frustration in his wake. He felt stupid for not doing what he was told. He felt sorry for what he did, though his intentions were pure. He just didn't want to let him down.

The sun began to set. The light in the sky shined so vibrant. Shades of red and orange stretched out from the low hanging sun, reaching far over Orson's head, to what appeared to be the end of the known world. He looked up from the stocks of the wheat field to admire it. He wondered who else looked upon such a thing, if they saw such beauty the way he did. He doubted it, thinking no more on it, and finished inspecting what few areas of wheat remained.

Through all the hours he sifted through the stocks, he only found one that he deemed unsatisfactory. Its stem contained dents and he saw splits formed in odd places. He feared that insects fed upon it, but he saw not a sign of them. He wondered if it were diseased, and that made him nervous for

Thomas, for disease spreads and he wondered if the rest of the crops were at stake. He felt guilt when he thought of that, thinking that he could've identified it before if he hadn't worked on that fence. He reasoned with himself that it didn't make much of a difference, Thomas would still find out that same day, but his heart beat wildly at the thought. He felt himself the reason the stock failed.

He looked away, off to the other side of the property. There, he saw the great oak. Its branches blew in the wind. Its leaves fell with a rushing gust. The glow of the sunset behind the tree created a halo that stretched from one side of its trunk to the other. It appeared ethereal, like a lone survivor out on the plains. The shadow beneath it no longer appeared so lengthy. Orson approached, wiping the sweat from his brow.

He finished his work, made up for the fence, as he thought. He still felt shame when he thought of speaking to Thomas and as he did as a child, he chose to wait to inform him for he feared the repercussions of his actions. He ran his hands against the hulking trunk. He did not see them from a distance, but small carvings sat within the bark, etched with a rough blade. He noticed a pig, small figures of people, a house with a chimney, a small dog, a few chickens, a sunset, and plenty of other things that he could barely make out. They were old by a few years, Orson gauged. He admired each of them though, running his index finger through each of their lines. He was careful, as to not pick up a splinter, but he found a love for the way the carved wood felt on the tip of his finger.

He circled the tree, examining each etch that he recognized, smiling from time to time and wondering what each meant. He stepped carefully for a few roots extended out of the ground, as if some sign of dominance from the tree that it wasn't going anywhere. He basked in the warmth of the fleeting sun, enjoyed what little shade he needed at the end of the day, and thought that he found some measure of peace out in the plains. It came short lived, for as he rounded the tree, facing out towards the far end of the property line, two crosses sat in the light of the sunset, not far from the base of the tree. They faced outward, looking out towards the falling sun, out towards the open plains. He knew them to be grave markers, he did not question it.

Orson lowered his hand from the tree. He touched his index finger to the tip of his thumb, rubbing away any feeling left by the etchings in the oak. He felt as if he desecrated such a sacred place and he felt ashamed of that too. He approached the wooden crosses, turning his back to the low hanging sun and looked upon them. Their names were hard to read, for they loomed in his shadow and the carvings in the wood looked worn, as if almost forgotten, though he knew that to not be the case. He stared upon the left one, hardly able to read it, but he knew what it said, "Tabitha Daniels 1870-1874." He felt a pit in his stomach. He could not imagine such a pain that Thomas felt. He would not even try to fathom it. He then eyed the one on the right, "Betty Daniels 1850-1874."

He didn't know if he should kneel to them, speak to them, or what any etiquette in any culture called for in a moment such as this. He just stood there, quiet, listening to the wind rip across the plains.

Chapter IX
On, Debt and Dying
1875

Thomas stood on the porch of his home. The anxiety about his crops subsided. He knew that he would have a good haul. He figured, somehow, if he at least cashed in more than half he could make back the majority of what he owed. He didn't want to get his hopes up, because the last time that happened, tragedy struck him. Though, it was the first time in a long while that he felt hopeful about anything at all, and to be hopeful for becoming debt free was a good daydream to have.

If he felt anxious about anything, it was more so concern for the boy in his employment. He felt himself too harsh on him, too condescending and mean. He feared the kid would leave his service, seeing him as nothing more than the other men he met in his past. He didn't know any of them or what they were like aside from what little Orson mentioned of his father, but he met a few plainsmen in his days, a few gamblers, a few businessmen, and a few of other career paths. He saw how they acted among the wilderness or the up and coming cities. There was something about that freedom that lacked empathy and turned men into the savages they were before civilization. He feared that is how Orson saw him, for that is how he saw himself upon reflection, though he did not know it was the furthest from the truth when it came to how the boy viewed him.

Orson moseyed towards the house. He looked worn and tired with a slight stagger in his step. Thomas knew that he worked hard, trying to make up for the mistake at the fence. Thomas saw that as *his* mistake in reflection and not one of the boy's. He smiled upon the sight of Orson and let out a quick sigh of relief, finding peace that the young man decided to stick around, "I was wonderin' where you was."

"I finished checkin' that field for ya," Orson said. He moved to the water barrel and spooned a cup to his mouth, "I didn't want to let ya down."

Thomas watched the young man for a moment, eyeing him as he drank that water from the ladle. He felt such guilt watching him. He saw the immense sweat flooding from his head and neck. He looked a bit burnt around his nape as well. He shouldn't have worked so hard, especially during a recovery. He told him, "I appreciate you fixin' that fence."

Orson looked to the man. He saw that the words were hollow. He knew that he really did not care for that fence to be fixed. He only said so in order to save face with him. Orson's honesty appeared once more, "I wasted time. I'm sorry."

"No need, Orson," Thomas said with a genuine smile. His frustration faded long ago, "It's alright. It was a kind gesture."

The kid felt the old man's sincerity. While he understood that the fence was a waste a time, he became a bit better about the whole thing. His intentions weren't misunderstood. He wasn't trying to get out of work. He only wanted to help Thomas, and it made him feel at ease knowing that Thomas understood. It lowered his defenses enough that he did not feel any guilt when it came to that stock he saw. He told him, "One of your stocks don't look so good."

"I'll check on it in the morning," Thomas said, looking out over the fields. He wondered which one. The anxiety crept in a bit as he thought about it. He hoped it wasn't a disease of some kind. He couldn't afford for it to spread. He also hoped it wasn't an infestation or the like with an insect or rodent or whatever else lurked across the plains. He shook his head, trying to remove those thoughts from it.

Orson moved past the old man, sitting in one of the chairs on the porch. He saw that anxiety slip into the back of Thomas's mind as he told him about the stock. He felt that guilt come back too. He regretted saying anything for a moment, but he realized that was selfish. He shouldn't have worked on that fence, he thought. He said as much, "I hope I didn't miss anythin'. I shouldn't have worked on that fence."

"Orson, I promise you, it is fine," Thomas told him,

turning to face him. His eyes were still anxious though, Orson saw that clearly, "I am just nervous is all."

"But you ain't mad?" Orson asked for clarification.

"Not anymore," Thomas spoke truthfully.

"I thought it would help."

Thomas watched as the kid removed a cigarette from his pocket. He plopped it in his mouth, then struck a match to the heel of his boot before lighting it. The kid was trying to relax, but Thomas knew him to be just as on edge as he was. He reassured Orson, "I know."

Orson shook his head, "I'm sorry it won't help none."

"Ain't nothin' helpin' me," Thomas stated. He felt the kid's open honesty rubbing off on him.

"Wha'chu mean?"

"I mean," Thomas hesitated. He wanted to be open with Newkirk. He truly did. Though, he found his plight to be a sad one. He viewed himself as pathetic, emasculated in a sense. He still told him, "I'm sick. I got somethin' growin' in me and I can feel it."

Orson sat up, leaning forward in his chair, concerned, "You seen a doctor?"

Thomas nodded, "Saw one up at Fort Hays a little while back. He says he seen't it before."

"You dyin'?"

"I'm dyin'," Thomas answered quickly. As the words left his lips, he felt a chill rush over his body. He never thought he'd say such a thing, or at least say it to someone who might actually care since his family passed. He continued, "That's why I'm so scared about these debts, my friend."

"But when you're dead, you ain't got no debts," Orson tried to put the man at ease. There's no ease that can be found in dying, but Orson still tried. There could always be a brighter side. He thought about dying a lot when alone on the plains, always tried to find the brighter side of it all. There'd be no more pain, no more suffering, no more work, no more trying to find a way. He still lived, and he knew that. There was always something better about life to him, something driving him that he couldn't find a way to close his eyes forever, so much so that he stopped thinking about death most of the time.

"Debt carries," Thomas told him. "I gotta sister up in Lawrence. She's married to a good fella. They're like me though, not a lot of money. They spent what little they could helpin' me get this place."

"They gon' make her pay for it?"

"That's my fear," Thomas felt a lump forming in his throat. He often thought of the situation, but never spoke it out loud. "Her husband's name is on some papers, somewhere. I'd hate for them to pay for my mistakes, you know?"

"I ain't got siblings. No debt neither," Orson admitted. He didn't mean to hold it above Thomas's head. He just tried to show that he could not fathom that sense of guilt. He felt guilty plenty, but he did not understand Thomas's situation.

"That's good on you. The debt, I mean," Thomas smiled. He thought for a moment, thinking of his sister. He admitted, "I'd just hate to be lyin' in the ground and she got to pay up."

"That does sound bad," Orson said, his honesty not helping with Thomas's anxiety.

The two stood silently for a moment, listening to the wind roll across the plains. They both looked out to the horizon. The sun could no longer be seen peeking out from the great beyond. Thomas moved and sat next to Orson. He took a sip from his canteen as Orson smoked the remainder of his cigarette. Nothing needed to be said anymore about his debt. Thomas wanted to just move on from it, though he found it hard.

Thomas reiterated, "I appreciate you stickin' around to help."

"What's 'er name?" Orson asked.

Thomas looked to the boy, confused, "Hmm?"

"'er name? Yer sister," Orson could not get his mind off what Thomas told him.

"Oh," Thomas realized that they would not move past this. He found some sort of peace in that, though he still felt shame, "Her name is Lilly, like the flower."

"I don't think I've seen a lily."

"Might have, but maybe just didn't realize it," Thomas nodded. He was sure the kid did. He had to. He saw so many things in the world. He must have seen a lily.

Orson thought on it, wondering what the flower looked like. He thought of sunflowers or daisies. He really wasn't sure. He stated, "Maybe."

And that was that. They spoke no more of it as they sat on that porch. They didn't say anything to one another for a long while. They just watched as the red in the sky faded to purple then to navy. They watched as the blue faded and the stars usurped the sky. Nothing more needed to be said and they sat in that comfortable silence, understanding one another.

The two ate dinner in silence. They ate stew again with a few cooked potatoes. They enjoyed the silence. Orson in particular. It made him feel that he understood the man on a deeper level, something he only experienced once before. There were a lot of things he wanted to say, but never said. There was only one time where he looked to another person, and they looked back, and neither needed to say a damn thing. He felt good in the idea that he didn't have to say anything to Thomas to be understood. Everything was in the air.

Thomas washed the bowls that they ate from. Orson moved over towards the fireplace, sitting on the floor next to Thomas's rocker. He stared at the flames, watching them lick the stone sides of the pit. He felt lost to their dance, lost to their warmth. Thomas looked to the boy, watching him as he watched the flames, "You can have the bed another night."

"Oh, that's alright," Orson said without turning to the old man. "I'm feelin' much better."

Thomas began to dry the dishes, "I sleep in that rocker

most days, anyhow. That growth I mentioned, it's somewhere in my back. I don't care much for layin' on it."

"It hurt?" Orson asked, still staring ahead into the fireplace.

"Like hell," Thomas responded. "Take the bed."

"Alright then."

Thomas finished drying the wooden bowls. He set them aside on his old wooden counter, stacking them atop one another. He dried his hands with the same towel, then began to make his way over to his rocker. He hobbled a bit. His back ached from not just his sickness, but from the long hours he spent in the fields. He grimaced as he sat in the rocker. It leaned back after accepting him, and he nudged his legs ever so slightly to rock himself back and forth.

He too stared into the flames, telling Orson, "When I was a kid, we used to sit down near the fire and always tell stories. My pa always had good stories. I never was much good at it."

Orson nodded, the flames of the fire reflected in his eyes, "Me neither."

"I bet you could tell a story," Thomas told him, leaning in his chair a bit to take the pressure off his back. He knew the boy had stories to tell. He saw things, things nobody would ever believe.

"Probably not a good one."

"My pa always said good stories come from experience. He'd seen all sorts of stuff," Thomas told the boy. He rocked his chair a little, lost to that thought. His father saw plenty of things. He didn't. He never would, not with the shadow of the ax hanging over his head for what few days remained for him. He admitted to the boy, "I never really saw shit in my day. That is, unless you want a story about growin' corn or maybe wheat."

Orson knew where Thomas was going. He wanted him to open up, but Orson wished not to. He wanted to keep his past to himself, unless it mattered. That silence and understanding is all he wanted. He didn't feel the need to rehash the things he'd seen or done. He just told Thomas, "Yeah, I ain't got much to tell neither."

"Any huntin' stories?" Thomas pressed.

The kid had plenty of hunting stories. Most of which he wanted to forget. He thought about telling him the calf story for a moment, wondering if the old man would change the way he saw him. He wondered if he was as weak as he thought, and the old man could tell him so. That thought only lasted a second, a quick rush across his brain. He knew better. He said, "Nah, not really."

"Really?" Thomas pressed, slipping back into his old curious ways. "I thought there'd be some."

He studied the kid as his face scrunched, thinking of something painful. He knew then he went too far. The kid responded, "Yeah...well, there ain't nothin' big or fancy or nothin'."

Thomas said quickly, wishing to change the subject to something more comfortable for the boy, "Alright. You know, I ain't never seen the ocean neither."

"Oh yeah?"

"Yeah..." Thomas thought. It was true. He hadn't seen a single ocean in his life. He probably never would. It stung to admit it, "Never did get around to doin' that. Good on you's for goin' while you're still young."

Orson thought, lost to the flames. He always wanted to go that way. It was something embedded deep within him. In fact, it was the only real reason he thought of going to Dodge. He never wanted to stay there. He thought he'd get money, then leave. That didn't happen. He feared he'd never go. He told Thomas, "Figured maybe I'd find work out there. Always wanted to work on a boat or something. My mother used to read me a story about a boat crew. Sounded like fun to me then."

"That's hard work," Thomas told him with a nod that Orson didn't see. "You'd be good at it."

Orson smirked at the compliment. He heard it, but he wasn't sure if he believed it. Boat work and plains work were entirely different beasts. He hoped he had what it took, because he'd hate to go so far only to find out that he didn't have the stomach or the ability to work such a job. He told Thomas, "Maybe...but, I really just want to see it, you know? The way that it was described in those books, so clear, so blue. I can only really imagine."

"I heard it's pretty," Thomas said, he too lost to the thought of what something like that would look like.

"I bet it's something to see," Orson nodded to himself. He really wondered, really hoped it would be just as he imagined. He thought of that cool ocean air washing over his body, washing away his past.

"You'll have to write me when you see it. If I'm still here, anyway," Thomas said.

Orson smiled at that, looking to the old man. He really did like that thought, having someone out in the world that cared where he was or what he was doing. He admitted, "I'd like that, but I c'ain't write."

"Maybe I'll teach you when we have the time," Thomas offered.

"Maybe," Orson responded. He didn't think they'd have the time. There was so much left to do on that farm, so much time to spend to make sure Thomas could live out his last days in peace and not having to worry about Lilly. He really liked that thought of writing him though, even if Thomas wasn't around to get the letters. It was just the thought of having someone out there who cared. It was then that it clicked: without Thomas, he wasn't sure if anyone cared at all.

Orson crossed his arms, resting them on his knees. He wanted to think no more of it. He didn't like the way his mind wandered, and so, he just stared upon the flames, listening as Thomas began to hum a soft somber tune under his breath.

Chapter X

Payment and Rumors

1873

Jack walked ahead of the boys. They moseyed through the railyards, a place that Orson only saw from a distance as he entered Dodge City for the first time. Empty cars sat idle on the tracks. Piles of bones and pelts laid strewn all over the place. Men sifted pieces from tall mountains of skulls. Pelts were carried and loaded onto train cars, waiting to be taken to their destinations. Men moved all around, working hard to make sure the shipments went wherever needed. Orson never witnessed such efficiency before.

Masters walked next to Orson. Jack only brought them two with him to the railyard. Over his shoulder, Masters carried a single hefty pelt, one that Jack deemed to be the best of their haul only a few days prior. Timothy kept his eyes forward, not looking to the workers that surrounded them. He only watched Jack, keeping in step with his boss. Orson, on the other hand, could not help but stare upon the mounds of death and destruction that overtook the railyard. Near the edge, with the empty nothingness of the plains on the horizon, a large mountain of skulls loomed. They all belonged to bison. Orson knew that much. The thick bone of the skulls glistened in the sun. Pieces of pink flesh hung from some, others still stained with red, and others still contained horns that went un-scavenged. The mound itself was taller than six men. It was not the only one either, for there were many that towered over the edge of the railyard. The young Orson could not look away. He wondered how many calf skulls were among the dead. He wondered if any were beaten with a club.

Jack stopped ahead, and Masters halted immediately. He reached his right arm out across the distracted Orson's chest, stopping him too. The boys stood roughly twenty yards away from their leader, who now spoke with some man in decent attire. The man possessed a large mustache, and he wiped his sweat from it with a rather nice silk handkerchief. Jack began to discuss something with the decent man, but the sounds of the railyard drowned out their conversation before the boys heard it. They just stared ahead, watching their leader conduct his business.

Orson lost interest quickly. The mounds of skulls called to him once more, and so he looked upon them. They appeared to grow again, and men worked atop them, throwing down skulls in some instances, and in others, piling more atop the mounds. The piles were such a brutal wonder to the boy as he continued to examine them from afar. He felt a sting in his heart at first, but it faded away as if he pulled the trigger on his rifle again. He cleared his mind, thinking no more of the calf, thinking no more of the bison he killed. He only saw the workers, the skulls, but told himself to feel nothing. And for a moment, he went numb, exactly what he wanted. Though, his heart jumped again, flooding his body with guilt and remorse, once he noticed a single skull, that of a canine, that of a coyote, among the pile. He felt all air leave his lungs as he looked to that lone skull, the odd one out from thousands of others. It couldn't be there. It shouldn't be there, he told himself. He blinked, thinking it was a trick of the heavy sun overhead.

Masters drew his attention, "Jack's happy with ya."

Orson looked away from the mound, shifting his eyes to Masters. He felt a sense of relief in that. He no longer needed to stare upon his mistakes, past or present. Also, the fact that Masters reinforced Jack's pleasure with Orson's work seemed to wash away any doubt the kid possessed in the first place. He asked for clarification, "What do ya mean?"

"He sees potential in you. He don't like that other one much, but he likes you," Masters informed him. He still did not break his gaze from Jack as he said, "He wouldn't have brought you here had he not."

Orson spoke honestly, "I just don't want to let anyone down."

Timothy still eyed Jack, as if he were waiting for a signal, but he spoke to Orson, "Do yer job and don't question the boss and you'll do fine, 'round here."

Orson felt good about that response. He knew he could do that. He knew he could listen to Jack because he respected the man. He gave him an opportunity and he wouldn't waste it. He wouldn't let him or his fellow hunters down. He refused to do so. He wasn't so sure about his acquaintance, "You think Charlie will be alright?"

"Who?" Masters asked, turning his head to look to Orson. He looked into the kid's eyes, seeing true concern. It was then that the Lil' Lamb's name came forth from the back of his mind. He scoffed and smirked, "Oh, that boy. Yeah, he's alright. I think everyone wants to cut 'em loose but Jack feels sorry for 'em. I kinda do too."

"Why?" Orson pressed. He didn't think of Jack or Masters to be the sentimental type. Charlie might not have what it took to run with the Tanner Party. Orson knew that. He knew that the calf broke him, the way it did himself, if not deeper. Charlie needed out, but he wouldn't go unless Jack forced him.

"You seen 'em? Fuckin' pathetic," Masters told Orson. Timothy chuckled at the thought of the young Charlie flailing that club and said, "He did beat the hell outta that calf though. Maybe he'll do fine. Hell, I don't know. That's Jack's job, ain't mine—"

Jack hollered to the boys from where he stood, "Timmy, bring that pelt up here! Newkirk, you get up here too!"

The boys did as they were commanded, approaching their leader in step with one another. Masters tipped his hat to the decent man, then threw the pelt down at his feet. He unraveled it, revealing the beautiful dark brown fur on the inside. It looked perfect, as any pelt should. Orson figured it to be Masters' or Jack's kill, for some reason or another.

Jack ran his hand over the fur, looking to the decent man as he did so, "See? It's fine as could be. Tanned it and all just two days ago. I got a whole wagon full."

The decent man eyed the robe. Jack saw his eyes and knew they were impressed. He smirked at that, giving Timothy a wink before looking back to the decent man, who said, "I don't know, Jack. I'm buying in bulk and you don't have all that many."

"I've got a little more than half a hundred," Jack replied.

The decent man wiped his sweat and said, "I need more than that."

Jack's demeanor changed. Orson half expected him to lose his temper and begin berating the mustached businessman in the middle of the railyard. However, Jack lowered his guard, raising his hands as if to plea with the gentleman. His voice softened a bit too as he said, "I got eager, that's my fault. I'm workin' some new boys in my crew."

"You told me last time you lost Ol' Ben," the decent man said to Jack. He then looked to Masters who nodded and hung his head, then to Orson who just stared back wide eyed, confused as to what he witnessed.

Jack lowered his head too, taking his hat off, "That we did, so I have to work around this a little. I can get you more. You know me. I am the best damn hunter 'round Dodge. My crew too, they're hardnosed."

The decent man eyed Jack. He felt sympathy for him. The mustached businessman had never been on the trail, or at least that is what Orson thought just by looking at him. He would never know the feeling of losing a friend to make a simple buck, an honest buck at that. He saw the sympathy growing in the man's eyes as he said, "Fine, fine. I'll buy this lot, but next time you need to bring me five times more than this. Every swingin' dick with a rifle is bringing me a pelt or two and I am tired of shellin' out 3 bucks a head."

"I completely understand and half a hundred pelts ain't nothin' to worry about," Jack said with a quick smile. He plopped his hat back on his head, turning to Timothy Masters quickly, "Go and fetch the wagon, Timmy."

Masters turned, exiting the railyard at a quick pace. He did not run, but Orson saw the excitement of the deal in the young man's steps. He watched him go for a moment, and then he felt a hand on his shoulder. He looked, seeing Jack looking at him for a second before turning back to the decent man and saying, "I've got a shooter here that claimed at least ten of 'em. We'll get'chu robes."

That made Orson feel good. Masters must've been honest with him. Jack must've seen something in him.

The decent man replied, "In bulk."

Orson looked off towards the railyard's edge. He stared

upon that pile of skulls one last time. He could no longer spot that coyote among the bison. Though, he felt as if all those bison skulls stared back at him, as if their spirits tried clawing their way out of his heart.

Jack nodded and reiterated to the decent man, "In bulk."

The wagon rolled down Front Street. Masters sat at the reins and Tanner next to him. They spoke to one another in soft voices and Orson could not hear them as he sat with his feet dangling off the back of the empty wagon. He looked down the street, still seeing the railyard not too far off in the distance and to the south of it. He looked upon what little of the Arkansas River he could see. Such a strange feeling he felt, for he still saw the bones stacked up facing the plains to the north, and all down the rail tracks he saw mounds and mounds of pelts. Some of the ones he claimed only days before now laid among them.

Parker, Bill, and Charlie stood near a small cigar shop as if they waited to enter. Masters pulled the wagon up to them, parking on the edge of the dusty street. Patrons walked by, some dressed fancier than others. Orson knew the plainsmen from the wealthy, and he also knew people could tell what he was just by sight. He hoped that they saw him as a seasoned hunter, and nothing more.

Jack leaped from the wagon and stood before his party. Parker stepped forward, spitting a bit of tobacco, "He take 'em?"

"Yeah, that skinny prick wants more though," Jack responded.

Parker's voice rose, as if frustrated, "More?"

"He said, 'industrial needs,'" Jack nodded.

Masters and Orson moved around the side of the wagon, regrouping with their fellow party members. Masters stood near Jack while Orson took his place next to Charlie.

Parker raised an eyebrow, looking to both Jack and Masters, "We gettin' paid though, right?"

Jack took his right hand, digging into his coat pocket. He removed a thick wad of bills. On the notes, the small text read in a waving pattern, "National Currency United States." Orson smiled when he looked upon the notes, seeing that he finally earned something he could be proud of. Jack smirked, "Yeah, you's getting' paid."

Jack took a few bills from the top with his left hand and extended them out towards Parker, "Easy on the girls."

Parker grinned and spat, then took his share.

Tanner then took another split from the top, then handed them to Bill, "Don't fuckin' gamble with this."

Bill pocketed the notes quickly then looked to his leader with narrowed eyes, "It's my money."

Jack wasn't having any of it. His eyes grew wide, annoyed that Bill even tried to counter his judgement, "And I ain't frontin' you shit if you lose it again!"

"Fine," Bill said with a nod. He dug into his pocket and removed a rolled cigarette. He muttered, "That's all fine."

Orson put his hands in his pockets as he eagerly awaited his stack of notes. Jack turned to him. His face still fumbling with frustration from Bill Chambers. He saw the excitement in the boy's eyes though and that washed away the anger he felt. He saw the eagerness of the kid earning his first honest pay in a long while, if not ever. Jack reached his hand out, holding the bills towards Orson who quickly grabbed them. He gave the kid a wink and a smile, "Learn to drink some whiskey."

Orson smiled at that.

Their leader then turned to Masters who he gave a cut to and said, "Enjoy yourself, Timmy."

Charlie stood next to Orson, watching all the others receive their pay. It hurt him, it truly did, but he did not question it. He knew he did not pull his own and he had to be punished for that. It still stung, knowing that he could've done more, should've done more, to make sure that he didn't let anyone down. He shook his head as he watched Bill count his dollars. He should've killed at least one, maybe more if he found the strength. He'd have something to show for where he'd been, at least.

Two single dollar notes hung from Jack's index and middle finger. He held them to Charlie's face, "Here's an extra fifty cents, boy. You did well on that calf."

He could buy plenty with that extra cash, and he felt happy that Jack offered him more than what he promised. He eyed the bills for a moment before snatching them from Jack's fingers. He stuffed the two dollars into his pocket, and he looked down towards the ground with a sharp grin, something he hoped none of them saw. He wasn't proud by any means, but he was thankful for what little mercy Jack showed.

Parker laughed, "Killin' that calf was 'bout all he did."

Charlie ignored Parker, speaking to Jack, "I'll do better."

Jack gave the boy a slight nod. Parker, however, refused to believe it. He leaned against the wagon, spitting and crossing his arms as if to appear dominate, "Bullshit, Lil' Lamb."

"Don't call me that," Charlie responded with a quick shift of his eyes to the scrawny Parker.

Parker unfolded his arms and stopped his lean. He chuckled to himself, enjoying what little Charlie did to defend himself and his actions. He shook his head at the thought and began to walk away from his crew. He had money to spend. Bill wasn't too far behind him.

Jack yelled after them, "'Ey, Parker."

Parker turned to see his boss.

Jack looked out to his entire party, raising his hands as if granting permission for them to be dismissed, "We all meet back here at sunup. Enjoy yer'selves!"

The saloon bustled with lively folk. A lot of them, by what Orson could tell, were hunters or cattlemen. They drank and sang and conversed loudly at the long-extended bar. Some wiped their mustaches with small cloths that dangled at the front of the bar's woodwork. The place wasn't lavish, but it wasn't poor in appearance either. It was adequate, Orson thought as he took a sip from a shot glass filled to the brim with a harsh sweet whiskey. He sat at a table, eyeing the folks at the bar. Parker was there and Masters stood next to him. They were drunk, slamming whiskey after whiskey.

Prostitutes were all about the saloon. They wore their girdles and their long flowing dresses. Some of them were well crafted and the women who wore them, if Orson didn't know any better, could pass as any lady on the street. Bill spoke to one, a good-looking woman with long blonde hair. She appeared young and well dressed. She also appeared to be disinterested in whatever Bill told her. Orson could not hear them speaking, but her body language, that of a quick recoil when he touched her arm, told the young man that she did not care for his company. She carried on in conversation with the burly man, nodding her head with a fake smile as he drunkenly complimented her, or boasted about himself, or whatever else he spewed out of his gob. It was honest work, Orson told himself, and she probably made good money doing that. It was her dignity that fought back, and he then began to wonder if his fought in his line of work.

"They hate me," a voice came from Orson's shoulder.

He looked, seeing Charlie at his table two seats over. A glass of water sat in front of him, half drunk. The boy hung his head after he looked to his companions around the room. He shook it after he told Orson how he felt, what he knew.

Orson told him, "They don't."

"Parker does," Charlie responded with a nod towards Parker at the bar. He took another drink of whiskey when Orson looked to him. Him and Masters paid no mind to the boys across the saloon.

"He hates *us*," Orson explained. "It ain't just you there."

Charlie eyed Parker from across the bar. His eyes danced with fury and frustration. He took a sip of his water, "He's a big ol' pecker, is what he is."

Orson found that funny and so he laughed. He liked that fire that grew in Charlie. It made him feel as if he weren't so alone in his thoughts and feelings.

Charlie shot Orson a glance as he held his water with both hands, "How'd you do it?"

"Do what?"

"Kill all them buffalo," Charlie replied quickly.

Orson didn't know. He thought back on the moment and thought nothing of it anymore. He fired that rifle in his mind without hesitation, watching as those bison dropped dead in the field. He remembered the blood, the buckling of the legs, the tearing of the flesh. He remembered the tuffs of fur, the skinned hides, the cloven head of the calf. At the time, he felt sorry about it, but that was days ago, he reasoned with himself and it would only be easier in the future. He didn't want to cast doubt to his acquaintance and so he told him, "I don't know. I just shot, I guess."

"You ain't feel bad?" Charlie asked.

Newkirk saw the water in the young man's eyes. As he looked to them, he saw that field of dead bison. At first, he felt something, as if it was a cold chill on the back of his neck that wasn't there. His heart felt heavy and his breath slowed as he imagined that killing field. He thought of his companions and that feeling went away, cold replaced by hot. As it did, he swore he heard the yap of a coyote mixed with the saloon piano player's high notes. He shook his head, still wanting to build Charlie up, not tear him down, "What's to feel bad about?"

Charlie hung his head again. His eyes stayed glued to the water in his glass. He watched it ripple and splash as he took another drink and set it back in front of him. He sighed, "I don't know..."

Orson watched Charlie closely, studying his every move. He knew he still struggled with something. Whether it was letting everybody down or the calf, that was what Newkirk wasn't sure about. He assumed it to be a bit of both, as if the ideas were conflicting and tearing their way through the boy's heart. Orson felt that too, though he felt one side winning and his weakness would soon flee from his body. It just took time, he reasoned with himself. It would take a bit more with Charlie, but it all took time.

Newkirk dug into his pocket, sliding a coin onto the table towards his acquaintance. He smiled to the boy, "Let me buy you a drink."

Charlie hesitated, reaching his hand out to take the small coin. His fingers danced across the edge of it as it laid flat on the table. He desired it and the whiskey or gin or beer or whatever he wanted that came with it. He felt that maybe that would wash away the feelings he had, and he could just move on with the party, move on and become whatever it was that Jack wanted him to be. As his fingers touched the face of the coin, he slid it back towards Orson, "I ain't earn it. Keep it."

Orson did. He took the coin, examining it before sliding it back into his pocket. His eyes danced around the saloon as he did so, and he noticed that Parker no longer stood near the bar. He now leaned against the wall, drunker than Orson ever saw one man. He nodded his head forward wildly and Orson feared his glassy eyes would fall from his skull. Before Parker stood a man, one rougher than anyone in Tanner's party. He wore a pair of fringed chaps and a rough looking shirt that had been re-stitched at the seams multiple times. The rough man ran his grimy hand through his oily hair as he spoke to Parker about something, which is what caused Parker's head to continuously nod. A smile lifted Parker's face and he let out a slight laugh, of which caught Charlie's attention. He too looked on from afar.

Charlie asked, "Wha'chu think they talkin' about? Think he's makin' fun'a me again?"

Orson watched as Parker's smirk faded as the rider told him something else. Parker adjusted himself on the wall, trying to appear somewhat presentable. The rider kept talking and Parker kept listening, kept nodding his head.

Newkirk glanced to Charlie and gave him a shake of his head as he said, "I don't think so. Looks more serious than that..."

The sun rose over Front Street. The streets basked in the orange glow of the Kansas sun. The water of the Arkansas reflected that hue back into the sky. The men stood near the cigar shop from the day before. They all huddled around, listening to Parker tell his story. Orson couldn't pay much attention at first, lost to the sight of the Arkansas in the distance. He then found interest in the tired expressionless faces of his companions. They all looked ill, too much drinking he figured. He didn't like whiskey, but he still drank it the night before. Two glasses over a long period of time. He wasn't sure how long, but he didn't feel as sick as his companions looked.

"...Then he says to me, 'took me three days to ride through the damned thing,'" Parker spoke.

Orson looked to the tall scrawny man. He stood at the center of them all. His hands raved as he told the story. Beads of liquor scented sweat rolled down his cheeks. He looked like hell, but he was excited about whatever it was that he reiterated to the party.

Bill spat a wad of tobacco, "Three days?"

Parker flung his arms upward in frustration, knowing he would receive this type of disbelief, "Tha's what he said! Ask Masters! He was there! He heard it too!"

Jack studied Parker for a moment before his eyes shifted to Masters. Masters just looked on, looking at Parker as well, reading the frustration as he pitched his wild and crazy idea. It was only when he felt Jack's gaze upon him that Timothy spoke up, "Tha's what he said, took him three days."

Tanner rested his hands in his gun belt. Sweat dripped from the tip of his nose. His back was slightly hunched, as if he swallowed stones the night before. His voice groveled, "Tha's what he said, but do you believe it?"

Parker threw his hands out, the back of his right patting Jack's shoulder. Jack turned to the wild looking Parker who spoke for Masters, "When's you ever heard of a herd that big? Three days to ride through? That's gotta be bigger than thousands."

"I don't believe it though," Bill spat again. He shook his head as he spoke his opinion. He didn't like the sound of whatever Parker was selling.

"If you's wasn't fallin' over whores all night then maybe you'd have heard it, seen his face," Parker said as he looked to the burly Bill with wide eyes. He then looked to his leader, the man who he pitched his idea to all along, "Jack, I'm a good judge a' character an' I trust this man."

Jack cocked his head to one side, really studying the face of Nathaniel Parker. Tanner ran his index across the tip of his mustache as he thought, looking to his loyal follower. Something didn't sit right with him and he knew, just by the way Parker acted, that it sounded too good to be true. He asked him, "You trust this man's story or you wishin' it were real?"

Parker took a step back, as if Jack hit him in the stomach with a haymaker. He calculated the question. His eyes squinted as those gears turned in his head. He didn't mean to say it out loud, but it slipped, "Huh?"

"You really believe it," Jack rephrased, "or you just hopin'?"

"I believe it," Parker said, putting his foot down on the matter. He had no doubt in his mind that he was right. He was always right, and if he was right about this, he'd never be questioned again. Maybe he'd get his own hunting crew. Maybe he could quit hunting all together. The amount of bison would be incredible. As Jack stared him down, a bit of doubt set in. Parker clarified it to himself with a question, "Why would he lie?"

"Boast," Jack said bluntly. He then followed up with, "Would also take out some competition 'round here. Indian Territory is a bit of a ways."

Masters chimed in with a fair point, "We'd need another wagon too, for all them pelts in bulk."

Jack threw his thumb over to Masters, as if pointing out the argument presented. He stayed fixated on Parker, "That's true."

Parker hung his jaw slightly, as if confused by the pushback he received from not just his leader, but his companions. He shook his head with one eye closed as he began to get a little frantic that someone doubted him and what he believed to be true, "Alright, let's figure he's lyin'. We keep huntin' 'round here for a few days, maybe get enough for thin dick to buy in bulk. Great. But what if he ain't and we let this chance go, boss?"

Jack laughed, "Then we doin' the same shit."

Parker stayed firm, "But…I'm tellin' you, it's real. It has to be. You've seen big herds, ain't nothin' that big but we can make so much with one trip. Ain't nobody makin' up that size of a herd. Ain't nobody gon' believe that shit."

"You do," Bill spat again with a grin.

The entire party laughed, Orson too. Parker didn't take kindly to that. He shot a glance to Charlie, who then halted his laugh. His eyes shifted to Jack again. He stepped forward, presenting his argument with such rigor, "Boss...it's at least worth a chance. Indian Territory, yeah...it's far. It ain't too far."

Jack eyed the loyal Parker. He never heard of such rumors before. He wasn't sure if he necessarily believed it. Maybe that man did ride through three days of bison, but herds move and maybe he was stuck among them. Maybe not. Either way, that was a large pack of animals that were three dollars a pelt. Hell, if he only took the tongues, he could still feed his crew for weeks. He didn't see retirement in that idea though. He loved to hunt. He loved to be paid. He loved to spend. That herd was nothing more to him than just a few bucks, and Parker was right, it wouldn't mean much to just look. Bison were everywhere and if it was a lie or a mistake, they wouldn't come back empty handed. He thought on it, thinking about all the time they could waste wandering the plains. He then thought of the money, the finely dressed businessman. He thought on it again, churning over all the pros and cons, all the possibilities. And then, he kept thinking on it.

Chapter XI
Ivory
1873

The men built a campfire before anything else. The flames started small, but as time went on and they unloaded their bedrolls and supplies from the back of their wagon, the kindle accelerated in its burning. The flames rose to something otherworldly for such an originally small fire. Jack tried buying two different wagons before they left Dodge City, but it became such an ordeal to try and haggle the owners to what little Jack had left over from his spending, and what little he pulled together from the others, that he gave up. They hit the trail with their one lonely wagon and Jack's horse. They carried more supplies, expecting to be out longer since they were heading to Indian Territory. Orson, Charlie, and Masters felt confined in the back of the wagon for their first day.

It felt good to stand by the fire. Orson crossed his arms, bent his knees, loosening up his stiff body from being crammed next to the others for hours on end. The sun set some time ago and the sky sat an empty abysmal black. There were stars though, but they seemed dimmer than usual, as if the light within them, however many miles away they were, began to go out. Orson stared up at them, basking in the hellfire glow of the campfire. His bedroll was slung over his back. His light jacket blew in the cold breeze that rushed across the plains. It chilled him to the bone, and he felt so small as he stared up at the sky, but he felt even smaller next to the rest of his party.

"Think we gon' get scalped?" Charlie asked. He knelt next to the fire. His young knees creaked and popped as he did so. He threw his hands over the flames, warming them from the cold dark night.

Orson misheard him, looking down to his acquaintance, "Wha'chu mean?"

"Indians," Charlie looked up to Orson, his face nervous. He continued, "They scalp white folk. You think we gettin' scalped?"

Pots and pans clinked over Parker's shoulder as he brought the cooking equipment away from the wagon. Jack wanted a stew made that night with their first set of provisions. The men didn't think that to be the best idea, but they went along with it. Parker took the equipment from over his shoulder and the iron clanked as it landed in a messy pile next to Charlie at the fire. Parker spat, "Ain't no one gettin' scalped, Lil Lamb. At least, not by Indians anyway. You hesitate at that big herd or you fuck it up in any way, I'll scalp you."

Charlie didn't bother to look to Parker. He looked towards the flames, their reflection dancing in his eyes, "I ain't gon' hesitate."

"I'll believe it when I see it," Parker laughed as he began to fumble through the cooking equipment.

Light thuds rolled across the flat plains around their campsite. They grew in sound, getting louder with each passing second. Orson turned, slightly nervous as to who or what it was. Out of the shadows of the darkness, Jack's Standardbred appeared and on the back of it sat Timothy Masters. A rifle rested over his lap. He held the reins in his right hand and in his left, he carried three rabbit carcasses tied together with a thin rope. He threw them at Parker's feet.

Parker said nothing, just looking to Masters with a scowl as if he were being treated as lesser than he.

Masters ignored the look and dismounted the horse, "Food's'ere."

The stew turned out alright. It wasn't the best Orson had, but it wasn't the worst either. Parker knew how to cook to some degree, but Newkirk would never compliment the man on it. He sat next to Charlie and Masters with their backs turned to the fire. They faced the wagon, watching the shadows of their other party members dance across the side of the wagon as they ate around the fire.

"It'll be a real adventure, this one," Masters told the two newcomers. He licked his wooden spoon as he stared at the dancing shadows. He nodded at a thought, then licked the bottom of his bowl.

Orson wasn't sure. He held some reserve about the idea of hunting something so outlandish. He wasn't an expert though. He knew that, but he trusted Jack and his decision. He replied, "Maybe."

"Oh, it will be," Masters put his bowl in the dirt, then pivoted his body to face Orson and Charlie. "I'm always lookin' for that, adventure. It gets yer heart goin'."

Charlie finished chewing his last piece of rabbit. He swallowed, then asked, "You done any adventurin'?"

Masters opened his mouth to speak. He looked excited by the thought. His youth showed, and Orson liked that. Yet, a shadow grew over the three young men and behind them stood Jack Tanner. He stepped over Charlie, then turned to face the boys. He knelt down before them and said, "This is adventurin'. Out here, untamed wilderness. Under the stars. It's all adventurin'."

Charlie nodded with wide eyes, "Oh, I see."

He didn't. He didn't understand that. He heard of great adventures in his youth. He often daydreamed about the idea. Yet, this was supposed to be an adventure. The slaughter of that first hunt was supposed to be an adventure. He didn't feel it. He didn't understand, and for a moment he thought that if it were so, he would never adventure again.

Masters smiled and nodded at Jack, "Best damn adventure I

know."

"Same here," Jack told him with a nod.

Orson studied his leader. The way he knelt before them, his thin legs looked longer than usual. He folded his arms over top them. His hat danced with the hellish glow of the fire, and the brim casted a shadow over his eyes. He looked as if he were some sort of infernal majesty. His nickel-plated Colt glistened in that same hellfire glow. The ivory handle appeared soiled and dirtier than before. The bending flames reflected on the cylinder of the weapon, and Orson could not help but get lost to the sight.

"I see you lookin' again," Jack told Orson with a smile. He joked, "You ain't gon' try and steal it again, are ya?"

Orson's eyes shifted to the dirt. He knew his leader tried to amuse him, but it held no effect on the boy. He thought back to those prostitutes in Dodge City and how he wondered if their dignity fought in their line of work, and if he would have any in his. He lost some dignity some time ago and he feared it all vacated. The joke from Tanner only made him realize that, remember that he lost a piece of himself somewhere along the road from home. He shook his head at the thought, "No..."

Tanner read the young man. He knew he stepped on a toe. He didn't really care all that much, but he cared enough. It wasn't Charlie he talked to. He held some respect for Orson. Nowhere near the amount of the others, but the kid showed promise in being a member, and he wanted to build him up rather than knock him down. He drew the revolver from his hip, giving it a quick twirl before pointing it at Orson's feet, finger off the trigger. He smiled, "Just teasin' ya, Newkirk. I know you ain't no thief."

Jack twirled the revolver again. The light of the fire danced wildly across the spinning metal. He grabbed ahold of the barrel, the ivory grip extended out towards Orson, who stared upon the weapon with such admiration. Jack gave the kid a nod, and Orson reached out, grabbing ahold of the grip.

Newkirk kept his finger off the trigger as he took the weapon in his hand. He soon cradled it in both, as if it were a delicate child. He saw his twisted reflection in the cylinder. The metal felt cool in his bare hands. The craftsmanship of the weapon appeared divine. Only one of a higher power could create such a thing, Orson thought. His pinky finger rubbed the smooth ivory as it rested in his palm.

The leader broke bread with the boy, "I used to thieve, ya know. Way back when."

Orson's gaze shifted from the revolver to his leader, who still knelt before him. He felt surprised by Jack's admission, "Oh, yeah?"

"Ran off from my parents when I was young. Came out here, snagged that off some Jayhawk back in the Bleedin' days," Jack nodded. Orson could not see his eyes under the shadow of his brim, but he believed them to be genuine.

"You kill him for it?" Charlie piped in, looking at the weapon that Orson held. He too admired it, hoping to own a weapon as nice someday.

"Maybe," Jack smirked to the boy. He turned his head to Masters and gave him a wink, the fire illuminated his eyes as he did so, "Maybe not. It's all ancient history. Yer past gets left at the door when you come out here."

Orson thought on that. He liked the way that sounded. He left everything behind, including that dignity he so regretted. He felt that, maybe, if he stayed out on the plains, that would be his new history, his dignity reclaimed, and he would be an honest man, an honest worker. He could be like Jack, free to do whatever whenever. He smirked at the thought, then he noticed Charlie studying the weapon. He extended it out towards his acquaintance, who reached for the weapon. Before his hand gripped the ivory, Jack grabbed ahold of the barrel and took it from Orson, giving it a twirl before putting it back in his holster.

Charlie felt a lump in his throat as he did so. He worried that Tanner too hated him, maybe as much as Parker hated him. Doubt set in. It made his heart race with an anxiety so fierce.

Jack removed his flask from his pocket, taking a quick drink. He buckled a bit in the knees. They were beginning to ache as he knelt before them, and his drunkenness didn't help much. He took another swig as he stared upon Orson, who he knew took his drunken words to heart. He knew the boy sat trapped within himself, trapped within whatever held him back, whatever he dreamed of, whatever he hoped for. Jack knew that all to be fruitless. All that mattered was money, the plains, that freedom and that life. The kid would see it. He wiped his mustache with his sleeve as he told Orson, "We all done bad things, we all done good things. I done plenty'a things I ain't happy about. I just knew then, I just knew...The world is wha'cha make of it. I wasn't makin' anythin' where I was."

Orson nodded at that. He took that as true wisdom. His eyes widened as the thought danced in his mind and all other things faded. He latched onto that last phrase and asked, "And where was ya?"

Jack stood, swaying with the cold nightly breeze. It rolled over him, sending chills down his spine. He rested his hand on his revolver, mostly to check that he had not dropped it in the dirt. He took one step forward and felt his boot buckle a bit on the loose earth. He took another sip, staggering as he took one more step. He smiled to himself, loving the drunkenness that overtook his mind. He cared about nothing or anyone and standing only made it better. He then realized that Orson asked him a genuine question, one of which he answered only once before and never again. Maybe he would, but he was a different man on the plains. His past life meant nothing to him, and he would never speak of it. He told Orson, "Maybe another time."

Orson watched as Jack staggered off back towards the campfire. Bill made a joke and Jack laughed wildly. He spat as he did so, then took another drink before collapsing before the flames. He lowered his head, thinking of something. The light basked over him as he knelt before the flames. It appeared to

Orson that his leader prayed, but he doubted that for Jack did not strike him as a religious man. If he did pray, he wondered what he prayed to.

"Tennessee," a voice came from the dark.

Orson looked over, seeing Masters beginning to stand. He dusted himself off as he told the boys, "At least, that's what he told me. He's from Tennessee."

Masters too wandered off towards the campfire. He sat next to Jack, kneeling before the flames. The original companions joked and talked to one another. Orson could not hear them, but he knew they were pleasant with one another. He and Charlie sat in the shadow of the wagon, looking over to them. Neither boy spoke to one another. They stayed fixated on their leader, whose head remained hung. The only light that touched his face beneath the shadow of his brim danced across the edge of his mouth. He smirked at something, a thought most likely, and Orson smirked too.

Chapter XII
The Weak
1873

Tanner told the men to stop the wagon at the crest of a shallow hill. They rambled for some time and dusk would soon be upon them. The golden grass lightly swayed back and forth as the men stood on the edge of the hill, all of them together, as they stared down on a small homestead surrounded by nothing but the golden ocean of grass. It appeared a modest home and by the looks of it, it had been there for some time and seen better days. A candle became lit near the back window of the home as the light of the afternoon faded and darkness overpowered all. The men paid no mind to whoever lingered within that small home, for their eyes laid fixated on a wagon near the rundown barn not far from the household.

Jack threw back his long coat, removing a rolled cigarette. He plopped it in his mouth but struggled to light a match with the whipping winds. He gave up, letting the unlit cigarette dangle from his mouth. He looked to Masters who stood to his right, "Y'said we'd need another."

"Yeah," Masters admitted, "not like this though."

"It don't make no difference how we get it," Parker chimed in, taking his place at Jack's left. He stared down Masters, "All that matters is that we get it."

"It do make a difference," Masters told them.

Jack stared forward, looking down upon the homestead. His eyes stayed hooked to that wagon. He still fumbled with that match, and finally lit it within his coat, placing the small dancing flame to the cigarette inside his jacket. He plopped it back in his mouth, sucking in the grey ribbons that spewed from the edges of the cigarette. He said, "Not much."

Orson stood behind his leader and next to him lingered Charlie and Bill. Jack turned to face them, but spoke to Bill, "Y'was right. There's a wagon down there."

"Thought I saw it," Bill nodded.

"Good eye for it," Jack nodded back.

Bill smirked at the praise over something so small.

Jack then shot his gaze to Orson, "You comin' with me."

Orson felt good about that. He wasn't sure where they were going, but he assumed where. Jack trusted him to stay at his side, that is all he really knew for sure and he felt proud by that.

"Boss, can we just discuss this a little more?" Masters pleaded.

"Ain't nothin' to discuss, Masters," Parker answered for his leader. "He said we doin' it, we doin' it."

"They just farmers," Masters moved to Jack's side once more, stepping closer to him as if his words would hold more weight that way. "They ain't hurt nobody."

"And we ain't hurtin' nobody," Jack responded.

Masters did not believe that. He held his dignity close to his heart and what Jack asked of the party was something he did not see as dignified. He too lived a hard life before the Tanner Party, and this made him feel dirtier than being covered in a week's worth of blood and guts. He tried to hold some morality when it came to man.

"They livelihood gon' be hurt," Masters pipped back.

Jack shook his head. He rolled his eyes as he did so. The young man who he admired dearly did not see the reasoning of Tanner. He didn't care much to be questioned either, especially in front of the others. He argued, "Ours gon' be hurt if we don't get that wagon."

Orson looked as Jack made his way to the wagon that they rode in on. He took off his coat, throwing it in the back atop the rifles and supplies. He rolled up his sleeves and took some dirt, throwing it on himself to appear as if he walked on the trail for some time. He looked to Orson, "You got something to say about this too?"

Orson shook his head. He did. He thought these things would be behind him, but he felt at ease with it for some reason. He figured it was because he wasn't alone in the act. They were thieving for survival, like he did, but it was a group effort and not one man's dignity at stake.

"Perfect," Jack smiled and nodded to Orson. He then moved past him as he made his way back to the crest of the hill. He looked over his party as he spoke and threw his thumb out, pointing to Orson, "I'll take this one and Masters down that hill and chat it up with the homeowner. He gon' invite us in. Parker, you and Bill show the other how we do it."

Parker nodded, "You got it, boss."

Charlie stood on, lingering on the edge of the group. He did not care for being with Parker. He did not mind Bill all that much. Yet, he felt some contempt there too. Though, Bill never really expressed verbally any issues with the boy. That made him feel alright about working with him. It was better than being left alone with Parker and being with someone besides the other novice.

"And what if they don't let us in?" Masters asked, giving his last hurrah of defiance against the plan.

"They gon' let us in," Jack smiled. "They just dumb farmers."

Tanner walked ahead of Orson and Timothy as he led them down the shallow sloped hill towards the homestead. He did not possess a care in his strut as he stared down onto the small farm. Masters and Orson walked side by side with shallow steps in the tall golden grass. As they approached the homestead, Orson saw it appeared not nearly as neat or modest as he originally thought. The wood was worn. Not a single living creature lingered on the property, livestock or otherwise. The barn loomed in disrepair and had the candle not glowed in the window of the home, he would have thought it abandoned long ago.

"You stolen somethin' before?" Masters asked Orson.

Newkirk nodded. He felt shame in that but spoke as if it didn't matter, "Yeah."

"You like it?"

"Not really."

Masters looked off towards the property. His eyes squinted as he stared at the wagon near the barn, "Me neither..."

Jack heard the boys talking but couldn't make out exactly what they said. He turned his head over his shoulder, speaking quickly to put them at ease with what they planned, "These are farmers. They weak. They ain't gon' survive much longer out in all this nothin'. No difference if we take it or not."

Masters didn't believe that.

Orson wasn't sure what to believe.

By the time the three men reached the broken fence of the property line, the front door to the small home opened and out stepped a tall lengthy man. His beard, peppered and long enough to cover the front of his neck, blew gently in the wind. A percussion dragoon revolver sat at the front of his trousers. His hand rested on the handle as he approached the three companions.

"Who are ya? Wha'chu want?" the man shouted as he marched to the property line.

"I'm Jack Tanner," the party leader spoke first. He threw

his arms out to present the two boys behind him as the man stopped on the other side of the broken fence. "These here are my sons, Orson and Timmy. We's travelers, a bit lost."

The bearded farmer stared over the two boys for a moment then studied Tanner. He asked, "Where's ya horses?"

"Thieves," Jack said with such a stern voice. "Damn 'em."

The farmer nodded. Orson thought he looked a bit slow, but he didn't really know. The farmer took his hand from the handle of his revolver. He continued to nod at Jack, "I see..."

Jack too thought the farmer slow, but he thought that of the man before he even saw him. He explained, "We been walkin' quite a ways, quite a long ways, really."

"Where ya headin'?" the farmer pressed.

"We was plannin' on passin' through Indian Territory down to Texas. Figured we start fresh down there."

"Where ya from?" the man continued to question. He believed Jack though, who he thought had no reason to lie.

"Kansas City," Jack said quickly.

The farmer raised an eyebrow to the boys' leader. He then looked to the young men behind Jack. He studied them too. He was apprehensive, Jack understood why, but the farmer appeared too trusting and too foolish. Jack made a lot of assumptions about the man based on his body language and what he perceived of all farmers.

The farmer spoke to the three, "Anne's cookin' some soup. We got plenty."

Jack smiled wildly with those dull yellow teeth, "That's mighty kind of ya."

"You and yer boys come on in, get'chu sum to eat."

As the farmer spoke, he turned his back on the three. He began to walk towards his modest home at the center of the property. Jack stepped between the fallen railing of the fence. He rested his hand on a split post, turning back and smirking at Timothy Masters. He gave the boy, who he appreciated more than all others, a small smug wink. He told him so.

The interior of the homestead looked rougher than the exterior. Pots and pans lined the walls. Some farming equipment hung in the home too. Orson figured it to be because the barn fell to such disrepair. An odor hung in the air, and the three thought it to be the soup, but it was something closer to death and rot. Something must've died under the farmer and his wife's un-swept floorboards.

They all sat at the best piece of furniture on the property, the dining table. It stood elongated, a long rectangle with only six chairs that only took up a small fraction of the length. One sat all alone right at the middle of the table. Two were pulled to the head of the table where the farmer and his wife sat. On the other end, three were pulled with Jack sitting at the end placement. Orson sat to his left while Masters sat to his right. The soup in front of them steamed and the men sweated as they ate, for it was a cooler night, but the inside of the homestead radiated a thick muggy heat that smelt of secretions. The fireplace crackled and hissed in the corner of the room.

"...said they was set upon by thieves," the farmer pointed to Jack and his boys with his dripping spoon as he explained the men's false plight to his wife.

"Oh, lord..." she muttered as she looked to Tanner and his fake sons. She saw them for what they presented themselves as. She could not see the predators that they were, Orson saw that much. His heart sank at the thought of it, but he dared not remove his figurative wool exterior.

Jack slopped his soup, "Yes ma'am. My thoughts exactly. Ain't much room for honest workin' men these days."

Orson took a sip from his spoon, wondering if that were true. Jack acted so well that he truly thought it to be his leader's honest opinion. Maybe he wasn't acting, Orson thought. Maybe honest work was just another façade that he believed in, that his father told him, that really didn't mean much at all.

"What's waitin' for ya in Texas?" the farmer asked.

"Beans," Jack replied matter of fact. He sipped from his spoon loudly.

"Beans?" the wife asked.

"Uh-huh," Jack nodded, wiping his mouth with the sleeve of his shirt. "My boys and I are goin' to Texas to start a bean farm. If you'll believe it."

The farmer appeared interested in what Jack told him. He liked the sound of a bean farm, any farm would do really. The farmer, whose property stood on its last leg, never really met anyone who shared his hardships, cared to hear him out. Those in town only wanted his money, what they could take from him. Either that or his crops, but when those ran dry, he held nothing more than a few dollars. The men in town were scavengers, willing to pick the flesh from his body before he even passed. He liked having another man around that farmed or that saw value in such a thing. He pressed with interest, "What kinda beans?"

"Well…" Jack thought for a moment. He looked to Masters for help, not really sure of what to respond with. Masters stayed quiet, eyes fixated on his soup and spoon. Jack just spouted off, "Any kind'a beans. Black beans. Pinto beans. Anythin' that'll make money."

The farmer laughed at that, knowing he too just wanted money, but the land was harsh, and it treated him as if he were its disobedient servant. He liked Jack's sense of security in his lies. He told them, "Yeah, we's been strugglin' growin' much of anythin' out here."

"Hush now," the farmer's wife pipped in, "we doin' just fine!"

The farmer shook his head as he took another sip from his spoon. He lowered the wooden spoon to the bowl, resting it in the murky liquid. He crossed his hands one over the other, staring down into the soup as if he saw his future in the muck. His voice shook, "We ain't. Life is hard out here for the honest, like you's said."

The man's wife watched him. She stared at his long face for a moment before she too looked to his soup. She saw what he saw, but still pressed optimism, "We'll be fine."

The oil rested atop the farmer's broth. It swirled and spun as if storm clouds, and in it, he only thought of his past, "Lost our boy, sickness took him. Lost our crops, God took them."

Jack carried not for the man's story or why he thought the way he did. He saw a bag of flesh in front of him, nothing more. He mocked the man with what knowledge he held for what he would do, and reveled in the man's ignorance on the subject, "Seen a barn out there."

"No livestock left," replied the farmer. "I sold my last two hogs up in Wichita just a few weeks back. We's runnin' out of money. We's runnin' out of time."

Orson felt for the man, so much so, he dared not look upon him any longer. He shifted his eyes to Masters who too no longer listened. He hung his head. His chin burrowed in his bright blue bandana around his neck. His lips ran along the edge of the cloth as he tried to focus on anything but the man's story. It made the farmer real to the boys. He was no mirage on the plains, no evil villain or tycoon of some corporation somewhere East. He was just a man, trying to make his way in the world as the boys were. Jack cared not, for he smirked at the man's tale.

The farmer continued, "We just...this land...it's unforgiving and it's harsh."

Tanner took his bowl in his hand, placing it to his lips as he drank the rest of his soup as if he suckled from a waterfall. The brown murky liquid ran down his cheeks. He wiped it away with his sleeve. He let out a slight belch, sliding his empty bowl forward onto the table. It slid and toppled. The crack of wood on wood startled everybody at the table, except for Jack who grinned with those yellow teeth, "You ain't gon' make it."

The farmer rose his head, leaning back in his chair. His lip twitched beneath his beard. His eyebrow raised as he looked upon the now menacing Jack Tanner, "What?"

"Like yer boy, he died," Jack said, leaning forward as he crossed his arms on the table. He nodded to those he spoke to, "Yer wife, she'll die. You'll die too."

The farmer wasn't sure what the stranger spoke of. It sounded insulting, but the way the man presented it, so matter of fact, as if he were some soothsayer of ancient days, made the farmer question his intent, "What you sayin' to me?"

Jack rested his chin on his fist as he stared at the farmer drunkenly, "This land, it's harsh and unforgiving, like ya said. It's brutal and it's rough. Only the strong survive out here. Only men who good enough, able enough to do what has to be done, they's the only ones who gon' make it."

The farmer said nothing. He just stared to the devil whom he allowed into his home. Orson still did not look to the man, but instead just stared at Masters who lifted his chin out of his bandana to glance at Newkirk. The young men stared at each other, eyes filled with regret and embarrassment for what their leader said.

Jack continued, "Yer weak, my friend. You always gon' be weak. Don't matter how many crops you grow. Don't matter how many pigs you have. It don't matter whether you have a wagon or not. You weak. You'll always be weak. This land will chew you up and pick its teeth with yer ragged bones. It ain't meant for you."

The farmer gritted his teeth. He knew now what he invited into his home. The stranger was no soothsayer, no man of great wisdom as he saw him. He was no farmer, no man of understanding or compassion. He embodied everything the farmer hated in the world. He cocked his head to Tanner, speaking with a harsher tone, "And who is it meant for?"

"Me," Tanner smirked, leaning back in his chair. He threw his arms out, resting his hands on the shoulders of Orson and Masters, "Men like me, and my boys here."

Jack opened his mouth, ready to continue to gloat to the farmer. As the first guttural sound meant to form a word slipped from his mouth, a loud crash echoed across the property. Swearing filled the night air. The farmer stood, as did his wife. He towered over the table. Jack stayed still. His hands tightened on the boys' shoulders. The farmer shouted, "Wha'chu tryin' to pull?"

Orson watched as Jack's hand left him and Masters' shoulders. His leader slowly stood, he too towering over his end of the table. He said nothing to the farmer. He only stared into those sad eyes, watching as the realization of what was happening seeped into them. Tanner enjoyed it, that much Orson knew. Jack turned and began to move towards the door of the home and the boys quickly followed.

As the three companions stepped onto the shadow swept porch, the hollering grew louder. No lanterns were lit. They just stood in the darkness, waiting for their eyes to adjust. Slowly, figures emerged around the farmer's wagon, which still rested near the barn. Orson recognized Parker's voice, "...gah'damn! Sum'bitch! Get on it, Lil' Lamb!"

They slowly came into view as the farmer and his wife stepped onto the porch. The bearded man stood armed with his old dragoon, looking on to his wagon and the figures that surrounded it. He saw the back wheel torn from the hull of the wagon. The chain he tied to it to prevent thieves worked, to a degree. He did not expect it to break the thing, his only last source of a possible livelihood. There it was, sitting in the darkness of the night, in ruins as if it represented his life itself.

"Sorry boss," Parker shouted as he dismounted from the driver's box. "It ain't goin' nowhere."

Bill Chambers wheeled the Tanner Party wagon next to the porch. Jack stepped towards it, climbing next to Bill in the driver's box. Charlie jumped aboard the back with great haste and Orson, along with Masters at his back, eagerly hopped in as well.

The farmer stood on his porch, dumbfounded by what he witnessed. He hollered out, "What the hell is goin' on here?"

Jack stood on the driver's box, watching as Parker too

climbed into the back. Once Parker was aboard, Jack turned to the farmer, "Now, you gon' be upset with me. You weren't suppose to know till mornin', but seein' as my other boys is fools..."

The wagon began to move away with a quick crack of the reins from Bill. Jack shuffled a bit as he stood, dropping his knee to the driver's box for balance. The farmer raised his dragoon, aiming towards the wagon as it peeled away. Sparks flew from the barrel, and a bellow of smoke enveloped his porch. He hollered something, but Orson could not hear it over the ringing of his ears. The men in the back huddled down as a round pierced the top panel of the wagon. Jack cackled and laughed as the men rode off. He shouted to the farmer and his wife, "Wasn't gon' serve you none anyhow!"

The party rode on through the night, only stopping to collect Jack's horse hitched to a lone tree not too far from the property. They kept heading south under the stars. Parker took the reins and Bill took over Jack's position at the box. Masters, the favorite of the young men, became lucky enough to ride Jack's horse, which he trailed closely behind the wagon. Nobody rode Jack's horse, nobody but Jack and Timothy Masters. He found pride in that, and Orson found himself envious, almost as much as Parker who occasionally shot dirty looks to the young rider.

Jack laid at the back of the wagon. His feet dangling out the back. They swayed with every bump and rut the wagon rolled through. Orson sat next to him, his legs too hanging from the back.

Charlie lingered behind them, smushed between the food preserves and ammunition. Orson looked out to the stars, feeling so insignificant in the presence of them.

Masters swayed with tiredness atop the horse, he spoke to Jack but lowered his head to hide his disappointment, "They ain't got it…we ain't got it. What was the point?"

Jack groaned and groveled, sitting up and resting his arms on his knees. He cracked his back and his neck, mumbling under his breath. He was tired. He spat, "The point is, we tried. We failed, but we gon' make it. We hard. That man and his wife? Farmers...they ain't gon' make it. I warned him. They'll be dead before winter ends."

Masters dared not look to Jack as he questioned him, "You c'ain't know that…"

Jack grew angry. He tried his best not to show it, but Orson felt it in the night air, as if it were a swarm of locusts vacating his body to ravage those who opposed him. Jack calmed his voice, "I do though. I seen the kinda men who can make it. I seen the ones who c'ain't. He c'ain't."

Masters finally looked to his leader. It was hard to see his face under the shadows of the night, but he asked him with full honesty, "Oh yeah? Mm'I gon' make it?"

Jack smirked, plopping a small cigar in his mouth. He lit it, and his face illuminated under the orange flame. Orson witnessed the anger in his eyes fade, replaced by that wisdom, false or otherwise, that he, for some reason, respected above all else.

"Yeah, you gon' make it," Jack said. He then patted Orson on the shoulder, "You too."

"I will," came a voice from darkness in the back of the wagon.

Orson looked over his shoulder, watching as Charlie shuffled in the dark to find comfort. Jack looked too, studying the boy who tried to defend himself. Jack honestly forgot he was there, and because of that, found no value in the young Charlie. He wouldn't make it, no matter how hard he tried. He saw him as no greater than that farmer, who Jack was certain would perish. Jack took a long drag off his cigar, "We'll see about that, Lil Lamb."

Chapter XIII

Kansas-Pacific and A Visitor in the Night

1873

They rode on and come morning, they sauntered not far from train tracks, the last they'd see any further south they went. They weren't the only ones, for when they broke the crest of a shallow hill on the plains, looking down onto the tracks, they saw a decent sized herd meandering near the steel pathway. There had to be nearly a hundred, maybe more, maybe less. The men discussed it among themselves whether they should stop and collect the pelts of the brown beasts. Chambers spoke from the driver's box, "We should snag a few, Jack."

Tanner, atop his steed since sunrise, whipped the beast around in a small circle as he rode in front of the wagon. He shook his head, "Save the ammo. Plus, we don't know how long it'll take to find the herd."

Bill shot back quickly with a glance to Parker, as if his look were to jab him in the ribs, "If it exists."

Parker whipped the reins, forcing the horses forward, "It exists. You seen big ones, real big ones. Bigger than this lot here."

Masters then chimed in from the back, kneeling atop the food preserves to peer out of the driver's box, "No three days big."

"No reason to waste time on hides that might soil," Jack responded to Masters. He turned his horse back towards the tracks as if to signal them to move onward without question. He then spoke over his shoulder, "We don't find that herd, we come back for these later."

The party leader looked out ahead as he began to walk his horse down the shallow hill towards the tracks. He did not get far before he stopped, for the clouds on the eastern horizon darkened from the base of the Earth. Shadowy smoke flowed upward as if the world itself split and Hell came forth. He stared on, knowing what he witnessed but he still found amazement in such a thing. Around the bend of the tracks, a great metal beast roared to life, whistle blowing and clouds of black bellowing from a large chimney. On its side Orson read, "Kansas Pacific" as the locomotive rolled towards the herd that collected around the tracks.

The horn blew again. Orson stood at the back of the wagon, watching as the train barreled forward. Its horn screeched, something he didn't expect to be so loud. The shriek cut the air as if it were a long-forgotten banshee, there to remind the travelers of its existence. The bison became startled by the sound, clearing away from the tracks slowly. Newkirk witnessed two men sitting atop one of the train cars. Rifles sat across their laps. One stood, eyeing the herd as it cleared away from the tracks. He said something to the other, then slammed his fist down atop the passenger car.

Jack muttered something to himself, then turned back to the men of his party, "Get down!"

As he shouted, the windows of the passenger car dropped and out flew plumes of gun smoke filled with lead. Rifles cracked the air. Orson stayed standing for a moment, watching as the hellish manmade fog formed around the side of the cars. The bison nearby began to buckle and cry in pain. Their screams, so human, so haunting, radiated upward into the heavens as their souls fled their bodies. Scarlet and crimson flowed from wounds, soiling the salt of the earth. Few could not clear from the tracks, as panic set into their feral hearts. The train cared not, for it pressed onward. Orson watched as one bison, a medium sized heifer, tried to steer its bulky body away from the rail line. It was too late, for the iron grate attached to the front of the metallic monstrosity lifted the beast upward, causing it to topple over. Its legs laid on the rails, and then it disappeared behind the train as it rolled on by.

The bison that broke free from the chaos rushed the shallow hill, swallowing the Tanner party in their presence. Orson saw the fear in their eyes as he continued to stand atop the wagon, looking down onto the beasts as the ran by. Their deep brown eyes shifted wildly and he felt as if they looked onto him for guidance, but he could offer none, for had he been given the chance, it would be he who would startle their wild minds, he who caused their panic. He would be that machine if given the chance. But as he looked upon them, their eyes crazed with such bedlam, he pitied them as if he were one of them, as if they were men and him a god.

Shots continued to fire upon the bison, even as they ran. Those aboard the train cared for nothing but what lived within their confinement. They fired upon them, rounds hissing as they flew by Orson as he watched on with such amazement of the disorder. Some beasts buckled and fell nearby. Others were struck, but only grazed and continued on, leaving thick trails of red atop the grass. The smell finally hit the boy as he looked on, gunpowder, and excrement, and urine, and iron, and blood, and fear, and panic, and death itself more prominent than all the others.

A hand reached up to Orson's, locking around his fingers and then pulled down with such a force. Rounds began to fly around the wagon. He looked up, seeing Charlie remove his hand from his, then ducked as low to the bottom of the wagon as physically possible.

Only a few rounds struck the carriage, but splinters flew wildly and peppered those that took cover beneath it. Jack dismounted his horse as it kicked upward, startled by all the commotion. He fell to the ground, and before him a great bull ran. He stood, fearful of being gored and ducked away as it moved past him, his back only brushing the fur of the beast's great ribs. He slid and crawled under the wagon, hiding among Parker and Bill. Dirt flew atop them as crazed hooves stampeded by. The thunder that came with them could not be heard over the wailing of the train car nor the cracking of the rifles. Though, as the three laid beneath the wagon, their chests pressed to the earth, they could feel that thunder as the world felt as if it would fall out beneath them.

The screeching grew louder as the train began to brake. The herd of bison began to clear, and all the gunshots faded. Wails and cries of bison began to be drowned out by cheers and excitement from inside the railcar. Orson closed his eyes at some point while cowering in the back of the wagon. He didn't know when, or if he even saw what he thought he did when he stood to watch the massacre. It was only when Charlie put his hand on his shoulder that he opened them and removed his hands from his ears. The two stood, looking out over the killing fields. Some bison laid wounded, a large number dead. Their black and brown bodies basked in the sun. A manmade fog of gunpowder rolled across the field. Blood laid splashed over all golden and green. The boys heard only one thing, the screams of the wounded, screams of the dying, for they sounded so human.

Tanner crawled out from under the wagon. Parker and Bill followed. The leader stood near the carriage, inspecting the damage done. He scanned the field, eyes nervous. A scowl stretched across his face and Orson saw he worried for something. It was only when his horse appeared near the rail line, miraculously unscathed amid the chaos, that a smirk lifted Jack's cheeks.

A scowl returned to the leader once he witnessed the door to the passenger car open. Off stepped a uniformed man. A thin mustache accented his pale complexion. He removed his hat, presenting forth the great dead beasts to those who began to scramble off the train. The folks aboard wore suits, dresses, and finer clothes. They wore their wealth with their pocket watches and the fine stitching of their garments. The train worker said to them, "Remember, one dead bison means ten dead Indians!"

Jack began to walk towards the train. Parker hopped onto the driver's box of the wagon, having the horses, still slightly on edge from the commotion, follow his leader. The party walked next to the wagon with their leader out front as they made their way through the killing fields.

"Take yourself a horn or a hoof as a reminder of this great journey West!" another train worker said as the people began to examine their kills. Some carried knives, others hammers, and others a variety of additional tools. They began to peel away at whatever they desired from the corpses. Some took a hoof or a horn from those still dying. The bison screamed in pain as they did so, but the folks in their dresses and their suits did not mind, nor did they mind what blood splashed up onto their gaunt, pale, corpse-like faces.

Tanner stood before a worker. The travelers stewed all about, paying no mind to the plainsmen. For a moment, Orson wondered if they died and become ghosts among the plains. That faded when the worker turned to Jack, raising his eyebrows and throwing his hand out to greet the man. Jack spat, and the man recoiled his hand. His raised eyebrows arched, becoming frustrated at the plainsman's hostility. He asked the party leader, "Who the hell'er you?"

Jack moved past the man for a moment, grabbing the reins of his horse. He pet the beast on its neck, shushing it. It immediately calmed. He climbed aboard the saddle, then paraded the horse around the worker for a moment, who looked up to the leader with such confusion. Tanner asked him, his voice boiling with such anger, "What the hell you think yer doin?"

"My job," the worker replied. "What about you?"

"You could'a killed us," Jack stopped his horse directly in front of the man. His party lingered behind him. They stared on.

The worker studied the party, seeing nothing of concern, "You ain't though? Ain't none of ya take a bullet."

Another worker disembarked from the machine. He carried a thick burlap sack under his arm. He stepped around the dead bison, those already stripped clean of what was desired of their corpses. He reached into the bag, showering small white pellets atop the carcasses, who would be long forgotten except for the small pieces or trinkets taken by travelers.

Orson watched as a woman received a horn from a well-dressed man. His gloves glistened, bloodied. Her smile radiated and eyes widened with joy. The young man wondered if they would truly remember that killing field the way he did. He doubted. He doubted they would even remember the bison that it came from. He wondered what they would do with that trophy and he envisioned it sitting in a desk, turning to dust and being forgotten as all things tend to be.

The boy's thought became interrupted as he heard Tanner yell, "You stupid asshole! I almost got trampled!"

The train worker crossed his arms. He refused to budge with his attitude, especially after the disrespect from Jack. He told the party, "But ya didn't. I don't see the problem."

Tanner crossed his hands one over the other, resting them on the pommel of his saddle. He looked around the killing fields, watching the trophy collectors go about their business. He knew he wouldn't get any sympathy from the train worker, there'd be no way. His party stood unscathed. He spat again, looking around, "This yer idea of huntin'?"

The train worker stared at the grizzled plainsman. He cared not for the man's opinion, and he knew his comment was meant to belittle him, "I ain't say it was."

"It ain't huntin'," Jack stared the man down, looking deep into his eyes.

The train worker smirked. He didn't care what some low rambler thought of him or his trade. He had a job, and he expressed it as such, "Someone's gotta keep them tracks clear. You boys sure ain't. You got guns. You ain't doin' nothin'."

The party leader's face stretched upward, eyes opening wide, as if hit in the jaw. His brow then lowered with anger and slight confusion. He didn't know what to say, so he replied, "You dumb. You know that?"

"Off wit'cha!" the worker yelled throwing his hands up. "The lot of ya! You's holdin' us up!"

Tanner did not move. His party did not move. They stared onward towards the worker. They did not take kindly to his antics, and their gazes were strong enough to let him know. He looked into them, each and every one of them. He felt his heart race a little more, but he observed one of the younger boys, Orson, staring off towards his coworker and his bag of chemical pellets.

Orson kept on watching the other worker sprinkle those white circles onto the corpses. He wasn't sure what they were, and he asked the man, "What is that?"

The worker with the sack under his arm heard the boy but ignored him for a second. It wasn't until he felt the gaze of the other party members shift towards him that he looked upon Orson. He examined the truth and honesty in the kid's face. He kept on working, but spoke as he sprinkled, "It's for the vermin. They're a plague 'round here."

The other train worker, whom Jack refused to take his eyes off, shouted to his colleague, "Jim, shut up and stop talkin' to these urchins. Get everyone back on the train. We got a deadline."

The passengers weren't eager to leave the killing fields, but the workers urged them to get on the train. They were heading somewhere West, and Orson thought that maybe they were heading as far as West would go, and maybe then he could see an ocean that he always dreamed of. His party stayed stagnate, watching as the folks boarded the train. The train worker, whom Jack continued to eye with disgust, was the last to board. He glared to the plainsmen, then slammed the door to the train car shut.

The locomotive began to roll onward, heading to wherever it desired. Nothing could stop it. Once it vacated from the front of the party, the men climbed aboard the wagon and began to mosey on. The killing fields surrounded them, larger than Orson originally thought, for they shot from both sides of the cars. Hundreds laid dead in the field. The white pellets sat atop their bodies as if a light snow fall. Death stretched out before the party and they pressed on.

Across the plains, the wagon followed the lone rider. They marched on through the killing grounds, seeing no more death or destruction along their way south. Though, Orson imagined the faces of the dead creatures all around him, as if they stalked him, begging to be remembered. Only murmurs or the occasional hum of a song cut the silent air as they continued their travel. The plains went onward, forever it seemed. Had Jack not announced their entry into Indian Territory, Orson would not have known any different. His leader could tell the difference that Orson could not, for the land, while open plains and pockets of trees scattered in the distance, felt desolate and cold. The earth, cursed and stained with red deep in the soil, spoke to none of them as they entered that land. Orson felt nothing of it, and it saddened him to some degree. Charlie too, for not once did he think of grabbing one of the many stones that lingered in the tall grass, seeing if it would speak to him. He'd given up on such childish things, such innocent thoughts.

By nightfall, the men set a camp in a small thicket of trees. Their fire, so mighty and majestic, roared wildly within the small wood. The men sat around, all of them drinking, laughing. Orson drank his whiskey from a tin cup, sipping what little Jack offered to his men. The young man did not need as much as the others, for he had three sips and felt his head lighten, as if a fraction of his soul fled from his body.

Bill Chambers cackled, leaning towards Jack and patting him on the shoulder. The two basked in the orange haze of the flames. Their eyes glossed with the effects of alcohol. Bill spat as he spoke, "...the look on that stupid sum'bitch's face when he got back on that train? He didn't know what he was doin'."

Charlie examined the two, sipping even less whiskey given to him by Tanner. He felt none of it in his head, only the burn in his throat with each sip. His mouth went numb, and he salivated heavily. He spat into the flames, asking Jack, "Would you have killed him?"

Jack glanced at the boy, taking a heavy drag from his rolled cigarette, then a lofty sip from his flask. He leaned back a bit, resting on his elbows as he laid in the dirt. He replied to the boy with a big grin, his voice rising with a joking manner, "I was madder at them buffalo for almost crushin' my ass!"

Every member of the party roared with laughter. Even Orson and Charlie cackled among their peers. It was the closest they felt to each of them and all it took was a massacre near a rail line and almost certain death. The alcohol helped too. It felt strange for Orson, for he admired the men around that campfire, but never felt as if he were one of them. Under the haze of bourbon, he felt that connection for once, as if they were all one, a true party. Jack's actions were his and vice versa. Charlie's, no matter whether they agreed with them or mocked them or belittle them, were that of the party. Orson felt comfortable with that, as he looked around, staring at his companions, for in that moment, out in the nothingness of Indian Territory, in that thicket of trees, by that fire, he felt at home for the first time in a long time. It would be the last for a long while.

Parker's laughing began to die down before anyone else. He became a bit stern, as if he gave the orders, "Avoid them tracks from here on, I say. Them assholes ain't no true hunters."

Timothy Masters leaned forward, his face almost touching the flames of the campfire as he stared down Parker. He ran his tongue across his teeth, smacking his saliva. He grinned and chuckled, "You ain't no true hunter neither."

The party laughed wildly. Charlie harder than anyone. He

reveled for the first time in Parker's own humiliation. Nobody believed that of Nathaniel. He was a good hunter, not the best, but Masters was better. He knew it. Parker knew it. Everyone knew it.

Parker stayed quiet, looking around the campfire at all those who laughed at him. He knew it to be a joke, but beneath the laugh and grin of Masters came a dagger that pierced his pride. He nodded at the thought, nodded as he looked to the drunken Jack now laying on his back in the dirt, laughing to the stars and branches above. He looked to Bill who nodded back in agreement with Masters as he cackled. He looked to Orson, who sipped his whiskey with a fat grin on his face. And he looked to Charlie, who roared wildly with laughter, more so than any other man. The others, Parker felt, deserved to laugh at him. They'd earned their place, but not him, not that little one who couldn't stomach the work. Parker leaned on his leg, stretching his neck towards Charlie. His face got close and he spoke between gritted teeth, "What you laughin' at, Lil Lamb? You ain't no hunter. I'm more a hunter than you."

Parker wanted to kill the boy. He wanted to throw his body to the flames, watch them consume him. He felt a rage rising within him. His hand balled into a fist. Charlie stopped laughing, but the others did not. He watched as Parker rose his fist, ready to strike. The boy began to sweat. A lump gathered in his throat. Though, a sharp comment from Bill cut between them, "That don't mean much, Parker!"

Everyone continued to laugh, and Parker leaned back to where he sat before, distancing himself from the young Charlie. Charlie looked to Bill who laughed wildly, and he felt thankful for the defusing of the young man's rage, but the truth of Chamber's statement struck him harder than Parker ever could. It was Charlie then who looked to those who surrounded the campfire, watching as they laughed at him. Even Orson, who smirked as he stared into the flames, grinned his teeth as he watched Jack laugh hysterically into the night sky. That hurt him. The only one who did not laugh was Parker, for they laughed at him too.

Jack sat up quickly. His hat rested on his lap. He grabbed it by the crown, throwing it into the dirt as he moved quickly to his feet. The men kept laughing, but Parker waved his hand as Jack stood. Nobody stopped for him, but they did when Jack gave the same gesture, all went silent. The trees moved gently in the wind of the night. All could be heard in the dead silence. Rustling began somewhere in the dark.

The nickel-plated revolver glistened in Orson's eye as his leader drew it from his holster. Every party member raced to their weaponry. Chambers drew his knife. Orson sat near the fire, resting on one knee. It was Masters who threw him his breechloader from the back of the wagon, Charlie's too. The two young acquaintances huddled near the fire, their hands gripped tightly on their weapons.

"I ain't the only one that heard it," Jack said, cocking back the hammer of his revolver.

"I heard it too," Parker replied.

"We all did," Masters spat back, raising his rifle and aiming off into the darkness of the trees around them.

Parker opened to speak, lowering his rifle as he did so. Jack interrupted him, "Shush now…"

Parker raised his rifle, he too aiming off in the dark.

Each man looked a different direction as they created a circle shaped barrier around their flames. Something stirred in the dark. It tried to stay quiet, for when a branch snapped or a leaf shuffled, the noise stopped for a second before moving once more.

Masters whispered, "What is it? Comanche? Cheyenne? Apache?"

"Ain't no Cheyenne down here," Parker informed him.

"This is Cherokee land…" Bill muttered in the dark as he squinted his eyes, looking for any movement amongst the shadows.

"We ain't gotta worry 'bout Cherokees, do we?" Parker asked.

Orson felt a hand grab his sleeve. He looked, seeing Charlie staring into his eyes so honestly. He whispered softly, quiet enough to where he thought nobody else could hear, "I don't wanna get scalped…"

"Ain't no one gettin' scalped, boy," said Jack. He then glanced to Parker and said, "Just cuz it's Cherokee land don't mean it's Cherokees."

Charlie removed his hand from Orson's sleeve, gripping the

barrel of his rifle tightly. His finger did not rest on the trigger. If he couldn't shoot a buffalo, he doubted he could shoot a man. Even if that man's intent was to bring him great bodily harm, he knew he couldn't do it, but he would try. He felt it in his bones that he would fail though, and he wondered what the crew would do if he fell. Nothing he thought, they would leave him to rot, for they cared nothing for him.

The rustling stopped. Masters looked off into the tree line. He saw something low to the ground, hunched it appeared. The light of the fire danced in its eyes as it stared back at him. He pulled back on his hammer, taking aim for whatever embraced those cold shadows. The figure moved forward slightly, enough to be lit by the roaring flames of the campfire. It was only a small coyote, one lost from its pack. It perked its ears, looking nowhere but to Masters. All the men looked to the beast, breathing a sigh of relief. They all lowered their rifles, all but Masters who fired upon the beast. The bullet struck a low hanging branch, severing it from its lifeline. It fell to the ground and the coyote disappeared off into the night.

Parker laughed, "And you's a true hunter? You's a shit shot, Masters."

Masters lowered his rifle, dumbfounded that he missed such a close and easy shot. It had to be his nerves, had to be. He scowled at Parker. He spoke, "You done pissin' yer pants 'bout Indians?"

Jack lowered the hammer on his revolver, tucking the piece back into its holster. He spat into the flames, then took a drink from his flask. He observed Parker move towards Masters with great hostility, fists at the ready to strike the young prodigy. Jack interfered, only with his words, "We gettin' too 'laxed. Timmy, you and Parker take first watch."

The two men stopped, looking to Jack. It was Masters that spoke first, "Why us?"

"Cuz ya'll won't shut the fuck up and won't stop bickerin' with each other," Jack responded as he sat back down near the fire. Bill followed suit.

"Why not the new guys?" Parker asked.

"You really want that little lamb watchin' you sleep?" Jack asked.

Charlie hung his head at the comment as he rested his rifle back into his lap.

"I ain't wantin' him—" Masters began.

Jack finished, "How about you do it cuz I said you do it. Good enough?"

Both Masters and Parker nodded, then moved to opposite ends of the camp. They both rested against trees, looking out into the darkness, the light of the flames at their backs. Jack shook his head as he continued to drink.

"I heard it's painful," Charlie told Orson quietly, "scalpin', that is…"

Tanner leaned towards the flames, basking his face in its warmth. The light of the fire danced in his dark eyes. He spat again. The wood of the fire hissed as he did so. His voice cracked as if it were the timber to the flames as he told the boy, "All death is painful, boy. The trick is how long it'll last."

With that, Jack laid down into the dirt, throwing his head back and covering his eyes with the brim of his hat, which he retrieved from the thicket floor. Bill sat near the flames, drinking silently to himself. He only eyed the boys for a moment, then acted as if they weren't even there. He began to hum a song to himself quietly, it was one that Orson never heard before. While Orson and Charlie wanted to continue drinking or talking or having a good time, all of that passed. They spent the rest of the night huddled next to the flames, clutching their rifles, jumping at whatever lurked in the outer dark.

Chapter XIV
The Fall
1873

The heat of the morning beat down on the men as they stood around the wagon. Everything came to a halt. The sound of thundering hooves roared somewhere in the distance. The clouds, white and sparse, stretched overhead, still and motionless. Bugs hissed, birds chirped, the land itself spoke to the men as they stood idle, listening to the herd. None felt the earth tremble at their feet quite like it. Whatever lingered on the plains was massive.

Jack rode to the crew on horseback. He stayed atop his horse, giving his men a quick nod. A smile stretched across Parker's face and he looked to his companions for reassurance. He received none, for they stared up at their leader. Sweat seeped from everyone's pores as the adrenaline began pumping through their veins.

Bill Chambers removed the harnesses of the horses attached

to the cart. Parker, not happy about his lack of attention, patted Bill on the back and said, "I told ya boys. I told ya it was real."

"He ain't said it was no three-day herd," Bill replied, leading the horses away from the wagon, stopping them at Jack's side.

Parker continued to argue, squatting down and resting his hand against the vibrating earth, "It's part of it. Has to be. Feel that…"

"Maybe," Jack said, spitting. "Either way, we're takin' this chance. It's big."

Parker stood, placing his hand in his pocket. He beamed with excitement. A satisfaction radiated from his skin, more so than the sweat. Jack looked down on him, shaking his head. He had no time for the man's boasting, stated or otherwise. He turned his head to Masters, "Saddle them horses up. You're comin' with me."

Bill stepped away from the horses, letting Masters take their lead as he removed blankets and saddles from the back of the wagon. Jack continued, "They's movin' quickly. Somethin' spooked 'em."

"Indians?" asked Charlie.

"Dunno," Jack shrugged, "maybe they out here huntin'."

"You ain't see any?" Parker pressed.

Jack ignored him, looking to Orson instead, "Can you shoot on horseback?"

Orson never tried such a feat. He never really had to in the past. He crossed his arms as he thought about it, wondering if it would truly be as difficult as it sounded. Other men could do it, so why not he, he wondered. Though, there's other men out there, stronger men, and he feared he would only let Jack down. He didn't want to express as much, "I can try. I mean, I ain't never really done it."

Parker spat, "You c'ain't be serious, boss."

Jack turned to Parker with a cold stare, leaning forward on his saddle. His head bobbed up and down with every syllable, "I've seen you do it and miss. Bill too."

Parker gritted his teeth. He was right about the herd. He was right about Charlie. Yet, Jack still wanted someone other than him. He became frustrated, but knew Jack spoke the truth, "We ain't used to be cavalry boys."

Jack continued on ignoring Parker. He turned back to Orson, "I didn't ask if you can try. I asked if you can do."

Orson thought on it. He felt the pressure from not just Tanner's gaze, but those of his companions. They all looked at him. He felt that his first hunt would be his only test, but now that the time came, he couldn't think of anything else but to not let them down. He felt torn, for no matter his choice, he could fail. He loathed the idea of Jack berating him like he did Charlie.

"I can do it," Charlie spoke up, stepping towards Jack's horse.

"I ain't ask you," Jack said, not taking his eyes off Orson.

Parker spoke up, finally feeling the heat taken off him, "Get back in line, Lil Lamb. He asked the orphan."

Charlie stepped away from Jack's horse, head hung. He only

glanced to Orson, and in his eyes, Newkirk saw such sorrow at being declined the chance. He would only have this moment, and this moment alone, to show he'd be willing to not just try, but do as Jack instructed. It was far more important than being able to show he possessed the guts to down a bison, that much everyone knew already. Orson hesitated no longer, "I can do it."

Masters climbed aboard one saddled horse. He nodded to Orson, then pointed with his chin to the other horse. Orson moved towards it, resting his hand on the nose of the beast. He fastened his foot in the stirrup and climbed aboard. It had been a while since he'd ridden, but he kept that information to himself. No more doubt he would cause, for he could see the nervousness in everyone's eyes already.

"We need to stop 'em. Shoot around 'em and cut off a piece of that herd," Jack said. "Just like cattle, alright?"

Orson didn't understand the reference. He didn't know how to break up cattle, or a herd of them. He figured it would be easy, but his heart pounded wild in his chest and anxiety told him otherwise. He nodded regardless.

Masters removed his pistol from his belt, a large Remington. He looked over it, then stretched it out towards Orson. He told the new rider, "Shoot it in the air 'round 'em. Tends to turn their direction."

Bill removed three rifles from the back of the wagon. He handed one to each of the three riders. He then gave each rider a small pouch of ammunition. Once they took the cartridges from his possession, he stepped back, leaning against the wagon. He wiped his brow of sweat, but his eyes danced with concern.

As Orson slung the rifle over his back, Jack told him and Masters, "We tryin' to stop 'em. If we don't, use them rifles and down as many as you can."

Orson and Masters just looked to Jack. He saw their fear. He wasn't sure why. He too felt nervous. Hunting from horseback wasn't his thing. That startled herd wasn't something he'd take a chance on had it not been the reason they came down to the territory. There were a lot though, a lot of beasts ready to fall. He had to take the chance, regardless if it went against his norm. The trip couldn't be wasted. He studied his whole crew, the gloom overhanging their heads. He cared not. It was his decision. They would reap its rewards no matter how they felt. He spat and kicked his spurs into the ribs of his horse, "Alright, let's go."

Tanner led his two riders away from the wagon. Those left behind walked towards the crest of a low hill. The crew stood, arms crossed, baking in the heat of the morning sun, watching as their leader and his two young riders broke across the open field that rose and fell in small patterns. The riders needed not go far, for the herd moved from one shallow slope of the plains to another. Dust kicked up around the beasts, filling the air with such calamity. Snot and drool flung from the nostrils and mouths of the creatures. They moved quickly, faster than any herd Jack ever saw. It wasn't the largest he'd seen though, but the roaring under his horse's hooves made him believe more lingered somewhere out in the morning sun.

However, Orson pulled up on his reins as he saw the great herd before him. There had to be at least three thousand, maybe more, all running in synch with each other. He could not be sure, for the dust that the herd left in its wake towered upward and blanketed the beasts as they moved ruthlessly across the plains. Orson stopped for a moment, watching as Jack and Masters rode on. He felt a lump in his throat, that fear setting in. He was unsure if he could do what Tanner commanded, but before his horse broke a trot, he kicked it in the ribs and carried on in great haste behind Jack and Masters.

As the riders approached, a section of the herd broke away from the rest, a good head of them, maybe one hundred, maybe two. Jack raised a hand, pointing to the separated group. He pulled the reins of his Standardbred, shifting his course towards the small pack of animals. Masters rode at his side while Orson tried to catch up from behind. Jack shouted over the roaring thunder, "Timmy, head to the front! Newkirk and I will get the flanks of it!"

Masters grabbed the excess of his reins, slapping them to the side of his horse in a crisscross pattern. His steed barreled forward, riding forth towards the herd. Orson mimicked the young man's motions with his reins, pressing his horse to ride next to Jack. As he finally made it to his leader's side, Masters disappeared within the growing cloud of dust, and within seconds, Jack and Orson too were swallowed by the herd's storm.

Grass and dirt flew upward into the air. Orson lowered his head, holding his breath as it swirled and swelled around his face. His eyes burned as they became peppered by the debris. He heard Masters shout and holler, which drew the young man's attention. He saw Masters riding alongside the bison. His silhouette, so dark, stood out against the brown cloud. He grabbed his reins, pulling them to the side and his horse kicked inward towards the center of the bison.

Jack pulled upward on his reins as he and Orson took position at the herd's side. His horse's legs ran in synch with those of the bison. They kept a steady pace, though it was the fastest Orson ever rode and he thought, in that moment, for just a second, he would never ride so hard or so fast ever again in his life. As Orson passed his leader, Tanner called out to him, "Stay along this side, Newkirk! I'll bring up the rear!"

Gunshots rang out, cracking in the air as if bullwhips. Orson peered back, seeing Jack firing around stragglers that broke from the side of the herd as he made his way towards the rear. The beasts feared the man, though they appeared thrice his size and could easily dismount him if need be. The stragglers returned to the herd as it continued barreling forward with no care for where it went.

Before Orson, a smaller bull broke from the herd. It rode directly in front of his horse. The hooves of his beast almost clacked with that of the bison. Orson opened his mouth, letting in a quick inhale of panic as he pulled on the reins swiftly to slow his horse. In the same motion, he removed the revolver given to him by Masters and fired it twice into the air. The bull looked back over its shoulder, eyeing the young rider. It feared him, Orson studied it in the beast's pupils. It kicked to its left, bucking slightly and slithered back among its peers as Orson rode on by.

Masters rode at the very center of the herd. He kicked his horse in the ribs repeatedly, still slashing at its sides with his reins as he tried to gain speed over the herd. His horse moaned, screamed at times, as he tried to push on through. The bison around him kicked up such dust, were so large, so bulky, so mighty, that his horse feared riding through them. Jack knew the skilled young man struggled to ride through, and shouted to him, "Get up there! We gotta stop em before they get too far out!"

Masters looked back, seeing Jack riding at the rear, peppered with dust and debris as he rode on. On the horizon, barely within sight of his poor vision, he saw the three others watching from the shallow crest of a hill. They looked small, and it was then that he realized that the herd moved faster than they all originally believed. He shouted to his leader, his voice cracking as he tried to drown out the thunder, "They already too far out!"

Jack screamed, his voice rattling with anger, "Then turn them, dammit!"

The earth stiffened beneath the feet of the great beasts. The dust did not rise as high as it did before. It lingered in the air only halfway to the bison's and horses' sides. Ahead, Orson watched as the bison gently turned left, avoiding a portion of the land off to their right. He observed a flat open field not far out, and beyond it, he thought he spotted other riders who watched on from a distance. Though, as he rubbed his eyes clear of filth, they seemed to have faded with the heat waves that rose upwards towards the sky.

Masters cut his horse right, firing his revolver in the air, shouting odd guttural noises. The herd began to shift lazily with him, startled by the gunfire from all directions. A great bull moved through the pack of animals, powering its way onward towards the front of the herd. It gored its own kind, panicked and fearful of what came. It moved faster than the horses, faster than its peers. Adrenaline rushed through the great beast's heart and it thrashed its head as it tried to save itself. Soon, that beast was on the heels of Masters' horse. He looked back, witnessing the mighty trapped foe. The young man gasped, fearful that he would be bucked from his horse and trampled beneath the hooves of his prey. He kicked his heels harder than before, his spurs spraying with droplets of blood, and his horse screamed as it carried him forward at such a great speed.

The young rider smiled as he looked back out ahead. That faded though, for as he stared out over the plains, the head of the herd vanished from his sight, an odd thing for sure. He squinted, seeing if it only a trick of the heat or the dust, but they were not there. It was then that he saw others disappearing before him, one by one, two by two, three by three, they slid from his view as if the world itself swallowed them before the young man. He could see it then, a great ravine stretched outward, downward, a long way too.

Masters pulled up on his reins. His horse skidded forward. Dust and gravel flew upwards from its hooves. The young rider whimpered something. It was not words. Though his horse broke, the bison behind it kept going, fearful of what fate awaited behind them rather than forward. Two struck his horse, pushing it forward, closer to that great edge, that steep drop. They were on the edge now, his horse bucked upward, trying one last time to halt before the fall. Masters threw his feet out of the stirrups, falling backward. He would rather be trampled, he thought. And so, within a second in the air, the great bull was on him and it reared its head upward with a great thrust, one that struck the backside of his horse and struck Masters in the chest with one blow. It was only Orson who saw the young rider disappear into the descent, and he witnessed through the dust and fear the body of Masters falling, twisting, turning, then fading beneath the piles of corpses, of wounded, of screaming bison.

Orson pulled his reins. His horse stopped immediately, and they stood five feet from the edge. He threw his hands in the air, turning to Jack, motioning him to stop, for he did not know what he would do if he lost him. He screamed and cried, "He fell! He fell, boss! He fell!"

Jack slowed, finally seeing through the dust that the herd vanished before him too. He stopped and yelled, "Where is he?

Where is Timmy?"

"He fell, boss!" is all he managed to yell, "He fell! He fell! He fell! He fell..."

The pile of dead and wounded stood tall, halfway up the ravine, leaning and resting against the red rocky surface. Thousands of pounds of mangled flesh seeped a deep crimson into the dirt. Gored sides, cracked ribs, torn flesh, basked in the heat of the sun as it crept over the sky. A horse laid among the buried, its hooves cracked, like those of the bison. The tongue of the steed hung from its mouth. The flies buzzed, drawn to it. Its coat stood out among the heap of black and brown carcasses. Though, all the companions looked upon was a small pale hand, half clutched loosely, that stretched outward from the center of the heap.

Tanner and his boys used large tree branches from nearby thickets to lift the bison and the horse upwards, straining to free their companion. It took hours, it felt like. Jack breathed heavily, barking orders and telling his men when to lift, how to lift, when to pull, when to free the fallen Masters as if there was some chance that he could be alive. He knew better, but the corpse of the boy meant something to him, or at least he said.

It was Parker who slithered the mangled crushed corpse of Masters from the heap, resting it in the brownish red dirt at the bottom of the ravine. Parker stood over the fallen one. He spat, his saliva hissing as it hit a sunbaked stone, "Stupid sum'bitch…"

The others gathered around the body. Had Orson not seen Master go over, he doubted he would've believed it to be him. Those young facial features were gone, crushed, and his skull cloven halfway from the crown. One eye dangled from a blown-out socket. It stood no chance against such weight. His nose laid flattened, broken, and blood seeped from it like endless waterfalls into his open mouth and down his pale cheeks. His jaw sat crooked, unhinged, and his skin appeared whiter than before, with hints of blue and purple that rested beneath his flesh.

Jack looked down on the dead young man. He could not tear his eyes away, "He wasn't stupid."

"He ain't seen it?" Parker question, stepping over the dead man. He moved away from the crowd that gathered, sitting near the heap of dead bison. He removed his hat, placing it on a cracked horn of an expired beast. He ran his hands through his hair, wiping sweat away from his forehead and into his locks. He began to smoke.

"I ain't seen it neither," Jack informed him. "Had Newkirk not called it out, I'd have gone over too."

A gunshot echoed. A dying bull grunted. The men looked towards the heap, and on the far end of it, Charlie stood with his rifle. He opened the breach. A shell shot from it, smoking and smoldering as it hit the dirt. He loaded another and fired into another bison. As the round struck the eye, a mist of red peppered the boy. He repeated the reloading process. He aimed again, but before he fired, Parker shouted to him, "Will you stop it, Lil' Lamb! Mercy killin' ain't killin' and you're driving me crazy."

Charlie lowered his rifle, looking to the men. He wasn't sure what he hoped to achieve by killing them, but whatever response he received was not what he expected, was not what he needed. He slung his rifle over his shoulder and ran his powder covered hand across his face, blackening his cheeks and smearing the drops of scarlet.

"Newkirk, get the shovels," Jack told Orson. He then nodded his head towards Charlie, "Take the boy with ya."

"You cain't be serious, boss," Parker argued, dabbing his half-smoked cigarette onto his boot.

"What you mean?" Jack pressed, though, deep down, he knew.

Parker raised his index finger. The last remnants of cigarette smoke seeped from his lungs and out of his nostrils. He cocked his head to one side, closing one eye, as if it helped him with whatever he was doing. All the men looked to him as if he were crazy. He took his left hand, resting it on the ground. He said, "Listen..."

And it was as if he spoke some magical spell, for Orson heard the low thunder of the herd continuing their journey across the plains. He felt the rattling in the soles of his boots. Parker's spurs rotated ever so slightly. He nodded to Jack with affirmation, "It's big. Headin' north too."

Jack, however, cared not for the thunder or where it went.

He spat, "I hear it."

"We ain't got time," Parker stood, taking his hat from the horn and plopping it back on his head. "We gotta pursue."

Jack listened. The herd was big for sure. He couldn't tell if it was as big as what was told in Dodge, but he felt that thunder, he heard that thunder, and with each rhythmic beat he imagined so many dollars, so many pelts, so much blood, and gore, and death, and the money to cover it all. But as he felt that distant herd's panic synching with his heart, he stared down onto the mangled corpse of Masters, his favorite, albeit never stated aloud. He felt a lump in his throat and his eyes water as he tried to recognize the crushed skull.

"You c'ain't be serious. We just lost Masters," Bill argued. "We gotta bury him."

"Why?" Parker dusted his clothes off. Red dirt fell from his coat and chaps, "It all rots the same."

"God says so," Bill argued.

Parker chuckled, "And when did you get all religious?"

"It ain't right," Bill moved over towards Parker, crossing his arms before the man. He towered over him, "We ain't gon' leave him out here."

Parker cared not for Bill's intimidating stance. He knew the burly man wouldn't touch him. He smirked at that thought, knowing his place over Bill's, "It ain't your call."

"I agree with Chambers," Orson spoke up. He couldn't help but think that he too almost fell from the cliff. He feared what would come for his corpse if not buried.

"Well, ain't nobody ask you, orphan," Parker shot a grim look to the young man.

Jack continued to stare down onto the body of Masters. The sun felt hotter than before. The dead flesh baked in the heat. A smell would come soon, bloating with it. Jack wondered what Timmy might look like in a day or two, seeing how that made him feel. He felt no different if he was honest with himself. He hardly recognized the corpse anyway. He asked Parker, "How far off you think they is?"

"A few hours, maybe less," Parker told his boss, trying to hide a small smirk. "It's big. That's our herd."

"Jack..." Bill turned to his leader, pleading.

"It don't make no difference now. He's dead," Jack argued.

Bill stepped back, raising his hands to his waist as if shackled. He moved them side to side as he spoke. It was an awkward gesture, one that showed his true confusion with Tanner, "Would you leave me out here? Parker too?"

Parker answered for his leader, "I'd let him leave me out here if I knew there was a herd the livin' could reap the rewards of. You weren't gripin' when it came to leavin' Ol' Ben."

As Parker stepped to Bill, they continued to argue to one another. Jack did not care for it. He made a decision and that was that. However, he felt the gaze of the young Orson looking upon him. He turned, seeing Newkirk lost to the wonder of death, the corpse of Masters, the stack of dead against the wall of the ravine, and Jack's callused nature about it all. It was then that he saw that honesty again, that simple trait that he respected so much. He saw a bit of Timmy in the boy. He saw a bit of himself too, as if Orson were a walking time capsule of days gone by, days Jack mostly forgot when he lost himself along the way. He pressed the boy, "You think it wrong of me?"

Orson spoke truthful, "I do. I'd want to be buried."

Charlie moved over towards Orson and the corpse, looking down upon it. He slightly gagged, then stepped away from Masters. He raised his forearm, hiding his face, but tried to appear tough. He countered Orson, "I don't think it's that bad to leave 'em."

Jack looked back to the body. He felt as if the spirit of Masters was long gone, left somewhere to wander the plains. It mattered not what Orson told him, what Parker told him, what Bill told him, or Charlie. He made his decision, though his heart struggled with it. He whispered to himself, Masters' last rites, "He was a good kid…"

"Boss," Parker called out. He knelt in the dirt, resting his hand against the ground. He spat, "It's getting faint. They's movin' on. We gotta go."

It was only thoughts, but Orson knew them to be true. Vultures rested atop the carcasses of the dead bison at the bottom of that ravine. Their beaks glistened with blood in the low sun of dusk. They chewed bright pink flesh ripped from the dark brown and black corpses. That horse, who accompanied Jack Tanner for however long, was fed upon too. Something gutted that beast sometime that afternoon and its entrails became nourishment for the scavengers. One vulture sat upon the chest of Masters. Its talons digging into his sternum as its beak fumbled with the eye that dangled from its crushed socket. Something startled the bird, for before it could eat, it flapped its wings wildly and screeched as it flew off somewhere else to feed on other dead. The corpse of Masters would lay undisturbed for only a moment before the coyotes came. Five of them there were, and they snarled as they bit into the pale mort flesh of the young dead man.

Orson tried not to think on it. Hell, he told himself none of it was true. He didn't know what honestly took place at the bottom of that ravine, but as he sat in the back of that wagon and it rolled across the plains so lazily in pursuit of a herd that they could not feel or hear no more, he felt such a weight on his heart that told him it *must* be the truth.

Jack rode out ahead of the wagon. Only one horse pulled the wooden cart and it moved slower than usual, lopsided too with one wheel swaying as it rolled. Parker sat at the reins with nobody at his side. He smoked as he slashed the reins downward gently onto the back of the remaining steed. He wanted to speak, but Jack was too far off, and the others cared not what he had to say, had to justify. Occasionally the young Nathaniel Parker exchanged a glance with Jack when he looked back to see how far he'd gone from the wagon. He never halted though, and soon enough he appeared to only be a small figure on the flat horizon. His face, lit by the setting sun, only showed determination. No signs of remorse or caution or fear or depression or anything that the others felt accented his eyes.

Newkirk wiped his tears as he continued his thoughts on the coyotes, his thoughts on Masters. His legs hung from the back of the wagon. He kicked them gently against the bending stocks of grass that rolled from underneath the cart. He dared not show anyone that he wept, however little it was. He stared upward, looking to the sky, so orange, so red. It helped him not, for all he wanted to do was weep. He wanted to weep for Masters, for the bison, for himself, because he knew if he'd fallen too that there would be no grave for him. He didn't know why that mattered, but it did. He figured because he didn't want to be forgotten like he'd forgotten so many others in his past.

Bill sat next to the young weeping Newkirk. He knew the boy cried. He did not hide it as well as he hoped. He said nothing on it. He gave the boy a pat on his leg at one point, light enough to be easily ignored. The burly man just sat next to him, he too kicking the tops of the stocks of grass as they passed underneath them. He felt like a child again in that moment, almost forgetting he was the second oldest of the party behind Jack. He enjoyed that, and he enjoyed that nobody spoke to Parker, for he knew that weeping would not be allowed on his watch. He found some sort of hope within the welling eyes of young Orson Newkirk. He didn't know exactly what it was, but it made him want to question his behavior towards Charlie.

"Wha's that?" Charlie's voice called from behind them. His arm flew forward, cutting the air between the two men that sat at the back of the wagon.

Orson looked away from the sky, looking out across that orange horizon. On it, the silhouettes of six riders, maybe seven, appeared. He wasn't sure of the number. Though, he knew they were no white men. They carried lances. He eyed their painted horses, marked with such strange symbols that looked so alien to him. One held a rifle, but his feathered war bonnet is all that Orson looked at. He'd seen them before, something he thought to be a mirage or ghost out on the plains as they drove towards the cliff.

"They's been followin' us since the ravine," Bill noted, lighting a cigarette.

"Cherokee?" Charlie questioned.

Bill shook his head, waving his match out in the air, "Them's Comanch. We shaved off a piece of their herd, I reckon. They's probably drivin' it to that cliff. They do that, ya know?"

Orson piped up, "Ain't Comanch supposed to be south?"

"They ain't carin'," Bill replied. "They go where they please."

"They mad at us?" Charlie asked, sliding closer to the two at the end of the wagon.

"Yeah," said Bill. "They's mad."

Bill looked to the boy. He saw the dust and dried blood

caked onto his face. He saw that he looked to be a hunter, but he knew how he obtained such warpaint. He still saw the glossy innocence within the young wannabe hunter's eyes. He thought of telling him about the histories of white men and red men. He thought of telling him about the various wars, removals, hunts, scalpings, the growth of bitterness and resentment. He thought of telling him about the things he witnessed, what he'd seen out on the plains. He thought of telling the boy in hopes of teaching him of how the world worked.

Yet, he chose to instead tell him, "You know they believe in some strange things 'bout the world. They believe all these buffalo were held by two people at one time, an old woman and her son. Well, the other people of the world needed the buffalo to survive. The Coyote didn't like what the old woman and her boy were doin', so he tricked the boy into taking him home, thinkin' Coyote would make a good pet."

Charlie kept his eyes fixated on Bill as he told the story, and Bill looked into them, lost to the wonderment that they held, "Well, the old woman tried to club the bastard to death since she thought all animals were tricky. Coyote ran away towards the large pens where they kept all them buffalo and let out a loud yap. Them buffalo got scared and broke free of the pen and flooded the earth with their thunder. Coyote slipped away and the boy was left with no pet and the old woman was left with no buffalo."

The young would-be hunter looked out across the plains, thinking on the story. He rested his head in his hands, wiping away at the dirt and the dried blood as he thought. He shook his head as something passed through his mind and spoke to Bill over his shoulder, "I don't get it."

Bill too thought on the story he told. He couldn't remember exactly where he heard it, somewhere maybe in the City of Kansas or possibly Lawrence. He even began to wonder if he made the whole thing up. He examined Charlie who still tried to process the story. Even though he was the one who recited such a foreign tale to the young hunters, it was he who lost the meaning of it all. Chambers just looked back out across the horizon. Those figures had vanished, leaving only the red and the orange, the darkness of the land. He knew not where they went or where they were going, but he knew not the same for himself. He stated, "Me neither."

All the while, Orson watched as those figures disappeared over the horizon. They blended with the outer dark that crept slowly across the plains. He heard nothing of Charlie's questions. He heard nothing of Bill's responses. He only heard the cackling of the coyotes, somewhere deep in that ravine so far away, as they tore the flesh of Masters and fed upon his still heart.

And he said nothing on it, only weeping quietly to himself.

Chapter XV
Ghosts
1875

Those coyote yaps haunted his mind as he thought back on Masters and that ravine. He hacked away at wheat stocks, caring not where they fell. His eyes watered with such anger, such hatred, such shame and regret as he continued to hack away at the wheat with his sickle. He wasn't sure at how much time passed since he started, but he knew he'd been at it all morning, for the sun sat at high noon, and his arm muscles wrestled with one another begging him to stop. He couldn't. He felt such pain as he hacked, yet with each slash he heard the breaking of bones, tearing of flesh, yaps of scavengers.

"Orson?" came a voice from behind the boy as he chopped.

Thomas observed the young man as he slashed at his crops. He damaged them. They weren't clean cuts on the stocks. He swung wildly. Something bothered him, disturbed him greatly. He knew by looking at him, and he feared the crazed anger that swelled within the heart of the man. Thomas tried to calm him as he approached slowly, as if speaking to a startled horse, "Orson…calm down…"

He stood not two feet from the young man as he threw the sickle back, ready to strike the crops with another crushing blow. It cut the air directly in front of the old man's throat. He looked down upon the glistening blade, so silver in the warm glow of the high noon sun. He stepped back as Orson turned around.

The young man wiped his eyes, hiding the tears that flowed from them. He threw the sickle down, aware of his potential accident. He looked upon the old man with wide wet eyes. They shimmered and welled.

"Why you sad?" Thomas asked sincerely.

Orson bit his lip. His cheeks rose as his eyes closed slightly. He shook his head as he barked, "I ain't sad! I'm mad is all."

"Well," began Thomas calmly, "wha'chu mad about?"

"We left him," Orson quivered his lip. "We left him out there and Jack didn't give a damn…even after all this time I think of it…think it bein' me…"

"What?" pressed Thomas earnestly. "Left who? Who the hell is Jack?"

The two quit working for a few hours. They sat on the Daniels family porch. Orson dangled his feet off the raised edge as if he sat on the back of the old Tanner wagon. He looked out across the fields as Thomas sat behind him, recounting his story. He explained Jack Tanner. He told him of Charlie and the calves. He told him of Masters, a man he admired and watched fall. He told him of Bill and Parker and of all sorts of things. He told him what he saw, what he did, but he dared not tell him all.

Once the boy recounted all the story, as far as Thomas was concerned, he stood and lingered behind young Orson Newkirk. He too looked out over the fields, looking for something to say. His eyes wandered to his family tree out by the property line. Nothing spoke to him. Nothing gave him any words to say. He tried though, "You can't worry 'bout it no more."

"I know that, now, at least," Orson told him, shaking his head. "I still feel bad about it though. I could'a swayed Jack. I could'a at least buried him."

"They'd have left you, if what you done said is true," Thomas spoke.

Orson nodded at that thought, "Lookin' back on it, probably should'a. Should'a just stayed, done what I felt right, not what *he* wanted to be right."

"I understand," Thomas said, sitting next to the boy. He too hung his legs over the edge and said, "It's hard though. Maybe that's why Jack didn't want to bury him. Burial is saying goodbye, and that is difficult."

"Nah," Orson spat, "Parker didn't want to do it. That's why Jack didn't want to do it. He wasn't a deep man."

"All men have depth," Thomas told him. "They just express it differently. They all love things, hate things, care for things, what have you. It's just that…some men…they just don't say it. They done keep it to themselves is all. Men are complicated creatures. Jack probably had good intentions."

"I think you givin' him too much credit," Orson stated.

"Maybe," Thomas replied. "I just know that I never said much and never told my girls how much I cared for them. Hell, I even found it hard to say goodbye and when they was buried and in the earth…I still didn't know what to say. It's hard, but sometimes men just don't know what to say or do. They bottle it up too much, ya know?"

Orson didn't know how to respond. He just apologized, "Sorry, I didn't mean it."

"Mean what? You ain't got nothin' to be sorry for," Thomas replied. "You c'ain't change nothin' no more. You can only change what's comin'. You c'ain't change Jack. What happened to Masters is a shame, but you c'ain't change that neither. You c'ain't bring back my girls and you c'ain't take back what you said, no matter how many times you say it."

"I didn't mean to offend you. I don't know nothin' 'bout you, your life."

"You didn't offend me. What'd you say? I gave Jack too much credit for havin' feelings? You a better judge of that. Or, was you implying that I ain't got feelings or that I shouldn't or somethin' like that?"

"I don't know what I was implying but it sounded bad, is

all, after talkin' 'bout your girls," Orson said.

"It's in the past. I like to think I moved on," Thomas chuckled, "Bigger better things, right?"

"You ever wished you said more?" Orson asked.

Thomas looked out over the tree, "The past is just that. It'll catch up to us someday."

The two sat silent for a moment. Orson watched as the sun moved gracefully overhead. The rays broke behind great white clouds. He felt at peace in that moment, more so than any other. It was as if just by talking to Thomas, he buried Masters somewhere out on the plains, though he knew that not to be the case. His bones laid scattered across the wasteland for all time. There would be nothing he could do about it now, and he felt sorry for it. He'd pay for it if he hadn't already. He came to peace with that.

"You hungry?" Thomas asked.

"I ain't finish my work after I beat them stocks to shit," Orson laughed to himself as he stood. "I gave you my word and I'll get them stocks sorted before nightfall."

"Good on ya," Thomas smiled as he stood. "I'll get it started and it'll be ready when you're done."

And so, for as long as the sun hung up in the sky, Orson worked for the rest of the afternoon, moving that wheat. He collected a bunch of stocks, put them in bundles, then carried them to a wagon near the property line. It took him a few hours, but he gave his word. And not once did he think of Masters, those coyotes, or the Tanner party while doing so. Though, he knew that would not last, for when he stopped for a break, he heard the bison grunting somewhere at the back of his mind.

When night fell over the Daniels family farm and the two ate soup for another night, they sat silently within the ruined home of Thomas. The wooden walls popped and hissed as heavy winds swept across the plains. The wheat that remained uncut rustled in the breeze. The fire crackled as Orson sat in front of it, throwing his hands out every so often to keep them warm. He became lost to the flames, something that always happened when he looked upon such a thing. He could not fathom how such a thing existed within nature, such a natural thing, and how man tamed it, made it their own, as if they invented it. They could conjure the flames at their will, control it, for the most part, and to Orson he felt amazed yet saddened by that.

Thomas stood nearby. His hand rubbed his lower back as he looked out the window of his home, looking off towards his tree. He watched as the moonlight danced across its magnificent branches, so green in the day yet so empty at night. The stars twinkled overhead, so radiant in their glow. He groveled something to himself, the pain in his back twisted his words to force him to speak. Orson could not hear what the old man spoke, but it drew his attention. He watched the man for a moment, looking upon him with such admiration, yet pity.

"Wha'cha lookin' at?" Orson asked, fearing he examined

the damage done to his yield that day. Orson's anger bested him, and he feared the old man's repercussions.

"My tree," Thomas replied, not turning to face the boy who basked in the light of the flames. "The family tree, I guess."

Orson admitted, "I seen't it the other day."

Thomas knew, "We used to spend a lot of time out there. Each of us had a carvin' or two in the trunk of it."

"I saw more than a few," Orson replied as he stood.

"I been addin' to it, was addin' to it. I find it more difficult now."

Orson moved over to the window, looking out across the farm. He too stared at the tree as it basked in the moonlight, swayed with the nightly winds. He asked, "What do they mean?"

"Just important days and whatnot, I guess," Thomas answered. "Like, the day we sold our first pig, Betty cut a hog into it. Just stuff like that, little reminders of what we done."

"I'd like a tree like that," Orson admitted. "Though, I don't think I'd be carvin' nothin' in it."

Thomas cocked his head, turning to look to the boy, "Why?"

Orson lowered his head, shook it for a moment, then peered out the window. He stared at that tree. He wanted to own something, a piece of the earth, a place to claim as his. He possessed a lot of dreams and a lot of desires, all of which he feared he would never accomplish, especially at that point. He spoke truthfully to the old man, not looking him in the eye, but beyond him, looking through that window instead, "Ain't a lot of things I'd like to remember. I was young, foolish more than half the time."

"You's still young," said Thomas. He then chuckled, "You still a little foolish too. I was too though. I'm old now, old 'n foolish."

Orson smirked. It did not last long. As he looked upon that tree, he heard the thunder in the distance. He heard hooves rattling the core of the earth. He heard the coyotes feasting, yapping.

Thomas read the anguish in the young man's face. He told him, "You got plenty a' life ahead a' ya, Orson. Ain't no point in thinkin' it's all over now cuz ya ain't happy with wha'cha done."

The young Orson said nothing.

Thomas continued, trying to ease the kid, "Plenty a' time to figure out wha'cha want, do wha'cha need."

As Thomas spoke to the melancholy boy, Orson witnessed a shadow move between the stocks of wheat. It stayed low to the ground, moving and weaving between the moonlit farm. Its paws made no sound as it slinked through the darkness. It moved as if unseen, but Orson saw it, for he felt it wanted him to. The moon danced within the eyes of the beast, revealing its cold colored fur and snout as it moved up to the Daniels family tree. The coyote bathed in the silver light of the moon as it rounded the tree two times, then three. It stopped, sat, and looked out across the plains as if waiting for something to come and carry it away.

"Do you believe in ghosts?" Orson asked as he stared upon the small beast.

The coyote yammered to something out in the dark. Nothing responded, but it looked back towards the farmhouse, looked through that window, Orson felt, and stared back at him for a moment.

"Maybe," said Thomas. He looked out to that tree. He spoke no word of the canine. Instead, he said, "It's a nice thought. Sometimes I think I hear Betty or Tabitha from time to time. I like to think they still here, like to think they still 'round...I just tell myself it's wishful thinkin'."

The coyote stood once more, yapped once more. Then rounded the tree for a fourth time. It disappeared amongst the shadows of the branches, vanishing somewhere in the outer dark. Orson looked away, moving back towards the fire, "I don't know if I believe neither."

"It's a nice thought, but I think God's judgement is it for all of us," Thomas said, he too moving towards the fire. He sat in his rocker, chewing on his unlit pipe, "No point in a ghost hanging 'round when there's more important things, right?"

"Maybe."

"The past catches up, whether it be through judgement, ghosts, what have you's," Thomas said, the shadows of the flames dancing across his face, the embers reflected in his eyes. "At least, that's what I believe anyway."

They spoke no more that night. They sat there by the fire. Each man dreamed of different things, different ideas of family, different ideas of adventure, loss, love, work, and anything else that scampered across their downtrodden minds. As that fireplace hissed and crackled, nothing stirred on that property. They listened to the rustling of the branches that basked in the darkness, swaying with those cold winds.

Chapter XVI
The Plague
1875

The harvest went along. Bundles of wheat laid stacked in the wagon that Thomas possessed on loan. Him and Orson worked the fields all morning, since before sunup. He felt able that day. His back still ached. He felt that growth somewhere deep inside him. His determination outweighed all of that though, for he felt guilty of having the boy do the majority of the work. Without Orson, he would've had to yield all the fields. He would've had to push through anyway, so he worked as if the help did not exist.

Orson took a bundle, slinging it over his shoulder. He walked through the cut field. He hardly recognized the ground where he worked. At least a third of it laid cut, bundled, and stored onto the wagon, which Thomas would take to Hays at some point. As the young man carried the bundle, he passed the old man who wheezed and knelt in the dirt. He wrapped the cut stalks of wheat with a thin rope, then stood to lift it in a similar fashion as Orson.

The young man told him, "No need, I'll come back for it."

"It's alright," Thomas replied. "I can do it."

"Your back actin' up?"

"It ain't so bad," Thomas said, grimacing as he lifted the wheat over his shoulder. He buckled, then set it back down.

"I'll get it," Orson told him. "You just keep cuttin', alright?"

Thomas laughed, "You in charge now? It your farm?"

Orson smiled and went on towards the wagon. Thomas hollered after him, "I appreciate you."

"Don't mention it," said the boy as he threw his bundle onto the stacks that flowed over the brim of the wagon. He rested against the wooden panels of the carriage. He took his gloves, placing them in his back pocket. He wiped his brow and sipped water from his canteen. He stood with the sun flooding over him. Though, the light faded and soon the young man stood in a long shadow. He peered upward, finding it strange for no clouds hung overhead. He looked out, seeing a bizarre sight. A cloud it was, had to be, but black was its color and strange its movement. It rose upward from the plains, up into the sky, and sagged downward then upward as if it breathed.

He looked overhead, seeing nothing but blue. The sky darkened only in the distance, only where that abnormal cloud blocked out the light. He held his hand out, half expecting rain to fall upon it. It didn't. The air felt just as arid as before. No rise in humidity. Rain felt doubtful. Thomas stepped forward. He too stared out at the oddity that rose from the plains.

"The hell is that?" he pondered aloud.

The cloud began to twinkle as it twisted and turned in the sky. Shades of gold and red reflected from the blackness at its center and around its edges. It moved quickly too, racing across those plains. Orson thought maybe it came from some prairie fire. He doubted that though. It looked nothing like the ones he saw in his past. It could not be smoke. All fell silent as it crept closer to the farm. Yet, as it grew nearer, a low faint hum began to radiate across the flat fields.

Thomas was the first to hear it, and upon doing so, he said to himself, "Oh, Lord..."

He knew. He knew what the cloud was. He stared upon it, lost to the twinkling gold and crimson. He heard stories over the past year, people spoke of the plague returning to Kansas. He thought it to just be talk. Yet, there he stood, staring upon the wrath of God Almighty in the form of millions, if not billions, of locusts.

The cloud moved once more, so unnatural in its formation and Orson realized that what he stared upon lived. He, unsure what they were, asked, "What is it?"

"They come!" Thomas shouted. He began to move away from the wagon towards his home, "I got some kerosene out behind the shed! Go on and fetch it! I'll get a flame!"

Orson cocked his eyebrow. He did not understand. Yet, he looked back to that cloud, which now towered over them. The sky turned black. The humming became deafening. The twinkling of gold and crimson as small rigid insects flapped their wings captivated him for only a moment, for he felt as if he looked upon some strange celestial void above. Thomas shouted again, "Get that kerosene! Pour it near the crops! Hurry!"

Orson began to run.

And, as if the earth split and Hell itself rode forward onto the Daniels farm, the locusts were upon them.

The black insects struck the boy, so mindless in their hunger. He felt five, then six, then more than that, then more than he could count, and then he fell. The air around him became alive as he laid in the dirt. Black wings hissed overhead. He hardly saw anything except for darkness that whizzed by. The creatures clung to his clothes as he tried to stand but peppered him again as he began to run once more. He tore at them. He removed two, and four appeared as if they were an erroneous form of the Hydra.

The locusts covered every inch of the farm. They landed on the wheat. They landed on the home. They hurled themselves, so mindless, against the windows, shattering them. They crawled along the porch, along the support beams. They overflowed from within the wagon. No golden wheat could be seen beneath them. Their small mandibles chewed the stocks, chewed anything they found. Orson looked back as he ran from the wagon. He saw nothing but black, almost appearing as if it were bubbling over the sides, falling into the dirt. The only gold he saw were that of their exoskeletons. The red glistened in what little light broke through the cloud, and they struck him again.

He struggled but made it to the shed. He threw the pests from his back. It mattered not. He threw them from the small red jug of kerosene that he discovered, right where Thomas told him it would be. He threw them off, but more continued to appear. He stopped as one clawed his mouth, another at his nostril. He grabbed them, crushing them in his hand and he wiped the remnants on his pants without thought. He ran again.

The boy bled. Small welts formed on his arm. The flesh cracked atop the small hills of skin. Crimson flowed down his arms, his neck, and a few lines down his face. They kept hitting him. They would not stop, for the air was alive and swarmed and buzzed. He looked to the fields. They were black. The wagon, black too. He struggled to keep running. He buckled with each small hit. He opened his mouth to breath for a moment, a deep inhale of nervousness and panic, but two locusts clawed their way in. He spat. He chewed the leg of one. He kept on.

He undid the lid of the kerosene as he stood before the moving crops. They swayed back and forth as they were devoured. He thought he heard them scream. It was his own. He poured near the edges of the field. The kerosene fell into small ditches the old man dug for irrigation, or as if he planned for this moment all season. The boy walked across the edges of the field, leaving a trail of that pungent liquid in his wake. He felt the metal container lightening.

He knew there wouldn't be enough for all the fields. He stopped, looking at all the distance he needed to cover with such little fuel. The golden fields were gone. All that remained on the farm was death, decay, destruction, and hunger.

Orson felt a quick sting at the back of his neck. He swatted. The kerosene container flung around. The liquid inside sloshed. He did not see it, but it splashed forward too, free from its confinements, thrown forth unto the destruction before him. He clawed at another insect as it climbed his jawline. The chaos, all of it, became too much for the boy to bear and in that moment, as he stood with the kerosene, swatting away at the plague that fell upon the land, he felt that he should've never been there. He felt that it was his doing, that it was he who brought such a thing, for he enraged the land. He followed a man who cared nothing for it. He feared everything was lost. And, in that moment, as he spat another insect from his mouth, he wished he died somewhere out on those plains, for the old man would not suffer for him.

Thomas approached. He too struggled to run. He carried a lantern, lit. Its flame glowed among the shimmering crimson and black of the locusts. They buzzed his ears. A few clung to his silver locks of hair. He shouted to Orson, "Get back! Get away!"

Orson did so, stepping away from the field. He fell to the ground, staggering as he did so. The kerosene laid in the dirt, still dripping from its prison. The old man rushed forth, as if his back no longer bothered him. Though, as Orson observed him before that field, he looked to be that of a corpse among the shadows of insects and death. With what little strength the old man possessed, he threw forth the lantern near the wagon, where Orson first poured the kerosene. A loud crash echoed across the farm, and for a moment, it was as if it drowned out all the humming and buzzing of the plague. The glass split. The flame rested in the air, free. The kerosene embraced its warmth and with it, the flame multiplied, expanding around the field. Thomas stepped away, watching as the fire rose. Smoke with it, and the consumed insects creaked and hissed in the inferno.

The orange flames wrapped quickly around the field. Orson too watched and Thomas moved towards him. It was then that they both witnessed Orson's small, unnoticeable mistake amongst the chaos. The trail followed the small ditch, the flames rising high, the smell of smoke and burning with it. Yet, as it came to where the container laid, the line of flames forked, one towards the open container, the other towards the field itself. Stocks soaked within the horrid stench of kerosene and they were set aflame before either the old man or the boy could say a word.

It took only seconds for the entire field to begin to burn. The flames consumed all within it. No golden could be seen, not even on the wings of the locusts. Their black bodies charred to the stocks. The flames licked their rigid exoskeletons. The heat hissed through them. Some popped. Some flew, their bodies aflame. The smoke and embers rose before the two as they watched the field become a heap of scorching flames. Orange dots, flaming insects or pieces of wheat, danced in hypnotic circles above the field. Orson saw them in the glassy eyes of Thomas as he stared upon such a horror. The old man's wrinkles became deep canyons on his face as the shadows of the flames waltzed across them. He no longer swatted at the insects that climbed on every inch of his shirt. He stood before the mighty field, those mighty flames, heartbroken and lost, but empty as if he watched a godly temple burn.

He could find no words to say, that much Orson knew. He stared at the man. He felt his knees weaken, his stomach churn. He vomited. The field, the locusts, the flames, they all became one among the eyes of the boy, a single entity of Hell. He fell to his knees. He knew it to be his fault. All of it was his fault. He vomited again. As he stared upon the haunting destruction, his cheek burned as a flaming locust flew from the heap and barreled into the young man's face. He grabbed ahold of his cheek, crying out in pain. He felt blood. He felt the heat of the blaze. The old man looked to him. His eyes still danced with those flames. He told the boy, "Run! Get away! Find shelter…"

The words echoed and bounced around the young man's skull as he stood. He began to run. He knew where not to go. He kept getting pelted. He watched as the flames of the field broke away, stretching across the property. The wagon burned. The locusts hissed together. They sounded like screams, so many screams. He ran. He kept running. He paid no attention to where he went. He just heard Thomas in the back of his head like some methodical chant, "Run! Get away!"

The boy climbed into the only cover he found, the abandoned chicken coop. He slid the door closed behind him, laying on the floor amongst the feathers and the excrement. He began to cry as he tore at his clothes, peeling the insects away from him. The locusts pounded on the outside. Coyotes cackled somewhere on the plains.

Chapter XVII

The Inferno

1873

The Tanner Party moved across the plains of Kansas, still in pursuit of a three-day herd. Days passed since Masters fell. None of the men spoke of him anymore. For the first few days, it was all they talked about when Jack wasn't around or when he rode far ahead of his party on his horse. They kept to themselves about the subject, not wanting to upset him. They feared his rage. Often, they stopped, listening to the light thunder ripple beneath the surface of the earth. Each day becoming fainter. Each day, the men wondering if it even existed. At times, Parker even wondered such a thing. He'd never admit it or speak his truth. He had to be right. Jack too, for he was always right, even in the wrong.

Conversation between the lot waned too. Those nights huddled around the campfire, smoking, laughing, and drinking became only memories of the Tanner Party. They just laid underneath the stars in silence. Orson stared up at the glowing orbs most nights, wondering if Masters was up there somewhere. He thought of asking his companions, but he knew they wouldn't have anything to say about it. He wondered if they acted this way when Old Ben perished.

As days passed, he no longer looked to the stars, but to the infinite void behind them. He felt lost amongst the blackness, lost to the abyss. He wanted it to take him some days, and then he wondered if that is what Masters felt. He thought of speaking to his acquaintance about it. He knew Charlie wouldn't have much to say, for he'd been staring at the dark in the sky since the calves. They hardly spoke anymore. Nothing needed to be said. They were men, and nothing needed expressing. They stood by each other, slept near each other, but hardly a murmur passed between their lips.

When morning broke over the plains of Kansas, the wagon rolled on. Charlie sat in the back with Orson. They both dangled their legs, feeling the prickles of the tall grass bite their ankles. The insects screeched. The crows cawed. They doubted they'd hear the call of a rooster again, songbirds, or anything else pleasant. A stench filled the air. They smelt it some ways out and it grew ever more powerful with each roll of the cart.

Jack turned back at some point. He started the morning about half a mile away from the wagon, nothing but a speck to those that wished to look to him, though the party often did. He wore a blanket over his shoulders as he sat atop his horse, marching onward across the plains, still somewhat ahead of his party, about fifteen to twenty yards.

Charlie and Orson shared a blanket, one meant for the horses. Their breath turned cold in the morning dew. A bitter winter was coming, Bill told them. He knew so because of the crystals atop the grass. They thought nothing of it. They kept on keeping on, moseying with that stench growing amid that cold morning.

They passed one dead bison. The morning wetness matted its unskinned fur. Something took to it, chewing away at its ankles, its underbelly, and its entrails that laid strewn out in the crimson grass that surrounded it. They passed another, which looked less scavenged, but the evidence of such beasts was present. Those small white pellets still sat atop a few of the carcasses as more came into view for the two boys at the back. The wagon bumped as it passed over familiar train tracks, and those killing fields were so much darker, wetter, redder, and grim than when they left them. Orson looked out the back of the wagon. Most of the dead bison appeared taken hold of by the scavengers of the plains, and those who were not, laid bloated, grim, and decayed.

The wind blew and with it the grass, and atop it rolled tuffs of grey and red fur. The party kept on, saying nothing as they moved through the killing fields. Orson wondered if they took the time to stop and skin them if they'd look so bloated, if they'd look so pitiful. He then wondered if Masters looked the same and the thought made him sick. He turned his head, looking downward, but as he did, he caught the sight of a coyote, dead, among the bison. It laid in such a strange posture, so unnatural. Its back laid arched. Its fur thinned and the young man saw the creature's ribs, its rigid spine stuck in that odd position. Its mouth hung open, a foam dried around the edges of its lips and tongue. Its tail laid most curious too, for it stretched straight out, stiff as a board. Its legs curved inward, as if it perished running, frozen still as whatever it ate took hold.

Then, the wagon passed another, and another, and another. Soon, Orson counted six, possibly seven, coyotes out in that field. All their fur thinned. All their tails extended straight out. All their mouths hung open with their tongues draped around the lower stalks of tall grass. Their rotting corpses blended with those of the bison. Soon they would rot into nothingness. Soon, there would be nothing left of them to be remembered across the plains. Those bison were trophies lost, Orson thought. Those coyotes, he didn't know what to think aside from the occasional image of his father, that chicken coop, and that cloven skull of the wounded one he had not the heart to kill as a child. He wished in that moment he could go back. He wasn't sure if he could kill that coyote, even now, after all that time. He wasn't sure why he wanted to do such a thing. He just knew he didn't know what to do anymore.

They kept on, until the killing fields and the coyotes claimed by it were long from view. The stench left some time after, but occasionally Orson smelt it deep within the fabric of his clothes. He would smell it forever, no matter the cleaning or the washing, he would always smell it. That much he knew too.

A day later, it was Parker who noted a haze on the horizon. The sun began to set with an odd purple hue. Yet, across the flat plains a great orange haze hung, and smoke towered above it. They all knew it to be a fire, but it was only Parker who even brought it to conversation.

He called out to Jack, who still trotted ahead, "Wha'chu think, boss?"

Jack turned to the wagon driver. He threw a hand in the air, curious as to what he referenced.

Parker pointed to the fire in the distance, "Think it's friendly folk?"

Jack halted his horse. Parker wheeled the wagon on, stopping at his leader's side. Jack said nothing for a moment, only staring out across those plains, watching that fire. He rubbed his chin, curious as to who or what it could be. He feared it to be Indians deep down, and he also feared it to be competitors. Their stores would get low soon, he thought, and a night at a friendly camp could save them some time and money on restocking. He nodded to that thought. He then told his crew, "It's worth checkin'."

They were met by guns as they rode up to the camp. The wagon rolled to a halt. Parker and Bill put their hands in the air. Orson and Charlie did the same. Jack, however, leaned forward on his horse, crossing his hands atop the pummel of his saddle. He spat as he looked out to the three men that greeted them on the outskirts of the lavish campsite. Two carried revolvers. One held a Remington rifle. It was a nice piece and Jack admired it. He looked over the camp, seeing many tents. Their fire roared wildly, enough to keep the fifty some odd men that watched from its glow warm. The shadows of the impending night danced around them. Embers rose and danced above their heads. The men ate. They sang before the Tanner Party arrived. Now, they just stared at them with cold faces and curious eyes.

The man with the Remington spoke first in some foreign tongue.

Jack spat, "English?"

"American?" Remington asked.

Jack nodded, "All of us are."

"We too," said the Remington man.

Jack studied the man's pale face. All of them were tall, lengthy, and gaunt. He knew they were hunters just by the clothes they wore, and the equipment strewn about the camp. He also knew they weren't as good as he. How he knew, he didn't understand, but he didn't see them as competition in the slightest, even with their large numbers. He shook his head, "That accent don't sound American."

"Swedish," said the man with a revolver on the Remington's right-hand side.

Jack spat, "Then you's Swedish, not American."

"We are citizens," said the Remington. "These are my friends and we came here for profit."

"All these your friends?" Jack asked.

The leader nodded and then threw his hand out to present the wagon and the crew with their hands raised, "Are these yours?"

"This is my party," Jack told him. "We's hunters, same as you."

"What you hunt?" the Swedish leader asked.

"Bison, mostly."

"And who are you?" the leader pressed.

"I'm Jack Tanner. Like I said, this is my party."

The Swede looked over the wagon crew who began to lower their arms. He smirked, seeing the nervousness his rifle created. He asked Jack, "And what is it that you want, Jack Tanner?"

"Well," Jack spat, "I done seen your fire from a distance. It sounded like a party as we's rolled up. Thought we'd see if you'd have us for the night."

"And why do you want to join my friends?" the leader asked.

"We ain't joinin' you for a hunt or nothin'. We's hungry. Our food is lower than usual. We need to eat," Jack told him.

The Swedish leader spat too, almost as if imitating Tanner, "You only want us for our food, yes?"

"Tha's right. We got's our own tents."

“And what if we are running low, same as you?” the leader asked.

“You ain’t,” Tanner told him. “I know you got some extra in there. Look at all them. You got more. I know it.”

“How do you know?”

“I just do.”

The Swedish leader laughed at that. He then turned to his friends and patted them on the back. They lowered their revolvers and he continued to chuckle, “You are stubborn, yes?”

“Yes,” Jack smirked.

“Is there a reason you do not have food?” the Swedish leader pressed. He dared not let coyotes into his coop.

“We’ve fallen on hard times, lost one of our own a few days back. We haven’t caught up to the herd we’re tracking and…” Jack trailed off. He thought of something. It didn’t matter. He continued, “And we’s lookin’ to relax and find some shelter.”

“Shelter?” the man asked.

“Tha’s right, I said shelter.”

“You have tents,” the Remington in the man’s arms swayed. “Is that not shelter?”

“Look,” spat Jack, “I ain’t here to play with words. You gon’ feed us or not? Like I said, we done lost one of our hunters and we lookin’ to sleep somewhere. Ain’t no city for miles. Our stores are low. We been trackin’ a herd but slowed because a boy done fell. You gon’ feed us? That meat smells mighty fine and I and my boys is hungry. If you ain’t, just say so. We’ll move on. I ain’t gon’ sit here and chatter with ya no longer. I'm tired. I'm angry. I ain't got no words left to say on it."

It was the most Jack said in days. Orson felt a warm rush of adrenaline in his body as he watched the Swedes stare down his leader. They kept their weapons lowered, but their faces sat stern as they mulled over what he said. "We can't talk business," said the leader. "We too are tracking a herd. Don't know if it is the same."

"Tha's fine," Jack replied.

"And you eat after us. We have a lot of mouths to feed."

"Tha's fine too."

"I only do this because you said you lost someone. You had the chance to bury them?"

Jack said nothing. He just stared at the leader.

The leader nodded at that, then gave a small religious gesture with his hands as he looked to the sky. His eyes then shifted to Parker, "You may park your wagon with our others."

Parker nodded, "Thank you."

The Swede nodded back and then turned to Jack, "Will you return this gesture if someone comes to your camp in need some day?"

Jack nodded, "Yeah, sure…"

"Come then," said the Swedish leader. "Have a drink. Mourn your friend. Have some meat."

A drizzle came and went. The fire did not dull, for its

flames were mightier than the droplets. The Swedes, as they drank, ate, and sang, began to take larger pieces of wood, throwing them to the flames. The orange haze grew, and once the water stopped falling from the opened sky, a strange halo formed around the pyre in an aura.

Orson ate meat and bread. The Tanner Party didn't receive much, but it would be enough to hold them over for the night. The young man basked in the flames, feeling the heat radiate over his cold body. He saw his breath. His clothes were wet, and his boots sat in moist grass with mud clinging to his soles. The Swedes set logs around the fire, most sat occupied. The young man and his acquaintance sat in the mud, crossed legged and eating in silence.

He watched Charlie chew his food. The boy dared not look to the flames, but rather through them. He studied Jack and Parker drinking with the Swedish leader, who gave his name but none of the men recalled it. The acquaintance said nothing as he chewed his last sliver of meat. He licked his fingers. His eyes danced away, looking to Orson who he caught staring. He waited for a moment, as if he expected Orson to say something to him. He imagined a thousand questions behind the young man's eyes, but none of them asked. Instead, Charlie inquired, "You think we gettin' close?"

Bill sat atop one of the logs near the fire. He spat into the flames, then threw a few tuffs of wet grass into them, watching for a moment as they hissed and burned. He shook his head, and did not look to the boys, "I'm thinkin' we ain't ever gon' find it."

Charlie looked to the burly man, curiously, "I heard it, same as the boss and Parker."

Bill nodded at that, the flames in his eyes swirled as they hypnotized him, "Yeah, I heard it too. Weren't no three-day herd, far less than that."

The boy's voice cracked as he asked, somewhat patronizing, "You ever heard a three-day herd?"

Bill's eyes glanced to the boy, still filled with the flames, "Have you?"

He looked away as Charlie bowed his head. Orson watched as Jack Tanner began to stumble away from the Swedish leader. He turned back for a moment, raising his hand, laughing, and said a joke in broken Swedish, something he practiced with the men of the camp. It was terrible, so much so, the leader threw his head back and drunkenly laughed with Tanner. Jack didn't see he was the butt of the joke. His drunken stagger and confused glossy eyes were enough to show that. Tanner threw his upper body forward as he kicked his legs outward, moving awkwardly towards the fire. He threw his hands out, warming them. He spat to the flames. His tone became somber as the drunken smirk faded from his face, "Lost 'em…left 'em…"

Bill glanced up to his leader, "Nothin' we can do 'bout him now. We gotta keep movin' on."

Jack's brow crumpled, the ferocity in his voice rose, "I ain't talkin' 'bout Timmy! I'm talkin' 'bout all them pelts we done left at them tracks, that we done left in that ravine!"

Bill lowered his head, giving it a small shake. He knew that to be a lie, but Jack would never own it. He began to think of a response, something he wanted to tell Jack for a while but couldn't find the words for. He felt tired suddenly, just the thought of talking to Tanner in his current state became exhausting, and so he didn't say anything at all.

Charlie, on the other hand, could not read the face of the bull in front of him, "You did what you thought was right."

"Shut up, you!" Tanner stepped away from the flames, moving over towards Charlie and Orson. He continued, "You ain't done shit since I picked you up in Lawrence. You know what I should'a done? Should'a done took you out instead of Timmy. That or I should'a thrown you off the fuckin' ravine when we was there."

Bill stood, but kept his distance, "Boss…"

Jack turned his back to the boys, pointing at Bill with such anger and frustration. Orson could not tell if there were tears in his eyes, but the flames accented the gloss enough that it became hard to distinguish. Jack shouted, "Wha? You taken up for him now? You ain't like him neither. He ain't worth a damn. He c'aint kill. He c'aint shoot. He c'aint do anythin' s'ept sit here and eat."

Bill stood tall, unphased by Jack's drunken anger. He'd seen it all before, "You're drunk, Jack."

"An' yer a fool," Tanner spat back. "I heard you sayin' we ain't near that herd. We is. We's close. Ain't that right, Parker?"

From across the camp, near the Swedish leader, Parker raised his glass, only catching a glimpse of the conversation. He wasn't positive of what Jack spoke of, but he needed affirmation, and

Parker was drunk enough to give it blindly. He said, "Tha's right, boss."

Bill didn't even bother to acknowledge Parker. He spoke solely to Jack, "We're close to a herd. It ain't wha'chu think, Jack."

"Wanna know what I think?" Jack asked, stepping towards Bill. He stood before the burly man, looking up at him. He poked him in the chest, the whiskey on his foggy breath hung in the air as he said, "I think you's scared of makin' a little money. I think you's scared what you'll do with it. C'ain't hang onto it. Gamble it all away, mostly. Spend it on whores cuz…you c'ain't think of nothin' better. You know you and you's scared a' you. Most of all, I think you's scared that I'm right."

Bill gave a little huff, then smirked. That faded as he spoke, "It ain't yer idea, Jack. It's Parker's."

"What I say goes," said Jack. His eyes danced over to Parker, who now watched intently as the stare-down between Jack and Bill intensified. Jack continued, "It's my call. It's my idea."

Charlie barked out, looking for some form of validation, "Ain't no one doubtin' you, boss."

Jack hurled his body around with great haste. He marched across the flames, staggering a bit, almost tripping into them to be consumed. He moved on by, stopping in front of the young Charlie. He waved his long skeletal index finger in the boy's face as he shouted, "Stop callin' me boss, boy! I ain't your boss! Ever since you done cried, all you been doin' is bein' 'yes boss' this and 'yes boss' that."

Parker emerged from the shadows of the camp. He took a drink as the light of the fire washed over him. He shivered as it warmed the cold beneath his flesh. He smiled with a crooked grin as he wiped the liquor from his lips with his sleeve, "You see the way Lil Lamb killed them wounded ones? Like it made him get some hair on his stones."

Jack laughed with Parker. They howled at one another drunkenly. Tanner threw his head back, laughing up into the starry night. His breath blended with the smoke of the flames as he continued to chortle. Charlie sustained his gaze upward at Tanner. A scowl stretched across his face. Jack saw it when he looked down on him and continued to mock, "You tryin' to impress me, boy?"

The Swedes began to gather around the flames, their leader watching from the shadows of his tent. They knew not what the Americans said. They cared not. They felt it in the air. A tension rose in the camp, somewhere near the outskirts, but swelled at the heart of the flames. The night felt still as they argued. A few spoke to one another in their foreign tongue, questioning what took place, for they felt a disturbance deep within the balance of the world, something so often ignored, and something the Tanner Party never felt.

Charlie spat back to Jack, "I'm tryin' to do my job."

"You ain't got no job," said Jack, still towering over the boy.

He continued, "You're worthless, boy. I hate to say it. You's worthless. Dumber than hell too. You ain't ever gon' be no man if you can't do a simple thing."

Orson sat silently. He dared not move, for he did not want the attention on himself. He'd seen all this before, experienced it all before. Not with Jack, but his father. If he learned anything as a child, it was to hunt and to avoid being hunted by the drunken stupors of a superior. He admired Charlie in that moment though. He saw that his face sank with such anger and frustration. Though the boy said nothing, his face told it all. Orson saw it. Jack saw it. Parker saw it. Bill saw it. All the Swedes watching saw it too. The young man's acquaintance stood, his fists balled, his eyes watered around the edges. His lip quivered with sadness and rage. As he stood, he quickly fell back to the wet earth, for Tanner raised his hand, striking the boy across the face with the back of it.

Charlie writhed on the ground for a moment. The Swedes closed in. He held his cheek, such a searing pain. He wondered if his cheek was broken. Orson wondered it too. He felt the strike as well, deep down somewhere within his body. He wanted to vomit. He thought of his father, whether he lived or died, whether he ever thought of his son, whether he ever thought of his mother, whether if he thought of all the strikes he'd given his boy, whether he ever thought of the cloven skull of that coyote or heard its yaps.

Jack loomed over Charlie, "You step to me, boy, you best

be willin' to take a hit. You're worthless. You ain't ever gon' do anythin' right."

The acquaintance looked to Orson. His eyes welled with many tears, but he buried his face within the mud to hide them. He still held his cheek. Shame seeped from every pore on the boy's body.

Bill appeared between the two, his back to Charlie and his front to Jack. He raised his hands, palms out and opened, showing that he meant no harm to his leader. He spoke harshly though, "Jack…stop, you're upset and you're drunk."

"I *am* drunk, dammit!" Jack screamed. His voice rattled as he did so. He stepped back, closer to the flames, "I am drunk. I ain't sad! I'm fuckin' mad! Mad at him! Mad at you for doubtin' me!"

Parker cackled as he watched the scene unfold. He took another drink. Jack heard him. He did not smile though. Their tether of humor shattered at some point during his drunken rage. All that remained were Jack and his thoughts, his emotions, which Orson began to wonder if he even had any. Tanner moved away from the boys and Bill, moving towards the fire. As he passed Orson, he looked to him, sticking his boney finger out in his face, "And I'm mad at you too!"

"Wha's he done?" Bill asked, taking two steps forward to let his presence be felt by his leader.

"He's too fuckin' quiet!" Jack shouted. He looked back towards Orson, he knelt, his face to his. The boy smelt the alcohol as if it were a part of the man. Tanner demanded from him, "Speak your mind, boy! Say somethin'! How you feel 'bout all this?"

Orson thought. He knew. He knew how he felt about everything, Masters, Jack, Charlie, all of it. He knew what to say, just not how to say it. He didn't bother to open his mouth because he also knew it wouldn't make a difference with whatever he said. He could agree with Jack, lie about his feelings. Jack would care not. He could disagree, show his true colors. Jack would care not either. He just sat, staring at his leader.

Jack nodded, standing back up. He chuckled to himself. There was no humor in it. He moved to the other side of the fire. He held his hands out to the flames, almost touching them with his bare hands. He studied the hundreds of eyes of Swedes who watched him. He didn't feel bothered or ashamed. They knew not what he said. He found peace in that. He stepped back from the flames, raising his arms. The flames rose with them, as if they bent to his will, he was the grand puppeteer. He shouted, "The whole lot'a'ya is tryin' to make me out to be a fool. I ain't no fool! This is my show and if you don't like it, off wit'cha then! This is my party! This is my hunt! This is my land!"

Jack stared down into the flames, his arms still held out over his head. Orson watched as his leader stood on the other side of the bonfire. He witnessed the flames dance across his leader's hellish face. He watched them swell within those glossy eyes as Tanner became lost to the visions in the flames. He saw something that caused his eyes to fill with tears. He examined a broken man beneath it all, but that rigid exterior loomed so powerful before the flames. All stayed quiet as they looked upon the man, daring not to challenge his authority.

A figure staggered behind Tanner. A Swede it was, who swayed his arms low. His back hunched over as he took shallow steps towards the flames. Blood dripped from the top of his skull where no hair sat, only a bloody glistening pool atop an exposed skull. An arrow hung from his shoulder, pierced through and crimson seeped from over his heart. He opened his mouth to speak, but only a haunting gurgling echoed across the camp. All watched him, their eyes taken from the drunken Jack who still stood with his arms out. He too looked, and those eyes no longer swelled with tears and anger, but with concern and a quick realization, followed by panic.

Out of the shadows, figures emerged among the Swedes. Their eyes did not glow with the flames, for they were the flames. Most stood half naked. Their red flesh decorated with black symbols glistened in the pale moonlight. They stood tall, proud, and their faces stoic as they wielded their lances, bows, rifles, pistols, and clubs. One, larger than the others, stepped forward towards the flames and the drunken Tanner. His eyes, so black with hatred, watched the man intently. His face stood painted in a dark red and a black handprint covered his mouth as if to silence him. In the great warrior's hand, he held a shimmering tomahawk. He rose it over his head as he approached Tanner with great speed. Jack went for his revolver. That is the last Orson witnessed of the ordeal, for in a moment, the Comanche were upon them all.

Shouting is all the young man heard as he fell to the wet ground. Foreign languages filled the air as the sounds of bones being crushed, gunfire, and splitting flesh overwhelmed Newkirk's ears. A fog seeped over the camp, gunpowder. It smelt so rich, so filled with iron, and the boy stayed low to the ground as he watched men being hacked within the darkness. Then, the horses were upon them. Strangely clad Indians rode through the scattered ranks of the confused and lost Swedes. Their horses, painted too, bore symbols of hands, dots, and their riders lightning bolts, animals, and other strange pictures. Some fired rifles. Others heaved lances. Others threw tomahawks. Others slashed with knives. Some leaped from their steeds onto fleeing men. They hooped and hollered as they took lives. Blood seeped from so many open wounds, mixing with the mud beneath the damp grass, the true salt of the earth.

In all the commotion, he lost Charlie. He stood. As he did, a horse raced by him, striking a frightened hunter who fell into the flames, knocking the burning pile into the dirt. The flames scattered forth, released from their manmade prison. The embers rose, hissing and cracking, as the fire began to consume all in its path. On the other side of the lake of flames, Tanner stood bloody and battered. He looked to Orson and Bill, "Get to the wagon you dumb sons of bitches!"

It was then that Orson discovered Charlie, who huddled near a makeshift bench. Bill reached down, grabbing ahold of the young boy and yanked him to stand by his collar. They ran, and Orson followed for a moment. Yet, after only a few steps, an arrow whizzed by his head, clipping the tip of his ear. Warm blood trickled down. He thought for sure he died, and he fell to the ground to accept his fate. The wet mud no longer felt cool against his skin and clothes, no. The blood warmed it so, and it felt as if Hell seeped upward from the earth to consume him. He felt a hand on his back, and he turned to see if some spiritual being were coming to whisk him away from such a horror. Bright eyes stared at him, beneath black and red lines of paint. The warrior's face looked gaunt in the light. His hand grabbed Orson's hair and the boy yelped as the man drew a roughly made blade from the back of his belt. Something struck the warrior from the dark before he brought the crude weapon to the boy's scalp. He fell into the mud and Orson felt the warmth of the dead man's blood on his face as he crawled back.

He rested against a wooden box, staying low and hidden. He thought of playing dead, for he knew he still existed in the realm of the living. He wet himself at some point. He cried out in terror as he watched tents go up in flames, burning so quickly as torches were thrown atop their canvas. Bodies littered the ground. Blood splatters covered everything he saw, so much red. The Swedish leader leaned against a wagon in the distance. Orson thought him standing his ground, yet upon the growth of the camp fires, he realized a lance sat within his gut, keeping the man pinned upward against his attempted escape. His skull sat exposed. His arms laid hewed from his body. His dead eyes stared back at the boy, a cold empty blue.

Another hand reached down to the young man, he screamed, expecting another blade to his head. Yet, as he looked upward to scream into the face of his would-be attacker, he saw the gashed and bloodied Parker. A wide wound sat atop his forehead. Blood ran down over his eyes, a warpaint of his own. He said nothing as he spat blood, but lifted Orson from behind the box with one arm and began to lead him through the chaos.

The camp swelled with a vibrant orange from all the fires. Parker kept his hand latched tightly around Orson's shirt, pulling him. Orson's feet kicked, trying to match pace with his companion. His eyes danced with the bouncing fires that surrounded them. They became lost within the maze of burning canvas. Swedes ran with them, around them, and past them. Each man possessed a wound of some kind. Dead laid scattered, scalped, mutilated. One dead man rested with his face down in the mud. His limbs hacked away. His head glistened with a crimson exposed skull. A tent burned overtop him. Small pieces flaked down, scorching his skin like a flaming snow. The two passed, continuing into the inferno.

A horse, rider-less, rode past them. Orson watched it. Blood seeped from a wound on its hind quarters. It went back towards the center, towards the now all-consuming bonfire. It was then that the young man saw Jack, staggering behind him and Parker. He was far back, but he moved as fast as he could. He fired that beautiful revolver at the shadowy riders who owned the night. It glistened in the orange and red.

To his side, following another pathway through the inferno, Charlie and Bill ran. A rider closed in on them. A rifle round tore into his guts. The horse bucked. He flew into a burning tent. The two companions kept running. Even among the chaos, the bloodshed, the screaming, the dying, Orson felt the earth rumble beneath his feet. He thought bison for a moment, but he looked back, seeing a great steed riding forth through the flames at a full gallop. Its rider, black faced and screaming with wide eyes, swung his lance at men who ran. He heaved it forward, striking Jack Tanner somewhere that Orson could not see. His leader fell into the bloody muck. He did not move. The rider dismounted from his moving horse, knife in hand. He began to hack away at others in his path, and somehow, he was struck by a round from some rifle out in the dark.

Charlie saw Tanner fall and rerouted his run to go back. He screamed and cried, for he did not know what he would do without him. He'd come so far, and yet felt worse of himself for doing so. Yet, as Jack laid face down in the mud, he could not leave him in such a place. Bill reached out, grabbing ahold of the boy and tossing him to the ground. He shouted, "They'll kill you too, boy! We gotta go!"

Parker did not stop. He did not lighten his grip either. He kept on dragging Orson, who began to feel the tiredness set into his legs as they kicked awkwardly as he ran. He feared he'd fall, and Parker would leave him, the same way he didn't question leaving Masters. His companion whipped his arm forward, throwing Orson behind a burning tent and a stack of wooden boxes that only began to burn. He too huddled behind it. He looked to Orson with those bloody eyes. He spat blood too, "You see it?"

"Huh?"

Parker shook him, waving his fist in Orson's face, "The boss! You see him fall?"

Orson nodded.

"He dead?"

"I ain't sure."

Parker looked out down the path between the tents. He couldn't see far, not with the blood in his eyes, the darkness of the night, the dead and dying scattered about. He whispered, "I ain't neither and Bill done left 'em."

"We c'ain't go back," Orson replied.

"If he ain't dead—" Parker began.

As he spoke, a great beast of a horse, so thick in legs and body, trotted before them and reared. Its rider, naked covered in painted handprints, waved a lance over his head. He brought it down, and if it were not for Orson, who grabbed Parker in a hug and threw himself back, the lance would've been driven home into the young man's head. However, Orson rolled, and the lance struck him in the lower calf. He screamed as he felt the warmth of his own blood. Parker drew his five shot Colt. He missed all his rounds as the rider stared down on the two.

The rider raised his lance, ready to throw. Another horse rode through, aflame and screaming in agony. It startled the rider's, bucking him upward. It was their chance, and they took it. No bravery or faulty courage lingered between the too, and Parker grabbed Orson once more and they continued fleeing.

Parker ran. Orson hobbled. Parker let go of his shirt. He slowed the man too much. Pain seared in the boy's leg, but he tried his best to keep up. They passed through the ammunition storage. The tents too burned and so did the ammunition crates. Premade cartridges burst, sending rounds flying off into the dark. Black powder, fallen to the earth, burned faster sparking and exploding in small pockets. A decapitated man burned nearby. His head cradled by the native that took it.

Not far in the distance, fifty, maybe sixty yards or so, the Tanner wagon moved. Orson saw it among the light of the flames. Charlie sat in the driver's box. Bill hung on the side. Some other horse had been hitched in and it panicked. It kicked its hooves outward as the wagon began to roll away. Charlie did not grab the reins and the horse moved at such speed, and thus the wagon too. Bill held on to the side for dear life. It rode on out of the camp. Orson saw no pursuers.

Orson said nothing, just pointing the sight out to Parker.

When he saw it, he shouted with blood stained teeth, "Wait! Wait, you assholes!"

An arrow cut between Parker and Orson. Parker stepped back, turned, and tackled Orson to the ground. A mounted native rode on by, whooping and hollering, firing arrows into the dark and into nearby Swedes. His beast trampled a man. Its hooves crushing his ribs. The sound could not be heard over the Swede's screams, the beast's, and the cries of the native.

From where the two regained their footing, they examined an opening before them. They lingered near the edge of the camp. The shadows of the night beckoned them, calling forth for them to flee and be consumed by it, to hide from the inferno. Parker arched his back, ready to dash. Yet, it was Orson who grabbed his arm, twisting him around. He shouted, "Wait! What about Jack?"

Parker's eyes examined everything, seeing all in just one quick look. His vision blurred with the red of his wound. The light of the flames flared outward in their haze, as if they were the long legs of arachnids, reaching for the darkness of the night. The halos of light all but shattered, and only odd images blurred before him. He only heard the chaos and spat more crimson, "He's dead, you saw it. I saw it."

"You said if he ain't dead—" Orson began.

Parker interrupted, "Stay then."

With that, Parker turned his back and dashed off into the night. Orson did not wait. He did not hesitate. He too ran after his companion, rushing into the cold blackness of the open plains. He ran as hard as he could. The screams of the camp felt closer the further he ran. He did not see Parker in the dark. He did not see himself either, only black. The earth rumbled with the hooves of the horses. He wept as he ran. He didn't care if Parker knew, for he swore he heard him weeping too. And so, they ran, ran until they could no longer hear the chaos or see the flames, only the darkness.

Chapter XVIII
Loyalty and None
1873

The night was cold for the two survivors. They huddled close together, neither sleeping, far away from the camp. They watched the orange haze fall on the horizon, then watched it mimicked as the sun began to rise. Though, under the light of the morning, neither spoke to one another, and they no longer huddled together under that lone tree. The Comanche left sometime in the night, they assumed. They watched dust trails in the dark as the war party left, heading to wherever their hearts desired.

Once he felt safe, Parker stood and paced around that lone tree on the prairie. He mumbled to himself, clicking his nails to his teeth, nerves still rattled from the night before. Orson leaned against the grey withered bark of the dead tree. He tore pieces off his shirt, wrapping them around his wounds, the same way he watched Parker bandage his headwound in the low light of the morning.

The two exchanged exhausted looks to one another. They both thought the same thing, go as far as they could together then part ways. They cared little for each other, though bound by blood and experience. Parker kept his murmuring, shooting small side eyed glances towards Orson. Orson said nothing, only looked back, holding his leg as if cradling it would, by some miracle, make it whole again.

"Wha'chu think?" Parker asked.

"Think about what?"

"Headin' back."

Orson shook his head, looking off towards the smoldering camp in the distance, the rising smoke greyed the growing blue. He said, "I think it foolish."

"Me too," defended Parker. "They might have somethin' left behind though. You know?"

"Indians," Orson reasoned.

"Them Swedes," Parker misunderstood. "Them savages couldn't have destroyed everythin'. Right?"

"I doubt it."

"Maybe they has horses there."

"I bet you they ran," Orson spat.

"Maybe. Maybe not. We c'ain't be sure," Parker said. "Bill and Lil' Lamb probably long gone. It's just you and me now."

"Think so?"

"Know it," Parker shook his head as he paced. He didn't like the thought he possessed, "With Jack gone, I'm in charge. I say we goin' back."

"In charge of what? It's just us now."

"The Party," Parker stopped moving, looking onto Orson. "I'm in charge."

"You mean me," Orson said, "seein' as the party is just us now. Right?"

"Yeah, guess that's so," Parker said.

"And if I said no to goin' back…just went on my way, what would you be in charge of then?" Orson asked.

"Looky here, orphan," began Parker, "I say we's goin' back and there ain't no question of whether you leavin' or stayin'. You goin' back with me, no matter how you done feel about it."

"But I could leave," Orson argued.

"Fine then," Parker said, waving his hand in the air presenting the open emptiness of the plains. "See how far you gon' get with that bum leg and no rifle. Them Comanch'll run you down."

"They gone."

"For now, more time we waste, they prolly gon' come back for seconds," Parker debated. "That leg'll rot off before they get here. You need supplies and that camp prolly done has some."

"Why c'ain't we just go?"

"'cus I said so," Parker reasoned. "You stickin' to the party or you gon' leave?"

"I was just sayin'," Orson replied.

"With me runnin' the show now, you ain't gon' be just sayin' nothin'. Either you mean to leave or you mean to stay. Which is it?"

"I mean to stay," Orson said, though he questioned whatever came out of his mouth.

"Well alright then," Parker said. "Let's get on back to the camp and scavenge. We gon' head back to Dodge after, I guess. I'll figure it out."

The two walked lazily across the plains. Orson hobbled with his wounded leg. He felt the gash split and move with each step. His bandage, tied tightly around the deep cavernous cut, felt as if it did nothing. He cursed under his breath with every step. Parker paid it no attention. He stayed fixated on the rising smoke and smoldering ruins as they grew closer.

There, on the horizon, something stirred. A lone wagon appeared, silhouetted against the bright blue morning. It moved slowly and Parker, once he shielded his eyes from the rising rays, saw two sitting atop the driver's box. He smirked, "Well, at least they came back. I'll give 'em that."

The companions said no more on it as they pressed towards the camp. Orson and Parker made it first, hanging around the outer ruins of the site. Bodies laid charred and burned. Some stood, nailed to boxes, wagons, or anything else that could hoist such a grizzly sight. Arms and legs rested about, hacked in the mud, flesh peeled back from flames, bones broken beneath hooves and weapons of war. The land appeared scarred, black, smoking from the extinguished flames. A stench there was too, thickening the air every passing second as the bodies baked in the rising sun.

The wagon wheeled forward. Bill sat at the reins. Charlie smirked slightly as he looked down on Orson, not so much Parker. Orson didn't return the sentiment, for he still wondered if he'd been slain the night before and if he and his party wandered the world as spirits. Parker raised his arm, signally the wagon to slow. Bill pulled the reins, and the lone beast at the front of the wagon stalled and stopped.

Parker rounded the beast, moving over towards the side of the driver's box. He spoke to Bill, "You had it in ya to come on back."

"You get stuck here?" Bill asked.

Parker shook his head, "Nah, the orphan and I made it out. Almost didn't on account of y'all not waitin'."

"Couldn't," Charlie piped in, "the horses were spooked."

"Uh-huh," Parker nodded. "I'll get on to you later, Lil' Lamb. Right now, we done need to scavenge what we can. We gon' get the hell out of here."

"Who left you in charge?" Bill asked.

"I always in charge when Jack ain't here. He ain't here. It's my party now."

"That so?" came a voice that slithered from across the

camp.

Parker turned, thinking it came from Orson. He told him, "Yeah, that's so—"

He couldn't finish, for, before the four survivors stood another. His long hair blew in the wind. His hat, once flat brimmed, folded up around the edges, worn and tattered as if the chaos formed it. His eyes sat within sunken sockets, beady, all-seeing, though the left one wandered loosely, cut and bleeding. His hands were bloodied. His back too, for his coat, once a great symbol of his sportsmanship, sat torn near the buttocks and blood stained the color. His tattered hand shook, gnarled from some weapon, as he plopped a cigarette in his mouth. Tanner lit it with a match from his coat, then sat atop some charred wooden crate. He said, "I ain't see it that way."

None of the men said anything as they looked upon him. He was dead, should've been by all accounts. Yet, somehow, Tanner, against all odds, sat before them, king of the ruins, the sole survivor. He spoke again, his voice raspy, "Wha'chu come back for?"

Bill pipped up quickly, "The horses were spooked. We came back lookin' for survivors."

"That didn't much matter to you last night," said Jack. He looked to Charlie in the driver's box, "Wha he tell you? He good as dead? Sayin' they'd kill you too, right?"

Jack stood, walking towards the group with a slight limp in his step. He stood before the wagon, keeping his eye on Charlie. He threw out his arms, mimicking the same presentation he gave the night before around the campfire. He said, "Well, Lil' Lamb…here I am, good as dead."

Jack then looked to Parker. He pointed his finger at him, the cigarette smoldering between his index and middle, smoke rising from it as if it came from the depths of Hell. He said, "I seen you run too."

His eyes glanced to Orson, "You too."

It was when he looked up at Bill, that Jack certified, "I weren't dead."

"Boss…" Parker stammered out, as he stepped forward.

Jack raised his hand to him, silencing the young follower. He kept his eyes, good and bad, fixated on Bill are Charlie. He fumed. They all felt it in the air. He spat flakes of tobacco from his mouth as he took another puff of his cigarette. He asked both Bill and Charlie, "You wantin' gone?"

Bill raised an eyebrow. He didn't quite get it, "Wha'chu mean?"

"You and that Lil' Lamb there took the wagon. You done left me. You done left all of us to die."

"Jack…" Bill began, "the horses were spooked…"

"You was scared'er than they were. Wha' was you plannin' on doin' if we was dead?"

Bill shrugged, "Don't know."

Jack nodded at that. He thought he knew the answer, Bill would just never say it. He would, "Gon' back to Dodge? Drink and gamble, whore yer'self to death?"

"I said, I don't know."

"Hell, Parker was gon' take charge! Were you just gon' leave him? You gon' leave Newkirk and run off to Dodge with yer new friend there?" Jack asked. He turned and looked to Parker and Orson, "He done left you too. Ain't you mad?"

Orson said nothing.

Parker let out a soft, "Yeah, I am."

Jack turned to face Parker, "And now you know how I feel after watchin' you and Newkirk run off without me too."

"Boss," Parker began, "we thought you was dead. You were hit, lyin' on the ground..."

"Well, I ain't," Jack said. He turned to Orson, "What's yer excuse?"

Orson still did not respond.

"Thought as much," Jack smirked and shook his head. He looked back up at Bill, "And was you gon' even take back up with Parker? You gon' stick around now that I ain't dead?"

"Depends," Bill spoke honestly. Jack didn't care for Bill's honesty as much as Orson's in the past. Bill continued, "We ain't got money. We ain't got supplies. Everything we had is burnt."

Jack threw his cigarette into the burned grass. He crushed it under his broken boot sole. He said, "So, yer plan ain't changed a bit then. Has it? You wanted to leave and head on back to Dodge. You still wantin' to."

"I ain't say that," said Bill, flustered. His voice wiggled as he spoke, as if he carried a frog in his throat.

"You ain't have to," replied Jack.

Bill looked to Parker, trying to change the subject, trying to find a way around the wrath of Tanner, "We need to—"

Jack interrupted, yelling at the top of his lungs, his voice boomed and shook, "We ain't need to do nothin', Bill! All y'all left me out here to die! All y'all done stabbed me in the back! Right now, I need to know which of y'all still loyal!"

The men stood silent, watching as Jack ranted and raved. He threw his hands in the air, at times he kicked the dirt while he shouted. Orson lowered his head, not wanting to look his leader in his crazed eyes. His brow lifted and arched as he continued to scream. The young man understood why he was so upset. Though, he wondered if the ghost of Masters, if it wandered the plains, felt the same way. He would. He figured he'd be dead if it wasn't for Parker. He owed him that much, and he wasn't sure what all he owed Jack, but it felt like it was more than his life.

"We close to that herd," Jack said. "We got rifles! I see that ammunition in the back of the wagon! Ain't nothin' gon' change. We keep on after it."

"Jack..." Bill began to argue.

Jack's eyes opened wider than before. Orson thought the wounded one would fall from the socket. He shouted, "Don't fuckin' talk to me like that, you fuckin' snake! Don't 'Jack' me, you fuckin' coward! You was gon' leave! You and that Lil' Lamb!"

Parker stepped forward. His head tilted to one side, slightly hung, as he said in defense of Bill, "We was gon' come back."

"Oh, shut yer mouth, Parker! I ain't talkin' to you yet, mister party leader! You dumb fool, couldn't even wait till I was cold in the ground!" Jack spat to the loyalist of his crew without question or thought. He ran entirely on feeling, spewing whatever came to mind.

Bill tried rationalizing, "Jack, I'm sorry. I really thought—"

"Well, you thought wrong!" Jack moved over to the driver's box. He snatched the reins from Bill's hands, throwing them down into the dirt. The horse stirred, startled by the show. His voice became gruff, "You thought wrong. You always thought wrong. First the herd, then me, now you wantin' to go back to Dodge."

Bill's cheeks rose as his mouth cocked itself to the side in confusion, "I don't."

Jack didn't want to hear it. He kept on, "Leave then. Leave and go on back. You can drink and gamble. You can whore yer'self stupid for all I fuckin' care. I won't hold it against you. I can't hold anything much more against you anyhow."

Bill scoffed, trying to find some humor in the irrationality of Tanner. He joked, "It's a long ride back."

"It's a long fuckin' walk is what it is," Jack didn't find any humor in the situation. "I ain't givin' you a horse. I ain't givin' you shit no more. Not if you leave me high and dry like that."

Every member of the party wanted to say something, take up for Bill in some shape or form. None did. Though the alcohol wore off, the nonsensical ramblings of Jack, the paranoia, stayed true. He didn't want to be questioned, wouldn't take any form of it. He spat as he turned towards Parker and Orson. He pointed to them, his finger shaking as he waved his arm between the two of them, "The same goes for the rest of ye'! You ever leave me again, I'll cut yer fuckin' guts out! Understand? I put everythin' I had into you lot and y'all repay me like that?"

Parker nodded in agreeance. He knew better than to argue, "It won't happen again, boss."

Charlie jumped down from the driver's box. Bill watched him closely as the boy moved towards Jack. He took the place between Orson and Parker, directly in front of Tanner. He too nodded and said, "Yeah, Jack…won't happen again."

Jack looked upon the three before him. He seemed at ease when his eyes danced over theirs. He still saw some honesty in there but wasn't sure how much. He said, "We pressin' onward. That herd is goin' North and we gon' follow. I ain't hearin' no bitchin' or moanin' from any of ya."

The three said nothing. They didn't move. They just looked upon their leader with blind eyes, accepting whatever he said. He let out a little smirk as he looked back, then turned to Bill, "You got yer options, Bill. You stayin' or goin'?"

Parker sat at the reins as the wagon moseyed on across the open plains of Kansas, the golden blades of grass that parted before the wheels still damp at the base. The earth that held them, muddy. Jack's horse was long gone. He spoke of the Indians crushing its skull with a rock and dancing with its entrails. Orson didn't believe that. He figured the beast knew better than they did, and it went off somewhere to escape, to wander the plains, to be free. Tanner did however find another, a pinto Paint, not far outside of the camp. Its Swedish owner didn't get as far as the horse did, and Jack saw no trouble in claiming it for himself. He saddled it, with one he took from the camp, riding behind the wagon, as if herding his crew onward.

Orson and Charlie sat at the back, looking out across the plains. Yet, Orson could not take his eyes off his leader as his horse trotted slowly behind them. Tanner kept his head low, his hat shielding his face, almost as if rain fell onto him. There was none, only a light breeze that waved the tall grass inward and outward, as if the earth itself breathed sighs of relief.

Stirring in the back of the wagon drew the young man's attention. He looked, seeing Bill laying on his back, staring upward into the sky. He breathed shallow. His eyes stared off, wide open, lost to the collection of clouds overhead. He thought of something. Orson wondered what, but he began to think about Jack's horse again and where it was and how it felt if it knew it received a replacement. He then thought it didn't matter much, it was just an animal and didn't care about all that. It wandered the plains somewhere out there. He just hoped it was alright.

Chapter XIX
Ruin
1875

He didn't know what to expect when all the noise died down. He laid silently in that coop, basking in the quiet of the plains once that plague vacated the Daniels farm. He stared up at the worn and rotted ceiling. Water damage took hold years back, but he knew better than to think of replacing it. He sat up, slowly crawling out of the tight space into the openness of the farm. He expected the worst.

He exhaled upon the sight, for it alone stole his breath. The ground laid littered with thousands upon thousands of locusts, some charred and withered. Others laid complete in their exoskeletons, dead from either overeating or bashing their small bodies against immovable objects. A smoke rose over the barren black fields. The ground itself, blackened and red, smoldered in ruin, the grey only parting as Orson stepped away from the coop. The wind blew, and what black husks remained of the wheat, broke apart, turning to ash and dust, cremated and buried by the earth.

What locusts remained living slithered and hopped around the darkened ground. The young man shuddered upon sight of them. He crushed a few under his boots, living and dead, as he approached the wagon he spent days filling. That too was burned. Nothing was safe from his mistake, his error. He knew it. It was all his fault. He ran his hand against the charred wood of the starboard side of the cart. Flakes of dried warm wood fell to the ruined soil. He could not distinguish crop from insect, for it all became one heap of black and grey that smoldered. A haunting smell came with it, dry and odd. He hadn't smelt anything like it before and would never smell it since. In the years to come, he would wake in the middle of the night, thinking he smelt that odd incense, though he would figure it to be imbedded deep within his skin, lingering somewhere within his soul.

The thick smoke that fogged the air of the farm rolled inward, then outward, parting and breaking as another gust of wind came rushing through the land. More ash broke free from not just the field, but the wagon as well, and it snowed onto the young man as he looked out across all of it. As the smoke parted, he saw the Daniels family home, decimated beyond any sort of rational repair. All its windows sat broken. Bits of glass hung within the frames. The corpses and guts of a million locusts peppered the side of the home. The wood, once a deep brown in areas, grey in others, sat caked in oranges, blacks, and greens. So abundant the innards were, the insect gore, that it appeared to be splashes of such a foul looking paint.

What living locusts left on the porch hissed and creaked as the young man passed them. One hopped forth onto his shoulder, its wings damaged from the chaos. He felt no mercy for such a creature and grabbed it with his right hand, crushing it without thought. He wiped the innards onto his pants, something he did as a hunter, and moved up through the front door of the ruined home.

The inside appeared no better than the out. Insects, some burned, others crushed, laid all over the floorboards. Some lived and they scavenged for whatever they could find upon the counters, tables, and even in the bed. Among them, in his chair as usual, sat Thomas. He looked down to the unlit fireplace, starring into the blackened charred logs of the night before. His face sat defeated, but his posture not so much. His hands rested, tightly gripped however, on the edges of his chair as he rocked forward and back. He muttered something under his quivering lips. His hair sat with the remains of locusts, legs and heads forming a mock crown. He sat there, and though he looked lost to the brutal wonder of the West, Orson thought of him regal. He heard the young man come in and he no longer muttered. He spoke softly though, "Not a stock left..."

Upon the sight and sound of the old man, Newkirk fell to his knees. The corpses of locusts crushed beneath his bones. He cupped his hands together, shaking them inward towards his gut then outward towards the old man, a plea of some sort. He stayed knelt behind the man, who dared not look upon him. Orson spoke softly too, "Thomas…I am so sorry…"

Thomas' voice shook. The young man heard the rage in there, something so familiar to him, though not from the old man. Orson fell forward on his elbows, as if begging for some sort of repentance from a man who offered none. Thomas said, "Ain't nothin' gettin' paid back now…"

Orson sat up, looking to the bleeding and guts covered old man. He studied him a moment, wondering how his face looked on the other side. He only guessed the worst. He took his right hand, placing it over his heart as he stared upon the man. His honesty showed true again, for he truly felt a certain way when he said, "This is all my fault…"

Thomas did not stir. He sat quietly in his chair. He waited for the young man to speak, for he had to know. He doubted that there was sabotage of any kind. The earth itself opened and the locusts came forth. Orson could not do that, though he did believe in superstition, he did believe in many things long forgotten. That did not matter to him any longer. Nothing mattered to him. He failed at everything he ever believed in, would ever believe in. And so, he said, "I don't know what I'm gon' do... A man should always look after his family, should always look after what is his... I got nothin', nothin' but a scorched farm... I have to do somethin' for Lilly and Joe...they c'ain't suffer cuz'a me..."

Orson heard him, but tried to continue his honesty,

"Thomas…"

The old man looked to him from over his shoulder.

The young man continued, "It's cuz'a me... They gon' suffer cuz'a me."

Thomas stared at the defeated Orson. He saw his sorrow, his honesty flowing from him in an invisible aura that filled the air with such a dread. Tears ran down the young man's face, leaving trails between the dirt and grime on his cheeks, revealing the white flesh beneath it all. As he stared at him, he wondered how many years of dirt that was, for it looked thick, sooty, and wondered if it rose to the surface from within the young man's body. He knew that to be ludicrous, but in that moment, he didn't know what to think.

"You said it. Ain't nothin' forgotten or forgiven. You said it," Orson then screamed, "You said it!"

Thomas stood from his chair. Watching the boy in such distress made everything that swam within his mind vacate. Only care for the young man became dominate. He moved towards him, yet Newkirk stepped back, throwing a hand out to signal the man to stop. Thomas found it peculiar, "Orson…"

Orson hid his eyes behind a hand, trying to shield the tears that fell as if it were instinct to do such a thing, "It's burned! It's burned and your wheat is gone! I done some bad things, Thomas! I killed a lot'a things for no real reason. I never made much money with Jack...I never did much of anythin'. Hell done followed in my wake. I knew it would. It always does. I knew I should'a just gone. You took me in though and I couldn't see myself doin' much different. And God...He comes here and He...it's all my fault."

Thomas shook his head, reaching out to the boy who swatted his hand away, "This is my punishment. This is my reckoning."

"It's mine!" Orson shouted. "C'aint you see? Ain't none of this would'a happened had I not stayed!"

"This ain't got nothin' to do with you," Thomas spoke, finally getting past the boy's guard and standing next to him. Orson kept his head hung low, still shielding the tears from Thomas's vision. They dripped to the floor, and Daniels watched them as they left small pools in the soot and grime on the floorboards. He continued, speaking softly and earnest, "This is my punishment for failin' Betty, failin' Tabitha, failin' Lilly and Joe. I failed everyone I ever met."

Orson looked up to the man, no longer shielding his eye. They weld with such water, such anguish. He told the man, strong and angry, as if it made a difference in how he appeared, "You ain't fail me! You took me in when you should'a left me to die out there in them plains! It ain't nothin' I don't deserve!"

"Don't talk like that," Thomas commanded.

"It's true," said Orson. "You, the one man who done good for me since I left home, the one man who showed me kindness...and, you get this? You get repaid with this awful...this awful thing? You ain't done nothin' but good...it's cuz'a me..."

Orson tucked his head back into his hand. He wept heavier

than before as he thought of everything he ever did and why he was punished for doing something he saw right. Thomas didn't deserve what he brought with him, that plague to the land, something he saw himself as, even after all that time. As he blinked, tears fell, and in them he saw coyotes, bison, Jack, and his companions. He saw all of it. He felt such a guilt as he thought back on it, thought back on what he deemed his sins. Thomas paid for them, something he didn't see as fair. He knew that, knew he could've done something different. Honest pay, he thought. Honest pay for honest work.

"Ain't your fault," Thomas told him. The old man draped his arm around the boy, trying to comfort him in his time of need. He looked out the shattered windows of his home, looking out towards his tree. It stood tall and strong, mightier than it ever looked for surrounding it was nothing but waste and ruin. He felt he could've done something different too, for he felt himself a betrayer. He wasted the boy's time. He could've been to the Pacific by then and it would've made no difference. It would've caused him no grief. He could die alone, failing everyone he ever knew because it wouldn't have made a difference no matter how hard he tried.

He repeated, "Ain't your fault…ain't nothin' you could'a done…"

The stars lingered dully, masked by the still rising smoke of the Daniels farm. The black clouds overhead, wispy yet thick, moved lazily in the cool breeze. It could be seen for miles and anyone who passed on those open plains would assume the worst. Even in the dark, a man could see such a thick shadow overhanging the farm. Nobody came to help. Nobody came to check. The old man and the young man were left alone in the devastation, of which both blamed themselves for.

It was Orson who began working first. They did not eat their usual warm food, but instead feasted on what little bread they had. It was after he had a slice that he took up a shovel and began to clean the land. He took the ashes, the locusts, the charred stocks, and heaved them into small piles for easy discarding, whenever that would be. He'd been at it for hours and only cleaned a few rows of the empty fields. The locusts and ash turned his brown boots black with dust. His hands and face became covered in soot. He did not mind. He saw it as the least of his worries. It would take days, if not weeks, to clean the entirety of the farm. He wondered if he died somewhere out on those plains and this was his Hell, to clean it all only for it to comeback and remind him of everything he ever did.

While the young man shoveled in the fields, Thomas swept the indoor of his home. He tried his damnedest to rid the place of every locust, living or otherwise, from the interior. That too would take time, for after he cleared the bed for Orson, he turned and found more nestled within the sheets, or legs under the flattened pillow. He found them in odd places, in cabinets and tins. He feared that years later, whoever owned such a place, would still find them and curse his name for being such a fool.

The old man gave up on the interior after some time. His back ached. He coughed too. He wasn't sure if they were related, but a tiredness took control of him, one he could not fight. He feared if he slept, he'd never wake. His vision clouded, as did his mind. He wandered the property for a while, mostly lingering near his family tree. He found peace in the moonlight that broke between the branches. He thought of lying down, falling asleep near those graves, under those carvings, and never waking. Yet, he looked out over the devastation and saw that young man, still scooping the remains of locusts and wheat. He knew then he could not do such a thing, not while he stayed, not while Lilly and Joe suffered for his actions.

Orson watched the man near the tree for a few moments but kept on with his work. He became so focused on shoveling and watching the bits of the destroyed crumble in the spade, that he didn't hear the old man approach him. Thomas kept his distance, he too watching as the blackened ash dissolved into small piles in the iron spade. He asked the young man, "You goin' on your way in the mornin' then?"

Orson kept shoveling, "There's plenty left to do."

"Not for me there isn't," Thomas expressed. "The farm...all of it...it's finished."

The young man stopped, holding the shovel with both hands at his waist. He turned to the old man, "You ain't wantin' me around no more?"

Thomas felt taken aback by that question. Upon a quick reflection, he understood how the boy came to that conclusion. He elaborated, "I didn't say that. I like havin' you around, Orson. It's just...you said you wanted to go West. There just ain't nothin' here to hold you up no more."

The young man stabbed the spade into the ground, crossed his arms, and leaned against the spade. He looked over the ruined farm. Leaving and not having to repair sounded alright by him. Yet, as his eyes danced over the old man, he felt a sense of dread leaving after such a thing, something he still felt he caused, "Well, I'll think about it. You want to come?"

"Me? Go West?" Thomas scoffed, "Shit…I'm an old man like ya said."

"I c'ain't send you no letter. We never did get around to you teachin' me to read and write and all that you mentioned," Orson replied. "So, why not come? See for yer'self."

"I can't run away," Thomas said sternly. He wasn't trying to be hostile towards the young man, but the thought of it made his stomach churn, his back ache, his breath short, "I owe money. Best I could do is...hell, I don't know...maybe go into Hays and try and make a deal with the bank."

"Think they'll understand?" Orson asked honestly.

"Hell no," Thomas scoffed. He placed his hands on his hips, looking down at the charred ground as if it gave some clarity, "But a man's always gotta face what's comin'. I'll find a way through it...I have to, for Lilly's sake anyway."

Before the old man even finished speaking, he turned and began to walk back to his home. He knew he had more work to do, though his body shook from exhausted beyond any measure. His feet shuffled as he moved, aching from being on them for so long. Orson watched him. He watched the pain and anguish hover over him like a cloud that blended with the darkness of the night. The crickets chirped and sang. A coyote howled somewhere on the plains and others howled with it. He began to hum a song to himself, one he didn't know the words to but one that he heard somewhere out on the plains. He only began shoveling once Thomas disappeared in the darkness of the doorway.

Chapter XX

Nothing to Forgive

1874

Months passed since the Comanche attack. The Tanner Party moved on silently through the fruitful plains of Kansas, then Nebraska, up into Dakota Territory. All that land they covered, all the bison they killed, they never found what they searched for. They moved mostly by night, hunting what little they wanted during the day. They skinned to eat and make blankets from hides. The rest rotted under the winter sun that lingered shorter each day. They kept to the stars, but Orson often felt they used the blackness between them for guidance, for they found nothing of worth in the world, found nothing of value. They hardly spoke to one another unless they argued. They became hollow shells of what they were, for their souls vacated some time ago, fleeing from the monstrosity of the plainsman. He wondered most nights if he were dead somewhere, if they all were, and if they too rotted in the winter.

Dakota was colder than he thought it would be. He'd never

been so far north before. He saw some snow in his past, but nothing near as much as the plethora that accented every tree, hill, and field in the territory. The party spent Christmas in a silent circle, shivering near a fire, peppered in the white flakes that fell from the weeping heavens. Come the New Year of '74, they held a quick celebration, traveling to gather whiskey from a trader's post. They drank it the morning of, and lost sight of any hunt they wanted to do that day. They slept instead, then carried on not long after.

It was two weeks past New Year's when Orson saw his first white bison. He never heard of such a thing. Yet, as he stared upon the magnificent white buffalo, he felt such an admiration for its glowing white fur. Snow caked to its sides, gathered around the base of its horns. He wondered if it was the only one, wondered if it could produce offspring so unique. He hoped it couldn't for its blue eyes looked into his and he felt connected to its majesty. A rifle shot cracked the air. Jack hollered out. The bison fell, and the immaculate white turned crimson, the snow scarlet, and the beast laid dead and alone out on that snow swept territorial field.

Jack led his hunters down from the dead tree line. He beamed with such excitement as he towered over the dead creature. He changed since winter began, not just from within his soul, but in his appearance. His eye healed, but he still wore a faded white bandage that hung over it. It protected nothing, hid nothing, for as the wind blew, it flapped wildly, revealing the milky white eye and the scars around it. His face grew older. The wrinkles on his forehead became great canyons. Those around his eyes stretched back. He became gaunt too, with sunken cheeks, and wandered the earth as if he were the living dead, so skeletal and sickly in appearance.

He rested his rifle on his knee and said, "Always wanted me one of these."

Orson found it difficult to look at him, something that developed sometime before the New Year. He shifted his gaze, watching as a small pack of bison, five to six, moved gently over the snow swept horizon. He nodded to them, seeing their worth for they possessed good clean pelts and plenty of meat, something they could sell. He asked, "What about them?"

Jack removed his knife from his holster. It glistened in the pale white of the landscape. He looked off to the moseying herd. He spat, the spit hissing and melting the snow it touched, as he said, "Too far off right now. We'll skin and eat this one, go after the others in the morning."

"We can get them now," Bill argued, bundling his chin under his scarf as if ashamed by the comment. "They may not be here come morning."

"Ain't what we's after," Jack replied as he plunged the knife into the gut of the white bison. Such red came from such purity, and Orson could not stand such a sight.

"And what is we after?" Bill pressed, his mouth fully hidden behind the wool scarf.

Jack said nothing. He heard his companion. He didn't care. The wind whipped between the group as they all began to watch Jack soil that white hide with red as he began to carve away underneath the flesh. Orson first looked to Charlie, who stared down at Jack, lost in a trance as he'd been for some time. It was then he felt Bill's look fall upon him, so heavy, so piercing. He glanced to the burly man who continued to keep his mouth hidden. The whites of his eyes became highlighted by the snow as he stared at Orson so deeply. Orson knew what he wanted to say, what they all wanted to say. It would never be said, and so he just watched Jack revel in what victory he found in Dakota.

When the night fell quickly, the men set camp not far from their killing grounds. They sat under a thicket of trees. The light of their fire could be seen for miles off, which would usually be a danger, but they cared not. Death was imminent, Jack told them sometime after the Indian attack. They all needed to embrace such a thing. Throwing precaution to the wind, they welcomed whatever wished to harm them with open arms. Yet, nothing came to their bait, and Orson began to wonder if they were so undesirable that not even death would have them.

They ate the cooked flesh of the white bison. It tasted no different, something that Orson thought odd, for he thought it something magical, something otherworldly, but that too was just a thought and not real. He found shame in it as he chewed his food, as he watched Jack chew with his open mouth. It was no different, he tried to reason to himself. It was nothing but an illusion, a different pelt.

Jack grabbed the white bison pelt that he slung over his shoulder earlier that night, bringing it down over his chest, and wiped his hands with it. He smacked his food, licked his fingers, and said, "Ain't seen 'em since we been up here."

Charlie spoke up, one of the few times he ever tried, "Think it's still 'round?"

Parker hopped in on the conversation, he too smacking his food, "'course it's still 'round, Lil Lamb."

Bill became bold, so worn over the cold, "I say we cut our loses, head south."

"What's south?" Jack asked, not looking up from the flames before him.

"Bison," Bill scoffed. "Same amount as up here, from what we've seen. We go back—"

"To what?" Jack's eyes shifted up to Bill as he interrupted, "Dodge? Ain't that what you been trying to do since you done left me?"

Bill shook his head, not wanting to meet Tanner's eyes. He knew better than to argue, but still pled his case, "I wasn't the only one to do so, Jack."

The other men glanced to Bill, unfavorable of his words about them. Jack long forgot that they all left him with the Swedes, all of them but Bill. At least, that is how he told the story.

Jack corrected the timeline in his head, fitting with how he felt, how he viewed their situation, "You was the only one wantin' to go back to Dodge, last I 'member."

"Jack," Bill began, "it's been months. Ain't no point in stayin' up here. We trackin' a herd that don't exist."

Parker chimed in, as if it made a difference, "Heard it down in Indian Territory."

Jack shifted his eyes to Parker. They appeared angry, but he gave a nod of affirmation to the hunter.

Bill continued, "Yeah, we heard somethin' in Indian Territory. Didn't sound like no three-day herd."

Jack looked around at all the faces huddled near the campfire. He watched as the orange glow danced across their faces and he spoke to them as if he were a prophet, "Herd that got Timmy..."

The men bowed their heads, as if he said something sacred.

Jack finished, staring at Bill, "That was big..."

Bill rose his head, speaking earnestly, "Not three days big, Jack. I'm sorry but I'll be the first one to say it, we wastin' our time up here."

Jack looked around to his followers. He studied each of them with his thin pupils. They shifted silently between the men. He chewed loudly, "First one?"

The men stared back at Tanner, expecting some sort of lashing. He didn't. He just chewed, digging meat from between his teeth with his tongue. Their leader sucked his teeth, then bit into another chunk of cooked flesh. He stared down Chambers, "Hell Bill, you're the only one sayin' it. You're the only one that's ever said we should go back, and you been sayin' it for a long time now."

"Months, really," Parker chimed in.

"Well then," Bill spat into the flames, "I'm the only one man enough to."

"Man enough to tuck tail and run," Jack chuckled to himself. "While I'm lyin' in the dirt, eye cut to shit, almost scalped...you tucked tail and ran."

"I came back!" Bill shouted. "We all left, and we all came back, Jack!"

Jack glanced to his other followers, then back to Bill. He smirked, disregarding everything the burly man said, "And you wantin' to cut and run again. Where we gon' go, Bill?"

"Anywhere! There's places out there, Jack! I don't know what we're doin'!" Bill kneeled forward over the flames. The orange tongues licked up at his dangling beard as his jaw lowered as he shouted.

Jack's brow arched and crumpled as he looked to the raging Bill. The leader stood, his makeshift blood-stained cloak fluttering in the wind. He did not yell or scream, as the men expected. Instead, he lowered his voice calmly, as if laying out an elaborate plan, though there were no details to be had. His voice sounded almost as if a whisper beneath the winds as he said, "We're close.

We carry on as we have been, Bill. We ain't goin' to Dodge. We ain't givin' up. Shit, we too far now. We lost Timmy for this. I lost my eye for this. We ain't leavin'."

The men all looked up to him in amazement as the wind ripped through their camp. Snow dusted the face of their leader and he wiped his growing beard clean of it with the back of his sleeve. He spat into the flames and adjusted his hat as it bent to nature's will. He shook his head as he looked down on all of them, and they looked up to him. He muttered something sour under his breath but did not bother to clarify. He turned his back and wandered off into the darkness, off towards the wagon where he would drink and be alone with his thoughts.

The men sat silently after Tanner left their presence. He was far from earshot, especially with the wind. Yet, each man sat, pondering their existence and why they were there. Though Tanner spoke to all of them, they each felt he spoke directly to them. No one else in the world mattered. In their silence, they stared into the flames, waiting for some holy vision to guide them through the dark. It never came, only the blackness and shadows cast by the dancing orange tongues. It was Bill who broke their silence first, "Parker...you gotta talk sense into him."

Parker's eyes stayed fixated on the flames, "I'm ridin' on this one, Bill. I agree with Jack."

"Why?" Bill leaned into his companion. He slapped him across the chest with the back of his hand, continuing, "You know you's full of it. Yer the only one he's listenin' to."

Parker's eyes shifted to Orson and Charlie. He scoffed, "For all the right reasons."

"You left 'em too…" Bill said between gritted teeth, leaning in closer to the second in command.

"I was gon' come back for him," Parker said. He then pointed to Orson with his thumb, "Ain't that right? Hell, Newkirk was gon' come back for 'em too."

"But you didn't," Bill argued.

Parker ran his hands through his long greasy hair, "Waited around a lot more than you did. You and that Lil Lamb..."

Charlie ignored the comment, a new tactic he picked up that failed on more than one occasion. He tried to deflect any negativity, any harshness among the group, trying to find some way to mediate as he said, "Maybe that herd moved south."

Parker raised an eyebrow. His jaw hung slacked as he shook his head as if Charlie said one of the dumbest things he ever heard, "To wha'? Get chewed up and spit out by the railroad? Hell no. They's up here."

Charlie shrugged, looking around into the night as if it held some sort of response. All he came back with was, "It's cold up here."

"Said the Lil Lamb," Parker mocked. His head waved side to side as if it were wheat in a southern wind as his voice rose and he stared down Charlie, "You c'ain't hack it, can you? Just go on then, boy."

Orson asked a ridiculous question, trying to pull Charlie from the depths of Parker's stare, "How many miles is three days?"

Parker thought for a second, trying to come up with a legitimate figure. He replied, "A lot."

"Why ain't we seen it then?" Orson asked earnestly. He could see Parker's face sink with frustration and so Orson tried to clarify, "I mean...not even from afar have we seen it."

"Oh," Parker began nodding his head and closing his eyes as if they hid him from the watchful harsh gazes of his companions, "Newkirk's doubtin' too..."

The second in command stood, brushing the snow and dirt from his pants. He shook his head, cussing under his breath. The light of the flames accented his fine points, creating deep cavernous craters on his sunken cheeks. He spat towards the flames, though it appeared to be aimed at Bill. He said, "Y'all forget that Jack's in charge. What he says goes. There ain't no question about goin' back to Dodge. There ain't no question of whether that herd went south or if we seen't it. Jack says we stayin', we stayin'."

Bill moved back, crossing his legs and hanging his head towards the flames, as if he wanted them to consume him. Parker stared down on him. He cared not if the burly man looked up when he spoke. He found some power in it all as he told Chambers, "We all might'a left him to save our skins, but we ain't leavin' him again. He done a lot for us. He's kept us fed, kept us alive. Ain't nothin' in Dodge. Ain't nothin' South. He's hard on you 'cuz you left 'em and you ain't never really come back, Bill."

With that last line, Bill's gaze looked up with such fury. He came back, at least he believed he did. Things were different, they'd been different since Masters fell, since the Comanche came, since they picked up Orson and Charlie, since they lost Ol' Ben. Things were always evolving and changing and that meant little to the fact that they chased ghosts across the empty waste. He wanted to tell Parker such. He wanted to give the thin gaunt man a piece of his mind. Though, when he looked up, Parker staggered off into the darkness, off to wherever Jack lingered.

The three remaining around the camp stayed silent. Bill turned his back to the shadows, to wherever Parker wandered off to. He rested his chin on his fist, lost to the flames as the boys were. He expected to be told what to do, but he didn't like what he heard. He wanted out, wanted somewhere to go. He lost hope somewhere out on those plains and needed some place where he could find it again. He whispered to Charlie and Orson, "I hope y'all can forgive me."

"Ain't no one goin' be mad about it," Charlie responded, as if he knew something that Newkirk didn't.

Orson stayed quiet, watching the two men speak with only soft glances for a moment.

Bill fumbled with a small twig in his hand, running his thumb over the rough wood. He snapped it, flinging the discarded end into the flames. He watched it become engulfed, then took smaller pieces from the fracture, then began to toss them into the swaying orange as well. The flames reflected in his eyes as he stared blankly ahead.

"Jack will…Parker too…" Bill said, then his eyes shifted upward, staring at Orson. "And what about you Newkirk?"

Orson felt he knew what the man spoke of. Even if he wasn't sure, if it went against Tanner's wishes, he knew the leader would be more than upset. Parker would blindly follow Jack off a cliff if asked. He told Bill as such, "Whatever it is, they ain't gon' be happy."

"I wasn't askin' 'bout them," Bill said, still staring into the soul of the young man. He took the fractured twig in his hand, pointing it to Newkirk. He asked sternly, "But what about you? I won't do it if neither of you is willin' to forgive."

It was then that Orson knew. His heart sank at the thought. He wanted to express how foolish it would be but knew that Bill would not listen. He saw it in his eyes. He was dead set on it.

Orson opened to speak, yet Charlie spoke for him, "Ain't nothin' to forgive, Bill. Right, Orson?"

Bill's eyes did not look to Charlie. He stayed fixated on Orson, as if he needed the young man's approval, some form of validation for whatever he chose to do. Orson didn't know if he could give it, partially because he could not bear to think of such a thing. He held his tongue under the man's gaze.

"Ain't nothin' left to be said then," Bill murmured, throwing the last of the twig into the flames. It crackled and hissed as it became consumed by the dying fire. The red glow weakened. The shadows moved like shallow breaths across the men's faces. They stayed quiet, for Bill was right. Everything had been said at some point or another. They needed no more validation from each other. Orson stared off into the dark, wondering where Jack and Parker lingered in the shadows and if he too should join them.

The light snowfall moved between the trees gracefully. He found some peace in that, though the dark felt so tremendously overwhelming. He heard twigs snapping, branches moving, snow crumpling. Something lingered and he feared it Jack, though it could've been anything, maybe a midnight predator or perhaps a coyote.

Orson shivered all throughout the night once the men took their places atop pelts strewn in far distances from one another. They'd have kept warm had they stayed together, but like all other sense of family that Orson ever knew, they dared not be close to one another. The young man used a small bag of flour as a pillow. It was better than resting his growing hair atop the snow dusted pelt he laid on. He used another skin to cover himself. He buried himself beneath both, leaving only a small pocket between the dried hides to breathe through. Each night he cried beneath those hides, and every morning he peeled them away, as if reborn in the presence of Tanner.

He cried not that night, and come morning, Tanner ripped away the top hide blanket and stared down on the boy as he stirred from his slumber. Orson looked up to his leader, rubbing the tiredness from the purple bags under his eyes. His hot breath turned to steam in the cold morning air. Tanner kept his arms crossed, tucked under the long bloody white pelt that hung over his shoulders. He asked, nostrils flaring in anger, "Where is he?"

"What?"

"Where is he?" Tanner asked again, kneeling before the young Orson, as if he held all the answers of the world and he were praying to him.

"Who?"

"You know who," Tanner said with a nod. He leaned in close to the boy as he laid on the buffalo hide, the look of confusion dared not daunt Jack. He then screamed as he quickly stood, "You know damn well who! Bill! Where is he?"

Orson sat up good and straight, looking out around the camp. Parker stood not far off. His arms were crossed as he looked on, watching Jack's confrontation. Charlie too sat on his bed of hides. His legs were crossed as he looked out over the open fields in the distance. He cared not for the squabble. Newkirk didn't see Bill, something that he wasn't surprised about when he truly thought about it. He spoke quickly to Tanner who fumed over him, "I ain't sure."

"You ain't sure," Jack mocked. "The Lamb ain't sure! Hell,

Parker ain't sure! Yet, Bill is gone!"

Orson looked for any way to calm the man down. He knew it not to be true, but he stated, "Maybe he is comin' back."

"He took my horse!" Jack continued to scream. He wandered around the camp, arms thrown out, as he kicked whatever he could find resting on the ground, "He took my damn saddle!"

Jack then moved towards the wagon, resting his head against it for a moment. He made strange guttural sounds as he raged from within. The lone horse that remained kicked its hooves in the dirt as Jack stood nearby, nervous as if he were a predator.

Orson stood, asking earnestly, "That all he took?"

"That all?" Jack's eyes shifted towards the boy, yet his head stayed in place resting against the wagon as if nailed to it. He then sprang to life, screaming and screeching in such anger as he barreled towards the boy waving his hands wildly like some mad man, "That all?! Yeah, Newkirk! That's all! That and the fact he abandoned us!"

Parker chimed in as he examined the supplies resting near the wagon, "He took a rifle too, boss."

"Shut your fuckin' mouth, Parker!" Jack hollered. "Ain't no one talkin' to you right now!"

Parker hung his head, "Sorry."

Jack stood in the center of the three. He crossed his arms, huffing to himself. He tried to lower his voice but couldn't. He still shouted, though not as loud, "That fat sack'a shit left and ain't none of you seen it? Heard nothin'? Y'all let him go?"

"None of us knew, Jack," came Charlie's voice. He still stared off across the empty snow-covered fields, daydreaming of something.

"I doubt that," Jack said, pacing in small semicircles. He walked one way, biting the gritty dirt beneath his thumb nail, then walking the other as his eyes darted back and forth, shuffling through every thought that ran across his mind. His voice finally seemed calm, "The three of ya didn't hear my horse startled? Ride? Nothin'?"

Orson and Parker shared a glance. The second in command's eyes told the young hunter to stay quiet, and so he did.

Though, Charlie turned his head away from the open fields, no longer lost to whatever possessed his mind. His eyes studied Jack. His voice sounded so secure for once, so honest, no longer trying to impress, "You ain't hear it neither."

Jack's eyes grew wide. His gait turned almost animalistic as he lunged across the campsite towards the young boy. He stood over him, smacking the boy across the head with the back of his hand, "So it's my fault then, is it?"

Charlie buried his head in his arms, all dignity and self-worth vacated him once again. He muttered, "I ain't sayin' that!"

Tanner grabbed ahold of the boy's arm, pulling him upward to stand before him. He got close to the exposed ear of the young man that could not be hidden beneath his other arm like the rest of his face. Jack whispered softly, "What is you sayin' then?"

The boy lowered his arm, peering out to his leader. Their eyes met. He studied the rage that lingered deep within Tanner's pupils. He examined the pain and the confusion. In that low morning light, Charlie swore he saw tears welling up within those eyes, and it was then that he felt some connection at long last to his leader. It was short lived, for Tanner smacked the boy again, this time on his ear with the open palm of his hand.

Charlie became defensive, realizing the beating would not stop if he kept speaking. It was fruitless, and so he said, "Nothin'...I ain't sayin' nothin'."

Tanner grabbed ahold of the boy's ear, screaming into it, "And you ain't say nothin' last night when he left!"

With that, the leader struck Charlie one more time with the back of his hand. It connected right to the young man's cheek. He tried to block it, but Tanner was too fast, too knowledgeable about the way to properly hit someone with their guard up. When the flesh connected, the bones collided and a crack echoed across the plains, Charlie fell to the ground. Tanner turned his back, storming off across the camp, muttering, "Fuckin' worthless boy..."

Parker watched as Tanner moved away. He took one look at Charlie, his eyes gave confirmation to Jack's statement with one lid slightly closing, and the disappointment seeped from around the purple tired edges. He stepped away from the wagon, chasing after Tanner. He shouted all sorts of things, mostly those that belittled

Charlie, or that confirmed that Bill was nothing more than a snake.

Orson cared not to listen. Instead, he looked out across those empty snowy plains the way that Charlie did. He wondered where Bill went. He wondered how far he got or if he ever wondered if he should turn back. Charlie's whimpers became drowned out by the whipping winds and by the great dreams Orson saw of Bill's escape, if that is what he wanted to call it. He thought long on it, wondering if he too could do such a thing. Once Charlie's whimpers were all but gone, and nothing but the silence of snow and the morning winds surrounded Orson, did he think better of that.

The wagon moved slowly through the snow, leaving a thick trail across the plains. It felt as if they wandered in a straight line, but upon looking out the back, Orson knew they went in large circles across the open fields. So many tracks there were and nothing else seemed to be around but them, and that is all he paid attention to.

The grey skies overhead cast such an ominous darkness overtop the wagon. Tanner sat in the driver's box next to Parker, who held the reins tightly in his gloved hands. Their breath were thick bursts of fog as they stewed and brewed with such frustration. Nobody spoke since they left their previous camp and would not speak until dinner that evening. Charlie would not move from the back of the wagon either. He just laid near the tanned blankets, staring up at the vast grey nothingness overhead. He was alone then, or so he felt. He and Orson held no power, and Bill, the only one who ever thought of turning back for him, left without him. He didn't know how to feel about that, or anything else for that matter. So, he chose not to feel anything at all.

It would be another day before they found a small herd of bison. The creatures grazed under a blue sky. No snow fell. It appeared serene, majestic. Orson wished he possessed some sort of artistic ability to capture that moment in time, for he felt envious of the beasts. That faded with the first gunshot from Tanner's rifle and a bison dropped. The men abandoned all they knew and began blasting away. The rifles felt warm in their hands. The black powder brought relief to their cold faces as it sparked and caked to their white flesh. Five black and brown carcasses tainted the snow before the others began to run in a frenzied panic. Tanner stepped forward reloading a cartridge into the breech. He fired and walked. He did not aim at the retreaters. The others followed suit, firing away at the hip, grazing a few, striking others with wounds that would not kill but maim. And they kept firing, long after the remainder disappeared over the low hills of Dakota.

Tanner slung his rifle over his shoulder. The men mimicked his motion. He stood. The white hide over his upper torso fluttered in the wind, soiled by the black powder and dried blood. The blood-stained plains brought no sense of happiness to the man. He looked towards his prizes in the past with such great admiration, yet that was then. He saw nothing but corpses on the plains. He spat, "Skin 'em if you want to. I don't really give a damn."

And with that, Tanner turned his back, marching away from the corpses, back towards the wagon. The three watched him stagger across the open field. He kept his head low, holding the crown of his hat down. His legs sank deep into the snow and he dared not lift them all the way out. Instead, he barreled through the wall of white as if it were no obstacle at all. It was when Tanner was out of earshot and when a big gust of cold air cut through the three that stood among the dead that Charlie asked, "The hell is that all about?"

"He mad, Lil' Lamb," Parker told him, watching his leader climb aboard the wagon's driver box and stare out the opposite way they came, not wanting to look to his crew and their prizes. Parker moved to a carcass and plunged his knife into the stomach of the still beast, "Now, shut the hell up and start skinnin' 'em or I will."

The men worked tirelessly for some time, skinning what they wanted. Parker cut the horns free from two of the bison. He left them in the snow and had not made up his mind of whether or not he truly wanted them. Orson began to finish the removal of the hide from the kill that he claimed. Charlie worked slowly on his, trying to be as accurate as possible with his blade. He found comfort in the warm guts beneath his knees as he skinned away.

Parker scoffed as he watched the young Charlie work away,

"You's lucky, Lil Lamb. Didn't look like you hit shit. Good thing Jack don't want nothin'."

Charlie did not look up from his work. He stayed fixated on his knife beneath the skin as he slid it from side to side, severing any tether of the pelt from the beast. He felt anger take hold of his heart, though he fixated on the blade, on the warmth of the blood of the beast. He kept his voice calm, trying to deflect any rising tension from Parker, "I hit somethin'."

"A fuckin' barn," Parker joked, "'bout'a mile away."

Charlie's eyes shifted to Parker for half a second. He saw the scrawny second in command looking down on his kill, the third that he claimed and skinned. He did not look to Charlie as he openly mocked him. Charlie thought him a coward for doing so. He would not say it, for he found power in the thought alone.

Orson flipped the skin away from his kill. He laid it flat atop the red snow. His eyes danced over the pink and white corpse before him. Steam rose from the still beast. He cared no longer to look upon it, and in doing so, turned his head out towards the wagon. There, he saw Tanner with his arms crossed, hunched forward, staring back. Their eyes met across that great distance, that much Orson knew. He wondered what Jack felt, that sense of abandonment. He wondered if his father ever felt the same when he ran from that small farm he called home at one point. He doubted it, and as he and Jack stared upon each other, he knew that Tanner held some great care for each of them, though he knew not how to express such feelings.

"Bet Bill is happy he done left," Parker said wiping his nose with the sleeve of his buckskin coat. He crossed his arms as he stabbed his knife into the dead creature before him. He leaned his body forward, resting, as he exhaled deep puffs of fog. He too stared at Jack as he said, "I imagine Jack thought each of these boys was that ol' lump a shit."

Orson looked away from his leader, moving over to one of the unsullied corpses that lay cold atop the soiled snow. He plunged his knife into the beast, claiming that one for himself. There was no clear way to tell, but he wanted to work, for being left with the thoughts of Jack or Bill or his father or his mother or whatever else cursed his tired mind felt worse than gutting another dead animal. He still felt Jack's gaze on him, colder than the winds across the open plains. He tried to ignore it, focus on his work, for that is all he had left.

Tanner crashed into a drunken slumber early that night. He covered himself in his white bison pelt as he rested his head against a rolled hide, one that Charlie collected earlier that day. Parker too slept, resting against a lone tree on the far end of the camp. A bottle of bourbon sat gripped in his thin red fingers, left exposed as his gloves sat on his lap.

The two young men sat near the fire that began to fatigue. They watched their sleeping companions for too long, wondering if their safety was in jeopardy for whatever they wished to talk about. It wasn't until Tanner began snoring and

Parker drooled coldly onto himself that Orson turned to Charlie, whose face danced with the shadows of the night, whose hair sat peppered with a light frost, and asked, "He say anythin' to you?"

Charlie looked back. Orson sat mostly hidden by the darkness around them. The dying fire did nothing to pull him from the shadows. He thought on Bill for a second, missing a person who he deemed a friend, and told Orson, "Woke me up before he left. Said bye. Asked if I wanted to go."

"Should've," Orson responded honestly and without thought. He looked to Tanner as he said it, wondering if the treacherous comment would be enough to stir him.

However, Charlie did not take it the way Orson implied. He was strong, he knew it, but Orson did not, Jack did not, and Parker certainly did not. It made his stomach ache, for he could hack it, he proved that much. He scooted closer to Orson in the shadows and asked, "He tell you too?"

"Said nothin' to me."

"Yeah," Charlie reasoned, "you's good with Jack and Parker though."

"So are you," Orson didn't see it that way. He figured if they stayed, they were all good.

Charlie scoffed, "'Lil Lamb'...they don't even know my name."

Orson watched as Charlie stared into the dying flames. He muttered a few words under his breath, something drowned out by the nightly winds. He asked the young Charlie a question in hindsight that he thought as stupid, yet he only wanted to press for honesty, "It bother you?"

"Why wouldn't it?" Charlie asked, tearing his eyes away from the majestic death of the flames to look at his companion. "I killed that calf, same as you. I killed bison. They still hate me."

He did not think of it when he responded. Had he, he probably would've said nothing at all, but for some reason, Orson pled their case as if he were a part of Jack, a part of Parker, "They don't hate you."

"They both do. They act like I don't exist. They act like I ain't no man cuz I ain't a type a way."

"Wha'chu mean 'type of way'?"

"You know it," Charlie said, bundling himself deeper into his coat. He crossed his arms, snuggling his chin down into his scarf as he stared back at the low swaying orange, "Just forget it, alright?"

"You don't like the work," Orson reasoned, as if it made a difference in the young man's feelings.

"You don't neither. I can see it in your eyes."

"It's work," Orson said bluntly. He did not stop staring at Charlie who refused to look back at him. He regurgitated what he heard from Jack, what he told himself since he took up with them, "It can pay, honestly."

Charlie spat into the flames, nestling his knuckles deeper under his armpits, "And we ain't gettin' paid."

Orson felt frustrated by Charlie's bluntness, as if it were a dig at him, a dig at their work, their crew. He did the same work as he, and it felt as if Charlie saw any of it as worthwhile, something that Orson wondered from time to time. He felt as if he argued with himself, "Why don't you leave then? You still got somethin' to prove?"

"Don't really know why," Charlie said. His eyes shifted, staring off into the dark, staring off to where Jack slumbered. He thought of something, what, Orson did not know. His eyes then darted towards the sleeping Parker, who stirred slightly, then laid drunkenly still. Charlie whispered, only for himself to hear, yet Orson heard it clear as day, "I c'ain't take much more of this."

The bitter cold seeped into their bones. Orson tried to comfort, "You ain't gon' freeze to death."

Charlie's eyes studied the drunken Parker. Snow fell from the overhead branches, lightly peppering the boy as he stared coldly at his rival. He then turned his gaze back towards the flames, which had become smoldering embers that laid deep within charred wood. He spoke normal, as if confident again, "I ain't talkin' 'bout the cold."

As the embers burned out, the two sat quietly in the darkness as it consumed them. Something stalked deep in the dark. The snow split quietly under its footsteps. The two boys did not fear, for they saw death and carried it in their wake. It would be a welcome at their camp for once, they both felt. And as they both thought on it, a coyote called somewhere in the outer dark.

Chapter XXI
The Lil' Lamb
1874

By dawn, the Tanner Party moved on again. Their wagon rolled through the shallow snow that began melting in the warm overhanging sun. The dense white became crushed under the large wooden wheels of the wagon, and Orson sat with his feet dangling out the back, watching as his boots scraped the top of the snowy earth. Parker kept himself at the reins, moving the wagon forward across the open fields. However, Charlie sat next to him in the driver's box. They did not speak. They did not look at each other. The coldness between the two could not be warmed by the morning sun, and the two looked incredibly uncomfortable being so near.

Tanner sat next to Orson, he too dangling his feet out the back of the wagon. They shared a cigarette together, one that Jack rolled sometime that morning. They did not speak for a long while, enjoying the fleeting snow, the orange and purple haze of the sunrise, the coldness of the breeze. Orson found peace in that. Peace from what, he still didn't know. It was Tanner who broke the silence as he handed the cigarette to Orson, "You doubt all this too?"

"Don't really know what you mean," Orson said, puffing lightly on the cigarette.

Tanner felt a sense of dishonesty in him, though with past experience he told himself it couldn't be true. He explained, "The herd. The cold. Me. All of this. You ain't goin' to leave me like Bill did, are ya?"

Orson handed Jack the cigarette, the grey ribbons of smoke danced around his fingers, "Don't plan on it."

His leader placed the half-burnt cigarette in his mouth, inhaling deeply, then exhaling. His saliva wrapped around and soaked the open end as it dangled from his lips, "You like it out here?"

"Not really," Orson said bluntly, not looking to Jack as he spoke. "But it's work and you've taken care of me this far."

"That I have," Jack smiled, then placed his right hand on Orson's shoulder. He handed the cigarette off with his left. He reached into his coat, removing his flask. He started early, as usual, and took a heavy-handed sip, "Don't forget that. I've looked after all of you like you were my own boys."

Orson felt awkward under the attempted sentimental conversation from his boss. He spoke honestly again, trying to change the subject, "I'm sorry about Bill."

"Me too," said Jack quickly, flicking the finished cigarette into the snow in their wake. "He can gamble and whore himself into an early grave for all I give a damn."

"Y'all was close," Orson stated, matter of fact. He felt awkward doing so. He had nothing else to say, so he stated the obvious.

"We was," Jack thought on that, "yeah...we was. Years ago, for sure. Somethin' changed in him though. Don't know what it was."

Orson thought of a million things to say, all of them the truth, yet all of them wrong in the eyes of Jack. He learned by that point to hold his mouth before speaking, and he learned that any small thing, any taste of insurrection, and Jack would cast him out. He held his tongue.

Jack continued, "Look...if you ever gon' leave, you need to tell me like a man. Don't run off in the night like some coward who don't have a sack between their legs. If you respect a man, you tell them goodbye."

"Alright," Orson nodded. "I ain't plannin' on it though."

He held some truth in that, for he saw himself with Tanner for as long as he would have him.

"Good," Jack smirked, removing his hand from the boy's shoulder. "I like havin' you around. You're good at what you do."

And Orson felt good about that, forgetting all else.

Jack reached into his coat, removing his flask. He took another heavy sip, then handed it to the boy, who took it without question. The leader watched as the boy took a swig, heavy handed as he learned from observation. He did not grimace or strain his throat in pain like he did upon his first taste of the brown liquor. Jack smiled as he watched Newkirk wipe the dribble away from his mouth. He felt proud of the kid, as if he were his own.

When they came upon another small herd, the crew opened fire like mad men. Jack never gave a signal and not a word flew from his quivering cold lips as he began blasting away at the head of twenty or thirty. The smoke from their rifles engulfed them in a thick steamy fog. Four beasts dropped quickly. The men's vision became obscured by the gunpowder, but it did not stop them. They kept firing, kept creating such a hellish cloud above the snow-covered earth. Their horse attached to their wagon bucked and screamed as it too became enveloped in the plume.

They slowed their shooting and the air began to thin. It was only when the fog rolled on that the men emerged, covered in soot and blackness and grime and grease. Fifteen dead bison laid before them. Tanner smiled to each of his boys and he moved among the dead, grinning wildly as if the souls of the beasts rejuvenated his own. The thunder of the living remainder vibrated the ground beneath the men's feet. The smoke and fog swayed and flowed inward towards itself as it dispersed to the south on the coattails of the wind. Blood seeped from each beast, soiling the earth and their boots as they moved to begin skinning.

The men took their time, enjoying the craft of their work, skinning slowly and methodically to not ruin any of their prized pelts, of which they seemed to no longer value. It was the work itself they valued, that of which they had not been paid for in months. Orson wondered as he skinned his beast if they would leave these pelts somewhere along the way, like they'd done with others. He figured it would be so, but as he carved away at the dead creature, he found some sense of worth, though he knew it fruitless.

"'Ay, Jack," Parker asked as he began to tear away the flesh from his beast, "how many you get?"

Tanner did not look up, but he spoke assertively, "Don't know. Maybe four. Could'a been five."

"You, Newkirk?" Parker asked.

"I got four," he said as he skinned. He didn't know if it was the truth. It was hard to tell through the thick cloud they created and shot through. He shot at four, whether he hit them was an entirely different story.

"You sure?"

"Saw 'em buckle through the smoke," he replied to the inquisitive Parker. That was true, though he did not know if they were his rounds. He assumed so, and that was enough for him.

"I got five," Parker gloated.

"So what?" Orson deflected, as if Parker took a jab at him

for claiming more.

Parker stood, moving over to the bison Charlie carved away at. He stood before him, presenting the boy to Orson and Jack as they continued their work, "That means Lil' Lamb here only got one, maybe. Maybe he got none at all."

Orson looked across the dead bison in the field. He counted them on his fingers. Five for Jack, four for him, and five for Parker. He thought on the numbers for a second, but before he concluded, he heard Parker ask the young Charlie, "Well, wha'chu got to say?"

Charlie did not look up. He continued with his skinning, but spoke firmly, "Nothin' to the likes a' you."

Parker placed his foot atop Charlie's claimed beast. He rested his left forearm atop his knee as he leaned in. His face, whipped by the cold, became beet red and Orson swore he saw steam rise from the man as he spat when he hollered, "The hell did you say to me? You ain't kill shit and here you is, skinnin' one like its yers to claim."

"I got one," said Charlie, still continuing with his skinning, not falling into Parker's allegations.

"How many shots you fire?" Parker pressed.

"Don't know," Charlie shrugged. "Hard to tell when we ain't doin' what we was taught."

When the last word left Charlie's mouth, Tanner stabbed his knife into the side of his beast. He stood, towering over his crew. He lingered far away, but his gaze was enough to bring Charlie's eyes upward to meet his leader. Jack raised an eyebrow. His eyes danced with the fog of brown liquor. He spat, "Wha'chu say, boy?"

Parker chuckled, looking down on the boy, "Yeah, wha'chu say?"

Charlie let out a deep sigh. He took his glistening red knife, stabbing into the pink flesh of the half-skinned carcass before him. He wiped his bloody hands on his pants as he stood, facing the two men that seethed with anger. He said, so confident and proud, "We ain't goin' bout this right. How am I supposed to know how many I get? How many I hit?"

"You count, you dipshit," Parker scoffed, removing his foot from the dead animal. He straightened his back, rolling his sleeves, as if ready to fight the boy.

"Maybe I shot yours," Charlie said, turning his head to look at Parker and Parker alone. "Maybe I shot one of Jack's. Hell, I could'a shot one of Orson's."

"Let's get one thing straight," Jack said, moving across the field towards Charlie. He stood over him, looking down onto the boy. He left no gap between them as he spoke softly, "What I say goes. What I say is right. I say we gun 'em down quickly, we do it. Got it?"

Charlie replied just as soft, looking down to the ground, that confidence faded, "Got it…"

Jack sucked his teeth as he studied the defeated posture of the boy. He cared not. He proved his point, and that was all he wanted. He turned away, heading back to his kill to finish his job. The young boy's eyes shifted upward, watching the leader walk off. Yet, they soon beamed to Parker with such rage. Parker stared back, a smirk lifting his sunken gaunt cheeks. The two glared at one another, all their frustration, hatred, seething into the air, though unseen, thicker than the gunpowder fog the crew created earlier.

It appeared a stalemate, neither speaking, neither of the men wanting to look away. It became a battle of the wills, but Charlie shook his head, rolled his eyes, then knelt down to dig his knife out of the carcass. As soon as his hand gripped the handle and his eyes broke from Parker's, the second in command spat onto the dead bison, "Nuh-uh."

Charlie ignored him, removing the blade from the beast and began to skin away.

Parker placed his foot atop the bison again, "I'm claimin' it."

"Piss off, Nathaniel," Charlie said as he continued to skin.

"Fuck off, Lil' Lamb!" Parker shouted, lifting his leg from the bison and moving around the other side. "It ain't yer kill!"

"Ain't yers neither," Charlie responded, not bothering to look upon him anymore.

Parker, out of words and patience, lifted his boot and with one swift kick, hit Charlie in the ribs as he worked away on the dead animal. Charlie gasped, a deep bellowing from his lungs, as if all air vacated his body. He fell to the ground, tears welling in his eyes. Parker then moved between the dead creature's four legs, as if he were going to finish the job. He reached for his knife, realizing he did not possess it. He looked down at Charlie's to take it, but the boy beat him to it.

Charlie stood, staggering as he did so. His knife sat tightly grasped in his hand. He still wheezed as he stared down Parker. Parker's eyes widened for a fraction of a second, as if he felt nervous, but as he looked on the boy, that all faded. He smirked, "An' wha'chu gon' do, Lil' Lamb?"

Charlie slowed his breathing. His eyes stayed fixated on Parker. He spoke slowly, that confidence returned, "I'm gon' stick this here knife in your throat, is what I'm gon' do."

"Go on then," Parker said, presenting his throat to the boy with a wide grin across his face. "Do it."

Charlie, so sure, so certain that he could do such an act, peered down at his knife. He watched the blood of the bison drip from its sharp edge. He imagined it being Parker's. He wondered if it would feel any different than killing a creature. He thought it would. He thought maybe it would make him feel better, stronger, a master of his own destiny, a true hunter for he could kill anything. He pondered no longer on it, for as he stared at the blade, Parker's fist collided with his cheek. He felt his teeth rattle within his mouth. He heard the haunting grinding of them as he fell to his side, atop the bison carcass. He tightened his fist, as if ready to stab, yet the knife fell from his grip during the hit. He lost hope and laid atop that carcass as Parker leaped on him, flailing wildly with fists that hit Charlie every which way.

Orson could watch no more. Parker's fist pummeled his acquaintance, striking him on the nose, the cheeks, the stomach, and one solid hit struck the boy in the groin which hunched him over and allowed Parker to begin lowering his elbows into Charlie's back. Charlie fell forward as Orson dashed from his position towards Parker. He grabbed ahold of him, locking his arms within his and raising them above his head. He pulled with all his might, tearing the man away from the obviously defeated Charlie. Parker's legs kicked as Orson lifted him upward, stepping back, creating a distance between the two. Parker shouted, "You lucky you's got one friend left, Lil' Lamb!"

Newkirk looked down onto Charlie who laid in the bloody filth and entrails of the beast. Blood dripped from his companion's nose. His eye swelled with such pain and blackness. He staggered forward to grab the knife, as if Orson held Parker to do him a favor. Orson knew the boy's intentions and shouted, "Cut it out!"

Charlie bypassed the knife, startled by Orson's words. He leaped forward though, his fist connecting with Parker's cheek. He then began to strike Parker in the stomach, blow after blow. Orson let go of his hold, not wanting to be a part of such madness. He remembered what Jack told him the day he struck Parker and feared whatever repercussions would come. He stepped away, watching as Parker grabbed hold of the boy and took him to the ground. They struggled and fought with such hatred. A gunshot rang out, echoing across the plains. They stopped.

Jack Tanner stood over his kill, staying at a distance from his men. His rifle laid across his knee, smoking from its barrel. He spat, looking at Charlie, who stood first, "Boy, get back to the wagon."

Charlie wiped away the blood from his nose with his sleeve, "He started it."

"It ain't yer kill," Tanner replied, staring deeply into Charlie's bloodshot and blackening eyes.

"It ain't his neither!" Charlie yelped.

"It's my party," Jack glared. "It's my kill. Now, get on back to the wagon."

Charlie dabbed two fingers at his right eyebrow. Blood began to pour from the small gash. The blood of the beast that coated his hands mixed with his own as he looked down upon his grimy pale fingers. He muttered something to himself, realizing the fight was all for not. He obtained nothing, would never obtain anything at all, not while he lingered within the shadow of Parker, of Orson, and of Tanner. He cursed, looking to Orson as he did so. He stepped away from the tree and began to walk slowly across the snow-swept fields towards the wagon.

Tanner looked to Orson, "It's your kill."

"The hell it is..." Parker spat, sitting atop the carcass that he tried to claim from Charlie.

Jack said nothing to him. He needed not, for his harsh stare pierced the heart of Parker. It was cold, colder than the air that ripped between them. Jack turned, moving slowly towards his unfinished work. Parker studied him for a moment, wondering what would happen if he stayed. He thought of all sorts of things, none of which he particularly cared for. He shot Orson a glance filled with pettiness and growing resentment. It felt no different than Charlie's to Orson. Parker lifted himself and stepped away from the dead animal, Orson's new claim, and spat into the snow. He wiped away what remnant dangled from his chin with his sleeve. He gave Orson a nod, as if he had some say over the matter, "Go on then..."

Parker too went back to work. Orson did not, for a few moments anyway. He stood near that half-skinned bison, watching Charlie sit atop the wagon across that field. It was only fifty yards away, maybe more, maybe less. Yet, in the light snow that began to fall, it appeared miles apart from the crew that worked and the poor boy that sat atop the driver's box. He stared out across the plains, never daring to look back to the Tanner party. He no longer saw himself as one of them, the same as they did not see him as part of them since the beginning. Orson saw that realization from that distance. He felt it. He pitied it.

The infernal glow of the campfire in the night basked over Jack Tanner as he sat with his legs crossed, arms laid atop his knees, as if he were some deity of the plains. He chewed his food with his mouth slightly agape. He stared into the flames and he felt them stare back, as if they were connected, as if they were the same being. Parker sat at his side in a similar fashion. He kept his knees high though, laying across his chest, but he rested his arms atop them and his chin atop his arms. He looked down into the flames, seeing nothing but orange and red, burning timber, smoke, and nothing at all.

It was Orson who sat across from them with a piece of bison meat stabbed to the point of his hunting knife. The flesh sat charred around the edges, and Orson picked at it with loose teeth. He chewed slowly, looking upon the two men across from him, the flames before them. He watched the shadows breath in and out between the three, as if the flames were some living being. He heard Charlie adjust his legs in the dark. He sat away from them, no longer a member of their party in their eyes and in his.

Newkirk peered over his shoulder, off towards the wagon and the boy enveloped in shadow that lingered beneath it. He took the meat from the tip of his knife, holding it in the palm of his hand for a second, letting the warmth bask over his bare palm. He then extended his arm out into the darkness, towards the young boy who he could barely see. He heard stirring, and it was then that Jack's eyes lifted from the flames to study the young Orson. He halted him, saying, "He don't work, he don't eat."

Orson hung his head at the comment, keeping his arm held out into the dark. He closed his eyes, hoping that Charlie would take something, but he felt the cold fingertips of his acquaintance wrap around his fingers, then closed them overtop the meat. He then felt the boy's palms rest against his closed fist and a slight gentle push back towards Orson. He raised his head as he heard the scuttling of Charlie in the dark as he retook his position below the shadows of the wagon. He let out a huff as he turned back the flames.

Tanner heard the distaste in the young Orson's exhale. He said nothing on it though, for his words were his and he was truth and the only justice within the party. He knew Orson would dare not leave, he had his word, and he still valued the boy's honesty. He smirked at the thought, then turned his gaze back to the nothingness of the flames. Parker looked off into the shadows, watching as Charlie stirred and shivered in the cold. He laughed to himself.

When the flames of the fire died some hours later, the men spread out across the open ground. Jack drunk, Parker too, quickly drifted into a deep sleep. It was Orson who stayed awake, watching as Charlie did not lay to rest, but rather keep his arms laid across his knees, mimicking Tanner's posture at the fireside. Newkirk wondered if his acquaintance would follow in Bill's footsteps. He then wondered if he too would follow, wandering back down to Dodge, or onward to someplace else, places he dreamed of. He thought it sounded nice, but they were just visions. As he stared at Charlie and his mind raced with all sorts of ideas, his eyes became fatigued, felt heavy from such a long and dreadful day. He closed them, and then he began to dream:

He saw a small hut near the edge of the shore where the sand met the brown withered grass. The building, large enough for one or two folks, stood proud in the distance, made of what appeared to be straw. Next to it, a rack of freshly caught fish danced and swayed with the light breeze. Orson stood in the sand, looking upon the small hut. He wondered if it was his and as he stared at it, he knew it to be so. He smirked at the realization. Then, the sound of waves rolling across the coarse sand caught his attention. He turned, seeing an infinite blue before him. The white peaks of the waves curled and rolled over into the blue mountains as they slid up the rough white sand, turning it dark brown and shimmering with such smoothness.

He stepped forward, embracing the wet sand parting between his toes. He looked down, feeling strange to be separated from his boots. He never thought he'd take them off. A gust of wind burst from the sea, the waves crashing forth with it. The invisible force slapped his bare chest. He continued to smile. He beat his chest with an open palm, inviting the wind to try again as he laughed deep from within his belly. The wind came again, slapping his chest. The mist from the clear blue ocean sprayed his ankles and clean denim pants. He giggled like a child.

The waves grew taller, still rolling forward. He felt no fear as he stepped closer to them, feeling his feet and ankles swallowed by the salty abyss. He kept walking. The waters were warmer than he thought. He slapped his open palm atop the waves as they rolled by him. He splashed as if someone were there with him. He kept laughing.

The waves met his knees, and that is when he saw something in the distance. At first, he thought it a ship on the horizon, but it shrank in size as the waves carried whatever it was. A dark mass rolled with the crystal blue waves as they carried it forward to the boy.

Orson turned back, looking out towards the hut. It no longer sat near the edge of the sand. Neither did the rack of fish. Nothing lingered, only an extended expanse of barren brown grass, withered over time, scorched by the low hanging sun. It was then that his feet began to burn. He looked down into the waves. Pink and red rose from beneath the water. He realized he walked through that brush barefoot at some point. He felt the saltwater cleanse him from thorns and grime that he brought with him from when he passed through that expanse for however long he walked.

The pain was too much. He thought of turning back. The shape laid still, carried closer by the waves. That was enough for him, for the oddity needed to be figured out. That is why, he assumed, he was there. That thing, whatever it was, called to him and he had searched so far, so long, to find it. There it was, carried by the waves of a sea only he could dream of, something he feared he'd never see. It came into view. The sound of the ocean died. Only the light breeze tickling his ears made but a whisper.

A rope danced atop the stilling waters. It slithered like a serpent, finely made from whatever craftsman created such a thing. The wake of the item stirred the waters and the waves began again. And when they rose and fell, whatever the rope laid attached to slinked forward from the sea, as if presented as a gift. It collided with Orson's knees as he stared down on it, bouncing with the current and he. A coyote, dead and long so. It decomposed and maggots feasted on its gums as its mouth hung open. Its tail stretched upward, stiff as he saw once before. Its eyes stared upward at him, cold. Tuffs of fur fell from the dead creature, washed away within the salty waters. Around its neck sat that rope. Whoever killed that poor animal was long gone. The dead beast, still cold and frozen in place, let out a haunting cackle of a yap that echoed for miles across the sea and into the depths of the poor boy's heart…

Orson shivered in the cold night. He tightened his grip atop the hide he used as a blanket, trying to wrap himself deeper within it. He swore he heard the cackle of the coyote across the plains, but it died out quickly, for another sound filled the air. A strange one, one he had not heard. It was a thrust of sorts, as if a fist met another. Though, it repeated, a deep haunting gurgle came after each soft clap. He opened his eyes when he heard a whisper, "Lil' Lamb."

There, standing atop Parker, stood Charlie. His blade glistened with the light of the moon mixed with crimson across its pale metal. He thrusted it forward again, connecting with

Parker's throat. Parker bled tremendously, red seeping from a necklace of stab wounds. He held his throat as Charlie retracted his blade, preparing for another strike. The second in command panicked, grasping at the pools of blood that seeped from him as if trying to ladle it back into his body. Charlie whispered as he stabbed the blade through Parker's hand as it covered his throat, "Lil' Lamb…"

He drew back, stabbing again, "Lil' Lamb."

And again, "Lil' Lamb."

And again, "Lil' Lamb."

And again, "Lil' Lamb."

He did not stop, not even after Parker fell cold where he once slept. Charlie kept driving the blade into the dead man's throat, which steamed warm as it opened in the cold frosty Dakota air. Tears ran down Charlie's face as the blade drove forth into the dead flesh. Parker's eyes stared off, half shut, pale and cold as the terrain.

Orson sat up slowly. He knew not what to say, but his heart raced, not just from the false peace of his dream, but from the darkness he witnessed come from his acquaintance. Charlie did not see Orson stir, and kept hacking away. It was only when Orson mustered the courage to say anything that he stopped, "Charlie…"

Charlie no longer hunched over Parker. He stood, the wind rustling the trees behind him, blowing his wild hair in its fury. He appeared proud, matter of fact, as he looked to Orson, "What?"

Orson looked away from the confident Charlie, that of which would not fade. His eyes stayed fixated on the still Parker, still as those waves from his dream. He felt sorry for him. No man should die that way, he thought. No man should die like a beast on the plains, but he wondered if it was what he deserved. He hated that thought, and lingered no more on it, for Charlie spoke, “I told him I’d do it.”

Fear overtook Orson when he asked, “You gon’ kill all of us?”

Charlie looked down upon the silent Parker. He smirked. He then looked over his shoulder, studying the drunken deep sleep that Tanner put himself into. He thought about it. He then looked to Orson, shaking his head, “No…I don’t think so…”

Orson nodded towards the sleeping Jack, “Well, he’ll kill ya…”

“Yeah,” Charlie said, looking towards Jack. He watched him for a minute. His hand tightened around the grip of his knife, “I know.”

Newkirk saw that Charlie thought about knifing the sleeping leader. He grabbed his attention with a question, “You leavin’?”

Charlie turned back to Orson, sheathing his knife in the leather scabbard on his belt. He nodded as he looked down upon the corpse before him. His eyes shifted upward towards Orson as his face stayed parallel to the body, “You wanna come?”

“No,” said Orson, simply and honestly.

"You like it here?" Charlie asked, halfheartedly.

"Most days."

Charlie looked down on Parker once more. He cocked his head as he thought on it, thought of leaving, Orson's declination, the whole situation. His head began to shake slightly from side to side, "I ain't never liked it much."

The young murderer stepped over the corpse of Parker, heading towards the wagon. Orson sat up straight, watching him as he moved over to Tanner. He eyed the blade in its sheath, half expecting him to plunge it into the throat of Jack as well. He didn't. Instead, the young acquaintance stepped over the drunken leader, grabbing a handful of supplies out of the back of the wagon. It was a parcel of wrapped food. He stuffed it into an empty bag, slinging it over his shoulder. He took a canteen too, throwing it over the other shoulder. He looked down on Jack, shaking his head at the sight. He stepped back over him, fearing nothing from him anymore.

Charlie then moved over to Orson, kneeling in front of him. He said softly, "I'll walk. He ain't wakin' up anytime soon."

"Where you gon' go?"

"Dunno," Charlie thought on it, looking down at his boots. "I'll find my way, I guess. Best you say you ain't see me."

Orson nodded affirmingly. He knew what Jack would do if he did speak truthfully on what happened. He feared for his life, and as he thought on it, he really wondered if he should leave with Charlie. He feared then that Jack would find them, and that was too much to bear.

"You was always kind to me," Charlie told him, staring Orson dead in the eyes, so matter of fact, so honest. "Maybe I'll see you around sometime, somewhere."

Orson didn't know what to say to that. He just nodded.

Charlie smirked at the idea, then reached out and grabbed Orson's shoulder. He gave it an awkward shake, as if it were commonplace, or like he'd seen other men do such a thing. He told him, "I hope so. Take care of yer'self, Orson."

The young murderer then stood, turning his back to Orson. He walked away, stepping over the corpse of Parker, who stared lifelessly up into the night. The wind wailed as it whipped between the trees. Snow peppered Charlie as he stepped closer to the edge of the outer dark. He then became engulfed in the shadows. It was too dark for Orson to view anything. He only heard the steps of the young man wandering out into the snow. His feet were heavy. The snow cracked and crumbled beneath his gait. Then, all fell quiet, and Orson sat alone in the dark with the dead and the drunk.

Chapter XXII
On, Fathers
1874

The snow kept falling all through the night. Come morning, the hide that Orson covered the body of Parker with in the middle of the night, long after Charlie's departure, sat caked with white. The tan skin of the hide peered through pockets in the resting precipitation, but it was few and far between. The snow laid thick, undisturbed atop the cold corpse, an inch or two deep. Orson stood by, not sleeping that night. He held a spade in his hand, one he removed from the back of the wagon. He rested against the bark of a tree, feeling it dig into his skin, his jacket feeling like no protection at all.

Tanner stirred, knocking off clumps of snow that rested atop him. His legs rested, uncovered from the blanket and he sweat from every pore on his face. Even in such a cold environment, the alcohol still made him warm, or so he felt. His mouth sat slightly agape, dry. He smacked his lips as he opened his eyes ever so slightly, blinded by the white light that bounced from the thick snowy landscape. All laid silent, something he found strange. Nobody stirred but him.

The leader sat up, throwing back the hide that covered him. He leaned forward, resting his face in his palms for a minute. His head hurt from dehydration. He reached for his canteen in the wagon. He could not find it. He spat, thinking it would make no difference. It was probably frozen anyway. He took a scoop of snow from the ground, placing it in his mouth. The coldness felt relaxing as it melted to the warmth of his drunken breath. He swallowed it and found some relief. Tanner took another handful of snow with his bare hands, feeling the sting of the cold. It was then that he caught a glimpse of the mound of snow and Newkirk leaning against the spade.

He looked to the boy, studying his sad demeanor. It took him a moment to process what he looked upon. He smirked at the thought, thinking that Parker finally got rid of the boy. He spat again, "That the Lil' Lamb? Where's Parker?"

Orson tightened his grip around the wooden shaft of the spade. His voice cracked, nervous of what Tanner would say. He wondered if he would receive a beating, some lashing from Tanner's forked tongue. He nervously said, with a nod of his head to the mound, "He's under there."

The leader stood, brushing his legs clean of dirt, grime, and snow. He stayed hunched for a minute, trying to process what the young Orson told him. He moved slowly, as if trying to not disturb whatever laid beneath that snow covered hide. He brushed away the snow atop it, grabbing hold of the cover with his right hand. He peered beneath it, seeing Parker shrouded in the shadow of the pelt. His throat was torn open, looked more like a beast did such a thing and not some lamb, he thought to himself. He saw the bone and vertebrae of his second in command's neck. The hollow cavity sat drained of blood and Tanner wondered if he could peer into it and see all that made Parker tick. Those cold dead eyes stared upward into infinity. He lowered the hide, covering his companion once more.

He sat quietly for a moment, resting his arms on his knees. He nodded at a thought, sucking his teeth. He looked to Orson, asking, "The boy do this?"

"Yeah," the young Orson replied, matter of fact. "He left in the night too."

Jack muttered to himself, "Fuckin' coward..."

The leader stood, brushing his pants once again. He stood over the covered corpse, looking down on it with such shame. His eyes darted up as he questioned Orson, "You see it happen?"

Orson froze, nervous by the directness of the question. He wanted to be truthful, transparent with his leader, the man he looked up to so fondly when he first joined. However, he knew what that honesty would bring and feared that far more. He shook his head, denying it all for he would rather lose the quality that Tanner grew so fond of, than face the berating or possible beating that could ensue.

Tanner said, "I'd have killed him if I'd seen it…or if he stuck 'round."

"I know," Orson said.

"He knew too…" Jack's face became stretched with a scowl as he repeated, "fuckin' coward…"

Orson watched his leader turn his back to the corpse, pacing slowly as he thought of whatever he dwelt on. He wondered if his leader felt guilt or shame or if he had a hand in the demise of his dead companion. He wondered if his leader would feel the same if it were Orson that laid beneath that hide. He wondered what he thought of Charlie or Bill. He wondered if Jack thought of anyone other than himself.

The young man cleared his head, trying to keep Jack focused on the matter at hand, "I was gon' bury him."

Tanner turned, looking at him with wide confused eyes.

Orson clarified, "I mean…we got time."

Jack scoffed, running his tongue on the inside of his bottom lip. He sucked his teeth again and spat, "The ground's too hard."

"What?" asked the young man, cocking his head to the right, confused by Jack's sudden detachment.

Jack turned, waving his index finger in the air, directly over Parker's corpse. He spoke of it as if it were just another dead animal. His finger ran from the top of the hide to the bottom repeatedly as he spoke, "You'll be here for two whole days diggin' that grave. He's covered. We got money to make."

Orson squinted one eye, so lost, so confused by the coldness of Jack. He grew to care for Parker, to some degree. He certainly had issues with him, but it was Parker who saved him from the Comanche. It was Parker who looked after him, in some sort of way, since he joined. Sure, Nathaniel Parker was hard on him, but he felt some sort of connection with the man. They were all in this together, at least that's how he saw it. He certainly didn't believe that Parker deserved what he got. No man did, not even Charlie who committed such a thing. He didn't know how to formulate all of that into a sentence, and so he just stated to Jack, "But, it's Parker…"

"He's gone," Tanner said turning his back to Orson. He moved over towards the wagon, searching to see what Charlie took in the night, seeing how far he'd been set back, "No point in wastin' the time…"

Orson looked down onto the covered corpse. Blood stained the hide. Where Tanner stepped within the snow, he saw the pink layers that soiled the earth in the night. He felt sick as he thought of Parker's death and how he did nothing. It was too late, he told himself. Charlie was determined and precise, finally figuring out what he could and could not do. There was no stopping it, he thought. He still didn't deserve it, and if Parker did, they all did. He looked to Jack as he rummaged through their supplies, looking for breakfast. He watched as his leader took a sip from his flask. He couldn't believe it. He wondered if he should've left with the broken Charlie. It's too late, he told himself.

Tanner slapped the reins forward, clapping them against the back of the lone steed. His face sat emotionless, empty of any feeling or thought as he stared out across the long void of white. Orson, for the first time in all the time he'd been with the party, sat on the driver's box. He kept his arms crossed, feeling the whipping wind pelt him with small bullets of snow. He felt exposed. All he wanted was to crawl into the back, dangling his legs out the rear of the wagon, sheltered by the low walls of wood. He knew that not to be an option. Though the two men did not speak and had not spoken since early that morning, it was clear to Orson that he would stay at Jack's side no matter what, so said the unspoken will of his leader.

They rolled on all morning into the afternoon. A small herd of bison caught their attention. Tanner stopped the wagon, saying nothing, and Orson followed him to the back where they removed their rifles. They fired like madmen. Shooting and reloading whenever they felt like it. The smoke of their rifles settled low to the white ground. They stood, looking out to their killing field. There, they could see at least ten dead. The survivors were nowhere in sight. They slinked off somewhere beyond the vision of the hunters, but neither cared.

It was Orson who began to skin the dead first. He paid no mind to Tanner as he cut away the hide from the dead beast. He thought to himself, reminiscing of warmer days, better days, days of when he first joined the Tanner party and days before.

He thought of his time in his youth when he wandered the Appalachian woods alone. He thought of his mother and the stories she told. He wondered about his father, if he lived or died alone. He wondered if he would be the same. He thought of meeting Parker and then leaving Parker under that hide. He thought of Masters and how he fell. He thought of Bill and if he gambled in Dodge. He thought of Charlie and that calf, and he thought of where he was at that moment. He thought of the ocean and how he wanted to see it.

His eyes lifted as he tore away the removed hide from the beast. He rolled it under his arms and as he did, he heard Tanner stabbing away at a bison. He turned, seeing his leader over the carcass. He plunged his blade into the side of the animal, between ribs and sometimes on them, for he stabbed repeatedly. When his blade became stuck, Jack hurled his fists into the side of the beast. His knuckles collided with the stiff ribs of the creature. As he reeled his fists back, Orson saw his leader's face, his eyes, filled with such anguish. He held back tears. His cheeks flushed red, either from embarrassment, the cold winds, sadness, or a bit of all of it. He kicked his boots into the gut of the beast. He lodged his knife free from the side and stabbed it back into the animal, yet the blade struck bone and Tanner's bare hand slipped onto the blade. He screamed in frustration, in pain, as his blood dripped over the ruined pelt.

The leader turned, holding his wrist as he let the cool air cleanse his wounded open palm. Orson stared at the gash, thinking it strange that Tanner bled at all. Jack looked up, noticing the young man watching him. He closed his hand, hiding the wound. He shut his eyes, as if to clear the tears that formed around the edges of them. He could not hide his face, though he tried by bundling his chin into his scarf, jacket, and that soiled white hide on his shoulders. He spoke to the young man with his face hidden, "What? Wha'chu want?"

Orson stood, holding his perfect hide under his arm, "You alright?"

Tanner removed his face from hiding as he removed his scarf and wrapped his bleeding hand in it. He kicked the side of his ruined carcass. He swore and spat at it. He screamed, face red from anger, "Yeah, I'm fuckin' fine! Just this…this fuckin'…"

Tanner stopped, thinking of if he should continue. He stared down at the bison. His brow rose as if he saw something in those cold black dead eyes of the creature. His lips moved subtly, as if practicing whatever he wanted to say. He looked to Orson for a moment, and in that moment, Orson saw the defeat, the confusion, the abandonment that Tanner must've felt for he felt that way at some time too. It was then that Tanner's brow sagged, and the leader's eyes widened with a fiery rage again. Whatever he practiced was thrown to the wind and he simply shouted, "I'm just mad is all!"

Orson knew not what to say. He wanted to comfort the man, for he did care for Jack, at least that is what he told himself. He did though, somewhere deep down. He may not have respected him as he once did, but he wished no ill will against him. He nodded, sighing a bit, showing the disappointment in his leader's reaction, "Alright…"

"Don't do that," Tanner said, pointing his index finger of his wounded scarf-covered hand at the young man. He spat as he spoke, "Don't act like I c'ain't get mad!"

"Wha'chu mad about?" Orson asked, as if he'd not understood his leader at all. He knew. He always knew. He just wanted Tanner to admit it, show him some type of emotion other than mad. He knew better, for he learned it all from him. Yet, he still tried, "You mad 'bout Parker? Charlie?"

Tanner looked upon the boy as if he spoke tongues to him. He shook his head slightly with a furrowed brow. He then nodded off into the distance, way beyond Orson. There, a great swirling black hung in the sky. Thick heavy clouds moved across the white open plains. Jack began to step towards the boy, looking down towards his hand, hiding his face. He muttered, "No, I'm mad 'bout that storm that's comin'."

The blizzard hit just before sundown. The two rode that wagon for some time, trying to outrun the whirlwind of snow. They stood no chance against the might of such a thing. They could not see their own hands directly in front of their eyes as they lifted their scarfs, burying their faces in their chests. Their gloved hands felt cold to the bone. Snow whipped around them in fat flakes. It came in all directions. The only light on that open plain came from their wagon in the night. A single lantern dangled from the side, bouncing and rattling atop the wooden side panels of the vehicle.

Tanner whipped the reins as fast as he could, trying to get the horse going. It did no use. The beast moved slowly, blinded by the storm before it, uncompelled by the urgency of its master. It lifted its legs carefully as it trudged through the thick white. Tanner kept whipping. Orson said nothing, for they both knew it wouldn't help. It mattered not if it was said aloud. Tanner would do what he wanted.

It took an hour or so before they found shelter. The storm lightened at one point, and the boy and his leader made out a small shape on the horizon. They pushed towards it, realizing that it was a small abandoned shack. The sight of it was the first time Orson heard Tanner laugh in what felt like years. Jack grabbed the boy's shoulder, shaking him as he realized that they found cover. He cackled and laughed, as if the old abandoned building were some savior to their plight, though the storm was only what lurked on the surface.

The cabin sat in ruin. The wood that made the walls of the structure sat filled with small holes from termites. The foundation of the building creaked and moaned with each gust of wind. The roof possessed a dozen or so holes, each frozen on the edges. What thick snow made it through sat on the floor in small piles of white dust.

When the two entered, they checked to see if any occupants, official or otherwise, lurked about. No one entered that condemned place in a year at least. Tanner took the lantern from the wagon, placing it atop the single table in the center of the room. Five stools lined the west wall and he took one, taking his place at the table. It was Orson that moved to the fireplace that sat undisturbed on the south wall. He took what he could from the supplies in the back of the wagon and made a small fire.

Orson sat directly in front of the flames, holding his hands out to warm them. Tanner cared not to warm himself, for his soul grew cold with time. Instead, he removed a small bottle of bourbon from his coat and set it on the table. He popped the cork free with his shivering hands and began to drink.

The follower studied the leader, watching as the light of the flames danced across Tanner's face. He saw beneath the wrapping over his eye a deep crater of shadow and blindness. He asked his leader, "We goin' to keep on after this?"

"Keep on after what?" Tanner asked, swashing a pull of bourbon in his mouth. He swallowed, "The herd? Three-day herd? You still believe in that shit?"

The leader did not bother to look at the inquisitive young Orson. He stared at the label on the whiskey he drank, as if he pretended to read it instead. Orson shrugged, turning back to the flames, "Guess not."

"Stupid of me to believe in that shit," Tanner said, lifting the bottle to falsely study it closer. "Parker just sounded so…I don't know, like it was real."

Orson didn't look back. He stayed fixated on the flames, thinking about that herd, thinking about how he hoped it all real. He knew it wasn't. He doubted from the get-go, but if the herd never existed, and they weren't going to chase it anymore, then he wondered if all of it was worth it. He wondered if Masters' death and leaving him was worth it. He wondered the same about Parker. He wondered if things would've been different. They had to be, he thought to himself. There's no way that the world would've turned out this way had they just stuck near Dodge. He wasn't sure if he believed that.

"My daddy was an idiot. I ever tell you?" asked Jack as he took another drink of his stiff bourbon. "No, probably not. Well, he was. He bought into all sorts of dumb shit. I'm talkin' like any swingin' dick could make a miracle happen. He bought elixirs and ointments for anythin'. He was a dumb fool. Spent every penny he had on stupid dreams. Such a waste..."

Orson stayed quiet, slowly looking over his shoulder to examine his leader. Tanner held that bottle in his hand, staring down at the thing as if it were some magical elixir itself, something that his father would've believed in. He acted as if he possessed the only thing in the world that could cure whatever ailment he suffered from. He took another drink, his eye shifting to the flame, then Orson, then back to the bottle.

He continued, "I told myself, ain't no ointment, ain't no magic potion that gon' make me better. I'd have to make my way in the world. It would be what I made of it. Well here it is, in all its glory."

Tanner then threw his arms out, presenting the darkened room, the emptiness of the cabin. He chuckled drunkenly, "Ain't shit here but darkness and cold. This is the world I made. But I got money, he didn't. I got..." he stopped.

Something rattled deep within his mind. Orson felt as if he saw whatever it was scurry atop the head of Tanner, somewhere beneath the brim of that hat. His leader's eye looked up to the boy for a quick glance, then back down to the bottle. Tanner shook his head, taking another heavy drink. He wiped away the remnants from his lips, "I wonder how his turned out…"

Tanner took his eye wrap, the makeshift eyepatch, and removed it from his head. He set his wide brimmed hat on the table in the process. He eyed both, his good eye mostly fixated on the worn white, the tanned and grimy rag that he held in his hand. Orson watched the flames dance over his milky white eye, seeing it move and the scar along the edges flicker with the orange. Tanner let his fingers loose, letting the rag fall to the dusty floor of the shack.

He took the bottle of bourbon, holding it in his hand again. He put the bottle to his lips, yet that milky eye danced over Orson. He then held the bottle out to the boy with a smirk. Orson turned, taking it and quickly took a drink. Gone were the days of grimaces. He held the burning liquor in his mouth for a moment, letting his taste buds sting from the alcohol. He then swallowed it without question.

Tanner smiled, "You got better at drinkin'."

"Yeah," said Orson taking another swig, then handing the bottle back, "guess so."

"Better at huntin' too," Tanner said. "But, I guess you done that before you got out here."

"A little, yeah," replied Orson.

Jack pressed as he took a drink, "Daddy teach you?"

Orson nodded, turning back to the flames, studying the dancing orange tongues. "Yeah," he said, "coyotes."

"Oh yeah?" Tanner cackled to himself, thinking of the young boy hunting the wild beasts wherever the kid grew up. He thought of all that entailed and thought of how glorious the kid may have been at slaying the creatures, "Mean sum'bitches."

"More of a bother, really," Orson corrected. He did not look to Jack, for the correction itself was enough to get him in hot water. He continued though, "They ain't much to be scared of."

Tanner leaned forward, resting his forearms on his knees. He held the bottle with both hands as if it were precious. He studied Orson's back, waiting for the boy to turn. He did, and Tanner looked upon him with both eyes, good and bad, and said with a stern voice as if to teach the boy a lesson, "I don't think you give them much credit. One by itself, yeah...maybe it leave ya be. A pack of 'em? Fuck, Newkirk, they could tear the world down."

Orson didn't know what to say. He just turned his back to his leader once again. They sat quietly for a moment, listening to the howling winds outside. The world sounded as if it fell apart out there and with each crackle of the fire, Orson saw his father. He saw his old homestead. He saw the life he left behind. He wondered where it would lead him, and then he saw that coyote, nipping at its hind leg, howling and yapping mad. He then saw its head split from his father's bullet. He wondered if it would always follow him and if he had a choice, or if he made the wrong choice somewhere down the line and it would haunt him forever.

Tanner interrupted the thoughts as he too kept his mind fixated on coyotes, "You get a lot of 'em?"

"No," Orson said, seeing that dead beast fused to the back of his mind.

Jack asked sternly, curious by the boy's response. He expected a boast, a true hunter's reply. He asked, "How many then?"

"One," replied Orson.

"That's it? Just one?" Tanner leaned forward again, staring at the boy's back. This time though, the kid did not turn to face him.

"Just one," said Orson, matter of fact, the honesty dripped from his lips as if it was a forbidden delicacy as of late.

Jack knew not how to respond. He studied the boy, seeing that something kept him from boasting. Something kept him from true expression of how he should feel in his eyes. He thought of laughing but could not think of how to find humor in the situation.

He rubbed his milky eye and sucked his teeth as he leaned back in his chair. He wasn't sure how the young Orson felt, but tried to give comfort the best way he knew, "Well, look at it this way, Newkirk...I'll tell you something you probably ain't know about them coyotes. One coyote, it might not harm ya, but they crafty...they really crafty. They can live by themselves, survive by themselves. They ain't like wolves that need a pack. You wound a wolf, the others come running. Easy kills, really. You wound a coyote...well, them others gon' leave his sorry ass behind. Why? Survival, cowardice too. Coyotes can hack it a long time out there alone, long time..."

Orson did not turn to listen. He stared ahead. Tanner expected a sign that the hunter felt comfort in his explanation of how he saw things. Maybe he thought the young man would laugh. When he thought about all that he said, he realized nothing stood out as funny. He took another sip, then slammed the bottle down. He finally found something to chuckle at, something he thought the boy would laugh at too. He told him, "A coyote is social when it needs to be, alone when it needs to be...you got that one though. He ain't tearin' down shit."

The young man before him did not laugh. To that, Tanner knew not what to say. He just sat there, studying the boy who refused to look at him. He found that awkward, and then began to study the bottle again. He laughed to himself about the situation, thinking the kid was too serious, too stoic, and that it would do him no good. He had a few more things to teach him, Tanner thought to himself, and he laughed at that too.

All the while, Orson sat staring at those flames, paying no mind to his drunken leader. He felt the liquor kick in a bit and his eyes felt heavy as he watched those flames sway side to side. The howling of the winds was what he focused on and they drowned out Tanner's yap of a laugh. Yet, as he stared into those flames, he envisioned the silhouette of the coyote. The embers that rose from the timber held the image in the air for only a moment, and the boy witnessed the coyote staring back at him.

Chapter XXIII
One Coyote
1874

The storm moved on by morning. Only the remnants of it lingered, a thick six to seven inches of hard white snow covered the entirety of the landscape. The wagon sat covered, ice sickles dangling from beneath its panels. The horse that regularly carried it moseyed out from the small door-less shed where Orson placed it the night before. Hunger fueled the horse's motivation and it began to kick its hooves to scrounge for anything it could find. A light snow still fell from the sky as it searched. The door to the dilapidated shack struggled open, a force pushed it forward, sliding the stockpiled snow to the side. Orson and Tanner emerged, and the horse would find no food that morning, for they were off to somewhere. None of them, animal nor man, knew where.

They carried on about their business. That lone horse pulled their wagon wherever Tanner saw fit. Most days, they wandered the white plains of the territory. Orson figured them searching for bison, but they passed plenty and Tanner dared not stop the wagon. They headed North, and when Orson thought that maybe they would be heading to Canada, Tanner had them head West, then South, then back North. They went nowhere in particular.

For weeks they wandered, living off the land. They established plenty of camps. They double backed more often than not and used the same sites on a few occasions. Tanner, in the dead of night, often woke from his drunken slumber. He called out in his sleep most nights, startling Orson. The boy hardly slept at all. He would watch his leader wake, dripping in that alcoholic sweat, then begin to wander the campsite. Some nights he ate whatever they had in their stores. Other nights he drank the entirety of his canteen. Every night though, whenever he finished whatever ritual that drunken night called for, he wandered through the trees surrounding their campsite. He'd run his hands across the withering bark. He'd sing a song to himself under his breath. He always kept his eyes down, from what Orson could tell, as if he scrounged the foliage for signs of something that passed through. Though, only he and Orson existed for miles and nothing wandered nearby. He searched for something, as it seemed he always did, but knew not what he searched for.

Orson, though he thought it, wasn't much better in the presence of Tanner and Tanner alone. Each night before they laid awake under their respective hides, the boy watched the flames of the dying fire. He reminisced about the days they had around the flames as a whole party. He, at first, thought them mostly good memories. However, as he thought on them, he could not recount a single time where he didn't feel miserable, didn't feel like an outcast, didn't feel like all of it was for not. Sometimes he watched the dancing flames and daydream that Tanner died at the hands of the Comanche and that it was Parker who took control. He knew it wouldn't be much better if Charlie and Bill returned though. And so, he daydreamed, not only of Jack's death, but that Charlie and Bill ran off, ran south. He liked to think they'd head to Dodge again. In all his fantasies of how things could've been, they all ended with him breaking free, breaking away from the life he lived. He would leave Parker when the time seemed right, seemed acceptable and Parker held no ill will about it in his dreams. He knew that probably would not be a reality, but in his dreams, it was all he hoped for. And once he was free from Parker, from Charlie, from Bill, from Jack, he wandered the plains alone and in each of the wild scenarios he dreamed up, he escaped. That escape, however he played it out, ended with him standing on the shore of some great beach, some great dream that his mother told him about as a child. He imagined it so vividly, telling himself he would make it there, if only he knew the way. Every night he thought of a new dream, a sad ritual that he knew to be false. He'd never leave, he thought. Tanner would not will it.

The first kill that Tanner claimed in a long while, he shot from the driver's box. He startled the boy and the horse. He cared not. That first kill too, he just shot in passing as they went from one old campsite to another. He left the bison to rot on the plains. It wasn't until the boy told his leader that they could make some money again by claiming the hides that Tanner showed any inkling of listening. They could sell the meat too. Tanner, when the boy told him this, acted as if he never thought of such a thing, as if his time in Kansas was only but a dream. He laughed at that, drinking his bourbon, before agreeing with the boy.

That night they danced and drank together, and it was Orson who thought that maybe things would get better. He could hunt and so could Tanner. They could kill what they wanted, make money, like old times, and maybe it was just the crew and the dynamics of it all that made the memories so bitter. Orson kicked his drunken feet near the flames, thinking on that. His stomach sat unsettled, filled only with alcohol. He cared not, for it felt that they started afresh. Tanner celebrated the thought of a new life, one of the same, but somehow, in that mind of his, he thought it would be better. The same with Orson, who danced and swayed drunkenly near the flames under the full moonlit night. Things would be better, he told himself. It would be a new start, and all would be right in the world.

They stopped wandering Dakota Territory, aimlessly anyway. They searched high and low for bison, finding small herds wherever they went. None were as grand or big as the ones seen south. He wasn't sure if the bison migrated somewhere or if it was all that was left. He didn't care though. He killed them without question or thought, as did Tanner. They skinned them, took what meat they wanted, horns for trinkets and the like, and moved on to the next pocket they found. Orson did most of the tanning, but soon their salt ran out. Tanner saw nothing wrong with that and instead of opting to resupply or carry on, he told the boy it would be best if they just kept hunting. Orson questioned him and he was met with a fist to his arm. It stung, and the boy remembered why he never questioned his leader. And so, they just kept on hunting.

The two stacked the wagon to the brim with hides they collected over the weeks. Tanner, being the way he was, wanted to keep going, keep hunting, to keep adding to the stack. However, it was Orson who pleaded that they stop to sell. They could resupply, get more salt. They could sleep indoors for once. What that felt like, the boy no longer remembered. Tanner, once the young Orson suggested this, harbored the idea as if it were his own and set his sights on restocking his bourbon. He ran low and needed to replenish before he ever ran out.

Tanner drove the wagon to a small settlement near the Nebraska border. They'd been hunting in that area for some time, yet paid no mind to the settlements or the settlers in the area. The town wasn't much to be proud of. It held a few buildings, a sheriff's office, a hotel, a butcher, a baker, and a few houses here and there. That was it though. The majority of the folks who wandered the muddy streets looked as if they were vagrants, eyes widened by cold and alcohol as they staggered about the one place that took them in for miles.

It was near the butcher that Tanner brought the wagon. A few tents, hobbled together near the open end of the main street where no buildings stood erect yet, appeared appropriate to the leader and his young follower. He stopped the horse and dismounted. The owners of the tents, who sold a variety of wares, watched as Jack threw his arms out as if presenting some holy relic to them. He called them forth to view what he brought them. None cared, for they saw Tanner's qualities and the quality of hides he brought with him. Only one stepped from beneath his tent, an older man with silver hair and a silver beard. He ran his hands through his long locks before placing his wool cap atop his head as he stepped free from his tent. Only he, the old merchant, gave Tanner the time of day.

The merchant studied Tanner for a moment. He looked him up and down, examining the grime that covered him. He then shifted his gaze towards Orson, who sat atop the driver's box. He gave the boy a nod, then moved to the back of the wagon. He flipped through the piles upon piles of hides collected. His eyes peered over every little detail, yet he did not take a single pelt from the wagon to hold to the light or examine any closer. The old merchant knew the quality and spat, "Can't give you nothin' for 'em."

The old silvered man turned his back to the wagon and began to make his way back to his tent. Tanner watched him and the rejection from the only one who gave him and his follower the time of day sat deep within his belly and began to fester with anger. He moved after the old man, his feet slipping and sinking deep into the muddy streets. He asked, reaching out to the merchant as if trying to grab him, "Wha'chu mean nothin'?"

"I mean they's ruined," said the merchant, stopping and pivoting with ease in the muck. He pointed towards the wagon, waving his finger as he spoke, as if to cast some sort of enchantment over the soiled hides brought to him, "Ain't really much to work with. I can't tan 'em. Should'a done tanned 'em yer'self. Now, I can't sell 'em."

Tanner stepped forward. His instep sliding in the mud. He gritted his teeth to the old man, frustrated at being told what he should've done. He said to him, "I got three dollars a pelt back in Dodge…"

The old man turned, waving his hand in the air as if to tell Tanner to go back where he came from, whatever hellish pit he slinked out of. The old merchant's voice crackled in the cold grey air as he said, "Take 'em to Dodge then."

Jack's face lightened. He no longer gritted his teeth. His brow rose with surprise and bewilderment at the treatment of him by the merchant. He shifted tactics. He removed his white pelt that he kept over his shoulders. He flapped it in the air, giving a firm pounding sound with each roll, as if some Matador to a bull, "What about this one then?"

The old man stopped, turning back. He looked upon the hide. His eyes stayed narrow, unimpressed. He smacked his gummy mouth open and close once, as if formulating something to say. He shook his head, but before he spoke, before the rejection came, Tanner countered, "White, eh? Would make a good coat. I done wore it as just an overthrow. Kept me warm through all this nonsense y'all call weather."

"More like a good rug in that condition," the silver merchant replied. "This ain't the railroad. I can't buy in bulk and I can't take nothin' less than pristine."

Tanner lowered his head, defeated. His strong jaw slid side-to-side as he gritted his teeth together, biting his tongue in his frustration. He hadn't given up on the sale yet, but he rose his head to look upon Orson. His eyes beamed with such anger, such disappointment, something that he had not seen from the man since Charlie belonged to their crew. Orson looked away, staring at the old merchant instead who did not look up at him. Tanner turned back to the old man, signaling him to follow after him. The silver merchant did so, and Tanner lowered his voice to calmly explain, "Look, I'm on my last leg here. I ain't got a crew no more. I need some sort of coin."

Tanner wrapped his arm around the old man, giving him some false embrace as if it would make any sort of difference on the sale. He turned the old man's back to the wagon. He could not see the goods, only Tanner, only Tanner's face of dejection and loss. The old man studied him, his heart swelling so and his brain fighting back with any ounce of common sense. He told the buffalo hunter, "You need somethin' to trade. I already told ya, I can't do nothin' with that lot."

Tanner nodded, as if the man made some type of decent argument. He didn't really believe that. He just knew how to sell. He pleaded, voice shaking in the cold, "Please. Take the white pelt, you said yer'self, it'd make a rug. Someone ought to buy it."

The merchant nodded slightly, finally feeling the sway of Tanner, "I can't give you a lot for it. It'd be enough though."

"Enough for what?" asked Tanner.

They ditched the soiled hides that nobody dared to trade for or purchase near the outskirts of town. The left them in a heap, left to degrade in the light rainfall that began. Small bits of snow collected atop the worn tuffs of hair. Such a waste, Orson thought. He wasn't sure if he spoke of the dead or if he spoke of the money.

The two moved back into town after lightening the wagon. With what little Tanner got for the white pelt and a few that were tanned before the salt ran dry, he bought whiskey and two cigars. That's all he had enough for.

The rain turned to snow around sunset. It wasn't much, just small flurries with fat flakes that spun like startled horses in the air. No tavern would have them, for Tanner, drunk on what alcohol he bought with his little earnings, began boasting loudly at each saloon. He said he was the greatest hunter. By no means did that upset anyone, but when nobody acknowledged the man, he began yelling, screaming, crying, about how all must recognize him as such. When they didn't, his fists began to fly to anyone who stood in his way. Orson waited outside. He smoked a hand rolled cigarette that Tanner offered him sometime before the brawl. He listened as the scuffle began indoors. He watched the snowfall, his smoky breath turn to fog. Tanner came out, bloodied and bruised on his face, his coat torn at the seams of his sleeves. His eyes were both black in the socket. His nose bled and he spat blood as he looked to his companion, "Where was ye?"

Orson said nothing.

"C'mon then," Tanner said, slapping the boy on the back. "Le's get goin'."

They slept under the wagon in the muddy streets that night. The smell of horse manure and filth covered them as they took shelter from the freezing precipitation. Tanner puffed on his last fat cigar. He smoked the other in one of the saloons before the brawling. He held his head as it ached. He watched the snow melt in small puddles, then begin to ice over time. He said nothing to Orson, and Orson nothing to him. They stayed quiet, sharing the occasional glance to one another as they laid flat in the mud, only a few soiled hides beneath them to protect them from whatever disease they may catch.

That nickel-plated revolver sat in Tanner's holster at the front of his pelvis, ready for a cross-draw. It did not glisten or glimmer. Muck, caked into every crevasse of the weapon, soiled any admiration that Orson once held for the piece. The ivory grip laid cracked up the center. Tanner felt the young man looking at the weapon and shot him a glance. He broke the silence with a roll of his drunken eyes as he stammered out, "Wha?"

"You really get that off a Jayhawk?" asked Orson.

Tanner curled his brow, confused by the question, "Wha'chu on about?"

Orson repeated, "Did you get that off a Jayhawk?"

Tanner just stared at him, lost by the question. He held no knowledge of what the boy asked him, "Don't know wha'chu mean."

"Forget it," replied the boy. He turned on his side. His hair fell into the mud of the street. He watched as horses and wagons rolled by, seeing only their lower halves. He played a game, wondering who rode what, wondering where they were going, with who, or what they'd see. The game itself made him sick to his stomach, so he closed his eyes, thinking of anything better than where he laid.

Tanner told him, "Shouldn't've used as much salt. Could'a sold them hides if you done used less."

"We ran out," Orson told him, eyes still closed.

"Yeah, cuz you done used it all. You used too much,"

Tanner clarified drunkenly.

Orson didn't bother to turn to speak to him. He kept his eyes shut, listening to the wheels of passing wagons and the hooves of wandering horses scrape through the muck. He replied, "You can do it then, since you know wha'chu want."

The young man heard Tanner snap his head to look at the boy. He felt that stare on his back. He listened as Jack dabbed his finished cigar in the mud, "Nah, you gon' learn to do it right."

"You didn't buy no more salt," said the young companion. "C'ain't learn much without it."

Neither man said nothing after that. They laid in silence, both daydreaming of places better than that. Though, Tanner saw himself atop the hides of great kills and Orson saw himself sitting on a beach somewhere off where nobody could find him. They felt lost to the dreams, and that was all the two felt that they had in common anymore. Gone were the days of the Tanner Party, that much they both knew. Gone were the days of chasing herds. Gone were the days of understanding and respect, but Orson wondered if those ever truly existed. Gone were the days of friends. Gone were the days of belonging.

They rode out come morning. A man had been stabbed outside one of the saloons. Orson and Jack stumbled upon him in the back alley. Tanner took the man's boots. He offered the dead man's coat to his young companion, but he refused, seeing it as soiled. Orson wondered who else would find that man, if they would be his family or strangers. He wondered what they'd do to his body, but he tried not to linger on that, for his mind thought of Masters and Parker bloating and rotting away on the plains.

They passed where they ditched the hides the day before. They looked worse than Orson remembered. Snow sat dusted atop them. Pockets of ice decorated and accented the edges. They were stiff, as if he could snap them in two, down the center, if he so desired. He shook his head as he looked upon them. Tanner didn't bother to look. He just clapped the reins onto the lone steed's back, watching its hooves move in rhythm.

Pockets of snow lingered in the flat plains surrounding them. The grey grass, tall and withered, swayed in the light breeze that rolled through. Ice dangled from their stems and blades. Some sat completely incased, un-swayed by the invisible force that pushed those free of such confinements. Orson continued to look back, watching as the town and those abandoned pelts fell from view. It took time, for Tanner kept the horse at a slow trot, as if he truly did not wish to leave such a place or as if he were hesitant to go back out into the wild.

They carried on, moseying all morning. Around noon, Tanner began to drink again, keeping his flask filled with the best bourbon he could buy cheaply. He sipped on it, offering some to Orson, who refused the proposition. They passed low rolling hills, that from their position seemed to be deliberately stacked between where one fell, and another rose. As Orson looked upon them, he envisioned those skulls back in Dodge City, stacked so neatly, so high, and so deliberate. He wondered if they looked like the hills at that point. They had to. So many bison were killed, so many scavengers would go and get those bones out in the fields. The piles had to be so high.

The sun moved overhead slowly, and with it, Tanner grew drunker. He leaned over the side of the driver's box. He spat, then whipped the reins as the wagon pulled forward. He told the young hunter next to him, "We'll get more and go back. He wants pristine. We'll show him pristine."

"Why?" Orson asked, still fixated on his dark dream of the hills.

"Why not?" asked Jack, turning his head slightly towards his companion.

"I mean," Orson began, turning his head to look forward. He refused to look to Jack as he offered up questions, "Why we not goin' south? We ain't chasin' a ghost no more. We can make more money outside Dodge. We ain't gotta sell perfect hides to the big fellers down in Dodge."

"Tha' what you want in life?" Jack asked. "Mediocre work and payment fer it?"

Orson hung his head, realizing there would be no bargaining with the man. Tanner said they would go back to that small territory town, and that was what they would do. He hated that thought. He felt his blood begin to churn in his beating heart. He felt so frustrated, so angered by the thought of being stuck in a place he didn't want to be with a man he grew to dislike.

Tanner dug the insult deeper with a sigh, followed by, "Boy, I thought yer daddy raised you better."

Orson turned his head slowly towards his leader. He studied the drunken man who looked forward from the driver's box. He whipped the reins a little too hard, a little too wild, and a little too often. He swayed as the wagon bounced, his eyes rolling as he did so. He was nothing more than a drunken fool, a drunken fool with a boastful ego. What he had to boast for, Orson couldn't think of in that moment. The young companion felt his crown turn warm as he became lightheaded. His vision blurred in his anger. He asked honestly, wondering if Tanner truly said what he said, "Wha'chu say?"

Tanner turned his head for a split second, his glassy eyes studying the boy briefly. He knew he upset him, and so he tried to mend what he could. He refused to look at Orson as he tried to explain his statement, drunkenly, "Your daddy raised you to hunt and you out here wantin' to pitch half assed pelts."

"You ain't know my daddy," Orson told Tanner with a stern voice that shook with anger. "Don't talk about him like you did."

"I know you's better than what he taught ya," Tanner smirked. "You an' yer one coyote…"

Orson knew not what to say. He felt as if Tanner's words were fangs to his heart, piercing with such venom. He thought on that, thinking of those days with his father. He remembered him standing over that coyote. He remembered the tears he shed. He remembered the way his father was, so belittling, so far from understanding his son's soft heart. He tried to bury that, tried to be as callus as the man. He recounted that coyote skull stacked in the mix of the bison skulls. He could not forget them frozen in place on the plains from whatever chemicals they ate. He thought on that dead animal from his childhood, head cloven from his father's bullet. The blood ran into infinity.

He shook his head free of the visions, yet his somber heart told him to speak his mind, and so his honesty came forth, something that Tanner always admired, "And you ain't nothin' but a dumb drunk, believin' in fake stories."

Tanner pulled on the reins, stopping the lone horse that pulled the wagon. He turned, good eye wild, bad eye slightly cocked outward. Orson smelt the alcohol on the man's breath as he poked the boy in the shoulder. He was angered, riled up by the honesty. He told the boy, "Tha' may be, but I'm tryin' to help you and you need to hear it. The way you actin', the way you wallow about, you better than one coyote. You can be a better man, out here, huntin' with all this opportunity."

"Opportunity?" Orson scoffed. He turned to face Jack. He shouted to the man, "Opportunity? What opportunity? I ain't seen any since we lost Masters! Ain't been no opportunity out here for me! Wha' we doin'? Killin'? We ain't in it for the money no more. What we in it for then?"

Jack's eyes studied the gaunt face of his companion. He felt betrayed by such words. He told the boy through gritted teeth,

"It's always been more than the money."

"No, it ain't, Jack," Orson continued to speak. His voice rose with tension as he let all the truth flow freely, "Don't act like it is. Don't act like it ain't ever been more than a few bucks. You left Masters chasin' ghosts. You let Bill walk—"

Before the young man finished, his face was met by the back of Tanner's right hand, silencing the boy. Orson, struck so hard, slid towards the edge of the wagon. His head spun and his vision darkened with black dots of rage and confusion. He could not find his bearings and fell from the wagon.

Tanner stood from the driver's box, climbing over the passenger's bench and hopped down next to the boy. He stood over him, watching as the young Orson held his cheek and began to lean forward, resting on his left arm. Jack pointed to his companion, waving his finger in the boy's face as he began to stand, "Don't you ever talk 'bout things you don't understand."

Orson found his footing, placing his feet a distance apart. He raised his fist, ready to strike Tanner if he tried such an act again. He told Tanner, "That's funny, comin' from you."

Tanner kept his arms down, staring at his companion. He knew the boy was frustrated and as such, spoke to him with a calm demeanor. He would not be left alone in such a place. He needed the kid more than he wanted to admit, and so he fought for him, "What I do, what I did, I did for the best for everyone. Including you. I did it all for your benefit, no matter how much it hurt me."

Orson lowered his fists, staring at the man. He saw the emptiness in both of Tanner's eyes. He wondered if there was anything behind them or if they just sat hollow for all eternity. He couldn't remember in that moment if it had always been that way, or if things changed somewhere down the line. He liked to believe it was Masters and the fall, but the more he thought on that, the more he thought that to be a farse. In the milky white of Tanner's bad eye, he saw the cloven skull of the coyote at his father's chicken coop and next to it laid the cloven skull of the calf, something he tried to forget as hard as he tried. It broke Charlie, and he wondered if he had been broken long before he ever left his father.

He came back to reality, furrowing his brow as he spat, "Yeah? Ain't nothin' hurt you, Jack. You ain't never let nothin' hurt you."

"Wha'chu sayin'?" Tanner rose his right eyebrow. His good eye looked the boy up and down. He knew what Orson told him, he wanted to see if the companion possessed the guts to clarify.

"I'm sayin," Orson began but stopped. He shook his head at his options. He knew it was time. There would be no going back. He became too honest with Jack and he damned himself for it. Though, what Tanner saw as damnation, Orson began to see as freedom. He said proudly, "I'm sayin' you ain't no different."

The young man stepped passed Tanner, moving towards the front of the cart. He threw back the dangling reins and began to fidget with the harness that kept the lone horse in place. He loosened it, and the horse stirred at the liberty Newkirk presented. Jack stood by, dumbfounded at what unfolded before him. Orson shot the man a quick glance, but mostly focused on the horse, even in such a proud moment, not able to speak directly to his face with honesty, "You just another drunk who thinks they know better when they don't know shit..."

Tanner watched as Newkirk grabbed the reins of the horse once freed, leading it a few paces from the wagon. It clicked for him, "So, you leavin' too, huh?"

Orson brushed the horse with the palm of his hand, "I am."

Jack's voice lowered, solemn, true for once, "Why?"

The young man grabbed ahold of the reins tightly, leading the horse towards Jack. He lowered his head, scoffing as he shook it. He glanced up at Jack from beneath the brim of his hat as if it offered some type of protection, "Even now, after all this time, you c'ain't even guess?"

Tanner looked upon the young man before him. He dug deep, wondering how it all came to this. His breath turned to fog as it flowed from his slightly open mouth. It reeked of brown liquor.

The kid looked upon the man, one he used to hold so highly, but as he stood there with his mouth slightly agape, he felt nothing towards him. He shook his head again, "You told me you was mad at me 'cuz I ain't never speak my mind and now that I have, you ain't listenin'."

"You ain't sayin' it," Tanner replied, sternly, as if he gave some last stand in his death throes.

"I ain't never had to," replied Orson Newkirk.

The young man then mounted the horse without a saddle. He grabbed the reins attached to the harness of the beast and motioned the animal past Jack. He looked down on him from the work animal. He asked, "You gon' stop me?"

Tanner didn't bother to look up. He reeled with such loss that he knew not what to do. He stood there, drunkenly, swaying with the wind as if it were all just a bad dream. He removed his flask from his coat, taking another sip, as if that would repair the problem.

Orson smirked, feeling the power of the freedom, "Didn't think so…"

The young man clicked his heels into the ribs of the great beast, and it moved forward at a medium trot. The wind whipped across the plains. The young man's shirt fluttered in the wind as he rode into the invisible gusts. He heard nothing as the wind whistled over his ears. He smiled as he looked forward, seeing only an open expanse, an empty void, something that he feared for so long. Yet, as he rode into it alone, he felt relief.

Tanner stood by the wagon for a moment, still trying to piece together how he ended up alone. He drunkenly moved towards the front of the wagon, as if to ready the horse. He then realized that no horse was present. He stood alone, with no horse, and a wagon full of degraded supplies and no pelts. He cursed under his breath, cursing Newkirk, the boy who put him in such a situation. He turned, facing out towards the plains. He watched as the boy rode on and he shouted after him, "Fine then! Go on! You ain't gon' make it! You just weak! The world is made for men like me! It's been built by men like me! You fools, you who just ride away without sayin' bye, yer nothin'! You'll always be nothin'! Yer daddy be disappointed in you, boy! You hear me?"

The screaming and hollering of Tanner could be heard over the whipping wind in Orson's ear. He didn't care though. He found himself proud, for he knew that if it were months earlier, he may have hesitated and turned back. He told himself he would go West, as far West as he could go, someday. He would replace the wind in his ear with that of crashing waves. The great empty expanse before him would be of water, not grass. He smiled at the thought as his horse trotted along.

Tanner, as if his rage sobered him up, spewed such hate at the rider in the distance, "You ain't gon' tear nothin' down! You gon' be nothin! Forever nothin', boy! Daddy's disappointment, tha's all you'll ever be! You're worthless! You coward! You fool!"

Orson Newkirk didn't bother to look back. He only stared forward. He focused on the wind in his ear. He cared not for what Tanner had to say or what Tanner thought anymore. The freedom made his heart swell. Yet, as he broke over a low hill and he knew he was out of Tanner's sight, the voice of his former leader slowly began to fade and became nothing but the yapping of coyotes somewhere in the distance.

Chapter XXIV
Payment
1875

The light of the morning slipped through the shattered windows and tattered curtains of the Daniels family home. The rays, so sharp and golden, rested atop the closed eyes of Orson as he stirred in his sleep. He awoke. He'd been dreaming again, dreaming of those days with the Tanner Party and the days without them. He wandered so long alone, finding odd jobs in Nebraska as he made his way south back into Kansas. He stayed in Dodge for a long while, not hunting, but finding work in the railyards. As he looked around the ruined home of the lonely farmer, he felt nothing but shame and guilt. He felt as if he should have stayed in Dodge, stayed in Nebraska, maybe stayed with Jack, and Thomas' life would be for the better.

A few locust carcasses still lingered about the home, crushed under boots, some charred, others as if they just laid down and died. Orson shivered as he examined them, rolling his legs out of bed. He slid his boots on, watching the wind whip through the shattered windows, fluttering the shredded drapes. He leaned forward onto his knees, stretching his back as he slid his shirt on and buttoned the few buttons it possessed. His eyes danced around the room, looking for the old farmer. The rocker by the fire sat empty. The fire went out sometime in the night. Breakfast hadn't been cooked, he couldn't smell it or the presence of tinder. Outside, the sound of leather turning, tying, and buckling seeped through the broken window. Orson stood and exited the home.

Thomas stood next to a tall bay. He wrestled with the saddle, struggling to get a few lines of leather in the right place. Yet, as Orson stepped onto the porch, he finally finished his task, stepping back and examining the great beast before him with such pride. Orson observed the sight before asking, "Where we headin'?"

The old man grabbed ahold of his lower back, thrusting his gut out forward as he tried to stretch what he could for a bit of relief. He turned his head to the young man on his porch. He looked upon him sternly as he said, " *We* ain't headin' nowhere. I'm goin' to Hays."

"Why?" asked Orson.

"They expectin' me to pay my debts," Thomas said. He looked around the ruined farm, the charred landscape, the corpses of locusts. He shook his head as he watched the wind lift dust and ash, carrying it off somewhere across the plains, "I c'ain't pay. I gotta tell 'em what happened."

"They gon' believe it?"

"No," Thomas said, moving towards his bay. He ran his hands through the mane of the creature, finding some comfort in the softness of it, "I gotta tell 'em nonetheless though."

"Well," said Orson stepping down from the porch, "I'll saddle up too."

"No need," said Thomas, turning to face the young man. "I need to face it all alone. They need to hear me out."

"You in some danger?"

"Physically? No."

Orson cocked his head, curious, "There any other kinda danger?"

"Plenty," said the old farmer. He looked out over his farm again, then back to Orson, "But…I need you to stay here. Finish cleanin' this place up if you can."

Orson too looked out over the farm. The ash rolled in the wind. The carcasses of locust wiggled in the breeze. He chuckled as he said, "I'd much rather go with ya."

"Please, do this for me," Thomas asked.

Orson turned to face the old man. He played with his handkerchief in his hand nervously, "Honest, though…I'd rather go with ya."

"Why?"

"What if you's ain't comin' back?" Orson questioned.

Thomas nodded sternly to the young man, "I'm comin' back."

"You say that," said Orson. "There's all kinda stuff out

there, and you's not in the best shape. Them fellers up in Hays, whoever they are...townfolk ain't like plainsfolk. I just am nervous for ya, that's all."

"I'm comin' back," said Thomas sternly. "I say what I mean. I told folks up in Hays and at the fort that I'd pay up. I c'ain't, and I gotta tell 'em why my word was broken. I have to face that."

"Just run," said Orson, speaking from some experience. "Just run away from it all. Come on to the ocean with me."

"No runnin' from this," said the old man, exhausted at just the thought of the ride. "I gotta face it, for mine and Lilly's sake."

The old man turned back to his bay, putting his right foot in the stirrup. He struggled lifting his weight as he climbed into the saddle, both hands on the horn. Once his stomach rested on the seat, he swung his other leg around awkwardly. He hadn't ridden in a long time and it showed. His body had too many miles, thought Orson. He would be gone before he knew it.

Thomas sat in the saddle, straightening his back the best he could. He looked down onto Orson as he put his floppy wide brim hat on. He told him, "Try and keep everythin' nice and cleaned up. I'll be back in a day or two."

"And if you don't?" asked the young man earnestly.

"I will," replied the old man, as he whipped the horse around and began to trot along.

Orson smirked, "Alright then."

He watched as the old farmer swayed in the saddle as the horse moved lazily across the property. The ash and dust peppered the old man as he rode on through the opening in the fence line, headed towards Hays. The morning held a darkness to it, though the sun held such a bright and vibrant aura. Orson knew not why. Yet, he watched the old man for a long time, watched until he and his horse disappeared over the low hills of grey grass in the distance. It was then, when he felt truly alone, that he sat on the edge of the porch, basking in the void of the plains that the farm became.

He did what he was told. He spent all late morning and afternoon cleaning what he could. He shoveled the dead locusts into tall grizzly piles of exoskeletons. They reminded him of Dodge City, of old friends, but he tried to ignore that as much as possible. He scooped the ashes and cut down the charred husks of the wheat that stood so still in the breeze. He too threw those into piles, separated from the locusts. He didn't know what he'd do with all of it, and so around the break of dusk, he began to dig a hole. He knew he wouldn't finish it by sundown, but he would at least start the task that he planned finishing in the morning. He shoveled everything into the pit that he could, expecting to seal it away as if it were some ancient secret to never be discovered.

The sun glowed a hellish red as it set off in the distance. He took the time to pause his work, resting for the first time throughout the day. He admired the site, watching as the red rays turned to purple among the low hanging clouds in the distance. He wiped his brow with his handkerchief. He thought about Jack and where he was. He thought about Charlie. He knew where Bill was, but he thought about him too. He wondered if Masters never fell and if it had been him, maybe things would've ended up different. He wondered how his life would've been different if he hadn't taken up with the Tanner Party. He smirked as he thought of something darkly optimistic. He realized that he would not be there on that farm had it not been for Tanner and the experiences with him. He would've never met Thomas, though he still felt that plague to be his own doing. And with that, he thought that maybe it would've been best that he died sometime before arriving in Dodge. His smirk faded. He felt that to be the truth. A lot of people, a lot of bison, a lot of coyotes would be happier without him, he thought. His stomach turned sour, so he just started shoveling again.

He didn't make it halfway through his pit before darkness truly overtook the land. He moved indoors of the Daniels family home and began to prep his meal. The meat stores were long gone and all that remained were an assortment of vegetables. He diced them with a small knife he witnessed Thomas use. He planned to make stew again, something he rather enjoyed.

Orson moved to the fireplace, lighting a piece of small timber. He watched as the flames within the confined space slowly rose to life. He stared into them, feeling the coldness of the outdoors seep through the broken windows of the home. The chill struck him to the bone, and so he held his hand out to the flames, trying to find some comfort. It felt different with Thomas not being in the home and he felt that he was a squatter again, in a small shack somewhere in the Dakota Territory. He heard a coyote yap somewhere outside.

The young man stood by the flames, turning to face the broken window near the front door. He listened for a moment, holding his breath to be able to take everything in that he possibly could. At first, the hissing and crackling of the wood amongst the flames was all that he could hear. Yet, after a brief moment of silence, and right as he exhaled, the cackle of a lone coyote echoed in the dark again. He stepped away from the fireplace, moving towards the window. He stared out across the shadow-swept farm.

In the darkness, near the family tree, a small lone shadow slinked about the horizon. It trotted slowly, its feet moving evenly with each step as if on the hunt. He knew that to not be the case, for it called as if looking for its pack. Once the short shadow reached the tree, it stopped, sniffed, then sat and basked within the dark. Its muzzle and eyes became illuminated by what little light of the crescent moon glowed between the thick branches of the tree. It stared at him. He knew it to be so, for the glowing reflective pupils of the beast gazed deep into his soul, beckoning him to come forth.

Orson stepped onto the porch. He did not bring his coat. He did not bring his boots. He stepped down into the ashen dirt of the farm, feeling the grit between his toes as it stuck to his skin. The coyote that sat under the tree did not move as the young man moved across the desolate farm. When he stood maybe six feet from the tree, the coyote stood, arching its back and straightening its tail in a very peculiar fashion. It froze for a moment, as if the young man startled it so. Its hellish glowing eyes blinked as it backed away, circling round the tree for a moment before it disappeared among the shadows.

He stood beneath that tree for a moment, running his hands against the carved bark, unable to see the images of life that the Daniels family left as reminders of their existence, but he felt them. The pale light of the moon basked the graves of Thomas' girls in its cold light and Orson stood over them, wondering what they were like. He wondered if he'd have a family of his own someday and if he did, if he'd be like his father, be like Jack. The coyote called again, causing Orson to raise his eyes and look out across the open barren fields of Kansas. He saw it in the dark, still slinking in the shadows. The small beast trotted along, moving up a shallow hill with tall grass that swayed in the chilling breeze of the night. The wind whipped against Orson's ears, and he heard the ocean, as if it had been carried thousands of miles to his location. He watched the beast as it turned around, eyes still holding the light of the crescent moon. It opened its mouth, and a fog, so thick, flowed from its open maw as it cackled again. The sound echoed across the plains, and somewhere off in the distance, somewhere in the outer dark, a pack cackled back.

The pit laid finish by noon on the second day. Orson stood in that vacating morning breeze as he shoveled the dried charred carcasses of the locust into the makeshift grave. He took the ash, the husks of blackened stocks, and he threw them among the dead. He felt only shame as he did so, for each locust reminded him of guilt. Each burnt stock told him it was all his fault. He denied it to the best of his ability, but he felt it deep within his wallowing heart that it was the truth. Once he placed all that he could within the pit, he began to use his spade to scoop dirt and cover it with the dark brown earth.

It took an hour or so for it to be covered, and once the pit looked only as if it were disturbed earth, Orson turned to look out over the farm. He still had work to do, for the soil still laid tainted with black. He missed some husks that lay in the waste, and he missed some stocks that stood straight up in the destroyed fields, swaying in the breeze as if to beckon him. The carcasses of locust still rolled when the wind blew, and the young man let out a sigh of frustration as he looked upon the farm. There would be no hiding the scourge of nature that took place, no matter how hard he tried.

On the horizon, a lone rider appeared on one of the shallow hills surrounding the farm. The horse moseyed slow, yet proud, as the rider swayed from side to side with the gait of the beast. The dark figure made its way down to the farm, and Orson, unsure if it were Thomas on his return, stepped away from the disturbed earth at his feet and moved towards the edge of the property. The rider approached the young man, and as it came closer towards the Daniels farm, Orson recognized the hat, the silver hair beneath it, the uncomfortable sway of an aging dying man. He knew it to be Thomas and he smiled.

Yet, Thomas remained cold, emotionless, as he rode the horse to a halt before the young man. The old man dismounted, staggering as his feet connected with the flat plains. He grabbed his lower back, hunching over. He swore under his breath, and the horse stirred as he did so.

"I'm glad you kept your word," said Orson.

The old man looked to him, eyes filled with such frustration, and he told him, "Kept it to you, but not to others."

Thomas grabbed the horse by the reins, leading it through the farm. He inspected the work that took place, noting how much Orson did. It still looked terrible, but it was not nearly as bad as the old man remembered.

Orson followed after Thomas and the bay, "How'd they take it?"

"Not well," said Thomas as he continued to lead the horse through the property. He could not bear looking the young man in the eyes.

"Wha's gon' happen?" asked Orson, honestly curious as to what Thomas and the folks of Hays concluded.

The old man stopped his staggering short steps. His grip on the horse's reins tightened as he bowed his head for a second. His eyes shifted and studied his destroyed home. Orson stayed behind the man, keeping the big bay horse at his side. He could not see the man's eyes, but Thomas' body language changed, and he knew that whatever news he brought from Hays was ill. Thomas then turned his head, looking away from his ruined property, out towards the edge of everything that he owned. He stared upon his old family tree. He blinked a few times as his eyes rested on the beauty. It appeared untouched by the plague, standing tall and would forever stand the test of time, or so he hoped. He lowered his head and began to weep.

They ate bread and vegetables that night. They did not speak all throughout the evening. Nothing needed to be said. The situation was bad, worse than Orson imagined. He knew not what to tell his friend, and so neither said anything at all. That is, until they finished their food and sat next to the fireplace, Thomas in his rocker and Orson with his legs crossed on the floor. They both basked in the heat of the flames, the orange hellish glow that came with it. It was as if Thomas felt some sort of rejuvenation through the fire, though, it faded quickly and his pessimism overpowered, "House will be theirs…farm will be theirs…my girls…"

Orson looked up to the old man. He saw the tears forming in his eyes. He knew the pain that the uncertain future brought. He tried to comfort him, "They c'ain't take them from you."

"They are though," replied Thomas, eyes fixated on the flames and the grizzly visions of the future that they presented to him. "That tree, it's theirs too..."

"Well..." said Orson, really not thinking before speaking. He paused, not sure of what to say to help put the old man's heart at ease. He tried to shift the subject away from the farm, whatever future it held, "You can still come with me then."

"I wish I could," said Thomas. He turned his head to look at the young man before him. He blinked once, slowly, then spoke calmly, "I c'ain't leave 'em. I feel like I done the right thing by Lilly."

"You did," Orson confirmed, as if it made any really difference of what he thought. He felt foolish for stating it, but he felt that Thomas needed some form of confirmation.

Thomas's eyes welled with tears. He fought them from falling as he said, "I ain't done what's right by my girls."

Orson tried to find some form of positivity in the situation, "The bank don't own you no more."

Thomas rejected the notion. He spoke the truth, "Cuz they done taken everything. There ain't nothin' left of me to own. Hell, Orson...they own my girls."

Orson studied the man as the tears began to slip from the edges of his eyes. He lowered his head, covering his eyes with his wrinkled hand as to try and shield Orson from seeing such a thing. Orson stayed quiet for a moment, listening to the soft whimpers slip between the old man's quivering lips. He knew not what to say or do, and so he just stated what he felt, "I'll miss ya."

Thomas did not look up. He did not break from hiding what

he found shameful. He knew the young man would be leaving. He knew he could not ride with him. He knew that his days were limited, and death felt closer than ever before. Had the young man arrived a year earlier, maybe he would've run off. Maybe he would've done things different. He did what he did, and he had to live with it with whatever time he had left. He made mistakes, and nature cursed him. He felt sick to his stomach as he thought of what he'd do. He too would miss the young man and the thought of being alone again made his heart ache. He should've done more in what little time he had. He apologized, "I'm sorry I never got around to teaching you how to read n' write."

Through the vast wild, a lone coyote walked. Its paws carried it through stream, meadow, forest, and then the plains. Its body swayed as it trotted silently across the open fields. Hairs fell from the creature's coat as the wind blew, a wild one. The beast passed pockets of snow that laid untouched by the coming spring. The tall prairie grass gave great cover for the animal as it marched onward, back hunched, body swaying with each step.

The beast only stopped when it came upon a food source, or so it thought. A great bison laid in the grass. Blood seeped from a massive wound in the beast's side. The coyote stared upon it, then raised its nose to sniff the air that flowed over the dead animal. It did not like what it smelt, decay and death, and so it moved on. As it passed, the maggots became clear as they fed away on the festering wound. The ribs did not look as delicious as they once did for the thick hide laid stretched thin against the bone. Its eyes sat eaten by scavengers, and the face sat dry as jerky under the hot sun.

The sunlight faded as the coyote continued its search. Only darkness and a great fog lingered on the prairie. The pockets of snow glistened in the starlight, holding no shape or form until the paw of the coyote graced the white with its presence and left its mark as it pressed onward. It came upon another bison. It sat deformed and mangled, as if it fell from the heavens. Its ribs sat opened, the heart of the animal gone, scavenged by others long before the coyote.

It found another bison not far off from the fallen one. The flies swarmed the decaying hulk. They buzzed wildly, landing on the snout of the coyote as it stared into the still face of the bison. The flies sprung from the nostrils of the great beast like a fleet of bats from a cave. The coyote nipped at the insects as they buzzed him, landed on him, pestered him. He moved on, knowing he could not feed on such a beast.

Another carcass laid discovered, and then another, and then another, and it was only then, when the coyote stopped and examined its surroundings, that it realized that it stood in a large killing field of bison. Hundreds laid dead in the cold night. Their bodies lingered motionless in the darkness, the light of the stars twinkling in the thick congested blood that accented the grey and gold stocks of grass. Only the wind could be heard on that plane.

Everything laid still and quiet, and the coyote moved so silently that it could've passed as a specter in the night. The smell of death that hung over the field like a low hanging cloud grew strong, so strong, and all the coyote smelt and saw and heard was death and the nothingness that came with it.

For what felt like hours, the coyote searched. It came across so many dead bison, some skinned, some not. He came across calves with cloven skulls, and mothers with milk that seeped from their dead utters. Nubs sat atop the dead animals' heads, their horns sawed for trophies, or so it appeared. Yet, the coyote found a pile of discarded horns, laying wasted in the tall prairie grass, never to be discovered by anything else that walked the prairie.

Not far from the pile of discarded horns, the small coyote found a dying bison. It laid on its side, ribs rising and falling slowly. Blood seeped from a sucking wound just beneath the beast's ribs. Crimson accented the grass, flowing from the behemoth's nostrils, creating tiny rivers on the prairie. Thick steam puffed from the great animal's mouth as it let out a slow deep bellow that sounded as if it came from the very soul of the dying animal. Then, the rising and falling of the ribs stopped. The fogging breath no longer seeped from the mouth of the animal. Its eyes stared upward, empty and hollow, save for the clusters of stars that reflected in them as the beast stared off into the void. The coyote arched its back, its tongue licking its black nose, its gums, and then the beast opened its mouth to feed.

A gunshot rang out. The coyote fell. It too claimed by the great killing fields. The beast watched as its breath slowed. Its ribs rose and fell rapidly. It yapped in pain as it felt the warmth of its own blood stick to its fur. No other beast called out. The coyote was truly alone as it sat in the darkness of the night, buried beneath that tall prairie grass. Yet, a figure emerged from the darkness, a tall lengthy human. They stood over the coyote, the last image of the beast. The man held a large rifle in his arms. The barrel smoked. He possessed one good eye, one bad one with milk white for color. When the coyote laid dead, the man, who once was known as Jack Tanner, knelt down and collected the dead animal.

He moved across the open plains silently, as if he too was a specter of the prairie. With the coyote slung over his shoulder, the man passed other dead animals, mostly bison, all decapitated. He made his way further across the open field and stopped as he approached a great and mighty structure, one he made with his hands, one he relished the sight of. A great mound of skulls stood before him. He knelt before it, as if to give some form of offering, and then he unslung the coyote from his shoulder. He hacked away at its neck with a large glistening knife.

With the beast's head severed, he stood covered in the blood of the animal. He grabbed ahold of the dismembered carcass, throwing it into the prairie grass, hoping it never to be discovered. He then grabbed the crown of the head, holding tightly onto the fur that brushed between his fingers. He stared into those dead eyes, seeing only a reflection of himself. The tongue of the coyote dangled, and the man laughed, thinking it would never yap again. He tossed the head onto the mound of skulls and mummified heads from where he grew lazy in removing flesh.

He waited a moment, looking upon the coyote among the bison. He then climbed the skulls, sitting atop the pyramid as he looked out across the great plains before him. He smirked. Both his eyes sat milky white as he looked out over the darkness that shrouded the land before him. The stars twinkled brightly. The earth sat silent. That is, until his smirk faded and a pack of coyotes yapped wildly somewhere off in the distance. It started faint, but grew louder, and louder, and louder, until it was all the man heard. It became all he thought of. It consumed him as he sat atop his throne of death and despair.

And then, Orson woke.

Chapter XXV
On, Saying Goodbye
1875

Orson sat awake. Beads of sweat rolled from his forehead, his chest, and under his arms. His thin cotton shirt stuck to his moist body. He blinked wildly, trying to clear his head from the horrible nightmare of Jack Tanner. He looked around the small dark home of the Daniels family, half believing that Tanner lingered in the shadows waiting to fire as if Orson was the coyote. Yet, no gunshot or plume of smoke erupted within the small home. The early light of daybreak moved slowly across the floor in an orange aura that fought back the dominate shadows that became reduced to the corners of the room.

Orson stood, throwing back the blanket as he did so. He stretched, looking about the room and seeing that Thomas did not reside in the house. The rocker laid still. The floors looked swept. Not a single piece of dust or part of a locust lingered within the home. The curtains writhed in the early morning breeze that pierced through the broken windows, chilling Orson. He made his way towards the shattered glass, peering out across the desolate waste of the farm. He saw the charred stocks that remained. He saw some locust lay still in the dirt. Yet, on the far side of the property, he saw that great oak tree. It basked in the orange glow of the rising Kansas sun. Rays of red and purple danced with the branches. Beneath the tree, a lone figure sat. At first, he thought it to be that coyote. Yet, as he stared and watched for a moment, he knew it to be Thomas.

He marched across the openness of the farm. The breeze cooled his body through his damp shirt. His boots parted the ash and dirt with each step. The tree swayed. The branches moved up and down, as if to beckon him. He did not hesitate and moved as fast as he could. He thought of telling Thomas of his dream, yet he found fear in that idea. He cursed to himself, saying he'd keep his dreams to himself, fearful of speaking them into existence.

The bark of the tree shimmered in the morning light. The hand of the young man brushed away dried sap as he rounded the hulking trunk. On the far end, facing out across the plains, sat Thomas. His back was to Orson, his front faced the graves, faced the plains. Orson did not want to startle him and so he kicked the heel of his boot atop a gnarled root that rose from the surface of the earth to announce his presence. He stated softly, slowly, "It's peaceful up here."

Thomas did not stir. He did not turn his head to see the

young man, as Orson expected. He sat, legs crossed, the grave markers before him as if he were an ancient monk at the ruins of some great temple. His head dipped forward. His chin rested on his sternum. The young man moved towards his side, looking out across the plains. The great orb of the sun moved upwards into the sky. The reds and purples faded, only blues and yellows graced the aether. Orson looked down on the man, asking, "Thomas?"

It was only then that he knew the farmer did not breath. The old man's hands sat clasped to his knees, paler than the snow of the Dakotas. His chest did not rise or fall. He sat motionless, cold to the touch of Orson's warm living hands.

The young man knelt down, knowing the fate of the old farmer. His eyes welled with tears as he looked upon the old white bearded face of his friend. His eyes sat closed, stiff, sealed for eternity. His face rested, calm, relaxed, as if somehow, in the void that is death, he found some comfort or peace. The way of the world is harsh. Thomas knew that, Orson knew that, and somehow Orson found relief in knowing the old man found rest. As he looked over the body, he wondered how it happened. He wondered if Thomas did it himself, or if the cold took him, or maybe the sickness, or maybe it was a culmination of all those things. He stood, looking down on his departed friend, who sat so regal before the plains, before the oak.

Something drew his gaze on the horizon. Three bison, two adults and a calf, moseyed slowly across the shallow hills of grass. The wind blew their fur as they carried on. The lead stopped and glanced over towards the farm. It did not keep its gaze, for it needed to find its herd, Orson assumed. If it didn't, it would be killed for certain. He smiled at their beauty as they disappeared over the hills. He wondered if they would make it. He wondered if they'd end up as pelts and bones in the railyards of Dodge, or if they'd rot on the plains. He wondered if they would die of old age, or sickness. He wondered how their lives would unfold, and then he wondered if it would be anything like his, or like Thomas's. He was unsure, but he found some comfort in that, for he knew it would not be him to end their existence.

He glanced back down at Thomas, the morning rays of light dancing across his motionless chest. He wiped tears from his eyes as he stared, for he knew he needed to carry on, and carry on alone at that.

The grave took a few hours to dig. The earth, soft, crumbled beneath the spade that Orson discovered behind the shed. The sun rested slightly to the west by the time he finished. He wrapped his old friend in the sheets from the bed. He wished he made a coffin. At least he buried the man, he told himself. He was no carpenter, but he did hold some dignity. He created a marker from old boards of the chicken coop. He spent time with his knife to carve the name of his friend. He spelled the name Daniels based off Thomas's previous work on his girls' markers. The first name, the young man dared not botch. He knew that Thomas started with a 'T', and therefore left the marker as "T. Daniels." He did not want to disrespect the name of a man he held so highly.

He staked the marker in the ground and covered the body with dirt. Thomas laid beneath the earth within a few moments, and Orson lingered about the grave, resting on the spade, wondering of what he should say or do. He looked off towards the horizon, as if that would give him some answers. It didn't. And so, he spoke from his heart, honestly, truly, as he looked upon the grave of Thomas Daniels, "Well...I never really said it, but I cared for you, Thomas. You were really the only one that never made me feel...I don't know, even though you gone it feels hard to say. I just...I just hope you off to them bigger better things."

The birds chirped between his words. The sky felt open and the breath of the world washed over the Daniels farm, as if it were the voices of the dead giving some sort of acknowledgment to the young Orson. He looked towards the tree, still searching for words.

"You was the strongest man I ever knew," Orson said, turning back to the grave. "G'bye, Thomas."

He laid the spade in the dirt. As he turned towards the tree, it felt as if the great oak spoke to him, as if it were Thomas. It did not say words, but the branches danced with his soul as he looked upon the old carvings. Orson drew his knife, stepping towards the tree. He began to carve into the trunk, far away from those of Thomas and his family. He stepped back, admiring his work. On the opposite end of the trunk, he carved a single coyote that yapped upward into the sky. He smirked, then turned back to the grave of Thomas. He brushed a tear away with his sleeve, then gave a nod towards the grave as his final goodbye. He was truly alone again.

Orson saddled his horse. He used Thomas's as a pack. He took his rifle and strung it to the side of the beast. He took Thomas's double-barreled shotgun, placing it in a scabbard on the side of the great brown beast. He took what little provisions existed in the home. He felt guilty at first, but he kept telling himself that Thomas didn't own anything anymore. He was off to bigger better things. If he didn't take it, the bank or whoever in Hays wanted it would claim it. It better he, a man who knew Thomas, than some shark somewhere that never appreciated the farm and all it brought.

With both animals ready to go, Orson stood at the center of the farm. He held the reins of each beast in his hands. He took a long look around the home as dusk began to take hold. He thought of staying one more night but could not bring himself to do it. The only reason he ever stayed was for Thomas. Without him, he too needed to find bigger better things. He imagined himself staying there forever, holding off the bank or whoever came to claim the property. They were just wild dreams and he knew it wouldn't make any difference. Powers existed in the modern world that he did not understand, but he knew them to be greater than he in every aspect. He stood no chance and to fight such things was foolhardy.

Dark clouds rolled in overhead. The setting sun drowned out by the light sprinkling that came with the grey anvils. Orson clutched his hat down on his head, throwing an old blanket over his shoulders at the same time. He saddled his horse, looking across the great farm that he grew to love. The desolate waste looked so cold, so foreign in the dark light of dusk. Even the great tree where he buried Thomas with his girls sat in the darkness of the oncoming storm. No golden light basked the branches in a warm glow. No sun reflected off the shattered windows of the home. No wheat remained to roll in the great winds. The place stood the ruins of a time that felt so ancient to the young man. He could not bear to witness it anymore. He tipped his hat to the tree, a final goodbye, and mounted his horse. He led the big bay behind him and on he rode.

He felt the rain followed him, for it did. His blanket rested on his shoulders, soaked. He kept his head down, feeling the cold droplets run down his icy flesh. His hands shook in the cold as he held the reins of the great bay and his own horse. He missed the nights by the fire. He missed the conversations with the old man. He missed waking in the morning with a purpose. He sat on that horse, riding across the plains, penniless and nowhere to go. He wasn't sure where he went, but he rode all through the night. He rode until it stopped raining. He rode until his mind vacated all thought of the Daniels family farm. The more he thought on it, the more he wished he stayed. He had to do right by him though. He thought only of great waves of the Pacific. He thought of what he could do out there. He thought of that small shack he wanted to build. He thought of all the fish he could catch to survive. He thought of a small measure of peace somewhere untouched by all the darkness he encountered on the plains.

As morning broke, the bellows of a rising smoke stretched across the sky. The sound of an engine cut the air, followed by the ringing of a bell, the tooting of a steam horn. He saw the train, the hulking mass of steel that he grew to hate, rolling across the emptiness. It hauled supplies, people, whatever else, to a small town that glistened like a beacon of hope. He knew the place, Hays, and felt a wave of dread overtake his heart. He wondered if he'd end up like Thomas, only finding chains in the place, or if he'd find the freedom he so long desired. The wheels of the train sparked and screeched as it slowed towards the small rail station of the town.

He watched as people unloaded supplies and passengers from wherever the train came from. He knew then that Hays, a town filled with predators who crushed the soul of Thomas Daniels, would be his only exit from such a life. He clicked his spurs into the side of his horse, heading down towards the wealthy plains town.

Chapter XXVI
Friends
1875

An older gentleman led a short pinto into the stalls of the stable. He held a carrot in his hand, ready to feed the animal that he grew to love since raising it as a colt. He closed the door to the stall, locking the hatch as the brown eyed beast peered back at him. He presented the vegetable in his open palm, letting the animal devour it in only a few bites. He smiled, speaking to the horse in a calm voice, stating how good of an animal it was to follow his command.

"I got'a couple of horse here," came a voice from the stable doors.

The stable worker turned, seeing the dark silhouette of a young man at the center of the large doors. In the stranger's hands, he held the reins of two beasts, both of which were decent horses. He wasn't sure if the boy was slow, for that was a strange opener. He told the young man, "That's good for you. They're both nice animals."

"I mean, I want to sell 'em," said the young man, stepping into the morning light that broke through the panels of the stable.

The stable worker studied the young man's face. He knew he worked the fields or the plains for some form of living, a life that required a good strong horse, which he possessed two of. He shook his head, curious at the enquirer's purpose, "Why?"

"I need the money," said the kid.

He continued to study the young man. He felt nervous by his presence. He questioned his intent, it being ill or genuine. He asked for clarification, "They yer horses?"

"Yeah," said the young man.

"Got the paperwork?"

The young man removed his hat as he tilted his head to the side. His face scrunched, visibly confused by the stable worker's question. His eyes darted from side to side, thinking of something. He didn't know what it all meant. He removed the wet blanket from his shoulder, throwing it onto the back of the big bay at his side. He looked back to the stable master, making only a quick sound of confusion, still not understanding what he meant after time to process, "Huh?"

The gentleman took two steps forward, trying to assert some dominance. He knew the laws and he knew he could not buy two stolen horses, if they were stolen. He witnessed problems before in the town of Hays over horses. Not just two days ago, two men were killed over horses, though that fool was caught. He wasn't sure if the man before him took them from elsewhere. However, the kid did not look to be the thieving type. He asserted, "Them's good horses. You got paperwork though, to prove you ain't no thief?"

"This one here was a gift," said the kid presenting the saddled horse. He then motioned to the bay, "and this one here comes from the Daniels farm not far out of town. I was his farmhand fer awhile. He recently passed and his farm is gone."

"You ain't steal either of 'em?" the stable worker pressed.

"No," said Orson honestly. "I ain't steal neither of 'em. They was given to me."

"But their paperwork wasn't?"

"Ain't no paperwork on the plains," said Orson, beginning to get annoyed with the man. He just wanted his money and to part with the horses.

The stable worker laughed at that. He thought it funny how honest and forthcoming the young man was. He wasn't sure if he was being played, but that logic made sense to him and he gave the kid a nod, "Look, I'd give you a good price for 'em if they had the papers. Without 'em..."

The stable worker trailed off, watching the young man's face morph into one of dissatisfaction and discomfort. The eyes of the young man dropped, looking down at the hay covered floor, letting out a short sigh that looked as if it was almost unintentional.

The stable worker continued, "How much you want for 'em?"

Orson shook his head, shrugging his shoulders. He knew not

the value of the horses he possessed. He wasn't looking to make a fortune to stake some claim out on the plains. He just wanted what he always desired. He asked honestly, "How much are train tickets 'round here?"

He sold his saddle and bags too. He carried his rifle slung over his shoulder. He kept the double-barreled shotgun in the scabbard that he carried at his side. He took all his weapons to a gun shop down the main street. He sold them all for what little the owner would pay for them, including his revolver. He didn't need any of it anymore, he told himself. They were all dead weight. He would hunt no more.

He had enough for train tickets and food to hold him over for a few days. He made his way to the train station. He felt lost amongst the plains city. The folks there paid no mind to him and went about their business as if it were Dodge City. Some folks dressed nice with suits and dresses. Others dressed as if they worked the fields or rode out on the plains. It was a hodgepodge of different worlds that all existed on that flat surface that he called home for some time. He couldn't wait to leave it all.

He bought a ticket to Council Bluffs. He tried to get one to California, but he could only get that ticket from the other railyard. The train left later that day and he became the happiest he'd been in a long while. To kill his time, he wandered the streets of Hays, reminiscing of the days gone by. He looked to every man and woman's face, wondering which of them would own the Daniels family farm. He wondered if they'd respect it. If they knew the man who once lived there, the man and his family that died there, they certainly would. He thought that wishful thinking, and so he tried to stop thinking about it all together.

The young man passed the jail house. He kept on, but stopped as he heard his name being called from a back alley, "Orson?"

It sounded familiar. He had to know the person, they knew him, recognized him. It had been some time since he'd seen anyone he knew. He halted, looking down the alley. The dust of the streets kicked up as a horse rode by, and he saw the silhouette of a man leaning against the jailhouse wall. When the dust settled, Orson did not recognize the man. He wore a nice vest with his watch hanging from the front pocket. His sleeves were rolled, and a badge hung over his heart. He tipped his hat to Orson but shook his head and nodded over his shoulder towards a cage that lingered a few paces back. In it, a tall lengthy figure lingered. A stubbled beard accented his jawline. His hair, longer than Orson remembered, sat on his shoulders. His eyes narrowed as Orson looked to him, and it was then that he truly recognized his acquaintance. Charlie smiled at Orson, gripping his hands to the metal bars of the makeshift cell.

The badge wearing guard that nodded the way asked Orson, "You know this kid?"

"I think so," said Orson as he studied the image of what Charlie became. He wasn't sure what happened. He had to be mistaken.

Yet, as he did not approach the cell, Charlie recoiled his hands, lowering his head. That same look of defeat that he always saw returned, and he knew without a doubt that Charlie Hawkins resided in a cage in the back alleys of Hays, Kansas. He clarified, "Yeah, I know him. Wha's he done?"

"Killed two men in a horse theft," stated the guard.

Orson rose an eyebrow as he glanced towards the sheriff, "Why you keepin' him ou'side?"

"Hangin' him later today," said the guard. "Little crowded inside."

The weight of the guard's information struck Orson's heart heavy. He wasn't sure how he'd react if he ever lost Charlie. Now that it arrived, he did not know how to process the information. He took a step forward, "Can I speak to him?"

"Wha'chu gotta say?" asked the guard.

"We used to hunt together," Orson told him.

"That all?"

"That's all."

The guard responded with a slight nod over his shoulder, signaling Orson to make it quick. He stepped slowly towards the cage, as if behind the bars resided some rabid beast, not an old acquaintance. When he stood before the bars, Charlie rose tall before him, not proud or full of confidence like the last he saw him, but beaten. He'd seen better days. The young Charlie's voice shook as he said, "Hey, Orson…"

"Hey, Charlie…"

"Jack with you?" slipped from Charlie's lips, as if he spoke some form of blasphemy. He clarified, "I don't…I mean, I just don't want him to see me like this."

"No," replied Orson, honestly and sternly. "I left Jack some ways back."

"Oh yeah?" Charlie's voice rose, curious to that answer.

"Yeah," nodded Orson, not wanting to speak on Tanner any longer. Though, he wondered if that is truly all him and Charlie ever had in common. He knew that not to be true, but he always lied to himself and said it so.

"Tha's good," Charlie told him. "You seen him since?"

"No," Orson said quickly. "Don't plan to neither."

"Y'all have a fallin' out?"

"No, well…" Orson began, "I just realized some things, that's all. I didn't need him no more."

"An' wha's that you realized?" Charlie poked, lightening up a bit and resting his arms on the metal bars of the cage.

Orson smelt the dirt and grime that accumulated on Charlie. It felt thick in the air as it danced around Orson's nostrils. He swatted some flies away as he said, "He was the same, that's all."

"Good for you," Charlie smiled. His teeth were beginning to rot around the edges. He would be dead before they ever fell out, Orson though and his stomach felt dense at the thought. The young acquaintance continued, "You look good. You look happy."

Orson smirked, "It's 'cuz I'm leavin' this place."

"Oh..."

"Headin' out to California after I go to Council Bluffs," Orson said proudly. He finally felt good about something he did.

"Where in California?"

"Sacramento, then I'm headin' to the ocean."

"I always wanted to see the ocean," Charlie said. He then let out a half-hearted chuckle, "Guess I won't get the chance now."

Orson crossed his arms, studying the strange figure of a kid he used to know. He cocked his head to the side, asking honestly, with no ill will. He just had to know, "Why'd you kill them fellers?"

"Why not?" asked Charlie. He watched Orson's face scrunch in confusion, and so he clarified, "I mean...Jack and them always wanted us to kill. They mocked me for not. But when I do kill, I'm punished. Ain't that funny."

"Ain't nothin' funny 'bout it," Orson told him sternly. He shook his head, the concepts of all they learned were lost on the acquaintance, "Animals and man ain't the same."

Charlie scoffed, looking curiously at Orson, "To some."

The confidence in Charlie's demeanor returned, as if he said something profound. As if, recalling the deaths of the men he recently killed triggered something deep within his soul, and he saw the world clearly. Orson didn't care for that, and with Charlie's confidence returned, he also asked honestly, "You ever think 'bout Parker?"

"Why would I?" asked Charlie, slightly annoyed.

Orson sensed the frustration, shrugging off the question, "Don't know."

Charlie lowered his head onto his arms, resting the crown of his skull against the bars for a moment. He glanced upward towards Orson, his mouth hidden behind his thin dirty arm. He then said, "I hear him, sometimes, like a bug in the back of my skull..."

Orson didn't know what to say to that. He stood there awkwardly for half a second, until Charlie dipped his head back down, hiding his gaze. He then stepped back from the cage, trying to appear proud before Newkirk. He asked, "Was Jack mad?"

"Oh yeah," replied Orson, "he was mad."

"You tell him you saw me?"

"Not really."

"Why?" Charlie asked, cocking his head to its side.

Orson spat in the dirt, "What difference would it have made? He wanted to gut you. Didn't matter what I said to him."

Charlie pressed, "Was you scared of him?"

"Yeah."

"I was too. Still am, I think," replied the acquaintance. "I hope he don't know what happens to me."

"Jack's long gone," Orson assured him. "We ain't gotta worry about what he thinks no more."

"I still do though," Charlie admitted. "I just...I just don't want to let him down."

"You done bad things, Charlie. He's done bad things too," Orson stated. "It ain't worth worryin' over what he thinks."

"And what do you think?" asked Charlie directly. He kept his head slightly tilted. The glimmer of his youth still twinkled in his eye as he stared into Orson.

"Huh?" Orson was taken aback.

Charlie elaborated, "You disappointed in me?"

"Why's it matter what I think?"

"I don't know," Charlie bowed his head, nervous now. He acted embarrassed, shy, like he and Orson never spoke a word to each other before, "I mean, it might sound kinda dumb or stupid but...I mean, I always thought we was friends. I mean...I thought you was my friend."

Orson stood before the young man in the cage. He stared at his long hair, the beady eyes that carried dirt around their edges. He thought on their time together, their experiences out on the plains, their hatred for Tanner, their hatred for the work. With Tanner and Parker in the mix, he could never associate with the kid he deemed only an acquaintance. He felt connected to the young man, but never spoke it, never admitted it. He feared being weak by proxy. He got along alright with the young man, more so than any other in the group. He questioned why he never called him a friend before. He figured he should admit it before Charlie never walked the earth again, "I am your friend."

Charlie looked up at him. The definitive statement

rejuvenated something within him. He smirked a little, but that faded as his serious questions continued, "Then, I'd like to know if you's disappointed in me."

Orson thought on it. He had to give an answer. It brewed inside his skull, trying to formulate all he thought. He thought about those calves. He thought about Tanner and he thought about Parker. He thought about Bill and how they all mocked Charlie for not being able to do the work. He wasn't cut out for it. Hell, Orson didn't think himself fit for the job. Yet, Tanner did not cut him loose. He wondered if any of that had anything to do with the killings. Charlie did tell him that he saw no difference. Orson wondered if he saw one too. He saw bison and coyotes behind his eyelids as he blinked. He sighed, seeing Parker's mangled throat. He blinked again, seeing Masters' crushed corpse atop that mound of bison. They left them like animals, the way they left those bison to rot. Maybe that's what Jack taught him all along. Man is the worst animal, maybe. Or maybe, man can be. Or maybe, it was all something different.

"No, Charlie. I ain't disappointed in you," Orson told his friend, looking at the scrawny young man behind the cage. "I ain't entirely sure it's all yer fault."

"I ain't no Lil Lamb no more," Charlie said with a smile.

The young man's lips curving upward sent a chill down Orson's spine. Charlie wasn't that Lil' Lamb. He became something different entirely, a predator, a beast to tear the world down the way Tanner wanted him to. His stomach turned at the thought of the first time they met. He never thought it would end like this, not for Charlie at least. He gave a fake smirk, as to not upset his friend, to not try to show disappointment, "That you ain't, Charlie."

"Think it'll last long?" Charlie asked, raising his hands to his neck, "When they…you know?"

"No," Orson shook his head, trying to put the young man at ease. "I don't think so."

Charlie stepped away from the edge of the cage. He nodded his head as he thought on Orson's response. He believed it, knowing that Orson spoke honestly. He admired that about him too. He admired more about his friend Newkirk than he ever admitted or would ever admit. He wanted to be like him, the way Newkirk wanted to be like Masters. It just didn't work out that way. He smirked at the thought of a quick death, and he smiled at the idea of telling Orson how he envied him. Yet, as he looked upon his friend through the rusty bars of the outdoor cell, he could not bring himself to do it. He found shame in admitting such a thing. He leaned against the cell, sticking his hand through, which drew the guard's nervous attention. They met eyes, but the guard went at ease as Orson grabbed ahold of the hand, moving it up and down, a final handshake.

Charlie smiled, tears welled in his eyes as he looked upon a familiar face one last time, "Take care of yer'self, Orson."

"You too, Charlie," said Orson. He would miss his friend,

though they were apart for some time. It made his heart slow at the thought of never seeing him again. There would be no one left aside from Tanner, wherever he was, that knew what they experienced after Bill's departure. There would be no one left that understood. That made his soul weep, and the thought of never seeing Charlie again only brought an ill feeling. He'd miss him, for he respected him. Maybe not what he became, but what he once was. He told his friend, "I'll miss ya, Charlie. Goodbye."

Charlie let go of Orson's hand and his eyes dripped tears from around the edges. He gave a nod, the final gesture. He wanted to hug him, but he wondered if his friend would reject that. It didn't matter anymore, for Orson tipped his hat to the guard, lowered his head, and began to walk back towards the main street. Charlie watched him go. He wondered what laid ahead in the world for his friend. He wondered if Newkirk would ever find what he searched for, because Charlie never found what he desired. It was only when Newkirk disappeared among the passerby, that Charlie sat down in the cage. He lowered his head, crying as hard as he could, for his long search was over, and it was over for a long time. All he ever wanted was a friend, and they were there all along.

When the time came, Orson waited in the train station. He grew tired of walking around Hays, wondering where everything went wrong with Charlie. He felt guilt, for he hardly thought of him since he parted ways with Jack, yet as the time of expiration grew closer, it is all he ever thought about. He wondered if that same fate lingered in his cards, or if he somehow broke free of the curse. Maybe all men pay for their deeds, he thought. He hoped he had more good than bad.

The train rolled into the station. The sparks flew from the brakes as the iron machine screeched to a halt. The young Orson boarded the mechanism, making his way to the railcar that he could afford. It was small, cramped, and filled with an assortment of people. The air felt thick, smelt awful. He cared not. He was leaving such a dreadful place. He felt guilty for that too. He sat down near the back of the train car, near a group of folks who spoke little to no English. They looked confused with each passing second, speaking among themselves in whatever foreign tongue they possessed. Orson too felt confused, not knowing where he was truly going or why. He began to wonder if he should leave, but then he wondered where he'd go. It mattered no longer. He was heading West, finally.

All the while, Orson sat on that train and thought of Charlie. Charlie too thought of Orson as two armed guards came to his outdoor cell, opened the lock, and began to lead the young man through the streets of Hays. His hands were bound. His head hung low, shameful, that confidence never really lasted because it never really existed. It never had a chance to blossom. The guards led the young Charlie down the main strip of the town. Folks of all walks of life stopped and stared at him. He did not have the heart to look at any of them.

He began to wonder why he killed those men. He didn't have to. He thought about how he crushed that calf skull, and he only wished that he left Tanner's party then. Maybe his life would've been different. Maybe it wouldn't for he knew deep down beneath that timid demeanor, he unleashed his true abilities. He felt nothing but rage when he killed Parker. He felt nothing when he killed those men for their horses. He wondered if he were left to wander if he'd feel anything at all.

The gallows stood tall on the outskirts of the main strip. A crowd gathered near them, all unfamiliar faces. The first guard led Charlie up the steps, his boots echoing on contact. They sounded as if they went for miles across the plains. Charlie felt the smooth wood against his bare feet as he stood before the crowd, his back facing the vast emptiness of Kansas. He looked out over the town. He saw people going about their lives, doing what they needed for survival. He just wanted to find his way in the world. He found it. It just wasn't as he thought. Something dark lingered in him. He wondered if murder always sat within the depths of his heart, or if it were planted. He wondered if all men possessed such evil, for that is what he felt he was.

The guard grabbed the noose that dangled from the beam overhead. He placed it gently around Charlie's neck, tightening it so the coils rested on his pale flesh. Charlie could not look to him. He could not look to the crowd. He only stared out across the town. He saw the train sitting in the station. He smirked, hoping Orson could find whatever it was he looked for out there in the world. The other guard placed a woven sack over the young Charlie's face. All he then saw was darkness. In that, he heard the screaming of buffalo, the crying of the calves, and he swore he heard someone in the crowd say he looked like a little lamb. His heart began to beat faster. He believed his chest would burst and the organ would flop on the ground. That would be a way to go, he thought.

The guards began to say his last rites. He knew the inevitable lingered just around the corner. He braced himself. He wondered if an apology would make a difference. It wouldn't. He knew that. He just toyed with ideas, trying to find some last chance to get out of the grave he dug. He blamed nobody but himself. It was not Tanner that put him there. It was not Parker that put him there. It was not Bill or Orson who put him there. It was all him and his need to prove himself, not to any of them, but to his own self. He didn't find comfort in that, as he thought he would, and just as he began to wonder why, he felt the floor drop beneath him. He heard a quick snap, then all went black.

Charlie Hawkins dangled by the noose. He swayed left to right. The grey clouds rolled overhead. The landscape appeared as drab as ever. Nobody in the crowd said a word as they watched him sway. His legs twitched, as did his hands. He convulsed for only a short while, but then laid still. At first, the rope squeaking as he swayed is all that could be heard for miles across the plains. Yet, just as the townsfolk of Hays turned their backs to him to go back to their lives, a coyote yapped somewhere out in the void. Then, from somewhere else in the grey, a great cacophony of yaps replied. So loud they were, deafening, as if a great pack of thousands lingered in the outer dark.

The townsfolk paid no mind. It was only Orson who acted as if he heard the strange pack of animals. He sat at the back of the train car, looking out the open door as more people continued to board. He saw the great open fields. He saw the endless expanse of nothingness. He could not wait to leave it all behind. He then witnessed a lone coyote walking towards the outer dark, walking towards the dark grey clouds on the horizon, following the cacophony of yaps. He stared at it for a moment, and the four-legged figure faded, and the animals stopped their screaming, crying, yapping. He then wept.

Chapter XXVII
Nothing to be Said
1875

Cigarette smoke filled the working-class car. Orson puffed a hand rolled cigarette, given to him by a German fellow who sat across from him on the floor. They kept a wooden box between them, shoved off to the side as to not trip the many people who paced like animals trapped in a rolling cage. It was night. He spent very little time in Council Bluffs, feeling that if he stayed, he'd never leave. He wasn't exactly sure where they were either, for when he peered out one of the few chest high slots, all he saw was blackness and flat fields. Sacramento felt forever away, but closer than ever before.

The German laid a hand onto the box, a flush of hearts. He said something in his native language to the young man who possessed a hand worth only a bluff. Orson gave a smirk and a nod, ashing his cigarette on the ground. The German took the cards, shuffling them, then handed them to Orson, who shuffled them as well. He placed them back on top of the box, and the German began to deal.

"Don't know why I'm even playin'," said Orson. "You keep winnin'."

The foreign gambler looked to him confused, then smiled and said something in German.

Babies cried on the car. Woman shushed them. Men snored. Orson felt like he could sleep for days, but for some reason, he kept himself awake, fearful that if he fell asleep, he'd never awake to see the ocean.

The German dealt a few more cards. Orson had nothing, of course. The stranger across the box removed a flask from his pocket, took a sip, then set it on the table as an offer. Orson raised his hand in declination, "I don't drink no more."

The German raised the flask, giving it a slight shake, as if to clarify that he wanted Orson to drink.

The young man shook his head, professing a new creed he took after he left Hays, "No thanks. I don't drink."

The German shrugged, taking a sip, then put the flask back where he found it.

The two revealed their hands. The German won again. Orson did not care. They did not play for money. He learned his lesson on that a long time ago. He watched as the German grinned, shoving the cards to Orson to shuffle now. He saw the delight the man possessed in winning, even if no stakes existed. Orson asked, "How you get so good at cards?"

The German said something.

"Cards?" Orson asked, then mimicked him laying them out on the table, then gave a thumbs up as if he gave him praise. He then pointed to the German, "How you get so good?"

The German said some long phrase in his native language, all of which Orson could not understand but one particular phrase, "*Dodge City*." It made his heart sink as he thought on the place. He hadn't been there in a long time, since before he made it out to Thomas's farm. The German asked him a question about Dodge City next. Orson knew by the inflection.

"Yeah," said Orson, "I've been to Dodge."

He puffed his cigarette, remembering back to the last time he was there. He left not long after the incident, if that is what he wanted to call it. He wandered Nebraska for some time before he ended up back in Kansas. He didn't care for the work he found. He didn't have much going for him. All he knew was the trade of killing animals, and all others seemed to fall to the wayside. He found no satisfaction in anything else, but he felt numb while thinking about killing. He went back to Dodge near the end of '74, hesitant at first, because he feared maybe Tanner would be there. He figured that Tanner had a point to prove to himself and wouldn't step foot back in that place.

He acquired enough money in Nebraska that he didn't need to worry too much, but he decided to try and double what little he had by attending casinos and bars, trying to make some form of income that he felt honest that wasn't hunting. He ran out of coin pretty quick. He did not know the gambler's trade and those that did took advantage.

The last night of his attempt, he went through ten dollars within an hour at some dark dank casino off Front Street. He kept what little he had left and began to order drinks at the bar. He heard a familiar voice, which caught his attention and he looked over his shoulder. Across the way, sitting at one of the poker tables sat burly Bill Chambers. A prostitute sat on his lap and he smoked a fine cigar. He looked the same as he always had. He did not clean up, and Orson wondered if the grime from Dakota still lingered on the man. Months passed since they last saw each other, and Bill raised his glass of dark liquor to his mouth, his eyes watching Orson at the bar.

Orson watched Bill play his hand. He lost, no fault of his own. The young Orson kept an eye on the lady who sat on Bill's lap. She poured him another drink from a bottle she kept on her person. She laughed and smiled with Bill. They seemed to be having a good time, or that's at least what Bill paid for. Yet, as Bill looked to his cards, she gave nods and winks to the dealer who sat across from them. Poor Bill, thought Orson. He wasn't good at gambling either.

The young man turned to the bartender, setting his empty glass down on the bar. He tapped the rim with his finger, "Another."

He stood outdoors after another whiskey. He smoked a cigarette, letting the liquor and smoke on his breath radiate out into the night, carried off by the cool Fall winds. He leaned against the wooden railing that lined the deck of the casino. He wasn't sure how long he'd be there, but he figured it wouldn't be much longer. He would have to find another line of work, either that or return to hunting. He didn't like that thought the more he pondered, but it would always be a fallback. He thought about leaving, but he wasn't sure where to go. Only then, in that thought, did he stare off down the back of the main strip. He saw that old saloon where he met Tanner, where it all began. He wondered if any other naïve boys were picked up at such a place. How far he'd come since then, thieving and all other lines of degeneracy without any dignity. He didn't think he possessed much dignity anymore, not after living on the plains. So be it, he thought. He guessed he would be no better than he ever was.

A commotion grew within the casino. He knew things were getting heated indoors and that it would be taken to the streets sooner or later. He learned that not just from Jack, but off in Nebraska too. He stepped away from the swinging wooden doors, leaning against the far wooden railing of the deck. A man was thrown from the entryway, down the steps, into the cold dirt streets of the city. Two men, guards of sorts, exited the casino and towered over the thrown man. As the man stood in the street, it was only then that Orson recognized him as Bill.

Bill threw his hands up, red in the face, drunk and angry as if he were Jack Tanner himself, "She was in on it, wasn't she?"

One of the guards spoke, "You need to get the hell outta here, fella."

"Y'all done cheated me!" spat Bill.

The guard spoke again, pointing down the street, off into the darkness, "Move on, you drunk fool!"

"Answer me, dammit!" Bill screamed, his voice shaking with such ferocity. Orson never saw such a thing from the man when he knew him.

"Ain't no cheatin' here," said the other guard, crossing his arms as if he stated a clear fact and it could not be argued.

Then the other guard spoke, his arm thrown out, pointing the way once again, "We ain't tellin' you again. Now, get!"

Bill studied the two, then raised his fists halfway up his chest as if ready to throw down. The two guards took steps forward, ready to scuffle with the man, but Bill, quickly realizing he stood no chance, lowered his fists. He took his hat up from the dirt, brushing it off on his knee, then placed it on his head. He spat in the street, "I'm gettin'."

The two men watched him for a moment, then turned their backs as he began to walk off. Only when they entered the casino, did Bill turn back around, looking to Orson on the deck of the casino. His eyes, drunken, swam with a cloudy judgement. He opened his mouth slightly, as if to say something to the young man. Orson watched him, waiting for anything to be said at all after that strange exchange where he saw a different side to Bill. Nothing needed be said, so nothing was, and Bill turned his back after a small nod, a gesture of simple acknowledgement. They saw so much, been through so much, traveled so far, but nothing could ever be said between them again. Nothing more needed to be said.

Then Bill turned his back, walking down the shadow swept streets of Dodge City. Nobody else lingered around. It felt as if it were only he and Orson within the grand city on the plains. Orson watched him walk down the center of the street, staggering, swearing under his breath. The stars overhead beamed brightly but did not penetrate the darkness that laid over the city. Soon though, Bill faded from view, swallowed by the blackness of the plains. That was the last Orson saw of him. It was his last day in Dodge City.

"Yeah," Orson told the German, putting his cigarette out on the ground. He crushed it under his boot. He let the damn thing burn to the nub and he rubbed the space where he held it between his fingers, "I ain't goin' back there no more."

The German chuckled, as if he understood what Orson spoke of, what he thought of. He said something in his foreign tongue, shrugged, took another drink, then dealt another hand of cards.

Chapter XXVIII
The Dream and the Reality
1875

The train arrived in Sacramento by morning. The place was alive with so many people. The folks of the higher paying cabins stepped down from the steel steps onto the wooden platform of the train station. They disembarked first, then came the lower-class cabin. When Orson stepped onto the platform, everything felt similar. The place swarmed with finer folks. The city itself, sprawling, exquisite, loomed over him as he stared down the many streets and studied the finer folks that walked them. He felt himself lost, as if he did not arrive where he believed he would. He listened to the station workers directing folks on where to go to clear the platform. He felt reassured that he truly stood in Sacramento.

He did not bother to stay in the city. He bought a loaf of bread from a local baker, a man who did not seem to care for the younger vagabond entering his shop. The young man used some of the last dollars he possessed. He ate a few bites as he wandered the streets, looking out across the bridge over the river. It gave a sense of dread, as if he stared at the old river near Dodge. He divided the loaf into small portions, placing them in various pockets on his person. He wasn't sure where to go, and so he just began to walk westward.

The fields outside the city were filled with low hanging grass. Their stocks were dry, greying, yellowed. The overpowering sun beat down on the young man as he walked. Heat waves rose from the earth, bending before the young man's vision. He only stopped to look back once. He admired the city a good moment. It would grow in the coming years, he thought, grow more than Dodge City ever could. It impressed him, but he thought about how far it would extend. He wondered if at some point, a large city would extend from Sacramento all the way to Dodge or maybe even New York, wherever that was. He thought that idea foolish, then turned his back to the town, then kept walking westward.

He did not travel by roads. He kept to the fields, the low hills, wandering up and down them. The air seemed thinner. He felt the world different in California, opposed to Kansas or the Dakotas or Indian Territory. Yet, he didn't get the feeling that he longed for. He hoped for freedom, or a sense of it, but nothing of the sort came as he wandered.

A thicket of trees lingered near the crest of a small hill. He moseyed towards it, sipping from his canteen, hoping to find some form of shade from the sun only for a short while. As he approached, out of the darkness rose a short figure. It leered at him, then hunched lower towards the ground. The sun broke between the branches, dancing along the tuffs of grey fur attached to the animal. The beast's ears perked upward on the sight of the young man, but lowered, tucked back as if to attack as he stepped closer. Its eyes glowed a pale yellow as it stared into him, stared into his soul. He passed the thicket, not wanting to mingle with the animal. Though, the image of the beast soon faded away.

And so, he kept walking. As his legs wandered, so did his mind. He tried to think of all the good times he had while out on the plains. He thought of Thomas first, sitting around the fire, eating stews and bread. He thought about their conversation about his father. He thought about the times that they laughed. He wished he learned to read and write with the man, but he knew that life got in the way. He daydreamed what the experience would've been like. He thought Thomas would be an excellent teacher. He didn't see any berating or scolding out of frustration taking place.

He thought about the ride down to Indian Territory. He felt good then, like he belonged to the party for the first time. He remembered Masters sitting before him and Charlie, talking about adventures. Had he known then where the adventure would've ended, he would've warned Masters, but that all meant nothing anymore. He thought about how he admired Jack and that revolver, how he showed it to them and how he told them some story of how it was obtained. It didn't matter. They were all lies. He scoffed at the thought.

He remembered his first payday in Dodge City. He tried to forget how he obtained such money, but it felt good to him that he earned an honest wage for the first time in his life. He thought on Charlie though, and how little he was paid. That made him sick, for he saw Charlie swing when he dwelled on the moment.

The first time he met Parker, he punched him. He finally realized that and laughed to himself as he lifted his boots shallowly off the ground, walking slowly across the great expanse. He chuckled as he thought about how he scrambled to his feet, ready to fight the young man. Parker was pretty mad. He laughed at how everyone else thought it funny too. Yet, the more he thought about it, images of Parker laying in a pool of crimson crept into his mind. He remembered those still eyes staring upward as a light snow fell. He saw the soiled pelt laid atop his body. He tried to think of something different, but it is all he evoked when he thought of Parker. It made him ill.

He walked for two days straight, only stopping to refill his canteen and to take quick naps wherever he found shelter from the sun. He found himself moving better at night, avoiding the heat. It wasn't practical though, for the darkness in California seemed darker than that of the plains to him. It was because he didn't know it, he argued with himself, and so he kept going whenever he could. Eventually, he followed the sounds of crashing waves as he made his way through a small shore town. He hadn't seen the ocean yet, but he could hear it as it called to him like a siren out in the great unknown.

The streets were paved in the small town. His boots clacked against the smooth stone. People were out and about, studying him as if he were some strange creature that rose from the abyss. He staggered, weak, tired, hungry. He ate all his bread during the trek, and now he ran on dreams and pride alone. The waves crashed in the distance. He smiled, yet as he envisioned the great rolling blue that he dreamed of so many times, he thought on the great piles of bison skulls in Dodge. He shook that thought free from his mind, keeping pace to reach the edge of the small town on the bay.

His mind felt clear, but he felt the dark thoughts creeping back in. He began to recollect his journey by train to California. Nothing eventful happened once he left. Nothing happened in Council Bluffs that he could dwell on. He thought of the train, the tracks, and then images of those dead bison rotting near the train tracks on their journey back into Kansas from Indian Territory flooded his vision. He heard the flies. He saw the bison bloating, rotting, decaying. They would be nothing but piles of bones now, and he envisioned that too. The coyotes, poisoned by those strange pellets, stayed stiff with their fur blowing in the light breeze. Their tails extended outward.

Orson staggered, feeling his knees buckle. He rested his arm on the side of a great wooden building, staring off down the road. He had so little to walk just to see his dreams come to fruition, yet it felt miles away. He removed his canteen, taking a sip, the last of his water. Better times, he told himself as he began walking again.

Thomas and him sitting around the fire, laughing, filled his head. He thought of working in the fields with him. He thought of how peaceful and serene that farm was. He smiled at the thought, but the locusts destroyed it all and nothing was left. He only saw the barren fields. He only envisioned the men who bought it arriving, spitting in the dirt, thinking no man could own such a place. They probably tore down the home. He saw images of men hacking away at that great oak with small axes. The carvings, the only reminders of the family's accomplishments, split under the iron beards of the hatchets. The coyote that he carved would be all that stayed untouched, but the oak would be gone, the coyote would be gone, and nobody would know about who once existed in such a place.

He followed an alley between two monstrous buildings that loomed over him. His pace slowed as he heard the waves grow louder. He kept on, eventually walking between two homes and their gardens. He ran his hands across their wooden fences, giving himself some slight support as he carried on. A street sat paved before him, and on the other side, a drop blocked by a fence. He only saw the great expanse of blue sky and so he slowly crossed the street, resting his arms onto the fence. He felt his knees buckle again, and he stood, looking out over the edge of the cliff. He kept his eyes close, not believing he finally made it to where he wanted. He listened to the rolling waves crashing into the shore below. He felt the salted ocean breeze kiss his skin as it flew by.

A grand boat horn blew. It cut through the air, vibrating the wind that danced around Orson. He opened his eyes, and the sound of waves crashing faded as if all just a dream. Instead, he heard only that boat horn, followed by others, and men screaming, cussing, and laughing. He looked out across the bay, seeing the blue ocean somewhere in the great distance, but in the bay itself, the waters were stained red and black. Large fishing ships stood idle, bouncing in the wake of each other's endeavors. They reeled in large nets, prey flapping wildly within. They gutted fish on the decks of their boats, discarding the bloody messes that they didn't want back into the sea. Smoke flowed from the ships' chimneys, bellowing upwards into the sky that eventually blocked Orson's view of the deep blue in the distance. All he saw were bloody oiled waters where the unwanted floated atop the low wake.

His heart sank as he looked upon it. He felt his knees weaken again and he found no desire to hold onto the fence. He let go, falling onto his knees. Sharp pain radiated through his body, through his soul. He knew not what to do, where to go, but he felt that he could not stay, for it was all just a dream and he wondered if any dream ever truly existed. He wept. And as he mourned, he listened to the fishermen laugh and chant in some unholy ritual that he became all too familiar with on the plains.

The horns blew once more.

Then, all fell silent, save for the sound of a coyote yapping somewhere in the distance…

Epilogue

1886

The scavengers came and went across the plains. They carried great carts with them as they picked the earth clean of the bones. In years past, men made money on hunting great bison herds. Now, they were mostly gone. Only a scavenger could make a wage, for the bones ruined the soil and the farmers complained about the sod. He made decent money for a full skeleton, though that felt hard to come by. Everything blended, bison that were skinned, those that weren't.

He, fourteen at the time, rode with the same crew for quite a while, and held them each in high regard, though none of them hardly spoke to one another. The Scavenger knew nothing of hunting, knew nothing of what happened on the plains only years before, but he felt grateful, or so he was told to, for he and his employers would not have jobs if the hunters did not do theirs.

They rode back to Dodge, their caravan filled with the

remains of so many different creatures. They took them all to the railyard which seemed so foreign to him. The bones were stacked high. And when the men were paid, they added to them. When the Scavenger looked out at his work, the mounds of skulls extended for what felt like miles. Hides and pelts lined the railways. Femurs, horns, and ribs were all divided into their own piles, them too extending for what seemed like an eternity.

He never got the feeling all that much, but as he looked upon the great expanse of bones, he wondered what it was all for. It didn't mean much to him, as he was told not to worry about it. They gave him seven dollars for his labor, and he drank it all away.

Made in United States
North Haven, CT
19 August 2022